# HAWICK
## AN O'BRIEN TALE

## STACEY REYNOLDS

EDITED BY
## JOYCE MOCHRIE

STACEY REYNOLDS

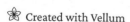

# OTHER BOOKS BY THE AUTHOR

The O'Brien Tales & Novellas

*Raven of the Sea: An O'Brien Tale*

*A Lantern in the Dark: An O'Brien Tale*

*Shadow Guardian: An O'Brien Tale*

*Fio: An O'Brien Novella*

*River Angels: An O'Brien Tale*

*The Wishing Bridge: An O'Brien Tale*

*The Irish Midwife: An O'Brien Tale (prequel)*

*Dark Irish: An O'Brien Novella*

*Burning Embers: An O'Brien Tale*

*The Keeper: An O'Brien Tale*

*Other Works and Spin-offs*

*His Wild Irish Rose*

*The Last Sip of Wine: A Novel of Tuscany*

*This book is dedicated to my readers.*
*Your support is both appreciated and heartwarming.*

# CHARACTERS FROM THE O'BRIEN TALES SERIES

**Sean O'Brien**—of Co. Clare. Married to Sorcha (Mullen), father of Aidan, Michael, Brigid, Patrick, Liam, Seany (Sean Jr.), brother of William (deceased) and Maeve, son of Aoife and David. Retired and Reserve Garda officer.

**Sorcha (Mullen) O'Brien**—of Belfast. Daughter of Michael and Edith Mullen. Sister of John (deceased). Married to Sean O'Brien, with whom she has six children and eight grandchildren. A nurse midwife for over thirty years.

**Capt. Aidan O'Brien, Royal Irish Regiment**—Son and eldest child of Sean and Sorcha O'Brien. Married to Alanna (Falk). Father of three children: David (Davey), Isla, and Keeghan. Serves active duty in the Royal Irish Regiment and currently living in Belfast, Northern Ireland.

**Alanna (Falk) O'Brien**—American, married to Aidan, daughter of Hans Falk and Felicity Richards (divorced). Step-daughter of Doctor Mary Flynn of Co. Clare. Mother of Davey, Isla, and Keeghan. Clinical licensed therapist working with British military families battling PTSD and traumatic brain injuries.

**Brigid (O'Brien) Murphy**—Daughter of Sean and Sorcha, Michael's twin, married to Finn Murphy. Mother of Cora, Colin, Declan, and Finn Jr.

**Finn Murphy**—Husband of Brigid. Father of Cora, Colin, Declan, and Finn Jr. An IT expert who works in Ennis and does consulting work with the Garda.

**Cora Murphy**—Daughter of Brigid and Finn. Has emerging gifts of precognition and other psychic abilities. Oldest grandchild of Sean and Sorcha.

**Michael O'Brien**—Son of Sean and Sorcha, married to Branna (O'Mara), three children: Brian, Halley, and Ian. Rescue swimmer for the Irish Coast Guard. Twin of Brigid.

**Branna (O'Mara) O'Brien**—American, married to Michael. Orphaned daughter of Major Brian O'Mara, USMC, and Meghan (Kelly) O'Mara. Mother of Brian, Halley, and Ian. Real estate investor.

**Patrick O'Brien**—Son of Sean and Sorcha. Married to Caitlyn (Nagle). Father of Estela, Patrick, and Orla. Currently residing in Doolin working as a Garda officer. Serving on the National Security Surveillance Unit on the Armed Response Team in Shannon.

**Caitlyn (Nagle) O'Brien**—Daughter of Ronan and Bernadette Nagle, sister of Madeline and Mary. Married to Patrick. Mother of Estela, Patrick, and Orla.

**Dr. Liam O'Brien**—Second youngest child of Sean and Sorcha. Internal medicine and infectious disease specialist. Married to Dr. Izzy Collier.

**Dr. Isolde *Izzy* (Collier) O'Brien**—Doctor/Surgeon, prior United States Navy. Married to Dr. Liam O'Brien. Born in Wilcox, Arizona. Close friend of Alanna O'Brien. Daughter of Rhys and Donna Collier.

**Sean *Seany* O'Brien Jr.**—Youngest child of Sean and Sorcha.

Serving with the fire services in Galway. Trained paramedic and fireman.

**Maureen** *Moe* **(Rogers) O'Brien**—American. Therapeutic riding instruction in Connemara. Married to Seany O'Brien.

**Tadgh O'Brien**—of Co. Clare. Only son of William (deceased) and Katie (Donoghue) O'Brien. Son William. In the Special Detectives Unit of the Garda. Married to Charlie Ryan.

**Charlotte** *Charlie* **(Ryan) O'Brien**—American FBI Agent with the International Human Rights Crime Division. Married to Tadgh. Son William. Sister of Josh. Currently working in Europe as the liaison to Interpol.

**Josh O'Brien**—American expat. Formerly Joshua Albert Ryan. Brother of Charlie. A lighthouse keeper with the Irish Lights. A rescue swimmer for the Royal National Lifeboat Institution. Married to Madeline.

**Madeline** *Maddie* **(Nagle) O'Brien**—of Co. Clare. Married to Josh O'Brien. Expert in Celtic studies at the National Museum of Archaeology. Sister of Caitlyn and Mary, daughter of Ronan and Bernadette Nagle.

**Dr. Mary (Flynn) Falk**—of Co. Clare. Retired MD, wife of Hans Falk. Stepmother of Alanna O'Brien and Captain Erik Falk, USMC.

**Sgt. Major Hans Falk, USMC, Ret.**—American. Father of Alanna and Erik. Married to Doc Mary. Retired from the United States Marine Corps.

**Maeve (O'Brien) Carrington**—of Doolin. Dual citizen of Great Britain and Ireland. Daughter of David and Aoife. Wife of Nolan, mother of Cían and Cormac. Sister of Sean Sr.

**Nolan Carrington**—of Somerset, England. Dual citizen of Great Britain and Ireland. An attorney residing in the London suburbs. Married to Maeve. Father of Cormac and Cían.

**Cormac Carrington**—of London. Dual citizen of Great

Britain and Ireland. An attorney residing in London. Son of Nolan and Maeve.

**Katie (Donoghue) O'Brien**—of Inis Oirr, Aran Islands. Widow of William O'Brien. Mother of Tadgh O'Brien.

**David O'Brien**—of Co. Clare. Husband of Aoife, father of Sean, William, and Maeve. The oldest living patriarch of the O'Brien family.

**Aoife (Kerr) O'Brien**—of Donegal. Wife of David O'Brien, mother of Sean, William, and Maeve. Originally from Co. Donegal.

**Edith (Kavanagh) Mullen**—of Belfast. Married to Michael Mullen, mother of Sorcha and John.

**Michael Mullen**—of Belfast. Married to Edith. A retired dock foreman. Father of Sorcha and John.

**John Mullen**—of Belfast. Deceased. Son of Michael and Edith. Biological father of Daniel MacPherson, the Earl of Hawick.

**Lord Daniel MacPherson, Earl of Hawick**—Northern Irish and English descent, raised in Hawick, Scotland. Sorcha's nephew, who was unknown to the family until recent years. Son and heir of the deceased Lord Robert MacPherson, the late Earl of Hawick. Biological son of John Mullen and Molly (Price) MacPherson.

**Lady Molly (Price) MacPherson, Countess of Hawick**—of Manchester. Surviving widow of Lord Robert MacPherson. Mother of Daniel, Gregory, and Elizabeth.

**Viscount Gregory MacPherson**—of Hawick. Son of Robert and Molly. Daniel MacPherson's brother and heir to the title of Earl. Brother of Elizabeth.

**Lady Elizabeth MacPherson**—of Hawick. Daughter of Robert and Molly. Sister of Daniel and Gregory. An author writing under the pen name Bethany Raven.

# PROLOGUE

Daniel MacPherson left the home of Edith and Michael Mullen in a sort of emotional fog. It had been a difficult day. A lot of tears and a heartbreaking sense of loss for everyone involved. He'd done it. He'd actually found the courage to contact his biological father's parents and sister. Daniel had an aunt Sorcha. John Mullen's sister, and now an O'Brien, who was living in County Clare in the Republic of Ireland. John's parents still lived in the North.

His chest was tight. All he kept thinking about was Edith Mullen's tear-soaked face. Michael Mullen's stricken eyes. Daniel had been very surprised when they hadn't lashed out at his mother, even though he couldn't even conceive of how betrayed they were all feeling.

The father who raised him had died a few years ago, and that's when his mother finally told him. Robert MacPherson, his beloved papa, was not his biological father. Daniel had been so angry at first, it had nearly buckled his knees. Then soul-crushing grief. First, his mother had taken one father from him, then she'd taken another. It wasn't anything John Mullen had done to her. From everything he'd learned of the man, he'd been a very good person. Would have been a good father and husband. But the politics of the time made the match unsavory. John Mullen had the audacity to be born and raised a Catholic. And his maternal grandparents were snobbish bigots.

Edith had taken Daniel's face in her palms, looking him over so thoroughly that it was a bit unnerving. He'd never looked like his mother. He had warm, brown hair, almost auburn. His father had told him it was his Celtic genes. He'd never actually said Scottish, which made sense. It had been his Irish blood. His aunt had taken one look at him, said the name *John* like she was talking to a ghost, and dropped into a dead faint. Edith's eyes were so full of pain and something that might have been joy. "You look just like him," she'd said. "A piece of him still with us. A piece of my sweet lad. You are the most beautiful thing I've ever seen." And for the first time since the day had started, Daniel had been close to weeping. It had been such a silly thing to say, but she'd meant every word of it.

He now knew that not only did he have family in Northern Ireland, but he had family in County Clare and County Cork as well. A few cousins were also living in Dublin, and one in Shropshire, England. He had a gigantic family who never knew he existed. And now the skeleton was well and truly out of the closet. The skeleton being him. He'd had to tell his employer. There was no help for it. But they were nothing if not discreet. Discreet is what they did best.

# 1

## HAWICK, CO. ROXBURGHSHIRE, SCOTLAND
### SEVERAL YEARS LATER

Daniel MacPherson rang off with his cousin's wife, smiling at the exchange. His cousin, Captain Aidan O'Brien, was getting ready to promote this week to the rank of major, and Daniel was trying like hell to make the ceremony in Belfast. He missed his new family, but he had doubts about the ability to make the engagement work with his schedule.

"What are you smiling about, brother dear?" His sister, Elizabeth, was sitting in his office with her feet on his desk. He gave her a chiding look, but she left her feet right where they were.

"My cousin's wife, Alanna," he said. "I'm going to try making it to Belfast next week if I can." He saw her face shudder, and he had the feeling this newer familial connection still bothered her. "Maybe you'd like to come along? Belfast has its own rhythm. You might like it. Something to write about. Put in those wildly successful books you keep writing."

Elizabeth smiled at that. He wasn't wrong. She wrote under a pen name, but she did well. She didn't need the money, but it was nice to earn something of her own. "Flattery will go far, brother, but I'm not sure I can go. I've got some work to do. I'm on a deadline."

Daniel tilted his head, knowing that there was more to her resistance. "You can talk to me about this whole thing, you know. It came as a big surprise to you. I had a few months to get used to the idea before I told you. But it's been over five years since I found them, and you've never met any of them. They don't replace my family here. The O'Briens and Mullens just added to it. It would make me happy if you had a relationship with them. You're my sister. I mean, Gregory even met my aunt and my other grandparents. Edith and—"

She cut him off. "And Michael. I know. And Sorcha's second son is named after him." Her tone was dry, but he heard the tinge of resentment. "You don't even talk to your own grandparents. You know, Mum's parents? The ones who are getting old?"

"Oh yes, right. The ones who tried to force my mother to abort me? Yeah, that's not your damage, dear Elly, but it is damage nonetheless." The ugly tale had come out during a fight, after he'd learned that little tidbit from his retired governess. His mother had confirmed it, which made him even more grateful to his papa. His sister was friends with one of the underpaid servants in his grandparents' Manchester estate. Elly slipped them an extra fifty quid when she came into town to reimburse the staff for looking after them. It was that friend who had relayed the entire quarrel, and Elly had been heartbroken. She'd known for a few months that their papa had claimed him, but not sired him.

Daniel had outright refused to keep it from them, despite his mother's protests. But this was a whole other thing. His papa had saved their mother from being disowned or pressured into having an abortion that she did not want. Their papa had been a dear friend to their mum. And after time, a true husband. In some ways, at least, because his siblings had come from the union. He'd seen genuine affection between his parents. Not a love match exactly, but a sort of partnership that he'd always respected. It was that father—the one who had raised him—whom he honored every day. Why he'd chosen the path he had. Secrets of another sort.

Daniel continued. "And I have spoken with Grandmother and Grandfather Price. So has our mother. A little civil discourse over the phone at Christmas and New Year's is all they are getting right now. Even after the way they'd treated our mother, she still calls and checks on them occasionally. And they still find a way to needle her. I wish Nana and Grandad were still alive. They were good people and I miss them, but they're gone. Our family is dwindling." The sadness in his eyes changed swiftly to a sideways grin. "Maybe there's a Prince Charming waiting for you in Ireland," he said with more levity. Trying to steer the conversation.

Elizabeth scoffed at that. "That is seriously doubtful, Danny."

Daniel laughed under his breath. "Well, you need to marry. One of you two does. I'm hopeless." Daniel had his solid reasons for not marrying. Reasons no one in the family knew about, but that was his burden to carry.

His sister exhaled. "I really can't join you this time, and you aren't even sure you are going. How about I think on it? Maybe I'll take a few days off and go to Clare with you. Or take advantage of that island cottage of yours." His face seemed to light up at that, and she suddenly felt guilty. "You've given me time, Danny. And I'm trying. I will try harder. Let's sit down next week and go over our calendars. Once I have this next draft turned in to the editor, I'll make the time."

The phone rang just then, and she could tell by his face it wasn't going to be a short call. His jaw tightened.

Daniel gave her an apologetic look as she left his office, then he answered the call. *So much for Belfast. Sorry, Aidan.*

———

## Belfast, Northern Ireland

Captain Aidan O'Brien watched the door to the meeting room. She was late. He knew why, of course. Brigid was whispering a play-by-play of Alanna's traffic issues while his father was standing in the parking lot, waiting to guide her in. He smiled apologetically at his boss. A colonel who made everyone's life hell with regularity but seemed to have a soft spot for Aidan's Southern belle. The door opened, and Alanna was out of breath. "I am so sorry, Colonel Patterson."

Aidan's boss just smiled indulgently. "Not at all, Mrs. O'Brien. We were just about to start." A bold lie, but he'd dare anyone to dispute the facts as he told them. Alanna was detangling Isla from her hip, handing her off to Aidan's mother. Aidan's da had Davey by the hand, and Alanna was attempting to get little Keeghan out of the baby carrier. Aidan held him while she unfastened all the buttons and clips. He didn't see it until she felt it. A cool shot of air at her wet chest. Two circles through her lovely silk blouse. Right where her milk factories were located. She just shut her eyes, exhaling. Then she looked down. "Sweet suffering baby Jesus."

The colonel was actually biting his lip. Aidan saw it. Trying to leave his wife with her dignity, for which he was grateful. Aidan just walked toward Brigid, who didn't see Alanna's front side, and he whipped her large scarf off her neck most unceremoniously. Brigid squawked, spitting lint out of her mouth and almost falling off her chair. She scowled, appearing ready to strike. Aidan ignored her and swept the scarf like a shawl over Alanna's shoulders. She swept one side over her chest like a runway model and said, "Adapt and overcome. Thank you, my gallant prince." Alanna then looked over at the colonel and said, "Carry on, sir. All is secure." The colonel could not hold his laughter inside, doing the remainder of the promotion ceremony with a smile on his face and a glint in his eye. Aidan was going to have to watch the scoundrel at the next unit gathering. He was clearly half in love with Alanna.

The reception that followed was lovely. His mother and grannies had done their special-occasion baking, which was appreciated by all his men. Brigid was milling around while the grandparents helped with the little ones. Not everyone was here, of course. His siblings had careers and school-aged children, but it was nice that Seany and Brigid had come. Seany was currently stuffing another berry tart in his gob. Aidan said, "You just wait, brother. Fifteen years from now, you'll not keep it off so easily." He patted his abs for effect. "Enjoy it now."

Brigid came next to Seany and said, "I thought Daniel was coming. What the hell do barons do?"

"For the fifth time, he's an earl, not a baron. And honestly, I have no idea. He rates a seat in the Lord Parliament, but he declined it for now. He'd be here if he could. He said something about needing to go to Amsterdam."

The truth was, as close as they all tried to get to Daniel MacPherson, he was private. Aidan's mother hadn't even known she had a nephew. More importantly, her brother, John, died without ever knowing about Daniel. A terrible thing, to be sure. But Daniel had been raised in the Scottish borderlands by his mother and her husband. A childhood friend who'd rescued her from the stigma of being an unwed mother and disowned by her family for taking up with a Catholic laborer from their Belfast mill. All that really mattered now was that Daniel found them. He was a part of the Mullen family, and by marriage, an extension of the O'Brien family. Aidan genuinely liked the guy. He was only a year older than Aidan. He and Alanna had even visited his Scottish estate last summer for a long weekend. Aidan wondered what on earth had been the cause of such a last-minute trip to the Netherlands.

# 2

## HAWICK, CO. ROXBURGHSHIRE, SCOTLAND

A quick knock had Daniel's office door opening to his butler. Davis said, "My Lord, you have a visitor." Daniel cringed, giving him a chiding look. He was technically an earl, but not some sort of royalty. It wasn't a particularly large or wealthy estate. And if they only knew the half of it. By blood rights, his brother should be inheriting the title. He'd run in the other direction. He was a terrible earl. He'd refused his hereditary seat at the Lord Parliament. At least for now, he was a no-show when it was time to meet or vote. He couldn't risk the exposure. The bloody paparazzi were relentless with their nosey questions and photos if you put yourself out there as a titled bachelor.

"Davis, do I have to fire you in order for you to stop calling me that?" Daniel asked.

Davis sniffed, almost a snort, and said, "My Lord, I'd like to see you try to run this estate without me. The younger men would have to cover their tattoos and take out their nose rings in order to answer the door. Now, about the visitor. It's Laird Douglas. Shall I send him in?"

Behind him, Daniel heard his old friend laughing. A deep, rumbling sort of laugh that set Davis's teeth on edge. The man said, "My Lord, it is none other than himself, the Duke of Roxburghe, at your service." He was, in fact, the Duke of Roxburghe. High ranking in the peerage, but he liked his secondary title of the Laird Douglas, from his father's side, and went by that most days. More to irritate his uncle in the afterlife, no doubt. And to his nearest and dearest, he was simply Douglas. As if the idiot hadn't been born with his perfectly respectable first name of Andrew. Douglas said, "Now, Davis, get that stick out of your ass and let me by."

Daniel choked on his tea, and Davis speared him with a look, despite the fact that he employed the crabby bastard. "Thank you, Davis. Please tell Donna there will be two of us for lunch. In here, if it's not too much bother. This will be a working lunch." The kind that allowed no servants to overhear, even ones who were more like family. Daniel smiled as his mate plopped down in a leather chair, his tie disheveled and looking a bit hungover. "Did you sleep in that suit?"

Douglas smirked. "I didn't, Danny. I slept naked with a Swedish yoga instructor balanced on my balls."

"If you slept through it, I pity the Swede. Send her my way if she needs a more lively bedmate." Daniel didn't mean it, of course. He didn't swap. Especially knowing where Douglas dipped his quill.

Andrew Douglas III, Duke of Roxburghe, was another bloody aristocrat who held the same secrets as Daniel did. One worth his weight in gold—not due to his estate, but due to his mind. The man was a genius. Douglas ignored the jibe as Donna and Davis came in with something smelling altogether decadent.

Douglas said, "How is it that I employ triple the staff and don't get nearly as much done?" He smiled as Donna came to them and kissed him on the top of the head like a small babe. He had women, young and old, eating out of his hand. They tucked into the hearty stew, and Douglas asked, "You got the message?"

Daniel said, "I did. I'm headed out tonight. I'm flying into Amsterdam out of Edinburgh. They just sent my itinerary."

Douglas nodded, blowing on his spoon. "I'm likely on the same flight. Economy, no less. So much for the privileges of rank."

"Yes, and don't go wearing those eight-hundred-quid boots. Try to at least appear inconspicuous. I know you're only an analyst, but make an attempt at looking like an everyday bloke."

"Only an analyst? Try the best fucking analyst the Crown could get their hands on, old boy. And not this time. They are putting me in the field." Daniel reared back. Unlike him, Roxburghe was more well known. It's why they hadn't let him work in the field. This had to be something serious. Daniel rose out of his chair, pouring his friend a finger of Scotch. Then himself one. He toasted.

"It's about time. Although, they'll be hard-pressed to replace you at that analyst desk," he said, taking a sip.

"Already have," Douglas said as he let that first sip warm his soul. "She's a looker, too. Under all the attitude and off-the-rack clothing."

Daniel gave him a dry look. "The people we work with don't have your family's money to fall back on. And you are a swine, besides. I'm interested in her job qualifications, not her cup size."

Douglas grinned unapologetically, and he wondered if the man would ever settle down. Jesus, Daniel sounded like his mother. Douglas said, "Well, then. I'll tell you everything I know."

————

**Glengormley, County Antrim, Northern Ireland**

Aidan walked through the front door of his grandparents' old house, and a missile shot from the sofa to wrap around his legs. "Davey, you're going to trip your old da, and then I won't be able to work."

Davey looked up at him, very serious. "Good. Then you won't have to leave." Aidan squatted down, getting eye to eye with him.

Aidan said, "I know it's hard, lad. But I'm counting on you to be a big boy and help your mam. Can I count on you? Your mother is very capable, but she has the baby. Can you promise me you'll help her with Isla? And help with the washing up and packing lunches and other things?"

The boy put his arms around Aidan's neck. "I promise, Da."

Aidan looked up to see Alanna's face, eyes lined with sparkling tears. He said, "It's not so dire as all that. It's training. It's only a month. We can do a month, can't we?" After all, Alanna had done several deployments with her father. She straightened her shoulders, inhaling the tears and putting a smile on her face.

She said, "Davey and I can do a month standing on our heads. And we've got your grandparents and great-grandparents and all those other O'Briens to hang out with. This is going to be a piece of cake."

Davey seemed to take some strength from that. Aidan said, "Belize is like a resort. It's training in the jungle, but it's also beaches and skin-diving and lobsters for dinner. It'll be like I'm on holiday. I wish you could go, but it's work. Training, but safe." In reality, Belize had one of the highest per capita murder rates in the world. It was small but mighty when it came to crime, and the Guatemalan border was dangerous for other reasons. They wouldn't be in the ganglands of Belize City, and it was a secure training area, but he'd have to watch over his men carefully. Curious boys often got themselves in trouble.

He saw Alanna's face tighten just a bit. Training could be just as dangerous as war, at times. It had to be if it was going to be effective. But they had no problem sugarcoating the situation to keep anxiety levels low for the children. He palmed his son's head gently. "And I'll bring back some fun gifts for all of you from the people who live there. They make things from cloth and wood and other interesting things. Would you like that? Some gifts from Central America to show your classmates?"

Davey's grin was huge. "Yes, Daddy. Can you bring me a sword?" Aidan heard a gurgled sound from Alanna. He wasn't sure if it was from humor or horror.

"Well, now. I can't bring you a weapon, but I'll be working with the Belize soldiers. They'll teach me things, and I can come home and teach some of it to you. I bet they'll trade a patch or shirt or something like that if you'd rather have something military."

Davey had a look on his face that told Aidan he still wanted a blade. God help him. But Davey just nodded. Then Isla made an appearance, and Aidan's throat tightened to the point of pain. Fair-haired and tousled from her nap, she rubbed her eyes. Then she put her arms out, wanting him to hold her. When she'd been born, her eyes were the blue of newborns. But in the last two years, they'd slowly transitioned to the green eyes of her mother's line. He stood as the child wrapped her tiny arms and legs around him. "Da." That's all she said as she laid her head on his shoulder. It's all she needed to say.

"Your mam told me you took your nap without a fuss. That's a good girl, Isla. It helps Mammy get your little brother to sleep if you're quiet, right?" Their house was small. The house his grandparents had transitioned into when they'd moved from the city. Three bedrooms and two small bathrooms, but it was enough. Branna owned it now, and Aidan was glad they'd kept the house in the family.

Aidan looked at Alanna, his heart overflowing. He'd leave in a week, and he had to admit he was excited. She said, "Don't worry about us, sweetheart. I'll check on Gran and Michael and Granny and David. I cut back my work hours for the month. We are going to be just fine, okay? Concentrate on yourself and your men."

———

## Amsterdam, Netherlands

"I hate flying economy. My fucking neck is all out of sorts," Douglas said.

"You should have actually taken the yoga instead of taking the instructor. Then you'd be more limber in your advancing years," Daniel said, avoiding a swipe from his mate. Someone cleared their throat behind them.

They turned in unison to see their boss scowling at them. "Morgan, so good to see you again." Douglas gave her a bow.

She smirked. "Save the ass-kissing, Douglas. I think you know Airmid Roberts, our new analyst and linguist. Airmid, this other devil is Daniel MacPherson. He'll be the lead operative today."

Daniel shook her hand absently, wanting to get to the harbor.

Roberts said, "Oh, yes. The two aristocrats. Well then, let's dispense with the courtesies toward the peasant class and get to it."

Daniel's gaze sharpened. He supposed he had brushed her off a bit, but she was cocky for a new guy. "A linguist? Full marks in French class, eh?"

She bristled. But before she could retort, Morgan said, "No. In fact, she's a prior soldier with the British Army. She attended the Defense Language Institute in Monterey, California. Spanish instruction, though she specializes in the dialects of Central and South America. Then to the Queen's University in Belfast where she studied three additional languages. Now, if you two are done with your pissing contest, let's be on our way."

Daniel had the good sense to feel a pang of embarrassment. It had been a stupid comment. The woman wasn't some schoolgirl. She looked to be about thirty and carried herself like a woman who knew her worth. He'd been half paying attention during the introduction, which was rude. And given that she knew his background, she probably took him for a snob. He turned abruptly, heading for his rented car. What the hell did it matter anyway? He'd befriended Douglas due to proximity and mutual friends. Had recruited Douglas into the agency, actually. This woman was going to have limited interaction via phone and secured Internet. They didn't need to like each other.

He said over his shoulder, "Belfast?"

She said shortly, "Derry."

Douglas interjected. "I haven't heard of that city. I've been to Londonderry. Is it nearby?" And Daniel had to fight to keep the grin off his face. Douglas was baiting her, and it had hit its mark.

Her spine stiffened and she said tightly, "Christ, deliver me from British aristocrats."

Morgan, who was Welsh by birth, just threw back her head and laughed. "I think I'm going to love working with you, Airmid."

————

The ship was not what Daniel had been expecting. Not a cargo ship, but a luxury yacht that had to be worth millions. Daniel said to Morgan, "The stern says Grand Cayman. I'd venture a guess the major business is happening in Jamaica. What's the country of origin for the boat crew and passengers?"

"Dutch, and we think somewhere in Central America. They

are saying Mexico, but it's not adding up. We've seized the ship, and the GPS should possibly give us the route. If not, we have their phones. For now, we need to start interviewing the men. That's where she comes in. She'll attend the interrogations as an interpreter and decipher the dialect."

Daniel raised a brow. "So, you can tell their country of origin by the way they speak Spanish?"

Airmid nodded. "Sometimes. It's not an exact science, but certain regions from Mexico down through South America have differences in wording and accent. More important for you is to find the weak link. Someone who will talk. Although, these drug cartels likely know where every family member lives. They may be too scared to talk. You haven't seen violence like this, I'd wager. None of us have. We had to learn about the nature of the crime and cartels during my training in Belize."

Douglas folded his arms, finally speaking. "What division of the army were you in, exactly?"

Airmid answered, "I was a linguist. I was attached first to the Royal Irish in Northern Ireland, then moved to a job with the Royal Dragoon Guards, as they needed an interpreter during training overseas. I didn't serve in a combat capacity, as they hadn't lifted the ban for women while I was enlisted."

"And would you have changed your path had it been opened to you?" Daniel asked, intrigued.

"No." That's all she said, with a look that told them all that she was done answering their questions.

Daniel said, "Okay, then let's head to the holding facility." He turned, starting to walk back toward the car.

Airmid said, "Wait. I need to go onto the ship. It will tell me a few things if I can access it."

Morgan said, "Lead on, then. Those lads aren't going anywhere."

Daniel watched her with fascination at first, then he caught on. She was looking at the food they served on the boat. When Douglas had opened one cooler, he yelped. Douglas asked, "What in the royal fuck is that thing used for?"

She was deep in thought. Airmid said, "This isn't a Mexican crew. This is a mix of European and Central American or South American foods and pantry items. That," she pointed, "is for cow foot stew, I'd wager. Popular in places like Belize and Honduras. We could be looking at a mixed group though. I won't know until we interview them." The only reason the Dutch Government was allowing them anywhere near this case was because the Cayman Islands are a part of the British Commonwealth. They left the ship and headed back toward their cars.

"You're here as an interpreter, not a field operative or investigator. Just leave the question-and-answer bit to us," Daniel said, clicking the unlock button on his key. He felt her bristle. The air practically crackled.

Her jaw was tight. "I understand, but if I do ask something that seems non-sequitur, don't be a tosser about it. I'm establishing speech patterns and minor vocabulary differences, and we don't have time to rehearse. Just go with it, Your Lordship."

And with that zinger, she got into her own rental car and sped toward the Interpol holding facility. Douglas cracked off a very obnoxious laugh, earning him a scowl from Daniel. Douglas just turned toward their boss. "I think you're right, Ms. Morgan. She's going to be great fun to work with. I like her already."

Airmid Roberts slid a file in front of the sodding tosser who was heading up this mission. Some smug Englishman with a title and land in Scotland. Christ, why wasn't he playing polo and trolling around on his own yacht? The both of them. Although, at least the Duke of WhereverTheFuck had a sense of humor. She liked the Welsh woman. She was tough, no nonsense, and very smart. An excellent boss all around.

"Your Grace," she said smoothly.

"You will address me as MacPherson or Mr. MacPherson." Then he wrote something and kept the cover of the notebook over it. She had to sit to read it at an angle. *I keep my ties to the aristocracy very quiet for obvious reasons. I don't need someone overhearing your attempts at a jibe and screwing things up for me. The last thing we need is the European press crawling all over me. So, that is your one warning. If we are in public, you call me MacPherson, unless I'm undercover.* "Do I make myself clear?" he finished.

He was right. She sighed. "Yes, Mr. MacPherson."

Daniel called Douglas over to him. "Go to the security desk, confirm the audio and camera are turned off for this room. The blonde security guard seemed to have an eye for you, so it shouldn't be difficult. If you doubt it, we'll take measures to secure the footage. I just want to make sure we haven't been monitored." He gave Airmid a pointed look. She exhaled, feeling like an idiot.

Douglas stopped. "Which blonde? The man or the woman?"

Daniel suppressed a grin. He said, "Just flirt with both. I think you'd have your pick."

Airmid changed the subject before he could make her feel even more stupid. "As you can see, they've disabled the GPS. All of the phones are burners of the simplest style. I'm not sure if they'd even be able to track them."

"There is a GPS. They disabled the obvious one. There's no

way they made this trip across the Atlantic without it. I'll have the harbor police keep looking. It's likely hidden. Or they ditched it when they got to the port," Daniel said.

"It's a good theory. Until then, are you ready for these interviews?" Airmid asked.

Douglas popped his head back into the room. "I got more from the lad. And no, I'm not taking one for the team. I think we are good to go. Although, you remember what Gordon always says."

He did. Assume every government building is recording everything everywhere.

———

Airmid had to give grudging respect to His Lordship the Asshat MacPherson. He was good at his job. He had a coolness that unnerved the detainees. He was also stupidly good looking. Tall and fit, with hair that fell somewhere between auburn and brown. Nice eyes, too. A mix of blue and green. Douglas was slimmer, but just as fit. His hair was darker, with fair skin and deep-brown, intelligent eyes. Well dressed and a good deal more charming than his mate. She was learning from them both, however. And from Morgan. She really liked the woman. She watched the Earl of Hawick mentally work this guy over like a seasoned agent, and she had to admit that she was glad to be working this case with him. Not that she'd tell him such a thing.

———

Daniel thought the interviews had gone well. Their analyst interjected very little with random questions. And now that he understood why, it didn't irritate him as much that she'd participated. She was, in fact, a very competent interpreter. She was passable in Dutch as well.

"Well, my guess would be Central America for a portion of the crew. Likely Belize, Honduras, or Guatemala. There are some Columbians as well, which, given what they were hauling, makes sense. Other than the Dutch who were involved locally, you also had two Jamaicans on board. Their story about a couple crew members being too ill to travel could hold water."

"Or they're dead," Daniel said absently. "If they did something out of line, they'd kill them and replace them. The Jamaicans were acquired mid-voyage as cleaning and cooking staff. They likely know how to keep their mouth shut, but I doubt they're deeply involved. The boat has been running on a skeleton crew for a vessel this big, and most of the men were there for security. The weapons we found hidden throughout the ship were pretty significant."

Airmid said, "The lab reports are in the file as well. The chemical markers for this load of cocaine match what's been coming into the UK. Particularly, purity levels, specific impurities that were present in similar amounts as in the last seizure entering through Cornwall. I mean, we suspected it was entering through the Netherlands, and I think this confirms it. At least the government is cooperating."

Daniel put the file aside. They were in a hotel suite now. "I am heading back tomorrow morning. We should meet at the Edinburgh office on Thursday."

Airmid stood. "I'm headed back tonight. We can video conference on the secured network if you need anything."

"Didn't they offer you a room?" Daniel asked, standing when she did. "They should have booked it when they booked ours."

Airmid didn't meet his eyes. She said, "They offered. I need to go back tonight." That's all she said. "My flight leaves in two hours. I have to go."

Douglas seemed as surprised as he was. When she left the room, Daniel called Morgan. She answered on one ring. She listened to his questions, then asked simply, "Do you need her anymore tonight?"

"No, but we all had a long day. Why would she fly back tonight? And why isn't she working out of the Edinburgh office?"

"Well, that's between Ms. Roberts and her boss. That would be me. Good night, Daniel." And the blasted woman just rang off.

Douglas said, "She did her job. Let the lass go home if she wants to. We have all we need. The Amsterdam office will call us if they nail the bastards down to a statement or find that GPS."

Daniel said, "I suppose. Okay, get your ass off my bed. You know I like to be near the door."

Douglas smirked. "You don't trust me to protect you?"

"I don't trust you not to sneak out and meet that blonde security guard. I saw those looks he was giving you." Bam! The pillow hit him right in the side of the head.

# 3
## EDINBURGH, SCOTLAND

Daniel walked the stone-paved lane, casually taking in his surroundings. Their office wasn't secured, but it wasn't advertised. He arrived at the four-hundred-year-old stone building to find his boss, Annabeth Morgan, wasn't alone. He said, "Ms. Roberts, I thought you were phoning it in?"

She was typing, ignoring the bait. "I was able to get away. Although I had to leave at five o'clock this morning."

He took in her face while everyone was distracted. Douglas was right. She was lovely. Minimal makeup, chestnut hair down to her shoulder blades, fair complexion, and bronze-colored eyes. He'd glanced briefly at her personnel file. She lived on the eastern outskirts of Newcastle-Upon-Tyne. Some coastal village in Northumberland. "It's quite a drive for you. Are you staying in the city tonight?"

She said, "No, I'll be going back." The woman gave away nothing. She looked up. "They found the navigation system. You were right. They'd stashed it in the false bottom of one of the closets nearest the bridge. They likely secured it once they got within view of the port."

Daniel liked the unique timbre to her voice. Northern Ireland had its own sort of dialect. Not like the classically musical sound of his cousins' voices, but more like Granny Edith. Just a bit higher in pitch. More liquid. The vowels were longer, and they accented different parts of a sentence. He thought about the drive she'd made. It was ninety minutes for him and not much shorter a drive for Douglas.

"Boss, what do you think about having these meetings at my home?" Daniel asked. "It's closer for Ms. Roberts. It's closer for everyone. I can sweep the place. I assure you, it's no less secure than this place and the food is better. There's less chance of Douglas getting tailed by media, as we are often seen together, and he lives nearby."

Morgan smirked. "And you can sleep in."

Daniel stiffened. "I, madam, never sleep in."

Airmid interjected, "Don't do this on my account."

"It's not for your account. I just don't want to base our work schedule around your travel time. You obviously have something or someone dividing your attention. All well and good, but this will shave ninety minutes off of your drive and about seventy minutes for myself and Douglas." The door opened. "And here he is. You're late."

"Sorry, I think I had a bloody, goddamn reporter following me," Douglas bit out. "I had to get creative with the traffic laws to evade him."

Daniel looked at his boss as if to say, *See.*

Airmid was still reeling from the smackdown he'd just given her. "I have it handled, Your Grace. My attention is not divided." She was actually gritting her teeth. She'd been looking for a reaction, and she got one.

He whacked the table. "You were warned not to address me—"

She leaned in with a devilish grin on her face. "You said in public. You said nothing about in a private meeting."

Daniel was going to strangle the little minx. He should have her thrown off his case. He could if he pushed, but it would make him look like he couldn't handle her and had been forced to shove her off to someone else's mission. Part of him liked the challenge, which was another reason he should be dismissing her from his team. He said tightly, "Well, I amend my bloody order. Tomorrow we will meet at my home in Hawick. Now that we are all here, cut the shite and let's get on with it."

Airmid just blinked at him. His blood was up, and he'd slipped with his accent. She'd thought him a transplant. His mother was English. But that was a lowland Scottish accent creeping in with his temper. Interesting. And hot as hell, damn him. He had a temper under that suit. Dealing with Irish men had taught her a thing or two about tempers, but she'd thought him above it somehow. When a grin slid across her face, she thought his head was going to pop off.

Morgan said, "Enough. Let's get to it. I might keep a place closer to the city, but I'm not in the mood for anyone wasting my time." Daniel knew she had a mountain cottage in Snowdonia, her place of birth, but the townhome had been a practical necessity. Her small row house in Berwick-Upon-Tweed was no farther from his home than this office, so she didn't have a dog in the fight, so to speak. "Until further notice, we meet at His Lordship's house."

Douglas actually choked on his tea, and Morgan seemed uncowed by his glare. But the blush on Airmid's face as she suppressed a grin was ... not charming. No. It certainly was not.

"Well, since I'm High Lord of this ridiculous group, I may as well reap the benefits. Someone, refill that coffeepot and let's get to it. According to the tech's report, they left from an outlying spit of land just northeast of the Jamaican Coast. My suspicion is that they swapped the navigation system there because there's no way that was where they originated from. I'll have our contacts in the Cayman's take a look, but the island appears completely uninhabited from the satellite pictures we have. So, the question is, where? The men we arrested from the continent aren't talking. I didn't think they would. They've likely got family back home with knives to their throats."

Airmid hated how these cartels scared people into silence at best, service at worst. She wondered if they'd kill the families outright because the boat had been seized along with the crew. Surely, they knew by now. She cleared her throat. "I've been digging into this. The most likely area is Honduras or Belize. We've seen activity coming into the Netherlands over the last few years. It's why the bastards have begun covering their navigational tracks. The port authorities in Amsterdam seized a commercial freighter about three years ago. A supplier who was sending drugs mostly into Scandinavia and France. Exclusively cocaine, which makes sense. The freighter started across the Atlantic from Belize City."

And the day went on, them piecing together a lot of *what ifs* and *maybes*. What they really needed was some operatives on the ground in Central America.

———

**Lisburn, Northern Ireland**
   **Thiepval Barracks, Royal Irish Regiment—2nd Battalion, Light Infantry (Army)**
   Aidan shook his head as he listened to a few of the lads

popping shit. He was commanding a company of soldiers during training exercises in Belize, but only a platoon was coming from the reserve unit in Northern Ireland. Most of the hundred and fifteen attending would be from his last assignment in Shropshire, England. He was glad to be back in Belfast, but he really did miss his men on the larger base in England. It would be good to train with them. The three eejits he was currently observing were just as dear and just as boyishly stupid.

"Corporal Cunningham, you'd work much faster cleaning those rifles if you weren't so busy being pleased with yourself."

The young corporal was a tremendous shot. The smackdown at the range had been pretty impressive. Some men just had the ability in their blood. Cunningham just said, "All I'm saying is that Lance Corporal Kenny is afraid of spiders. And by spiders, I mean the wee ones in the corner of your carpark or in the lav. The spiders in Central America could eat that yapping lapdog of his in one bite. And when the spiders come after him to feast on his bollocks, he best be hoping I'm at his back."

Aidan was not going to laugh. Nope. God, this kid was a cocky bastard and twice as funny. He was not going to laugh. He put his chin toward his chest, not meeting their eyes. "I heard all of that. Thank you, Corporal. If you're done caressing your big rifle, go over the gear checklist with Sergeant Willow. He's in the loading bay. At 1500 hours, I want the platoon lined up and ready." Corporal Cunningham hated paperwork, like all active boys.

He looked at the other two. "Kenny, Rivers, you two are to go to admin and make sure the paperwork for these rifles is sorted. Every magazine, every box of ammo, and every weapon is to be recounted. You have until 1500 hours, so don't dally."

They all three arose from their seats. Aidan said, "You're good soldiers. It's why you were chosen. I'm proud of you. And it's going to be good craic altogether. Despite the spiders." He didn't miss the pale-faced lance corporal taking a hard gulp of air. "And I look much prettier in jungle green than desert cammies. It brings out my eyes," he said for levity. The men chuckled, and as they walked away, Aidan swore he heard the corporal say, *That must be how he got that hot wife of his.* Men really were pigs, but he couldn't deny the truth of it. He had a flashback of sprawling Alanna over that beach house sofa, shoving her bikini aside and taking her with his boots still on. Had it been the cammies? Maybe he'd wear them home tonight and test the theory instead of changing into his civilian attire before he left work.

———

Alanna was panting, sprawled beneath him. Aidan had taken her hard and fast, shoving her shirt over her head, bra off, yoga pants and panties thrown somewhere. He'd at least removed the camouflage blouse beforehand. He didn't want her to get poked with anything. He had his boots and pants still on, the fly open to free himself. His undershirt was ... wet? Yep, covered in breast milk. Her sex was still gripping him, twitching around him. She started to laugh.

He propped up and looked at her. "You started it, love."

She narrowed her eyes. "You are shameless, Aidan O'Brien. You knew exactly what you were doing, swaggering in here all booted up and ready to go. You were tenting out your trousers as you walked in the door, so don't tell me I started it."

Aidan played with her blonde hair, splayed out on the bed coverlet. He just smiled. "I hate leaving you."

Alanna's eyes softened. "I know you do. And I hate when you leave. But we've been lucky. This is the first time in years you've been away for more than two weeks. I understand." And he knew she did. She was a Marine Corps brat. She worked with veterans and their families. She would support the kids through this.

Aidan said, "Davey will need the most help. I know you know that, but I feel like I have to say it. Maybe see if one of my brothers or Da can come visit. Or take the kids to Doolin."

"It's already planned," she said, smiling. And that's why he could do this. Live this life and still have a family. He'd convinced himself, once upon a time, that he had to choose between a life as a soldier and the path of a family man. But his mate had been waiting for him. And the emptiness in his chest had finally been filled. "I love you, *mo ghrá*."

Alanna said, "I love you, too, you big, Irish stud. And with that in mind, you're going to have to take your time tonight. I consider this the appetizer and must insist on a proper goodbye bedding when the kids are asleep."

Aidan kissed her soundly. "Do ye think I'd do any less than a full-course feast, love? It's a date."

———

### JHC FS Aldergrove
#### Co. Antrim, Northern Ireland

They all said their goodbyes and were loading on the plane that would take them to the army base in Catterick. There, they'd meet the rest of the large group of soldiers who were headed to Belize. Royal Dragoon Guards and Royal Irish Regiment, along with a large group from the medical corps, would be doing jungle warfare training in the rainforest and rivers of Belize.

It was different than anything Aidan had ever done. The platoon he'd brought with him were reserve troops, but they did humanitarian missions and disaster relief in various climates when called, so they needed this training. He'd had to fight to get them included when he'd been invited to help train the men. Aidan's work with the US Marines for embedded training team missions would help, but this was new for him as well. He'd learn just as much. And he'd come face-to-face with the challenges that his brother Liam and his wife, Izzy, dealt with in South America. Aidan couldn't wait. He saw the nervous tension in the group for what it was. They were all ready for an adventure. He took a sip from his water bottle, nudging his lieutenant.

"How's the vaccine site?" he asked, knowing he'd nudged him in his sore arm.

Rubbing his arm, Lt. Kearsley said, "With all due respect, ye're a prick, sir. And it's better. The last two nights were shit. Between the arm and the baby, I've had about ten minutes of sleep."

Aidan always checked on his men if they'd made a sick call. Kearsley had suffered a nasty reaction to the yellow fever vaccine. "Yes, well, savor those sleepless nights. Soon enough, your daughter will be bringing home valentines from boys at school." Kearsley made some mumbling comment about a body bag, and Aidan laughed. He said, "Seriously, though. Have doc check the site again over the next couple days. And if it hurts, ask him for an ice pack. I mean, if it hurts other than when your prick major elbows you."

They wouldn't be dicking about in the tourist areas. Well, not for most of the time in Belize. They'd be in the bush, training in jungle warfare. The mosquito-borne illness was nasty, and Liam had volunteered to do a zoom call from Brazil to brief the team on everything from spider bites to malaria. They'd all needed vaccines of one sort or another.

They all settled into the utilitarian seats, their gear secured in a large cargo area. Operation Maya was officially beginning. Their first stop would be the base in Catterick, England, then they'd take a larger aircraft together with the other platoons. Aidan had worked with the dragoons before and thought this was going to be a great experience for the men under his command. And so, in the time-honored military tradition of *hurry up and wait*, they strapped in and waited for takeoff.

---

### Hawick, Scotland

Donna was following Daniel around, firing questions at him. She and Davis lived on the estate in small rooms just past the large kitchen. She was widowed as a young woman, and Davis was a lifelong bachelor. The only other staff he kept were the two local girls who came in twice a week to clean, a full-time groom for the stables, and a gardener for the mammoth gardens his mother favored. Donna asked, "Did you ring your mother? She's called twice."

Daniel said, "It's on my list. Now, back to the meetings. It'll be every day this week. They should arrive around half seven, and I'm not sure how late they will go. Prepare a couple of rooms just in case, but I doubt anyone will spend the night."

"Yes, and about the meals. My intent is to serve three meals and a light tea if you think they'll be here for supper. If not, there will be leftovers for lunch. It's no bother."

Daniel smiled at his housekeeper. She managed the cleaning staff and did the cooking. He didn't need a cook, but she needed the work and a place to live. Her husband had died young and without a pension. So, she'd been forced to survive on very little until Daniel had promoted her ten years ago. He'd keep her here until she met her Maker, if that's what she wanted. Give her his best suite. She'd lived here since he was a small boy and she'd been a live-in maid. She was twenty-six when she was widowed. The same age as his mother.

When his parents moved down to Bath after his sister graduated from secondary school, he'd taken this on as his permanent home. His siblings lived in their own flats and had an allowance from the estate as well as their own careers. His brother, Gregory, was in a long-term relationship with himself, still sowing his oats. Elizabeth stayed single as well. By choice, but he didn't know the reason behind it. She was the baby of the family, ten years younger than Daniel. Gregory just turned thirty-one, and he was the apple of their mother's eye. The true heir to their father's title, but he'd stubbornly refused to take it. Elizabeth was, in fact, a Lady and could inherit his unentailed estate, but the actual earldom could only be passed to a male relative, which was ridiculous. The peerage really did need to catch up.

He stopped, turning to Donna. "I have about twenty things to do before I go for a jog around the village. Is there a question in there somewhere, love?"

She patted his lean face. "Cheeky. Yes, food allergies. Or God help me, a vegan in the group. Have the answer in fifteen minutes. I'm going to the market."

"Have Davis drive you, Donna. It's raining," Daniel said. She waved him off.

"Says the addlepate who's going for a jog around the village," she said over her shoulder. She was a couple years shy of sixty, but she had the fire of a much younger woman. Her back was still straight, and she ran his household with care and efficiency.

"I mean it, Donna. Have Davis drive you. He can load the parcels." He gave it a fifty-fifty chance that she'd follow his order. Stubborn woman. And with that thought, he went to ring his mother.

———

"Daniel, darling. It's about time you called your poor, old mother," Lady Molly MacPherson said across the many miles from Bath to Hawick.

"How are you, Mother?" Daniel asked, suddenly missing her very much. He'd been so angry with her when his father had died. Then the anger had cooled into something they could both live with, but something less. A month after his beloved papa had passed away, she'd rocked his entire universe with her confession. In one conversation, she'd taken something very precious from him. His father. His lineage. Two fathers, really. The father who had raised him and the father who had never known about Daniel —John Mullen of Belfast. A young mill worker and his mother's first love.

His tone was softer than it had been in years. He only had one parent left. She was young compared to his schoolmates' mothers. Had gotten pregnant just out of her girlhood. But even young people got sick. Look at his father. Robert Daniel MacPherson, Earl of Hawick, had died in his early fifties. Cancer had taken him away, and after his death, Daniel's mother had decided to tell him the truth. He both respected and resented her for it.

His mother answered, "I'm doing well, love. I miss you. I just saw your brother and thought maybe you'd like to visit."

And for once, Daniel wasn't lying. "I'm sorry, Mum. Truly. I'm swamped at work."

She sounded sad. "I see. It's important work. Your father would be so proud. I'm calling to let you know there is a parcel coming for you. It should be there tomorrow. Just something of your father's that I thought you'd be interested in."

He was surprised. Daniel said, "Okay, I'll tell Davis to look for it. What is it?"

She paused, just a moment. His mother said, "It's a set of three journals. From age twenty-two to age thirty-one. He stopped keeping one after that. I think he just got too busy with his work and three children. I just thought you'd like to read them. You were always so close to him, and I don't think he would have minded. I didn't read them. I couldn't." Her voice caught, and Daniel hoped it was because she'd really loved his father. He just didn't know.

———

Junior Agent Roberts and Supervising Agent Morgan arrived early, within minutes of each other. Daniel was surprised that Douglas was on time. The man would be late to his own funeral. Airmid seemed tense, and he wondered if it was the house and staff. The house was old and beautiful. He knew this. He loved his home. Had grown up here. And he wouldn't be made to feel awkward or apologetic over the grandeur.

Donna broke the tension by wheeling in a tea cart full of self-service breakfast. Porridge, bannocks and scones, jams and butter. A simple fruit salad and some warm-boiled eggs. He introduced Donna to Airmid, as she was the only one who hadn't met her.

Morgan and Douglas filled their plates and came to the small conference table. Daniel said, "Please, Agent Roberts. Help yourself."

She looked exhausted. Given her travel time over the last week, he understood it. She poured herself a cup of tea and took a scone, sitting down while Daniel finally served himself. Airmid said, "Thank you, Donna. This looks gorgeous altogether."

Donna said on her way out of the room, "You're quite welcome, Miss Roberts."

Morgan said, "Right, then. If we don't mind setting our courtly manners aside, let's get right down to it. Airmid, if I dropped you in Jamaica right now, could you get by with the language?"

Airmid seemed to think on it. "Not perfectly, but enough to prove effective. Patois is a unique English dialect formed from two other influencing languages—Spanish and French. There are some influences from the African languages as well, but I can't remember the specifics. Most of the Caribbean Islands have their own dialect, but the official language in Jamaica is English. Do you need me to listen to something?"

Morgan raised an eyebrow. "No, I need you on the ground. First Jamaica, then possibly in Central America."

The collective jaw dropped as it took a minute to settle in. Daniel and Douglas said it in unison. "Hell no."

Airmid bristled, but said to her boss, "I'm an analyst and a linguist, not a field agent. I can work as an interpreter, but my specialty is listening and deciphering."

Morgan talked over the two men in the room, who were shaking their heads and rumbling protests. "The three of you would stay together. You wouldn't be without protection."

Airmid stood, starting to pace. "That's not the problem." And she gave her boss a pointed stare. "And you damn well know it. I can't just pick up and leave."

Daniel looked at Douglas, then at her. Airmid said, "None of your business."

Morgan said, "The pay is substantial. A temporary windfall, as it were. You'd be paid a junior agent's wage with a hazardous-duty bonus. Think about it carefully before you deny me outright. If you can't do it, I understand. But if you can't do it, you're off the case. I'll try to find—"

Daniel interrupted. "I am squad leader on this case. Do you two mind not being so bloody vague?"

Airmid just asked, "Timeline? How long would I be gone, and when would I depart?"

Daniel answered, ready to strangle them both, but determined to take control of this stupidity. "We leave in five days. Once we've finished in Jamaica, we will come back to the UK, regroup, and meet with the remainder of the team here. The rest is fluid, depending on what we find out."

Airmid seemed to be calculating. Weighing. She shut her eyes, fighting some sort of panic or emotion. "I'll do it."

Daniel said, "She's not sufficiently trained. This cannot be amateur hour, Morgan. There's too much at stake."

Morgan said, "I disagree. She spent some time in Central America with the army. And she can take care of herself. She'll pose as your wife, and Laird Douglas over there will be her stepbrother." Daniel was scrubbing his face, obviously unhappy with the assignments. "Or we can reverse the roles. Douglas, you can be the spouse and—"

Before Daniel could stop himself, he snapped, "No!" He shook off the urge to strangle his best friend. "No," he said more calmly. "Leave it. He's as inexperienced at fieldwork as she." He couldn't read Agent Roberts's expression. What was her opinion?

Airmid said, "I'll need a break at around half ten to make some phone calls. I have to prepare."

*What the fuck did that mean?* Daniel's next task was to thoroughly read Airmid Roberts's personnel file, cover to cover. He was missing something. "Morgan, this is a bad idea. This is not rookie hour for a bit of extra pay."

Before Morgan could say a word, Airmid whirled on him with her finger point dead at his chest. "Do not condescend to me, Your Majesty. While you were taking tea with the other lords of Parliament, I did six years in the British Army. I trained in the jungles of Central America, did one tour in Afghanistan, and guarded aid workers during the Ebola pandemic in Africa. You know exactly shite about my life, so if you are going to insult me, then do me the courtesy of speaking directly to me!" Then she continued to chew him out in flawless Spanish. He narrowed his eyes on her, recognizing at least four curse words. Something about a royal pig-fucker being the most insulting.

Morgan stood, putting her hands up. In her clipped Welsh accent, she said, "Everyone calm the fuck down. Lass, go make your calls now. I need another cup of something before we continue, and you both need to cool off."

Airmid's eyes never left Daniel's, and grudging respect blossomed in his mind. She was a bloodthirsty harpy wrapped up in a pretty, little package. Daniel just nodded slowly. Once. And Airmid took her phone from the secured locker and left.

Then it was Morgan's turn at him. She said, "What has gotten into you, Daniel? You have never treated another agent like this. Even the agents who were way more wet behind the ears than that one. Whatever your issue is, get it together. She goes. And you will goddamn like it."

Daniel ran his hands through his hair as he watched her leave the room as well. He could feel the knowing eyes of Laird Douglas boring a hole into him. "Well, well," Douglas said in his low, deep voice. "It appears you've got a taste for feral Irish women."

Daniel walked over to the wet bar, poured a Scotch, and downed it in one gulp. "Fuck off."

———

Daniel offered the women a spare guest room, as they remained late into the evening. Morgan stayed. Airmid didn't. He'd apologized to her when she came back from making her mystery calls. She accepted, but her demeanor was cool. It had been distant before, but he'd drawn a line with her and embarrassed her in front of two coworkers. Unlike the frostiness of the English women he knew, she was now hard, brutal ice. And he couldn't say he was completely to blame. Whoever she'd contacted, the phone calls had fouled her mood.

He was sitting in front of the fire, despite the unseasonably warm weather for springtime. A fire at night always centered him. And this old house was drafty even without the windows opened. Daniel looked around his beautiful home and tried to see it through Airmid's eyes. Unapologetic wealth. And despite being in the borderlands, she saw him as English. There was a thousand years of history that made this relationship stressed. But she'd joined the British Army. She'd let British Intelligence recruit her. So, she wasn't anti-Crown so much as anti-Daniel. *Fuck me. You really stepped in it.* He suddenly wished he could talk to his father. As if on cue, he heard the front door motion sensor chime. Then Davis opened the front door.

Davis knocked on the open door. "Not meaning to disturb you, My Lord, but you have an overnight parcel."

Jesus. His father's journals. He couldn't do it right now. No way. "Just place it on the desk, Davis. Thank you."

Davis did so, and as he bid Daniel good night by handing him a tumbler of Scotch, Daniel laughed. That damn butler knew him better than most. "You look like someone took a piece of hide off you, if ye don't mind me saying."

Daniel asked, "Davis, do I ever act like a royal pig-fucker?"

The gurgled noise coming from Davis might have been a laugh. Davis said, "I find that in these situations, it's best to assume the question is rhetorical. You're a good lad. If ye've behaved like a royal pig-fucker, ye ken it." The butler dropped all pretenses of being a well-trained butler after seven o'clock at night. His burr coming out with the fatigue of late day.

Daniel said, "I suppose I do."

As Davis left, Daniel heard him talking in the common room. Davis said, "Good evening, madam. If you require anything from the kitchen that isn't readily at hand, don't hesitate to ring myself or Donna. There's a tray of meats and cheese and some apple tarts in the kitchen for the taking."

Daniel stood as his boss entered the room. He poured a rum and tonic for her, squeezing a lime over it to finish. He handed her the icy drink and she smiled. "Thank you. I needed a drink. I thought I'd find you in here, sulking."

The corner of Daniel's mouth twitched upward. "I'm not sulking. I'm brooding. It's much more dignified."

Morgan cracked off a genuine laugh, which was rare. He noticed she was carrying a file. She handed it to him. "Some light reading. I took the liberty of printing Junior Agent Roberts's personnel file, as I'm sure you'll be too nosey to stay out of it. She's new to your team, so you're within your authority to study her."

Daniel was almost afraid to take the damn file. He said, "I read the top layer, so to speak. But I'm guessing there's something in here I missed."

"Go to page eight. The family and dependent section and tax information," Morgan said.

He narrowed his eyes, almost refusing. Then he sighed, knowing his interest was too piqued. Was she married? That would certainly simplify things. But he didn't think so. He flipped through pages until he found the section. *Marital status: Single. Dependents: One child, age four.* Then he read the tax information. No veteran disability, or she'd never have been hired. *Single family income.* Child support column said a big fat zero.

Daniel felt like vomiting. "No support from the father of the child?"

"He's dead," Morgan said shortly. "A training accident in the army. She was six months' pregnant and had already ended her tour in the military to go to school. They hadn't married yet. He still had his parents down on paper as getting the survivor benefits. She got nothing. And when her daughter was born, the child got nothing. Not even a flag."

Daniel rubbed a hand over his face. He thought about his cousin Aidan and his three children. "Christ, that's a bloody travesty. His parents don't help her?"

Morgan said, "Let's just say their helping hand came with strings. Five hundred quid and they take custody of their granddaughter." Daniel jerked. She shrugged. "Apparently, they're English. They didn't like him taking up with an Irish girl. Hence the delayed marriage. He evidently thought they'd come around, but then it was too late."

Daniel's throat was thick. He thought about his own parentage. "Yes, I can see why you told me. I'm assuming this all came out during her screening?"

"Yes, it did. Getting a top-secret clearance is a rigorous background check and interview. They look for any leverage that could be used against a person with sensitive intelligence access. She was very open about it. Her only debt is a loan she took out for her car and a small one to pay her legal fees when the bastards tried to sue for custody."

"Fucking rotters. Jesus, people really do suck," Daniel said. "So, the phone calls. They're about care for the child, I assume? A daughter. Jesus, I should have guessed it was something like that."

"Yes, apparently her childminder is married and getting on in years. She can't do overnights. She has a few days to get this sorted."

Daniel nodded absently, feeling like a rotter himself. Or in this case, more accurately, a royal pig-fucker. No wonder she bristled at the idea of him. British aristocracy treating her like less in his huge, fucking manor. Goddammit. "I have some serious arse-kissing to do, don't I?"

"Yes, you really do," Morgan said. "Sláinte." And they both took a hefty sip.

# 4

Andrew Douglas, Duke of Roxburghe, rarely knew when to hold his tongue. "Christ, Derry girl. You look like shit."

And if you could disembowel a man with a look, Airmid did it. But he wasn't wrong. Daniel took in his new agent's face and had to agree. She was beautiful, as always, but she looked completely exhausted. She said, "Thanks, Douglas. Now, can we get on with things?" Her tone was sharp, and Douglas had the good sense to look contrite.

"Sorry, love. You look as though you could use a lie-down. I'm sure we can have—"

But she cut him off. "I'm fine. I just had a long night. And not in the Swedish yoga instructor way of having a long night. A shit night. So, believe me when I tell you that your life depends on the next words that come out of your gob."

Daniel did not love when her Derry accent got thicker. Nope. He didn't. "Enough. Now, Agent Roberts, your itinerary is in the file in front of you. I pushed departure back a couple more days, as you had such short notice."

Her face tensed, and he couldn't fathom why. He continued. "We fly into Kingston. I've rented a live-aboard sailboat, which is how we will be able to come and go from the area of the GPS coordinates without raising suspicion. We also have two rooms booked at a resort in Montego Bay."

"Why are we flying into Kingston instead of Sangster?" Douglas asked.

"Because our boat can't be delivered to the other side of the island. Our agents in the country have arranged another 'crew member' to help us navigate the waters. So, dust off your deck shoes, old boy."

"Of course, you both know how to sail. Jesus wept," Airmid said with a snort. "Well, I can't complain, can I? Just tell me which rope to yank, and I will do what I can for you." Daniel had the absurd urge to laugh, and Douglas's eyes bulged. Before anyone said anything, Airmid said, "That came out way more provocatively than it was meant. Forget I said it."

"It's a line, not a rope. If you are going to pass as a sailor's wealthy bride, get the basic terminology down. I won't have a ditsy gold digger for a fake spouse." Daniel was trying not to smile.

Airmid gave him the first genuine smile he'd seen in two days. "Was that a joke? From you?"

"Smart-ass," he said under his breath, and they went on.

————

It was about lunchtime when the call for Airmid came in. She entered the room, and Daniel could tell she'd been crying. He stood and asked, "What is it?"

"It's nothing. I'm handling things. What time will we be done today?" Airmid wouldn't look at him, and he thought he saw shame on her face.

"Morgan, Douglas, a minute, please?" He said the words gently, and they didn't question him. But Morgan approached him on her way out.

She said, "How you handle this situation will set the tone for this entire mission."

After they left, he turned toward Airmid. She snapped, "I said, sir, that I had this handled."

His voice was uncommonly gentle as he asked, "Is it about your little girl?"

"Don't be nice to me right now. The change could push me over the edge," she said, closing her eyes. "I prefer the English wanker. At least I know who I'm dealing with then."

"I'm only part English. I think you'd be surprised by the rest of that story, but not now. Maybe not ever. Now, Agent Roberts— Airmid, tell me what's amiss? You look like you've had no sleep."

She folded her arms over her chest. "I see you've briefed yourself on my situation. And what is amiss is that it is allergy season. My daughter has the sniffles. A small cold at best. But my aging childminder doesn't want to take it home to her husband. He's in poor health, and it's completely understandable. She's also not able to take care of her while I'm away. She just called, and the neighbor is coming over to finish out the day. Then I'm on my own."

Daniel had been thinking about this all night, after he'd read her file. "You're not on your own. If I may, I'd like to offer a solution."

As if on cue, Davis came to the office door and knocked. "Davis, just the man I wanted to see. Just set the tea tray down and come back in fifteen minutes."

"Whatever you need, My Lord." He was going to strangle Davis because he felt Airmid tense next to him.

When he'd thanked the smirking, old coot and closed the door again, Daniel turned toward Airmid. "This driving you are doing and the childcare situation can be simply solved if you'll indulge me. Why don't you bring your daughter here? I can arrange a local girl, and Donna, who I think you're comfortable with, to entertain and care for her while we are in meetings. You can stay in the guest room with her."

She paled. "I couldn't do that. It's unprofessional. I can handle this on my own."

"I'm sure you can. You've always done so. But this is a simple solution. And it's not unprofessional because your two bosses are not complete wankers. I can figure out a process for interviewing and hiring a nanny, who will be here during the day and then come here during our time away to live in-house. Someone you approve of. And for the next few days, at least, the lass is sick and needs her mum. She must be missing you, as late as you've been returning home." That did it. Airmid's eyes were rimmed with crystal tears that she wouldn't let fall.

Daniel said softly, "This isn't the Dark Ages. Working parents shouldn't be penalized for being parents. And your head will be more in the game and you'll be more well rested if we take this one simple step."

Davis knocked again and Daniel met her eyes. She just nodded. "Thank you, Your Majesty."

He cracked off a laugh, and she finally stifled a giggle. Daniel said, "Well, I have to say I prefer that title to royal pig-fucker any day of the week."

Morgan came into the room behind Davis, looking like a mother bear protecting her cub. Then Douglas. "Davis, if you would take the Land Rover and drive Miss Roberts to Newcastle-

Upon-Tyne. She'll be collecting her daughter and some luggage for an extended stay. Also, have Donna go to the market for some child-friendly snacks and family dinners. Thank you."

"I can drive myself, MacPherson," Airmid said.

"You're exhausted, and it is a round trip twice in one day. This is easier and safer, as you'll be transporting—I'm sorry, what is your daughter's name?"

"It's Erin. And I think this is likely a major inconvenience for Mr. Davis. I can just finish the day and come in the morning."

Morgan interjected. "Actually, I was planning on a late-evening video conference with our Caribbean agent, and it would be better if you just went now and settled in for the night. If you don't mind missing a few boring conversations over the next three hours. I can brief you later."

Morgan winked at Daniel when Airmid wasn't looking, and for once, Douglas was silent. When Airmid left the room with her purse and his butler, Morgan turned toward him. "Well done, MacPherson."

———

Daniel spent a good amount of the next hour on the phone with his family. His sister, as threatened, had gone to ground in order to meet her deadline. He didn't want to involve his mother. So, he called his aunt Sorcha because he trusted her judgment and quite simply adored her. He hadn't filled her in on Airmid's backstory because it wasn't his story to tell, but she'd given him some sound advice.

She'd also dropped a bomb in his lap about his cousin Aidan. The family news he'd missed due to canceling the last two gatherings was that Major Aidan O'Brien was on his way to Belize for training. Likely, the same training base where Airmid had been an interpreter several years prior. Operation Maya was jungle warfare training that took place with the Belizean military. For fuck's sake. Jamaica was the starting point, yes, but they'd narrowed down the departure city to three harbors in Central America—Belize City, Puerto Cortes in Honduras, or Cortina in Nicaragua. The meeting tonight was with the teams who were in place to head to Cortina and Puerto Cortes. Morgan supervised the entire group, and they all needed to be on the same page. Only Douglas, Airmid, and Daniel would be going to Jamaica, but after that, they'd cast a wider net.

This was going to get very complicated for his female counterpart, as she was a single parent. Daniel had made up his mind that after Jamaica, he was going to give her an out. Despite his temporary solution, this was not an easy career for a single parent. She'd been recruited as an analyst and linguist, not a field agent. And he was passable in Spanish. Barely. Daniel had a better grasp of the Russian tongue and could speak a little conversational Chinese. Although, admittedly, he was rubbish at reading both. Douglas could speak French and German, which did dick-all in this case. Right now, with the country of origin not narrowed down, they needed a good linguist. Interpreters were easy enough to find, but what Airmid did was so much more of a refined skill set. Daniel needed her, but he bloody well wished he didn't.

His phone rang in his hand. His personal phone, not his secure work mobile. It was a Belfast number he recognized. "Alanna, love. How are you and the bairns?"

She giggled. "Oh, you know how I love it when you go all Outlander in your speech patterns. You must be stressed if you are letting that Scottish slip."

Daniel rubbed his forehead. "Enough with the head-shrinking, woman. I like it just as much as that cousin of mine likely does."

"Touché, big guy. Rumor has it, you need a big ole distraction for a four-year-old," she said in that sweet, Southern way she had.

"Auntie called you, then? I thought she'd call Brigid," he said.

Alanna said, "Well, she may very well call her. I know Cora has a swim tournament this weekend though. How about we come for a short visit? Davey has school next week, but I can spare a couple days if you're okay with four kids in the house at once. It might make your coworker feel less like a burden if it's just a bunch of kids hanging out. I think it's wonderful that the foundation you work for is offering to hire a nanny, but accepting help is likely giving her the scratch."

Daniel said, "Well, I suppose head-shrinking has some perks. And you are welcome here any time. I'll have the groom expect some small riders. I know the neighboring estate has two highland ponies for the smaller ones, and I'm boarding a couple as well. And Davey can ride King Louis. He could use the exercise."

"Oh, you won't have to ask him twice. That's very kind of you. And Daniel. My advice for a comfortable workplace is to put my brood and your coworker as far away from the workspace in the house as possible. Maybe up on the third floor. Mommas always worry their kids are annoying people. You've got that old nursery up there that we can put to good use."

Daniel said, "Donna is already on it. And she may have bought stock in sweeties and cheddar biscuits. And I think I saw her come into the house with a sackful of toys like Father Christmas."

Alanna giggled. "I knew I liked that woman. It's a good thing you're doing, Daniel. Single parents need to be supported by their employers. Now, all that said, if her daughter isn't feeling better in two days, I will not be bringing the little ones. And if my kids suddenly get sick, the same applies. No need to share the love, so to speak."

"Good point. Well, then, we'll keep the plans fluid," Daniel said. "But I hope it sorts itself out. I think little Erin would be less unsure of the situation if she had some playmates." Daniel found his throat growing a little tight. Because this made him feel like he was part of the family more than any other of his interactions. For once, he was reaching out to ask for help, and the O'Briens were rallying.

———

Airmid was quiet for most of the drive, and if Davis noticed a sporadic dash of wetness under her eyes, he said nothing. It was about halfway to her home that he finally stopped the niceties and spoke plainly. "You know, Miss Roberts, our Daniel is not the sort to make gestures with strings attached. He will not allow this minor challenge you are experiencing to in any way measure your work performance or readiness. He has no children or wife, but he's not without compassion and a modern understanding of a working parent. Don't fret over this. In all honesty, it'll be nice to have a little one running around the place again."

She said, "How long have you been with the family, if you don't mind me asking?"

"Well, let's see. I was hired on to assist the household's butler twenty-two years ago. When he retired, I moved into his position. The previous earl and his wife kept a larger staff back then. They had three children running around, after all. But when Daniel took over the home, after they moved to Bath, he didn't replace the staff that moved with them. It was mostly single people who needed to retain the job and liked the weather better in Bath. He only keeps the rest of us on because he's one man and it's a big house and property. But the time for footmen and nannies is over for the household. At least for now. He can't get rid of me, and he would never part with Donna. She's like a second mother to him. She's been with him almost her entire adult life."

Airmid smiled at that. "She is a lovely person. And from what I've seen, he could never part with you either. So, you both live on the grounds?" she asked. "I'm sorry if that's too nosey."

"Not at all. We were both given quarters on the sub level. It allows us some privacy from the household and each other. Back when they built the estate, there was a separate servants' wing for the men and women. Three rooms in each hall. So, I have a library with a daybed for when I rarely have a guest. Daniel doesn't stick with the old ways, and I have a teenage nephew who will come visit on occasion. Donna uses her two extra rooms for God knows what. I never had the nerve to ask her."

Airmid giggled. Davis smiled and said, "It's good to see a smile on your face. We're almost home, and you'll want to put on a happy face for little Erin, I suspect."

"Yes, I suppose you're right. Thank you for this, Davis. Truly," she said. "And I promise we'll try to be low impact on the household. No juice on the good rugs and all that."

He smiled at that. "That house was meant to be lived in, my dear. Children leave their own sort of patina, and the house will be more beautiful because of it."

————

Donna came over the intercom just as they were ending the video conference with the rest of the agents assigned to this mission. The others were officially on standby until they returned from Jamaica. Morgan and another interpreter, who was stationed out of London, were going to go back to Amsterdam to have another crack at the detainees from the yacht seizure.

Donna said, "Daniel, I believe Davis has just pulled up to the front of the house."

Daniel got up from his chair, telling Morgan and Douglas, "I'll see to her. Just continue on and I'll catch up. I think she won't appreciate an audience until the child is settled and comfortable."

He'd been right. Airmid looked even more exhausted, and the child was sprawled over her chest, knocked out cold. He had a partial view of a flushed, chubby cheek and long, amber lashes. Her face was smashed against her mother's shoulder, and her riotous, blonde curls were trying to make their way up Airmid's nose. She wiggled her nose, and Daniel used a hand to move the child's hair away from her mouth and nose. She smirked. "Thanks for that. I'm sorry we were gone so long. She talked Davis into just about every stuffed animal she owns going into the boot. It was like negotiating with a terrorist."

Davis smiled just a bit. "Not at all, miss. Now, are you sure I can't help you? You are tired yourself."

Daniel swore the old boy was blushing. "I'll help her, Davis. If you'd just take care of the bags."

"I have her, Mr. MacPherson," Airmid said. She'd never call him Agent Macpherson in front of the staff, and maybe she thought dropping the mister sounded too familiar.

Regardless, Davis said, "Daniel, Miss Roberts." For now at least. They'd get their passports tomorrow. He was afraid to see which stupid name his admin person had come up with. He'd used his personal passport for Amsterdam, which was normally a no-go, but he'd feigned work stuff with the customs people. Non-profit do-gooder from the UK.

Daniel said, "Okay, then let me take the bag off your shoulder." He slid the strap off her shoulder and she groaned.

"Yes, that's grand. Jaysus, this child and her toys," she said.

And that Derry accent was more pronounced. Probably because she was tired.

Daniel said, "If you want to get her settled, Donna can sit with her while we brief you. Then you can rest until tomorrow. Did you eat?"

Davis said, "I offered to stop, but she just wanted to get back to work. I'll make sure she's got a hot meal waiting in your office."

Airmid said, "Davis, if you keep sweetening me up like this, I'm going to propose."

"Yes, miss," he said.

"I've told you to call me Airmid about a hundred times," she said.

Daniel grabbed the largest bag and huffed a low laugh. "Good luck with that one. I think he calls me 'My Lord' just to watch the annoyance bristle across my brow." And if they both heard a little grunt of laughter come out of Davis, no one acknowledged it.

Donna was waiting at the door, her heart in her eyes. "Oh, my. What a gorgeous little girl. Come now. Let's get her settled, and I'll bring a tray up to her. Davis, the third floor would be grand. There's a large suite up there and a nursery for her toys next door. We haven't had a child in the nursery since our little Elizabeth was playing with her dollies."

When they got to the bottom of the stairs, Airmid said, "Third floor, eh?"

Daniel fumbled over his words. "Oh, you don't need to be on the third floor. My cousin said you might enjoy a bit of privacy with your daughter and the use of the playroom. It's got another three bedrooms where she and her children stay. We can put you wherever you like. Closer to the kitchen or—"

"MacPherson, I'm sure I'm going to love the third floor. I'm just selfishly considering waking her up and making her walk. Just give me a minute."

But before she could argue, Daniel set the luggage down and said, "Hand her over before you fall over with the poor thing in your arms."

She sighed, letting him take her. "She's heavier than she looks. And she's got a cold. Don't say you weren't warned." But with surprising gentleness and skill, he took the four-year-old.

Daniel noticed the look on her face. "I might not have children of my own, but my extended family in Ireland has enough small children to form an army and launch another rising." And with that little truth bomb, everything she thought she knew about the Earl of Hawick started to blur.

———

### Doolin, Co. Clare

Brigid Murphy hated being the last to know things. She prided herself on her ability to be a nosey peahen when it came to her brothers' lives and, by extension, her male cousins. She knew Daniel MacPherson was a private but very kind man. He wanted to get to know the Mullen side of the family. And because his only Mullen aunt lived in O'Brien country, the entire clan just accepted him as a part of the family. But he gave little away. She knew he worked for a non-profit. Some sort of big-wig on the board of an international charity group. Aid workers and emergency funding for disasters, famines, pandemics, etc., in developing nations. He traveled a lot. That's all she knew.

But for once, he'd asked for advice. For help. Instead of being the rich cousin who did things like buy a cottage on Inisheer so that Katie had somewhere to go, the man had actually called because he was in need—not needed. And that was huge.

Apparently, a female coworker was a single mother and needed to bring her child to stay with her at Daniel's estate. That way, she could monitor her and be close by. When they traveled, Daniel wanted to ensure she had not only a nanny, but his sweetheart of a housekeeper to keep an eye on the child. He was a saint, no doubt. But this was a very grand gesture for someone who was a mere coworker.

She had to go to Scotland. Had to be boots on the ground, as Aidan would say. Daniel was a gorgeous, unmarried, thirty-nine-year-old man—and single. She'd prodded to see if perhaps he preferred men. And although he'd assured her that he'd be comfortable sharing that fact with the family, he was, in fact, a garden-variety heterosexual. So, why was he unattached?

Finn's voice broke through the clinks and shifts of her brain at work. He said, "Jesus, woman. You look like your head is about to combust. I can smell your scheming as it leaks out your ears. Leave that man to his own business."

Brigid said, "Shut your gob. I'm just thinking about how to help the lass. She's in quite a pinch, trusting strangers with her child."

He raised his brows. "How magnanimous of you, love. My apologies." Brigid saw the sarcasm for what it was. She made an obscene finger gesture at him, and his smile was devilish. "Maybe after my Zoom call." The dominance in his voice made her toes curl.

"That's not what I meant and you know it. And I have things to do. You'll have to wait," she said.

"You are a delicious brat, Brigid Murphy," he said, low voice rumbling over her bones.

She hissed in a breath. Damn him. "What time is that Zoom call done?"

———

**BATSUB Headquarters, Belize**

Aidan O'Brien took a quick shower before toweling off and adding another layer of bug spray and sweatproof sunblock to his exposed skin. They'd been mostly in the classroom today, being briefed on the month ahead. He checked the windows, making sure everything was sealed up tight. The officers' quarters had a mobile AC unit, thank the Holy Virgin. The barracks were less accommodating. They had relatively new ceiling fans and one window unit, which barely put a dent in the heat, but it was better than nothing. They all had mosquito nets as well. Best not get used to it because they'd be camping in the bush in a few days.

Tomorrow morning, the Belizean training team would be working on combat knife training. Using rubber knives, of course, but teaching them valuable, close-combat fighting skills that were a part of their army's infantry training. He'd done some similar training at Camp Lejeune with the US Marines.

Aidan often thought of that summer in North Carolina. Across the Atlantic from his native home, but almost as dear. It's where he'd met Alanna. Where he'd forged lasting friendships with men he still kept in touch with almost weekly. He missed them all— Hector, John, Doc O'Malley, Drake, Washington. He could pull their faces up in his mind so easily. Not just the photos on social media, but the moving pictures of the men they were. The laughing eyes of Washington. The stern, no bullshit way that Hector had of cutting right to the heart of things. And his best mate, John. As dear as a brother.

Aidan's computer started to chime, and he ran to it before he missed the call. His Alanna or maybe Davey, who had learned to call him on the computer with embarrassing ease. The kid was a whiz with computers. He answered the video call to the face of his devastatingly gorgeous mate. As pure a soul as ever drew breath. "Hello, love," he purred, and he delighted at the flare in her eyes.

How the hell was he going to go a month without her? He really was becoming a hopeless sap.

————

Aidan heard Cpl. Cunningham grunt with a blast of air as the instructor laid him on his ass again, fake knife having targeted his kidney area, then his neck. And because the universe loved to even the score, LCpl. Kenney had a front-row seat. Kenney was mad for the mixed martial arts competitions and took some sort of Jujitsu in his spare time. He was good with a knife. Aidan heard Kenney say, "Best not drop that rifle or run out of ammo when the giant snakes and spiders come for you. Because you are absolute rubbish with a blade, mate." The Belizean interpreter was laughing as he filled in the instructors about the finer nuances of British shit-talking.

Cunningham said, "Yeah, yeah. But I'm good with a staff. At least, that's what your mom says." And off they went. Every time someone hit the floor, someone else's mouth was flying. Except one lad. Lt. Kearsley was focused and downright nasty with a blade. He caught on fast, and he honed every lesson until he was proficient. He did most things with this sort of intensity. That was good. It would keep him alive if they ever did have to go into a hot zone. On that note … "Cunningham, Kenney, if you worked your combat skills the way you worked your gobs, you'd be invincible. Now shut your holes and pay attention."

On cue, the instructor, Lieutenant Ramirez, destroyed Kenney in two swipes. Then he poked a finger on the lance corporal's forehead. "The fight is here. Not here." And he held up his rubber knife. And wasn't that the fucking truth with most things.

# 5

## HAWICK, SCOTLAND

D aniel smirked as Douglas scratched his back on the doorjamb like a bear on a tree. "So, we're going to go trekking on this abandoned island looking for what, exactly?"

"Underground cargo containers or a hidden shack. Think of yourself as a pirate or a smuggler," Morgan said lightly.

"I'll have you know, I have some distant relatives in Cornwall. I very well could have some smuggling blood, not that my uncle would ever admit such a thing. He never did like my father," Douglas said. He stretched like a big cat, and Daniel caught the shift.

Daniel moved his eyes to Airmid's face, and she was discreetly taking in the duke's muscled arms and chest. He tensed, saying just a little too roughly, "If you're done with your morning stretches, let's get to it. We break at ten so Agent Roberts can interview two local childminders. Donna will be there to help, if you need her. She has all the tea on the locals, and she can look over their references."

Airmid's entire body tensed. "I'm still not sure about this arrangement. Having her here during the trips seems too much. Not just for her. For everyone."

Morgan interjected, "The agency will be paying the childcare expenses. This is a travel expense for a mission you didn't sign up for and were given almost no notice. It's perfectly legitimate. Your girl will not only be cared for by the person you hire, she'll have Donna and Davis to keep an eye on her. And when we aren't traveling and we have a late night, she's already comfortable. This place may as well be a historic inn. It's not like Daniel is using the rooms. Let the aristocracy earn their keep for once."

Daniel just smirked because he knew that coming from another woman, she'd get through to her. Airmid just closed her eyes, needing to think. "You're right. But once this Jamaican trip is done, I should go home for a couple of days. Just to get out of your hair."

Daniel said, "Whatever you need, Agent Roberts. This is your family, and you're in charge. I just want you to know this isn't an imposition. You just tell me what you need." He turned toward Morgan. "Did we get the credentials for travel?"

Morgan said, "We did." She slid an envelope over to Airmid, then to Douglas as he sat down at the small conference table. She slid the third to Daniel.

Douglas said, "Douglas Ruthford. That'll make it easy."

Airmid said, "Tara MacMillin is it? And who is my beloved?"

Daniel said, "Jonathon MacMillin." His voice was rough. Morgan's face blanched. She knew his biological father's name. Using the middle name of an agent sometimes made it easier to cement into their brains. MacMillin, from the O'Maoiláin clan. Mullins, McMillin, Mullane, and of course, Mullen. All derived from the same original clan name.

His undercover name was, for all intents and purposes, John

Mullen. Daniel looked at Morgan and she just shrugged, then gave a brief shake of the head. Only she and Douglas knew his story. The father who raised him, Robert, was on his birth certificate. They'd married quickly and discreetly because his mother had been pregnant already with another man's child. Daniel cleared his throat. "John MacMillin it is. Now, learn them, remember them. There's a brief history. Stick to the truth as much as you can without giving away anything important."

Daniel had copies of all three profiles in front of him. "They've changed you to a Belfast native, Tara. And that's another thing. From now until this is over, we will refer to each other by first name—Douglas, John or Jonathon, and Tara. As Dougie boy sounds like a dandy, he'll be a stepbrother, as we discussed before."

"Hey, look who's talking," Douglas said.

"Aye, but I've always been better at pulling up that Edinburgh brogue when we were trying to separate the coeds from their knickers."

Airmid, a.k.a. Tara, clapped a hand over her mouth and turned so red that she finally gave in and started laughing. Douglas grinned, saying, "Yes, you always did pull that out when you couldn't get them fair and square." Daniel winked at him, and suddenly, that tight-faced aristocrat and senior agent was gone. Was this who he was with friends? Or when playing a part for his work?

But just like that, it was gone. Daniel looked down at the paperwork. "Still working for the Terrance Foundation. I'm the CEO this time. Very nice. Douglas, you're on the board and working as a full-time playboy. Tara, you're my trophy wife."

"A plain girl from Derry is your trophy wife? They'll never believe it," she said with a snort.

"You're from Belfast, love. We met when you volunteered for

one of our overseas missions. And don't sell yourself short. The Irish certainly have their charms."

She tilted her head and asked, "And when were you going to tell me you were part Irish?"

"It wasn't relevant," Daniel said. "Now, let's go over education and a very basic family history. After lunch, we'll review fundamental boating terms and some very simple Jamaican terms. It's only five days, but I want you to brief us on what you know. Just to get by in case we get separated. Did they give you self-defense training when you were recruited?"

Airmid said, "They did. And in the army."

"Grand. Later, I want to talk to you about the training unit you were with in Central America. Perhaps sometime this evening. I know you'll need time with Erin, so I'll let you take the lead on that." Daniel glanced down at the profiles. "Now, Douglas. You're an Eton man, just as in real life. Like every British tosser I've ever met." Airmid spit her tea onto her jumper, and Daniel actually smiled. Just a tip of the mouth, but it happened.

———

Erin came in at about half nine, still in her nightgown and holding Donna's hand. "She wanted to see you. She told me you always pick out her clothes, so I thought we'd come see if you could take a break for a bit of company?" Donna looked apologetically at the group.

Airmid only had eyes for her little girl though. Her hair was so much lighter, but they had the same creamy skin, and Daniel's throat seized up at the sight of her bronze irises. Exactly like her mother and accentuated by her amber lashes. He wondered if this girl's father had been the blonde.

Daniel said gently, "Good morning, Lady Erin." This was, of

course, in response to the girl's hazy question, *Is this a castle?* The manor house was hardly a castle, but he supposed to a small child, all this stonework, chandeliers, and winding staircases would seem castle-like.

She tilted her head, just like her mother, her riotous curls bouncing. "I'm not a lady. I'm a girl."

"Well, since you've come to stay in my castle, I think that makes you a lady."

"I'd rather be a princess," she said. Cheeky as her mother, this one.

Airmid choked a little. "Erin, that's rude."

Daniel said, "No, no. It's a common mistake. Your mother would have to be a queen, or your grandda a king, in order to be a princess. But I suppose since I make the rules, we can do as we like. Princess it is."

That seemed to satisfy the child. She climbed in her mother's lap to settle in for a cuddle. "Do you have any other children here, Mr. Fearson," Erin asked.

"It's MacPherson, love. Mr. MacPherson," Airmid said.

"Minfearsom."

Daniel smiled and said, "My family and my very best mates call me Danny. Is that easier, do you think?"

"Danny," and the Irish accent was about as adorable as it got. Even Douglas wasn't immune, and he normally hated kids.

Erin looked over at Douglas. "Ye've got a beard."

He smiled. "I do, sometimes. Other times, I shave it off." He ran a hand over it. "What do you think? Should I keep the beard?"

Erin seemed to consider it. "I don't know what you look like without it."

Morgan said, "He has dimples. He tries to hide them because they make him look less scary. Men are silly, aren't they?"

Erin eyed him speculatively. "I think you should shave it. I want to see your dimples."

Davis came to the door. "Miss Roberts, your first interview is here. Perhaps I could take the girl for some breakfast."

The child climbed out of her lap begrudgingly. "I don't want to eat alone. Can't you come too, Mammy?"

Daniel stood. "I could do with a bigger breakfast. Do you mind, Princess Erin, if I showed you to my kitchen?" She smiled, and to Airmid's surprise, Erin took his hand.

————

Daniel came into the kitchen and said to Donna, "The first interview is here for the nanny position."

Donna cleaned her hands. "You can feed the sweet girl, I assume? And just for transparency, what is the wage your non-profit will pay?"

"What is a fair wage? For one child and some overnight stays?" Daniel asked.

"Probably a little more than the board will want to pay," she said dryly. "If you want someone experienced who will pass a background investigation and a drug screening, you'll have to pay well or go with an agency markup."

"I don't need to know the reimbursement rate. Hire the most competent person. I'll"—he looked over at the child, who was listening—"supplement." Surely a four-year-old wouldn't know that word, right? He didn't want Airmid's pride getting in the way of this process. Donna just smiled, and it was those smiles that reassured him that he wasn't such a royal pig-fucker.

————

Airmid had been stirring for hours, but she couldn't settle. Truth be told, she'd been too wired to eat much during dinner. And bloody exhausted. She'd crashed at half seven, then woke at eleven, ready to murder some sort of meat and potatoes. Maybe there were apple tarts left? She put her lips to her daughter's forehead, and there was no sign of a temperature. No cough had developed, and she hadn't needed to blow her nose since she'd picked her up at home.

She looked around the room, able to see due to a Disney princess nightlight that Donna had procured for their room. The woman was a saint. Not wanting Erin to wake up in the dark in a strange bed, she'd offered a little comfort where she could. Erin was out cold, and Airmid knew she wouldn't sleep until she at least had a snack and maybe a cup of herbal tea.

Airmid crept out of the room, heading down two floors toward the kitchen. The lights were bright when she turned them on, but luckily, no one was about. A midnight kitchen raid in someone else's house seemed like it should be a secret. Ridiculous, but it just was. Airmid padded over to the refrigerator. One of those subzero, restaurant-style coolers and deep freezers that you only saw on cooking shows from America. "Let's see. Lots of produce. That will not do at all."

"She keeps the good stuff on the third shelf, toward the back." Airmid yelped at the deep voice, throwing her hand over her heart.

"Jesus wept, MacPherson! Ye'll give me a coronary! What are you doing up?" She hissed the words, which only made him smile. It was a stupid thing to say. It was his house, after all. Why the hell had she agreed to this?

Airmid swallowed hard as she took in the sight of him. Flannel pajama pants and no shirt. His chest was ... She wasn't going to think it. Her eyes left his defined pectorals and met his eyes. He had a brow up and a smug look on his face. Daniel said, "Sorry I gave you a fright. I was just going to bed when I thought I could use a snack. We kind of worked through supper, didn't we?"

"Yes," she said finally. Her tone more civil. "I'm sorry. You probably want some peace and quiet."

"What I want is a shirt. Forgive me, just a moment." She watched him walk over to a closed door, heard him open the dryer door, and re-emerge, sliding a plain, white T-shirt over his ridiculously beautiful chest and abs. Daniel had to be pushing forty, but he looked like a finely honed athlete. He walked over, hair rumpled, and pulled the refrigerator door wider. Airmid was so used to seeing him in a suit. She couldn't clear her head.

He put his arm deep into the third shelf and began pulling things out. Mashed potatoes, white sauce, and some sort of sausages. She smiled and said, "Now you're talkin'."

Daniel said, "That's not the best part." He grabbed a stool and climbed up to reach the very top of the press beside the laundry room door. He took out a tin and gave it a little motion to check the weight. "Bingo." She leaned in as he removed the lid.

Airmid moaned. "Chocolate biscuits. Homemade, no less. I'm sorry, MacPherson. I'm going to have our household packed up and will be moving to Scotland. If Erin sees those, you'll never get rid of her."

"Well then, Mrs. Tara MacMillin, we'll have to save her a few." He gave her a chiding look.

The side of her mouth tilted up. "Right, Jonathon it is." Practicing was a good idea, but it was so strange answering to another name. She really hadn't had any ambitions to work in the field. "So, Jonathon, why don't you show me where the flatware and dinner plates are located, and I'll start heating this third-shelf contraband."

She felt him smile. Which sounded ridiculous, but there you

are. She felt it. He was not a man of grand or loud language. He wore his strength and intelligence quietly. His dominance, too. But it was there. Oh yes. And it was not hot as hell. Nope. Definitely not simping on her squad leader.

Airmid removed a plate from the microwave and hissed, setting it down and licking the hot potatoes off her thumb. Not enough to do any damage, but enough to get her attention. Daniel's face darkened as she popped her thumb out of her mouth. She said, "Sorry. I'll take the one I stuck my thumb into, and I promise not to eat with my hands."

Daniel's eyes were glowing with something. She wondered, stupidly, how many single debutants were circling, hoping to catch a handsome earl. Though, he certainly kept out of the public eye. Roxburghe had it a little rougher. He outranked Daniel in the eyes of the peerage. Had media vultures following him occasionally. She suspected the only reason he was able to do this assignment was because it was so far from his homeland.

"Where in Ireland are your family relations?" Airmid asked.

He paused, considering. "Belfast," he said. "And extended family in County Clare and Galway. Some in Dublin as well, when they aren't in Brazil."

"Brazil?" she said, surprised.

"They're doctors. They live part time at a Catholic mission," he explained. "I think I have distant family in Cork as well, though I've never met them."

"Your father was an earl. Scottish and English, right? I thought your mam was English? Is the—"

Daniel carefully made some herbal tea as he talked. He thought about her situation with Erin's father and decided to take a leap of faith. "You'd never find any official record of what I'm about to tell you. And I'm not ashamed. The people who need to know, know. I do it out of respect for the privacy of my parents."

"MacPherson, you don't have to tell me. I'm sorry. I shouldn't have asked," she said.

"It's okay. I'm the one who brought up my Irish ancestry. My father's name was Jonathon Mullen. The father's name on my birth certificate was Lord Robert Daniel MacPherson, heir to the title. He knew my mother was pregnant when he married her. They were old friends. He did it to save her. To save us. No one outside the families ever knew. He claimed me and never did anything but love me. He was an MI-6 agent. High ranking until the day he died. It's how I was brought into the agency."

Daniel let that sink in and waited. When she didn't ask any questions, he continued. "My mother's parents owned a large mill in Belfast. My mum's first love was a Catholic mill worker. The young and dashing John Mullen. A simple man, but I believe he was a good one. I think he loved my mother.

"She never told him about me. When the family physician betrayed her trust and advised her parents that she was pregnant, she told them he worked at the mill, and then, after some interrogation, she confessed he was a Catholic. She didn't give his name, but it was all they needed to hear. They took her back to their estate in England and tried to pressure her into getting an abortion. She refused. She also refused to reveal the man's name. They would have fired him, and then where would he be? He wouldn't have been able to provide for them if he lost his job. At least that's how she justified it. He was only twenty-one years old.

"He died of cancer several years ago and never knew about me. And I never knew about him until my father died. My legal father, I mean. He made my mother promise not to tell me. She did, finally, but only after he'd died as well. After both fathers were gone, and I was just left with questions. So, the Mullen family members are in Belfast and Cork, and my aunt Sorcha married a Clare man and they live there now. A big, boisterous family. They've been adamant that I'm an honorary O'Brien as well as a Mullen," he said with a lift of the shoulder, trying to lighten the mood.

Airmid's face was pale. "I'm sorry I've made so many cracks about your title, MacPherson. It sounds like the father who gave it to you was a wonderful man."

"Yes, well, I was angry with my mum. She sort of stole two fathers away from me with her secrets. But at the same time, she gave me two. So, I'm still working on my feelings about her."

Airmid said, "Speaking from experience, being alone and pregnant is not so easy. She was forced to make some hard choices without the support of her family, and she was a lot younger than I was with Erin. If your father valued their friendship enough to throw her that lifeline, then I understand why she took it. If her parents were well-off English people, an unwanted pregnancy was likely a huge scandal, even in the early eighties."

Daniel said, "Yes, I suppose you do understand more than most. Does your family support you?" he asked. "Help with the lass?"

"They did help a little. I've always had to work, but they assisted a bit with childcare at first. But since I've moved from Derry, they really haven't been able to do anything for me. No going to Granny's house for the weekend and all that. They both work. And Erin's father ... well, let's just say his parents weren't thrilled that he took up with an Irish girl. I have family in the North and in the Republic. I'm a Catholic. It didn't bother him, but it certainly bothered them. I mean, they don't even go to church. Not even on Christmas. But the idea of me is what is repugnant to them.

"My parents aren't rich or well educated, but they are good people. My brother is a good man. He's with a major oil company doing something in the Middle East. We are good people. But evidently, not good enough to raise Tommy's child. I might raise her to sound a little too Irish. Might get my blue-collar germs on her. And don't get me started on what they thought about a woman in the military. Apparently, and I quote, 'You're just a bunch of randy, little sluts, working with all men so you can let them pass you around.'"

Daniel hissed. "Jesus, Airmid."

"I thought it was Tara?" she said, smiling. "And it's nothing to think on. I know my worth, and so did Tommy. They don't deserve to lick my boots or Erin's. And clearly, the court psychiatrist agreed."

Daniel lifted his teacup in a mock toast. "To family drama and court-appointed shrinks."

She laughed. "Cheers."

He added, "And I'm very sorry that you lost him. I'm sorry Erin will never know him."

Airmid smiled, and he saw her fighting the tears as she said, "Me too. Thank you."

After they cleaned up, Daniel watched her walk out of the kitchen and up the stairs toward the third floor. She was wearing cotton shorts and no shoes. The Derry City Football Club T-shirt she was wearing was just thin enough to tell him she wasn't wearing a bra. It had taken every ounce of spare energy he had to not keep letting his gaze drift there to her swaying breasts. Her hair was chestnut, almost the same color as the English Thoroughbred he had in the stable. Her shining, bronze eyes were mesmerizing. Somewhere between brown and gold. Her hair was thick and wavy, but nothing like her daughter's.

Daniel and little Erin had something in common besides liking chocolate biscuits. They'd never known their fathers. He suddenly wanted to hug the child. She had a good mother. And so did he, regardless of how she vexed him sometimes. Airmid had given his mother the grace that he'd been missing. He suddenly wanted to hug his mum as well. Daniel shook himself. He was becoming a complete sap.

"Good night, Airmid."

"Tara!" she said over her shoulder as she rounded to the next set of stairs.

Airmid smiled as she walked up to her room. That was the second time he'd called her Airmid instead of Agent Roberts or by her alias. She liked how he said it. He didn't roll his *r* properly, but that just made it more endearing. Had she really called him a royal pig-fucker in Spanish on her first day? Yes. Yes, she had.

Daniel watched her disappear, then he swore he heard her laughter echo in the stairwell. He probably didn't want to know.

———

Daniel was surprised to hear the engine of his sister's compact Volkswagen speed up the drive. He'd been passing the front entrance to the house when she came through the door. Well, then. This was going to get interesting if she had a mind to spend the night. Alanna was going to be here by teatime with three bairns in tow.

He managed to beat Davis to the door, which never ceased to irritate the old curmudgeon. Daniel said, "Hello, love. You're just in time for breakfast. We have a full house, so come in and meet my colleagues."

Davis said, "Lady Elizabeth." And took her coat. She kissed him on the cheek. Then she turned toward her brother, brows raised in interest.

She said, "Colleagues? From your charity? Perfect. I never get to hear about your work."

Daniel felt like a rotter. He'd always hated this part of his double life. The lying to his family part. Lying to his partners. It's why he never sought a deeper relationship. Granted, there were married agents and their spouses knew about their work. But at his age, even if he found someone whom he was serious about, he'd have to initially lie to them for months, if not years. And once he did tell them—once it became a "forever" type of relationship —how would they ever trust him again?

His sister followed him into the dining room, and he watched Douglas's face transform. The bastard had a boy-size crush on his little sister, and he'd had to threaten him more than once. Douglas rose from his breakfast and scooped Elizabeth up for a twirling hug. "Hello, my future wife."

"Douglas, you are such a hopeless womanizer. Don't try to charm me with your muscles and your title. I'm not biting," Elizabeth said. But she kissed his face anyway. Her eyes landed on little Erin and Airmid. "And who is this?"

Daniel said, "You know my boss, Morgan. And this is Airmid and Princess Erin."

"What pretty names. And a princess, no less. My, my, your highness. May I ask about your kingdom?"

Airmid smiled. "We live in Northumberland. My childminder fell through, so Mr. MacPherson has been kind enough to let us stay until our current project is through."

Daniel knew this was smart. Tell her right away, control the narrative. Try not to confuse the child. Elizabeth looked at him, her face showing just how surprised she was by this turn of events. Daniel said, "A local girl will be handling childcare during our working hours, and also when we fly internationally. We have a new project that involves a few of us going to the site. Anyway, please sit and have some breakfast. How is the book going?"

But Elizabeth was not going to be distracted. "Is that an Irish accent, Airmid?"

"Yes, I'm from the North. Did he say book? Are you an author? What a wonderful thing to be," Airmid said. And Daniel knew she was volleying the conversation back into safer waters.

"Yes, I write under a pen name," she said, blushing.

Daniel smirked. "You may as well come out with it. Don't be shy, sister. I'm proud of you."

Airmid asked, "What genre? Novels or nonfiction?"

Elizabeth cleared her throat, but Douglas just couldn't keep his mouth shut. "She writes deliciously dirty romance novels. I've read every one, and although it's not my normal genre, I drank in every word. She's a vixen, is our Elizabeth."

Elizabeth looked like she was ready to murder the duke. "I prefer the term *spicy*, not dirty. And please refrain from any detail. There is a child at the table."

Daniel watched Airmid's face transform. No shock, disgust, or even judgment. She said, "Now I have to know your pen name. Spicy is the only"—she glanced at her daughter and seemed to amend her statement in her head—"pleasurable reading I am getting right now."

Erin asked, "What is spicy? Like the curry? I don't have curry in my books, Mammy." Morgan choked on her sausage and Douglas was unrepentant.

He said, "Not curry. More like habanero."

Elizabeth said, "Shush, you. So, Erin. Tell me, what is your favorite book?"

Erin smiled and said, "It's about a girl pirate!"

Douglas, on cue, said, "Didn't you write a girl pirate book, Elizabeth?" And on it went. Thankfully, the new nanny arrived and took the child to the nursery to read some age-appropriate stories. As soon as they were gone, Douglas said, "Her pen name is Bethany Raven."

Airmid's jaw dropped. "You are THE Bethany Raven? The

*London Times* and *New York Times* bestselling author? I'm sorry, MacPherson. I hope you know you are in the presence of smut royalty ... sorry, spicy royalty. Give up any thought of impressing me when your sister throws this big of a shadow."

But Daniel didn't mind the ribbing. His pride was evident in his eyes. He rustled his sister's hair. "Agreed. And they are not just spicy. Her plotting and character development get full marks. It's why she's so successful. You are an amazing writer, love. Although, let's not tell the grandparents you've been crowned Smut Queen. Nanna will have a coronary. Mum has a hard enough time with it."

Elizabeth said, "Too right. Nanna reads my books and hides them in her bureau. She has no idea it's me who's written them. Can you imagine what it's like to live a double life like this? I've had to deceive half the family!"

You could have heard a pin drop in the room. Morgan broke the tension. "No, I can't imagine. It must be difficult indeed." Then Morgan took a huge gulp of her tea.

———

"Mammy, I like my new childminder. She's nice. She is going to take me on a pony!" Erin said.

Donna interceded. "I'm sorry, she's a bit better at eavesdropping than I anticipated. She'd make an excellent spy." Daniel choked down a laugh.

Airmid gave a tight smile. "She would at that. I take it you were going to okay it with me before telling her?"

"Yes, of course. Again, so sorry. We can certainly find something else—"

Airmid interrupted. "It would be grand, Donna. She rode a

pony at a friend's birthday party. But someone held on to her. Is your groom okay with children? Should I come along?"

Daniel said, "Actually, my cousin's wife and three children are about a quarter hour from here and will be joining you. Alanna has riding experience, so she can help. And my sister has agreed to go to the stables as well. Divide and conquer and all that. But if you'd like to go down, or even go riding, maybe we can delay until after tea?" He looked at Donna. The nanny, Constance, was taking a small refreshment break for lunch.

Donna said, "I think that would be a perfect time. And it's been dry for three days. No mud to speak of. I'll let you all get back to your lunch."

Daniel was surprised at the stirring of emotion he felt as he watched Airmid with her little girl. He'd never put much thought into what they were asking of Airmid. She'd signed on as an analyst, not a field agent. The most she did was interpret during interrogations. But she'd agreed to this mission. He wondered about the solicitor fees Morgan had talked about. She wasn't so in debt that she was a security risk. The agency didn't clear people with large amounts of debt. But England was expensive, especially considering the child. Schools and playgrounds and village life instead of a flat in some dodgy but affordable area.

The child loved her mother. That much was obvious. She nestled under her chin as her mother struggled to eat with one hand. Daniel heard the doorbell chime and knew it must be Alanna and her brood. Perfect timing. Davis brought them right to the dining room, assuring Alanna that he'd handle the luggage.

This made Erin perk up. Isla was first to approach. She was about Erin's age. Maybe a few months older. "Hello, my name is Isla."

Erin wriggled out of her mother's arms. Airmid leaned down and said, "Love, say hello to everyone and tell them your name."

The child stood up straight, as if well-rehearsed in manners. "Erin Roberts! I'm four!"

———

Alanna O'Brien was drop-dead gorgeous. Even with a messy bun and a baby hanging off her, she was stunning. Airmid suddenly felt dowdy and plain, which was stupid altogether. What did it matter? Airmid said, "You're from the American South. Is it Georgia or South Carolina?"

Alanna's brows shot up. "That is incredibly accurate. Both, actually. I have family in both states. And I lived in North Carolina on the coast for part of my life as well. And other places. A military brat. And wife, now, come to think of it. I've never been one to stay put."

Airmid's interest was piqued. "Which branch was your father or mother?"

"Marines, and it was my daddy. He retired in 2014 and married an Irish family doctor. I married into the Royal Irish Regiment. Daniel tells me you also served in the British Army. The accent is Northern Irish, I think. Maybe you know my husband?"

Airmid said, "I might at that. What is his name and rank?"

"He's a freshly printed major. Just pinned on. Aidan O'Brien," she said.

Airmid said, "I actually have heard of him. He was in Shropshire when I was in the North, so we didn't end up in the same unit, but I know the name. He is quite decorated. Awards in Iraq and Afghanistan. It's a true honor, Mrs. O'Brien. I wish the army had a million just like him." Alanna's eyes misted and Airmid said, "Oh, I'm sorry. I didn't mean to make you cry!"

Alanna just waved a hand dismissively. "Sorry, I'm hormonal.

Aidan's gone right now and I miss him. It's only been a week, and I'm already missing him something awful."

"Where is he, if you don't mind me asking?" Airmid asked. She saw Daniel tense. It was subtle and no one else noticed.

"Belize for jungle training," she said. "Not in combat. Unless you count mosquitos and killer snakes." Alanna shuddered.

Douglas's fork froze halfway up to his mouth. Morgan knew. That much was obvious. Well, this was interesting. Airmid said, "Operation Maya. I did a stint there several years ago as an interpreter for the Royal Dragoons. I didn't get to do all of the actual combat training because I'm female. The rules have changed since then. I pushed my way into some of it though. Mostly, I worked with the interpreters and linguists on the Belizean side. Truthfully, seeing those lads come out of the bush every day didn't look all that appealing."

Alanna smirked. "Don't let them fool you. Those barbarians eat it up. As much as he complains, there's no place Aidan would rather be than on the ground with his men."

Douglas mumbled something and got an elbow in the side from Daniel. And she could guess easily enough. The jungle was probably second place compared to Aidan O'Brien being in his wife's bed. But the woman seemed oblivious to how she affected the men. Alanna said, "So, Erin. I hear we will be riding horses today! I'm so excited. And Constance has been nice enough to hold little Keeghan while I ride. Do you like horses?"

Erin pulled a toy from her pocket. A little, plastic horse. She showed it to Alanna, and the woman just gasped like it was the best thing she'd ever seen. "Oh my! You'll have to play with us after lunch and bring your horse. I think Davey brought his, too, didn't you, buddy?"

"Yes, and I have some toy soldiers. I wanted some real weapons, but Da said no," Davey said matter-of-factly.

Daniel said, "Yes, well, you might want to get a tad older. You'll be giving your mum grey hairs with that talk."

Airmid noticed that the English influence slipped a little when Daniel talked to the children. His guard came down, and a bit of the lowlander accent came through.

They finished lunch, and Constance came to the dining room to take Alanna and all four children to the third floor. Douglas watched Alanna leave and didn't hide the male appreciation. Daniel narrowed his eyes on him. "Have I mentioned that my cousin is about six foot three and about sixteen stone?"

"Lucky man," Douglas said unapologetically.

Elizabeth just snorted. "She's really nice, Danny. I like her. Now, I'm done watching Douglas make an ass of himself. Airmid, it was a pleasure meeting you. I'm off to my flat to let another man humble me." She winked at Airmid. "My editor. He's ruthless."

"Goodbye, and happy writing, Elizabeth. I can't wait to read it," Airmid said.

Daniel watched his sister leave and offered a warm smile to Airmid. She'd been altogether pleasant to all of his family. The idea that he'd be playing her husband was starting to make him nervous for no particular reason.

———

They'd decided to take a stroll before dinner, and Daniel had given the staff a few hours off by inviting the entire group out for dinner. Constance was seizing the opportunity to wipe down the toys after so many children were playing with them. Donna and Davis had the time to themselves. They packed up the children, ordered Tony's Takeaway for fish and chips, and spread three large blankets in the Wilton Lodge Park. They played on the magical playground, explored the gardens, and took the path along the Teviot River.

Airmid noticed Daniel staring at a beautiful fountain, hands in his pockets. When she approached, she saw a plaque on a pedestal near the fountain. *In Memory of Lord Robert Hawick, the 7th Earl of Hawick.* So not a particularly old title, comparatively. One of the honorary titles bestowed on some wealthy aristocrat a few hundred years ago. But it was important to Daniel. Important because his father had given the responsibility to him.

She said, "It's a beautiful tribute." It was a sculpture of a group of fae children, hands clasped together to form a circle.

Daniel said, "He loved children. He loved us so very much. He told me the key to happiness and a long life was to marry a good woman and have lots of children. And to have a purpose. I think he was a happy man. I hope so, at least. And he certainly had a sense of purpose. I miss him. Every single day, I miss him. So sometimes I come here. His ashes were spread in this park. He loved it here. He used to jog along this footpath. Said the river cleared his mind."

Airmid smiled at that. She looked along the path, thinking it was indeed a wonderful place to clear your head. She didn't say anything else. She didn't have to. She left Daniel to his memories and went to play with her daughter. They were, after all, leaving tomorrow.

# 6

## KINGSTON, JAMAICA

The humid blast of heat was both a welcome and a curse. The balmy Caribbean air was thick and exotic. It was also causing Airmid's button-down to stick to her body in a most unattractive fashion.

"Tara, love. Let me take that bag," Daniel said. And it was so odd to hear him play the part of a doting and chivalrous lover. Or husband, in this case. She'd never been married, but she wondered if Daniel's rescuing behavior was more nature or nurture.

"That's grand, mo ghra. Thank you. Did you hire a car?" she asked. She knew he hadn't. They had someone picking them up who worked for their local agents.

"Mr. and Mrs. MacMillin?" a short, fit Jamaican man said in English.

Daniel gave the previously agreed upon response. "Ah, you must be our new best mate."

The man gave one nod, smiling for show. "This way. And

please, let me take the bags. You have one more in your party, yes?"

Airmid said sweetly, "Yes, my brother was just waiting on a bag. He does love to overpack."

Douglas appeared with an oversize suitcase and a huge camera bag. "Ah, he's here. Please, my good man. Take me to the closest rum."

———

The home, in an affluent part of Kingston, was modest compared to the neighbors, but the security was good. "Apollo, how good to finally meet you in person," Daniel said.

The man was about sixty, had a Mediterranean look about him, and sounded like he'd just stepped out of Convent Garden. "John, Tara, Douglas, welcome to my home." It was aliases from here on out. No exceptions. They'd been practicing for the last four days, so it was becoming second nature.

The man continued. "The boat was delivered to Montego Bay this morning. I managed to sort it for the right amount of coin. You've met my driver, Lawrence. We've booked a standard suite for you, Douglas. The happy couple will be in one of the larger suites. Your extra crew member will be a fellow charity worker. His name is Peter Dubois. You can't miss him. He looks like a fucking pirate. Long hair and a stupid earring. He's gone a bit feral after three years. But he knows how to sail the boat, and he'll act as a dive guide if you have need of it.

"There's a man staying at the resort who is a person of interest. A potential ... donor. His name is Karl Jensen. A Dutch national who spends a lot of his leisure time going between the Caribbean and South and Central America. He's obscenely wealthy. Owns homes in five different nations and is a partial owner in the resort you'll be spending your land time enjoying. Don't act like someone on a mission. Drink. Dress your wife in something enticing. Mingle with the other guests. Act like newlyweds. Jensen likes to surround himself with money and beautiful people. He may not be our man, but I'd bet my left bollock that he knows who is."

Airmid interjected. "I'm going to need to go shopping. I live on the coast of Northern England, for pity's sake. I don't have the sort of clothing this is going to require. They're still wearing jumpers at night."

Apollo said, "Your beloved, Jonathon, has already taken care of it. There will be an assortment of items for you to try on in my guest room, as well as a better set of luggage. Whatever you don't like will go back to the store, so don't get that look on your face. This is the job. You are playing a part, and although you are lovely, you are lacking the polish you're going to need for the *Azul Real*." *The Blue Royal.* "The stylist I called is the best on the island. This resort is an adults-only, very exclusive resort. You must be dressed to the nines."

Excluding most people because of the price tag, she thought about her old bag from Harrods. It was a bit shabby. Jesus, could she really play a rich man's wife? This was where their sailboat was anchored, and it was also where their person of interest spent his time.

She looked at Daniel. His face wasn't exactly apologetic, but understanding. Daniel said, "I didn't pick the stuff out. I just asked Donna what your sizes might be and had them send a selection of stupidly expensive clothing. It's yours to choose or send back."

"Yes, yes," Douglas said dryly. "Chop-chop, woman. We've got some hobnobbing to do."

Apollo smirked. "And John, your new clothes are in the room across from your wife's."

Airmid asked, "You don't already have stupidly expensive clothing?"

Daniel said, "We're still wearing jumpers in Scotland as well. And my resort wear is a bit outdated. I spent the last two missions in the Ukraine and the Baltics."

She looked at Douglas. He said, "I shopped in London. And unlike this workaholic, I love a good holiday in the Caribbean or the Seychelles. Now, enough chatter. Go. Wear something light and pretty, but something you would have traveled in. Freshen up the hair and makeup. Make it look effortless, lass. You're not in an English village any longer." She bristled, even though she'd been concerned about all of these things, and more. She couldn't go into this new life with her old skin.

———

Airmid was way out of her comfort zone. The clothes were amazing, and the sizes weren't the issue. This wasn't rayon sarongs and speedo swimwear. Jesus, the luxury that hung in this closet could pay her rent for six months. But goddamn if she didn't love the feel of it on her skin. Soft, linen trousers, silk dresses and blouses, and three swimsuits that were not ready for her pale complexion. Even lingerie. The little, black dress fit her like a glove. She wasn't thin. At five seven, she wasn't petite either. She'd played football in secondary school. Done martial arts in the military. She took care of herself and she was strong. But she'd never really thought about what her body was going to look like in a two-piece swimsuit. The truth was that she wasn't showing off her stretch marks in this atrocity. She looked at the other one. A rash guard that showed a bit of her belly and some fairly respectable bikini bottoms.

A knock came at the door. She was finishing up her makeup and smoothing her hair with some anti-frizz serum when Douglas came through the door. He started looking at the discarded pile, then what she'd placed in the small, designer suitcase and garment bag.

"Take the bikini. Don't be so uptight," he said.

Airmid smiled into the mirror, meeting his eyes. "Is that your brotherly advice?"

"No, that's my professional advice. No one expects you to have a tan. Porcelain skin is revered as the exotic in this part of the world."

"No bikinis. Unlike those women you'll see in the hotel, I didn't have my plastic surgeon erase any signs of childbirth. MacPh—I mean, John and I have no children."

He sighed. "At least take the one-piece."

"The ass is missing," Airmid said smartly.

"Oh, the ass will most certainly not be missing. And the plunge neckline will make up for you not having the balls to wear a bikini." Airmid threw a makeup sponge at him.

Douglas said, "Careful. This shirt is Armani. I'm going to need it again when we go to part two of this mission. And I look amazing in it."

She slammed the bathroom door in his face. Daniel appeared in the open door and asked, "Is she almost ready?"

"Yes, she's getting dressed. This is ready to go." Douglas pointed at the luggage. Daniel took both pieces and carried them down to the waiting driver. Douglas waited for Airmid. When she came out, the breath shot out of his lungs. He said, "He really is a prick for making me play the stepbrother. Nice wheels, Tara darling."

"Thanks, brother dear. Where is my luggage?" Airmid asked.

"Your new husband carried it down. He looks rather dashing. You'll look good together. Just remember, you have to BE good together. You're young and in love. Don't get all testy if he's affectionate with you."

"I know that!" she snapped. She'd thought of little else.

"Yes, but your Royal Irish, ass-kicker case of resting bitch face is what will give you away. Look smitten. Blush occasionally. Flash him a look across a crowded room."

Airmid gritted her teeth. "Douglas, stop giving me advice."

They walked down with her new purse and designer Dopp kit, and Airmid struggled to acclimate to the new threads and heeled shoes. She was happy to see some flat sandals and leather ballet flats among the shoe selections. Heels were not her norm, and she wouldn't be able to pull it off every day. As it was, the Italian-leather heels she was currently wearing weren't stupidly high, or she'd be towering over half the population of Jamaica.

Her shift dress was pale-blue linen with a banded collar around her throat. The collar tied at the side and was actually very pretty in an understated way. The only thing that gave Airmid pause was the length. The hem came to mid-thigh. Coupled with the heels, the ensemble showed a lot of leg. And it hugged her through the hips and chest more than she was used to.

Airmid had smoothed and added a bit of curl just at the bottom of her hair. She'd put on some tasteful makeup and blush lipstick. She was fairly certain she passed muster. Daniel's face seemed to tighten when she appeared on the stairway. Apollo whistled. "Now you're ready."

She wouldn't meet Daniel's eyes. Didn't want to see what he thought. If he was regretting this whole thing. She walked toward the car, and Douglas was discreetly given the push as Daniel opened the door for her. She raised a brow as he saw her into the car.

---

### Azul Real Resort and Spa
### Montego Bay, Jamaica

They walked the corridor leading to the couples' suites. Apparently, the resort placed singles in equally luxurious suites, but in an area where they could mingle among other single guests. It was strange to look out at the swimming pool—as gorgeous as one could imagine—and not see one child. She understood it. Some places were designed for a kid-free retreat. But an absurd part of her felt guilty. Like she was taking a holiday without her little girl instead of working. Proper holidays were such a rare thing for them, between work and money. Daniel put a hand in the middle of her back and it startled her. He leaned in, saying, "Woolgathering?"

She swallowed, trying to compose herself. The touch hadn't been overtly intimate, but in a way, it had. She hadn't been touched a lot in the last five years. Not by a man, at any rate. "Yes, sorry. I was just looking at the pool and the gardens. You spoil me, John."

The man carrying their bags and the female concierge smiled. The woman said, "My name is Agnes. I will be your daytime attendant. Anything you need, whether it be a ride or an extra pillow, don't hesitate to call my extension. Your nighttime attendant will be Irie. She is young and sweet and very happy to help you."

Agnes was a lovely, fortysomething woman with smooth, brown skin and lively copper eyes. Her hair was long, given the size of her bun. She opened the door to the suite, and Airmid choked back a gasp. The large windows looked out over the turquoise sea. They couldn't see the people next door, but instead had a private patio that led to the beach. There were fences about twenty feet out before the beach opened up to the surf. A honeymooners' paradise. The bay was to the left, if you peeked far enough.

Airmid surveyed the expansive room. A cream-colored sofa, a door leading to a luxuriously appointed bath. Another bath, which had a small shower, was along the far wall where she noticed a stocked wet bar. She'd read the brochure, but the idea of it all seemed ridiculous. Such opulence.

Goose bumps prickled to life on her skin and Daniel asked, "Tara, love, are you chilled?"

She was. But not from the air-conditioned space. More from the king-size bed that faced the large windows. "I'm grand. Just jet-lagged, I think."

As they spoke, a man came through the door with a chilling bottle of champagne. "I'll leave you two to start your holiday. Ring me if you need anything. And if you'd like to see the sailboat before tomorrow, it's down in the marina under your room number."

After that, it was under a minute before Daniel and Airmid were alone. Daniel glanced at his phone. "Douglas said he's going to have a drink and a nap. We'll meet for dinner at half seven."

Airmid said blankly, "I'll tend to my unpacking, I suppose." She bent to retrieve her bag, and Daniel's hand came over her wrist. She popped up, her heart racing. "What is it?"

He gave her an understanding look. "You are as jumpy as a kitten. You start every time I touch you. It's something you're going to have to get used to, I'm afraid. Just come, Tara." God, she hated that name. Loved the name. Very Irish. But hated that it was a lie on his lips. That this was all for show. "Come sit on the sofa awhile. I'm not going to bite you."

Airmid tensed, bristling. "I'm not a scared kitten. It's just going to take a bit of getting used to. The only one who touches me with regularity is my four-year-old."

"You don't have a lover?" Daniel asked, appearing surprised.

She closed her eyes. "I don't have time for a lover. Do you?"

"I don't currently, no. I suppose that's better. This job could be a bit trying if one of us had entanglements. But it's a job." Daniel watched her sit, then went to the bar and cracked open the Perrier Jouet, pouring them both a hearty glassful. He turned. "I don't know about you, but I could use some liquid courage."

He walked over, handing her a glass. Airmid smiled, saying, "I'm Irish, mo chroí. It's what we do."

"Well, then. Sláinte from one bloody-minded Celt to another," he said. They clinked glasses and sipped. Daniel put his glass on a side table, then took a wooden chair from the desk. He sat on it, straddled, with the back facing Airmid. "I want you to be comfortable. And I'm sorry we didn't have more time to grow accustomed to each other."

"Do this a lot, do you?" Airmid asked dryly.

"No, actually. Only once. With a woman in the Ukraine," Daniel said. "More to keep the honey traps at bay than anything."

The Eastern Block had perfected the seductress method of gathering intelligence or even assassinating foreign spies. The le femme fatales became known as honey traps, back during the Cold War, and the name stuck. Daniel put out a hand, palm up. An offering. A start. She placed her hand in his because she trusted him. She just wasn't used to someone so buttoned-down playing this part. The bloody Earl of Hawick, touching her like a husband who had every expectation that she'd welcome the contact. Encourage it even. Daniel turned her arm, wrist up. Then he ran his other index finger lightly from the inside of her elbow to her palm. Then he met her eyes. "Is this okay?"

Airmid nodded dumbly. Considered asking if he could do it on her inner thigh. What she hadn't said was that she'd only had one lover, very short term, since the time she'd had Erin. A mutually beneficial fling to scratch the itch. But it had been two years since she'd graduated and been recruited by MI-6. She tilted her head. "I didn't mean to recoil. It wasn't repulsion. It's just been a while since a man has touched me. You just surprised me. It won't happen again."

"And if it does, you're going to cover," Daniel said. "Just say you've had too much caffeine or something. We're going to play this by ear, and you'll be great. And I didn't tell you before, but you look beautiful. I mean, you are beautiful. I know this second skin will take a little getting used to, but just enjoy it. And at least pretend to enjoy your new husband." He extended a hand to her, fingering her thick, dark hair. A warm brown that reminded him of autumn. He ran a thumb over her collarbone. "I won't take advantage of this. But there will be some unavoidable intimacy if we are going to convince the world we're newlyweds who can't keep their hands off each other. So, if you want to take a tally and slap me later, just give me a running start."

She laughed because this Daniel was disarming. He was tender and patient. "And what about you, darlin'," she asked softly. "Will you recoil at my touch?" She needed to just get it out of the way. Do something other than sitting here like a dolt. She stood, and he watched her with a predator's gaze. She put a hand on his shoulder as she walked around behind him. It seemed safer, somehow. Not being face-to-face. Then she wrapped her arms around his neck, putting her face in his hair. He leaned into the touch.

Daniel thought he'd die from this. He was in actual pain.

Other than his cock, which was starting to strain against his trousers. Completely inappropriate, but he couldn't seem to control it. It was the soft way she'd embraced him from behind. Not sexual, but its own sort of decadent pleasure. He exhaled, leaning into her. He could smell her hair. Her own unique, womanly scent. Warm skin and soap. This mission was going to kill him. Especially given that he'd be chastely sleeping next to her tonight.

"What do you say we go enjoy that pool before the real work starts tomorrow? Let's go get some stupidly fruity drink and be seen."

She groaned. "I'm afraid that's not going to do much for your reputation. I am as pale as a snowstorm, and I don't have a plastic surgeon on speed dial."

He turned and stood, cupping her head with both hands. "Confidence is the sexiest part of you. And you shouldn't need to hear this, but I'll say it anyway. Your body is one of the top five reasons that this entire assignment is going to kill me. Now go put on your swimsuit and sunscreen, lass. And let me show off my new bride." He'd accentuated his lowlands upbringing in his speech patterns, and it curled her toes a bit.

———

Airmid needed the other swimsuit tomorrow. The rash guard-style two-piece that concealed a little more and was perfect for a day on the boat. The other one, a one-piece, could barely be called such. Jesus. *Confidence is the sexiest part of you.* She slathered everywhere she could reach with sunblock. She was not dying of skin cancer for the Crown. Then she put the suit on. Holy God. Why would Apollo do this to her? Maybe she could check out the suits in the lobby shops.

"Get out here, love. Don't be shy. Time is wasting," Daniel said. Was he flirting? Yes, he was.

Airmid grabbed the gauzy cover-up, delaying the inevitable. Then slipped on a pair of low-heeled sandals. She removed her mascara, just adding some tinted lip balm and trying to finger-comb her hair.

When she came out, he just stared at her legs, on full display despite the cover-up. "Confident is the new sexy. Right?" She lifted her chin and he moved in close. He ran a hand over her hair. "I can see your freckles again. Took off the war paint for the pool, I see."

"Yes, and they'll multiply under this sun." She grabbed her sunglasses. Then she turned before they walked out the door and downed her champagne in one gulp.

———

The problem with exclusive resorts was the lack of population, Airmid reflected. Bigger, more well-appointed rooms for the elite. Less of the everyday Joes. No spring breakers or families cluttering up the estate.

Daniel was wearing a loose button-down and a pair of simple, blue swim trousers. She envied him that. They came to their assigned lounge areas, open to the air but providing sun protection above if they needed it. Daniel took off his shirt with not a moment's hesitation. Airmid sat, removing her sandals like a lady instead of kicking them off as she normally would. She took off her sunglasses and met Daniel's stare, despite the sunglasses he wore. He pulled them off, cocking a brow. Daring her to be brave. Confident. *Cocky bastard.*

Airmid stood, moving close. He was several inches taller, now that she'd removed her shoes. His chest had a dusting of hair, brown and coppery like his hair. He was in phenomenal shape. She placed her hands on his chest, and her mouth touched his ear. "Your body has never been required to grow an entire human. So, uncock that brow, love, or the slap tally starts tonight." Daniel turned his head, hovering over her mouth.

He fingered the hem of her cover-up. "This is rather fetching, but may I do the honors?" Her breath hitched in her throat. And like he served her, and only her, Daniel slid the shift slowly up and over her head. Her face was flushed, and he put his mouth against her hair. "You stop my heart, Tara love." He put a hand on her waist. "Whoever chose that suit should be arrested."

"I did, if you must know." Daniel jerked and looked to the side to see Douglas walking in with a rum drink.

"Don't they have a singles' pool for annoying big brothers?" Daniel asked.

"Of course they do. I just wanted to see how my sister was settling in after that long flight. That suit is fabulous, as I knew it would be."

Daniel did not want to know if Douglas had seen her in the suit while she was trying things on at Apollo's home. He was going to assume he'd pressed her into it after the fact. The alternative made him want to strangle his best mate. But Douglas was a pro. He didn't play the flirt as he normally would. He was supposed to be her stepbrother, for God's sake.

Airmid tried to steal his drink, and he twisted away like a five-year-old. "Get your own. Did you put on sunscreen? You'll turn into one big freckle if you don't."

She flicked her fingers at him. "Go peck at someone else. And yes, I did. Do you think I keep this flawless skin by burning like a teenager? I got everywhere but my back."

Daniel didn't miss a beat. He sat on the lounge chair, taking her by the hips and sitting her between his legs. He swept her hair aside and started rubbing sunblock slowly into her skin.

Douglas said lowly, "Well, well. I see you two are enjoying married life. On that note, I'll be heading back to the fun crowd." Airmid tried not to gawk as Douglas stood from the other lounger and left them. He had a spectacular back and ass. He likely had a private gym.

Daniel's voice rumbled behind her. "All done," he said as he squeezed her arms. "How about a swim?"

Airmid noticed that most of the women didn't swim. They likely didn't want to ruin their makeup or hair. But she was hot and her muscles were stiff. She let Daniel lead her into the pool. He walked backward, and his eyes raked over her body like a languorous kiss. The suit had a plunging neckline. When they were knee-deep, he said, "I like the new suit, love. Turn around and let's see it all."

She refused, blushing. "You've seen it all before." He kept pulling her deeper, but he started circling her, putting a hand on her belly and dragging it around until he was behind her. He thumbed her lower back, where the bottom of the backless swim-suit started. Just low enough to hint at the sumptuous backside, but not quite obscene. From the back, it almost looked like she wore a tiny bikini bottom and nothing else. The ass of the bikini was narrow, showing off way more cheek than he wanted anyone else to see. One swift current, and this suit would be off. One pull of the straps off her shoulders, and she'd be bared to him. He led her back, deeper into the pool, until she floated against his chest.

Airmid let herself go. Her eyes heavy-lidded, she was still aware of a few others watching them. She felt exposed. So having Daniel solidly at her back was a comfort. He grazed his teeth on the tendon between her shoulder and neck and she shuddered. She couldn't stop it. He nibbled her ear. Daniel said, "Pretend I'm giving you obscene ideas for after dinner." She grinned, letting him nuzzle her. He said, "There's a man at my ten o'clock. I believe"—he kissed her under her ear—"that is our Dutchman. Apparently, he has private parties for guests who interest him." Daniel tickled her ribs. She squeaked and he laughed, husky and low.

She turned, looking murderous, but not able to keep the corners of her mouth from turning up. Airmid splashed him. He snatched her against him. She whispered, "Who told you?"

He didn't kiss her. He just spoke against her lips. "A certain four-year-old who remains in witness protection."

———

They returned to the hotel to clean up before drinks and dinner. Airmid was starving. "Is this one of those situations where I have to pretend that I don't eat?"

Daniel's brows turned inward. "Absolutely not. It would look odd if you didn't partake in a bit of wine or a couple of cocktails. You can't do that jet-lagged and on an empty stomach. If my suspicions are correct, we'll have at least a couple drinks comped tonight. Jensen, the rotting bastard, couldn't keep his eyes off you."

Airmid shook her head and said, "You're taking a piss."

Daniel's eyes sharpened. "I'm not, Airmi—Tara."

"Well, given the buffet of flesh on display at the pool, I think you're wishful thinking. We should be so lucky," she said lightly.

Daniel said, "I'm serious. If we end up getting an invite to one of the VIP parties, I don't want you out of my sight. Men with this kind of wealth often think they can take whatever they want."

She gave him a sharp look. "I'm not helpless or an idiot. And would you be talkin' about yourself and Douglas by any chance?"

Daniel threw his razor down, wiping his face. "Men like this make men like us look like paupers. With the taxes on our ... positions," he said. "Estates like ours barely stay solvent. We are wise with our situations, but we are not like these men. Men like this don't work. They rule."

Airmid squirmed under his regard. "Sorry. That was a bit below the belt. I shouldn't assume things. Especially given how you've chosen to live your life. You're a good man. I'm sorry," she said again. "And you may as well know now that I'm downright vicious when I'm hungry."

He put his hands on either side of her, cupping them on the edge of the bathroom counter. "Do you know what makes me vicious? The thought of someone like Jensen cornering you in a hallway or bathroom and putting his hands on you. Sexual harassment or assault should not be a part of your job."

"I've been taking care of myself for a long time, darlin'. I'll be careful. You should be more worried about some cougar who isn't getting enough attention cornering you in the lav."

Daniel couldn't stop himself from touching her. He thumbed the pulse at her throat. "Good thing I'm a newlywed who's got a fiery Irish girl with legs for miles warming my bed. No cougar needed." He backed away, saying, "I'm going to move my stuff into the smaller bath and give you your privacy."

"I can take the smaller one," she offered, although she didn't want to give up the tub.

"It's done, see?" Daniel picked up one small Dopp kit and backed out. Airmid looked at the catastrophe of female products strewn all over the bathroom and smirked.

"I suppose you're right," she said, continuing with her ablutions. She shouted over her shoulder, "What time did my brother say he'd be meeting us again?"

"Half seven. You have ten minutes. He's already in the bar,"

Daniel said. He appeared behind her in the bathroom doorway. He was wearing a pair of low-slung, linen trousers and an open shirt. His chest and abs on full display. He buttoned as he spoke. "He's been emailing me on the company network. He didn't want to call, even though we've swept the rooms for surveillance equipment. It's how I knew about Jensen's reputation. He's on his second wife, but she stays in Finland with her lover. And he won't care if you're married. It might be half the challenge for him."

"Why would he look at me with all of these young, thong-clad women around?" she asked. "And that's not false modesty. I know I'm not half bad, but honestly, I think you're overreacting."

He came closer behind her. "Because you're different. You're sexy and confident, yes. But you're also game for a bit of teasing. You splashed me, for God's sake. You don't use skin bronzer or Botox. You actually got your hair wet. You are also supposedly wealthy, definitely educated, and extremely beautiful. Well dressed and well made. But you aren't conforming to their mold. You are purely and exquisitely you. And people like to brush up against that kind of magic. I meant it when I said he was eyeing us. He watched us, love, but he devoured you. Stay with me or Douglas. I mean it. He owns the police in this area. We have each other and that's all."

When she came out into the bedroom after getting fully dressed, Daniel hissed through his teeth. He ran a hand through his hair. Red silk. A slip of a dress. It was longer than the blue one she'd worn this morning, but sexy and one of those dresses that made a bra impossible. She wasn't overly busty, but it was enough to fill a man's hands. Her nipples were tight buds against the silken bodice. "Fucking hell, woman. I'm going to kill Apollo."

# 7

Thank the saints for a decadent prix fixe menu. After Daniel discreetly advised her what exactly amuse-bouche entailed, she was happy to know she only needed to choose an entree. Airmid said, "I'd like the citrus-basted lobster, please." The rest of the evening would be course after course of small delicacies. Douglas ordered the beef selection.

Daniel said, "A bottle of your Alsatian white wine, please, and I'll have the duck." Douglas mumbled something about liking a pint of bitter with his steak, but Airmid kicked him under the table.

The waiter said, "And if you'd care to select a cocktail from our VIP menu, our esteemed owner, Mr. Jensen, would like it to be his compliments."

The waiter motioned across the room to a large table near the window. Apparently, Karl Jensen was holding court. He raised his glass. Airmid smiled graciously, then met the smug gaze of her very fake, very fine-looking husband. Douglas said, "MacCallan No. 4, neat."

Daniel didn't look at the menu either. "A Hendrick's martini."

Airmid snorted. She spun around, looking at their host. She smiled and turned toward the waiter, and in an over-the-top Irish lilt she said, "What does himself recommend?"

"Very well, madam." The waiter was smiling like a boy at Airmid. Then he walked to the Dutchman to get his recommendation.

Daniel smiled tightly at his beloved. "Tread carefully with that charm, girl."

She stroked his bare arm, leaning in. "Do you want an invite to party with the cool kids or not, lover?"

Douglas gave a low chuckle. "Tara of the Emerald Isle. You are making this look easy."

Daniel had to give his mate some credit. He hadn't looked at Airmid's spectacular breasts even once. Au naturel instead of the silicone aftermarket buffet that surrounded them. Either that, or the women were barely into their twenties and probably the previous nannies. But they had nothing on Airmid. And just about every man in the room appeared to keep glancing toward her. Jensen's attentions hadn't gone unnoticed. The waiter brought their drinks, and Airmid's arrived with a tropical flower, handed to her with a bow from the waiter. She tucked it behind her ear, and Daniel was ready to walk over to that table and beat the Dutchman half to death with his fists. She asked, "And what is the drink?"

"It is our Appleton Estate, 21-year aged rum with our locally sourced sugar cane and limes. It is simple and elegant, like madam."

She took a sip and closed her eyes. "It's gorgeous altogether. Thank Mr. Jensen from all of us."

Airmid wanted to laugh. Both of the men sharing her table had tight jaws and looked like they wanted to throw their hands on their man of interest. She leaned in, taking another sip. She slid the drink over a few inches. "Would you like a sip, darling?"

Daniel narrowed his eyes on her. The devil was in his eyes. She heard Douglas say something like, *here we go*. Daniel leaned toward her, meeting her across the table. He put a finger under her chin. "I much prefer it from right here." Then he kissed her. A brush first, then deeper. He pulled away, but not before he ran the tip of his tongue along the seam of her lips. "Not bad. You've improved it, I suspect." And if that didn't send a signal to their host, then Daniel hadn't done his job.

He actually looked ready to go in for another go when Douglas cleared his throat. "Our first course is here. Can you stop snogging my sister's face off before you spoil my dinner, please?" Daniel removed his finger from the delicate skin under her chin, loving that for once, Airmid Roberts was absolutely speechless.

She hadn't lied about being starved. She delighted in the five-star dining. Bite-size portions of coconut lobster soup, seared barracuda on truffle polenta, heirloom tomato salad, and a sorbet palate cleanser.

As it was, there was no VIP gathering this evening. Or at least that was the intelligence Douglas had heard from the barman at the singles' pool. It was best. After some stiff cocktails and a bottle of wine, the three of them were dead on their feet. They sailed tomorrow, after breakfast. Daniel charged the bill to the room, then she noticed he put forty-thousand Jamaican dollars on the table in cash. About two hundred pounds. When they got out of earshot, she asked him why he'd paid the gratuity in cash. "I'm not being nosey. I just want to know what I should do in case I'm alone."

"These resorts take a cut of their tips. A processing fee that far exceeds that of a credit card. It's utter horseshit. This way, I know it's going in his pocket and not Jensen's."

"You're a good man, John." And Daniel wondered if they were in a different profession, somewhere alone, somewhere she could call him by his own goddamn name, if she'd say the same thing. "I mean it. Most people wouldn't have bothered to even care. They wouldn't have checked the hotel practices."

Daniel opened the door to their suite and stopped. When he closed the door, he didn't turn the lights on. He put a finger to her lips. Then he looked around the dark room, lit by moonlight. He checked the vents, the television and cable box, and the telephone. No cameras. He went to the drapes and closed their view of the water. Next, Daniel removed the detection device from his camera case. He swept the entire room. Nothing. Yet. But he didn't like the prat who ran this place, and he didn't trust him. "Clear."

He started unbuttoning his shirt, and Airmid was trying like hell not to be distracted. She took her shoes off. Daniel said, "It's important to find out those kinds of details for two reasons. Disgruntled and underpaid employees can be a hell of an intelligence source, even for small things like whether there's a VIP party tonight, and how often Jensen has his tea sent right to the room rather than taking it in one of the dining areas. What his favorite drink is. But also because if we aren't trotting the globe, trying to make it better for everyone, what the fuck is the point?" He slid his shoes off.

"You seem out of sorts," Airmid said.

Daniel turned the light off again, needing to see the sky. He opened the drapes, and the moon shone bright. "I *am* out of sorts. But it's not your fault. I just don't like the way he looks at you."

"And how does he look at me?" she asked. "I'm not some

blushing virgin. I recognize lust. I'm a shiny, new toy. He'll get bored before the five days are up. And if taking a sip of his best rum and flashing him a smile gets us the information we need, then there's no harm in it. I can handle him. I was a soldier for six years. I know how to handle pig-headed, arrogant men. Now let's get to bed. It's late, and I'm an early riser."

Daniel smiled at that. "Do you want to call Erin in the morning? It'll be lunchtime in Scotland."

"Yes, I'll do it first thing. I should have called her when we got here, but we just went right to work. I won't tell her work involved a large swimming pool. She'd never forgive me."

"You're a good mother," Daniel said softly.

"How do you know that? I could be a horrible shrew behind closed doors," Airmid said.

"Well, we're behind closed doors now. I haven't seen you sprout horns yet. Now get on with your flossing or whatever it is that you do. I'll meet you in ten."

———

"What are you reading?" Airmid asked.

Daniel looked up, smiling sadly. "My mother sent it to me. It is my father's journal. Robert's journal, I mean. Not the original, obviously," Daniel said as he lifted his e-reader.

"That must be hard to read. But it's a gift, I hope," she said. "What part of his life is it from? Is it about his work?"

Daniel shook his head. "No, he'd never have written about that in a private journal. My mum knows about what he did, and she knows about me. She's the only one in the family who knows what Papa did. My sister and brother don't. If I wasn't also with the agency, he probably would have told them before he died. But it's better this way, I think. Anyway, the journal is from his younger years, when he first married my mother. I think there must have been ones before this, but she gave me this one for a reason." He shook himself. "What are you reading?"

Airmid smiled. "Your sister's last book. It's quite good."

"Is that the one about the Cornish smuggling family?" he asked.

"It is. It's really good. I mean, she's a wonderful writer," Airmid said.

"It's a good book. She's working on the sequel as we speak. She seems to be really happy with it. She spent a month in an old house on the Cornish Coast doing research for the book. She's good about her research."

"You sound very proud of her," Airmid said.

"I am very proud of her. I'm proud of both my siblings. I love them more than anything. They are my heart," he said. "That's how you Irish say it, right? *Mo chrói*. My heart. I hear my family say it to each other. And it takes on a different meaning, I think, when they say it to their mates. I mean spouses. Not mates as in friends."

"Their mates? That's an interesting way of putting it. Most would say partner or wife," Airmid said with a smile.

Daniel nodded, the corner of his mouth turning up. "It is, I know. But the Irish are a superstitious lot, I think. The O'Brien family lore goes back centuries. Back to the time of the Irish kings. They believe with all they are that the O'Briens have one mate they are destined to find. Only one. It's serious business, this mate thing. And my male cousins are like a horde of barbarians when it comes to their women. Not chauvinistic. The women in their family are fierce and smart. Just in the overprotective and territorial sort of way. They're all very happy in their unions."

Airmid glanced at the journal in his hand. He followed her gaze. Daniel said, "Yes, well, with my other branches of the family, I'm afraid it wasn't so clear-cut. As I've said."

Airmid said, "It rarely is. Believe me, I know. I'm sure you're just enough of a good snoop to have heard most of my tale. And Erin's."

"I know enough," Daniel said. "And I think you are incredibly strong. And for what it's worth, your Tommy should have married you despite what his parents thought. People like that don't tend to come around on a matter like this. They have their prejudices, and that's how they stand. He should have told them to sod off and married you straightaway. You deserved that, and so did his daughter."

Airmid felt the hot prick of tears. And he was right. "I was mad at him for a long time. As much as I loved him, I was still mad at him. He could have changed his beneficiary despite the fact that I hadn't given birth yet. Despite the fact that he hadn't married me. He knew he had a daughter on the way. That should have been enough. He left us with no support, and his parents didn't need the money. But now, I'm glad. I don't want to owe his family anything.

"I loved him. And I forgave him a long time ago. But he didn't deserve me or Erin because he didn't have the spine to stand up to his parents. He was twenty-seven years old, but he wasn't enough of a man to fight for us. So, I'm okay with it just being me and Erin. I'm enough most days, and she will always be my top priority."

"I'm glad you know your worth, Airmid," he whispered. And the sound of her real name on his tongue caused her fingers to curl around her book. He was reclined next to her in sleeping shorts and a T-shirt. She highly doubted he slept in this on the daily.

"Do those pajamas still have the tags on them?" she asked, just to try to make light of their awkward situation.

"A Christmas present from Donna, actually. It came with slippers and a robe. I've worn them to actual bed exactly once," he said, the dimple on his right cheek making an appearance. "And are those from Apollo's treasure trove?" He nodded at the uninteresting, summer-weight pajamas she was wearing.

"No, actually. These are mine. We won't talk about what I abandoned at his house. I'm not actually a newlywed, and things would have gotten extremely awkward." She fingered the neckline of her pajamas. "These were a birthday gift from Erin. And by Erin, I mean I chose them, told the clerk at the department store to show them to my four-year-old, take her up to the counter, and let her hand her the money."

Daniel's throat thickened. He'd never really thought about what it was like to have no one around to take a child shopping for their mother. What did she do for Christmas? Maybe her brother or mother helped? Or a friend? His face softened. "They look rather fetching, actually. And comfortable. As for awkwardness, I usually sleep naked as a wee babe, so I think we can agree some adjustments were in order."

Airmid's face lit up as she laughed. "You know, sometimes you are so bloody proper. Then I get you behind closed doors and you're dropping the F-bomb and talking about full, male nudity. I can see where your sister gets her daring streak. You are a man of many layers, John." She said the name deliberately. As if to say, *earl by day, clandestine agent by night.* The whole thing was almost too much to take in. Everyone thought MI-6 was running from Masad and KGB. But they did international counter-narcotics missions as well. Especially after the influx of deadly heroin and the cocaine epidemic had infected Europe.

"Yes, well, we all have our vices. With Douglas, it is women. Mine is behaving, on occasion, like a royal pig-fucker."

Airmid put a pillow over her face. In muffled words, she said, "I'm never going to live that one down, am I? Well, I suppose my vice would be my temper. And the fact that I can cut loose on someone in several languages just makes me more deadly with my tongue. Ye should hear me in the Irish."

Daniel laughed. "Oh, I'm getting well versed in Irish cursing and insults. I have a lot of cousins. And the female cousin is the worst. Brigid will actually be there when we get back home, so you'll meet her. She's coming after Alanna."

"She sounds like my kind of girl. I'm going to have to do something special for her and Alanna. It's nice what they are doing. I feel guilty."

"Why on earth would you feel guilty?" Daniel asked.

She said, "Love, I'm a mother. If I'm breathing, I'm feeling guilty about something."

———

## Hawick, Scotland

Alanna smiled as Erin rang off with her mother. Donna had used her own cell phone to keep in contact with Danny and Airmid. They had some international phone that they traveled with. Pretty spiffy for a non-profit. She started as her own Face-Time app began ringing. "Davey, Isla, it's your daddy! Hurry!"

"Hello, mo ghra. How's my mate doing without me?" Aidan crooned.

Davey popped his head in view. "Da, stop talkin' all mushy to Mam. I'm a child!"

Aidan gave a husky laugh. "Davey, you'll have a mate someday, and you're going to remember this conversation."

Davey said, "No way. Girls are gross."

"Hey! The girls are offended by that comment," Alanna said.

Davey rolled his eyes. "You and Isla aren't girls. You're family." He turned back to the camera before he saw his mother hiding a laugh under her hand. "Da, are ye having fun? Did ye get to shoot a gun? Are the spiders really big like Uncle Liam said?"

They spoke for a while, then Aidan noticed a small head of blonde curls in the background. "Where are you, and who is this pretty lass?"

Alanna said, "Aidan, this is Erin. We are helping with some fun playtime while your cousin Daniel and his colleagues are on a business trip. Erin's mommy is raising her alone, so Daniel hired a nanny and brought her here. Isn't that exceptionally sweet of him to do for a colleague he just met?" She gave Aidan a knowing wink. He just shook his head. The women in the family have been dying to mate poor Daniel off to someone worthy.

Davey interrupted. "And we rode horses! Well, I rode a horse. The two little ones rode some sort of Scottish ponies. I got to trot! That's when you go faster, and it was awesome, Da!"

After a while, the children went back to their toys, and Alanna left them in the care of the nanny, Constance. Alanna said, "How is the training? Is it raining constantly? I miss you, sweetheart. How are the boys holding up?"

He told her about the work with maps they'd done yesterday. "These lads are so dependent on GPS, you'd swear they didn't know north from south. This is good for them. Really good. And our medics are getting a whole new set of skills. From foot fungus to unexplained rashes. They've got a small cooler with morphine and anti-venom of a few varieties."

Alanna shuddered. "Makes tick season seem sort of paltry, doesn't it?"

Aidan's smile was devilish. "Oh, but I do love doing a buddy check on you. One can't be too thorough. Those ticks could be hiding anywhere."

"So you've said," she said with a smirk.

"You never mentioned where Daniel went," Aidan said. "Where is this out-of-towner with his new coworker?"

"It's not just them. Another man is going as well. Some Scottish Laird or something," Alanna said. "And they went somewhere in the Caribbean. The Caymans or Jamaica or somewhere like that. They were sort of vague. Erin's mother is an interpreter. She knows several languages, including basic Arabic, but she specializes in Spanish. She was in the Royal Irish for a time, Aidan. She also did a tour with the dragoons. This was several years ago, but she'd heard of you. Apparently, my husband is a pretty big deal."

"What's her name?" Aidan asked.

"Airmid Roberts," she answered. "She got out before she had a baby. Donna said Erin's father is dead. I think he might have been military as well, but I don't know his name."

Aidan thought about it. "Airmid ... and you say she's a linguist? She must be smart. The training is top-notch and difficult. I'll ask around. You've piqued my curiosity. I've got to go, but I just wanted you to know that I love you and the training is just grand. It's slightly miserable and a good time altogether."

Alanna laughed. "You military people are twisted. You really are. And I love you too, baby." She blew him a kiss. "You can check me for ticks when you get home."

————

## BATSUB Headquarters, Belize

Aidan stood over his battle buddy, admiring his work. He'd managed to treat a fake laceration and splint an arm while kneeling in the pouring rain and mud. He turned toward the lieutenant colonel, who was the commanding officer of the entire program. He lived in Belize full time on a joint base with the Belizean Army. "How long have you been here, if you don't mind me asking, sir."

Lt. Colonel Mason was from Liverpool, and Aidan respected the man. "Let's see. Coming up on nine years, I think. They'll let me stay until I retire next year. Why do you ask?"

"Well, I was wondering about your time with the dragoons. Have ye heard of a female linguistics soldier, got out about six years ago. Airmid Roberts from Northern Ireland."

Mason's brows rose. "Yes, as a matter of fact I have. She actually came with the dragoons as an interpreter. Sharp kid, if I remember. She did some time in Afghanistan and Africa as well. It was a shame about her man. Staff Sergeant Tommy Devon. He was a communications tech. He died in a training accident with a child on the way. A vehicle flipped over in a river and he was pinned beneath. The poor sod drowned before they could get him freed."

Aidan cursed under his breath. "My wife is staying with my cousin in Scotland. Airmid Roberts is a colleague, and the child is staying at the estate with a nanny while she's out of town. My Alanna seemed to like the woman, and the little girl is adorable. It's a terrible thing that he didn't live to see her born. Apparently, they hadn't married yet and the child got nothing. His parents took everything, and Airmid has been left to fend for them both. It sounds like it's all turned out okay, but it's still a pity. His parents are real pieces of shit, if you don't mind me saying so."

Mason rubbed his jaw. "Yes, but some of the blame can lie with him. She was pretty far along when he died. For a man in love, he sure as fuck didn't seem in a hurry to do right by the girl and his child. It's the entire reason these lads have to be taught about how to have their affairs in order. Why they have to do a will before they deploy. Such a pity. But she was a good soldier and an altogether wonderful, young woman. I'm glad she's doing okay. And you know what I'm going to do? I'm going to have my admin guy make some calls. There have been some new

benefits that may be available to his surviving child if she can establish paternity. Let me do this for her. We aren't supposed to leave a man behind, and that goes for his children as well."

"Aye, well it's good of you to do that. Let me know what you find out, and I'll pass it along to Alanna. And it's also good to hear that you thought highly of the woman. Alanna is tenderhearted. I just wanted to ask around. It's a pity the lass got out of the army. Being naturally gifted with languages is a skill that's hard to come by."

"True enough. After nine years, I'm still learning. Well, now. How about we show these young lads how to find their ass with both hands. That map and compass lesson was ghastly."

Aidan chuckled. "Aye, and I changed the Wi-Fi password in the barracks. A little incentive to pass the next test." And as he said it, he could hear the young men start complaining that their phones weren't working.

Mason threw his head back and laughed. "You are heartless, Major O'Brien. I like your style."

———

**Caribbean Sea**

Airmid was exhausted. Sleeping next to Daniel had seemed like no big deal. He'd done everything possible to put her at ease. This was a job. She'd shared quarters with other women so many times, and in the field, they'd all been racked out near each other. She'd been a soldier for six years. Things like modesty and vanity went out the window during training or a mission.

But all she'd kept thinking about was that Lord Daniel MacPherson, the Earl of Hawick, normally slept completely fucking naked every night. Whoever normally shared his bed was a lucky woman. Especially if that rum-soaked kiss was anything to go by.

Airmid closed her eyes to the wind, the warm sun soaking into her skin. She was wearing the long-sleeved rash guard and bikini bottom from the island boutique. She'd tied a sarong around her waist, wanting some semblance of modesty while she walked through the resort and to the marina.

Now the agency assigned a *crew member* to help Daniel and Douglas sail the thirty-foot sailboat to the stretch of sea between Cayman Brac and Jamaica. They were going to sleep on the boat tonight, five hundred meters from the uninhabited island that served as a blue iguana preserve. Apollo's tech person was hacking the system right now, ready to shut down the cameras for the twelve hours starting at eighteen hundred. A "down for maintenance" message replacing the live feed. Apparently, it happened all the time, so no one would think twice about it. Until then, they'd eat, pretend to drink copious amounts of rum, and skin-dive off the back of the boat. Douglas and Daniel were scuba certified, so they'd likely be beneath her, getting the real view of the reef.

Their crew chief, Badrick, was of partial Jamaican ancestry going back five generations on his father's side. His mother was British. He was recruited by Apollo ten years ago and worked exclusively in counter narcotics. Airmid had a thing about names. She always wanted to know the origin and the why of it. It was

English and meant *ax ruler*. She smiled at him when he'd been introduced. When he told her what his name meant, she laughed and said, "Perfect." Airmid pointed a thumb at him and said to Douglas, "If the shit hits the fan, I'm with Badrick."

Badrick was currently tying the boat to a mooring buoy, his long, dark braids swinging around as he worked. In this area, they tried to protect the reef by not dropping an anchor indiscriminately.

Airmid brought out a tray from the galley, containing tall glasses with mango and pineapple juice. Sans rum, but there was the occasional boat going around, and it was best to appear on holiday. She had fresh coco bread and meat pastries from the resort bakery. The meat pies were spicy and flavorful. A perfect contrast with the juice. Airmid said, "Finally, I can eat large portions with my hands."

Douglas handed her a napkin. He said, "You are adorable when you stuff your face, sister dear."

"I need my energy. It's going to be a long night," she said. "So, after our lunch, it's in the water. What are we looking for exactly? Should I go closer to the shore since you'll be at depth?"

"You'll stay near the boat where Badrick can see you. You shouldn't swim alone," Daniel said like a mother hen.

"I did a resort diving course when I went on holiday with some mates. Just let me go down with you. It'll come back to me."

Daniel looked at her dryly. "It's been ten years, and you weren't open-water certified through any sort of reputable association."

Douglas interrupted. "How many dives did you do during your holiday?"

Airmid said, "I don't know, maybe five? This is ten meters at the most. Just let me go, for fuck's sake. Get the stick out of your ass."

Daniel stiffened, but Douglas said, "She can dive with me. I've got a double regulator. We won't be down more than a half hour. I'll share a tank with her."

Daniel gave him a murderous look. "The. Fuck. You. Will." The entire group froze, and Daniel seemed to check himself. "I went through the instructor course. She'll dive with me." He stood, wiping his hands on his napkin before descending into the boat's cabin. Airmid's brows were down, Badrick's brows were up, and Douglas was grinning like the Cheshire cat.

Badrick said weakly, "I brought my gear. She won't need to share."

———

Daniel's jaw tightened and his gut twisted. Or maybe it wasn't his gut. Airmid took off the damned cloth she had wrapped around her waist and was walking, bending, and stretching all over the boat. Her swimsuit was a white, long-sleeved, cropped top that zipped from her neck to her midriff. The bottoms were not nearly as skimpy as the suit she'd worn in the pool. It was more athletic and utilitarian. But all Daniel could think about was how quickly he could have that zipper down. And how absolutely stunning her ass was in those white bottoms.

Airmid may as well have been packing groceries into her car or folding laundry. She was focused on getting ready for the dive, not paying the three men with her any mind. This was the soldier. The woman who'd likely hiked until her feet blistered, dirty and tired, with her fellow soldiers. Who'd skipped showers and slept rough during an Ebola epidemic in Africa. She obviously didn't even consider how alluring she was. Douglas being Douglas took every opportunity to rake his gaze over her legs when she wasn't paying attention. It was like the man was trying to provoke him.

Daniel took the weight belt out of his best mate's meaty paw and turned toward Airmid. "I'll start with ten pounds, and we can shed weight if it's too heavy. It's easier to shed it than add more once we start descending. You stay glued to me. Do you understand? We take this slow. You need to make sure your breathing is steady. Don't hold your breath—ever. Do you remember how to clear your ears?"

"I do," Airmid said calmly. "Why are you so stressed out about this? It's been a while, but I just spent the last twenty minutes refreshing my memory on the equipment and safety measures. It's like riding a bike." She shrugged. "I'm not going to get the bends diving for forty-five minutes at twenty-five feet. And you've got a dive computer. So, let's quit with the fretting and do this."

Daniel wouldn't meet her eyes. He pointed at the tank. There was a band around it at the base with a hard, plastic ball attached. Douglas, being an idiot, said, "I know what you're thinking. Daniel left his ball gag lying around, and someone thought it was scuba equipment."

Airmid stifled a laugh because Daniel really didn't think it was funny. She said, "Despite the fact that I believe those are your teethmarks in the thing, I know what a tank banger looks like. Keep your kink preferences to yourself, Dougie."

Daniel said, "If you see something of note, or if Supergirl starts being consumed by a shark, bang your tank to alert the group. The visibility is good today, but stay within twenty feet of us, Douglas. I mean it."

Badrick said, in his smooth native tongue, "Come, Supergirl. Let's get your equipment on and get you in the water with these two fools."

———

Airmid slowed her breathing, deliberate and steady. Loosened her jaw around the mouthpiece before she bit through the silicone. She'd had to stop at about seven feet when the squeeze started, but Daniel had patiently waited for her to figure it out. She cleared her ears and finally descended to twenty-six feet, finding the sandy bottom.

The reef was all around her in large mounds of organic life. The water was about twenty-six degrees Celsius, and she was suddenly wishing she'd brought a little layer of coverage. A shorty or even a simple lycra skin. But her body acclimated to the water, and she felt the stress leak out of her as she took in the gorgeous sites around her.

Then she started toward a large coral head, deciding to see the sites before getting more detailed in their search. The anxiety tightened her chest, realizing that she really shouldn't be diving without a refresher course of some sort. But Daniel was beside her, and she knew, come what may, he'd put her safety first.

She felt a gentle hand on her arm, and she looked at her dive buddy. He drew her toward a craggy part of the reef, pointing. That's where she saw it. A spotted moray eel heaving in gulps of water, then releasing as its mouth gaped open. It was kind of cute. She disliked snakes immensely, but this seemed a little more palatable. She looked up to see a stoplight parrot fish crunching on some dead coral. She and Daniel swayed with the sea, just looking around them at the glory that was the ocean floor. She thought they'd go closer to land, but they followed Douglas away from the shore and out from the starboard side of their sailboat.

Airmid felt Daniel take her hand as the water got deeper. At about ten meters was where it lay. A shipwreck that she hadn't seen on her research of this island. She gripped Daniel's hand as she saw a solitary reef shark just above the wreck. It wasn't big, but the sight still jarred her. They approached and the shark drifted away, not liking the racket of their air tanks and the turmoil of their bubbles.

Daniel made the symbol with his hands to swim through, and then to watch. She would go in after Douglas, and Daniel would watch her back. The large, gaping hole in the hull, which time had eroded and made wider, was plenty big enough. But she felt her breathing speed up as she swam through. She felt Daniel behind her. Knew without a doubt that he'd stayed right on her heels. Or fins, in this case.

Douglas stopped her and motioned to his fins. She watched as he put his ankles close and did small flips instead of the long sweeps they'd normally do, where they had their legs alternating up and down. Small flips, so as not to stir up the bottom. It made sense. The visibility was good, especially with their dive lights. But it wouldn't stay that way if she came in here flapping her legs like an amateur.

Daniel came next to her and gently sank to his knees, taking her hands. She did the same, letting her body sink gently. It's then that she noticed how fast she was breathing. He looked at her tank and saw that she had plenty of air. Then he did the funniest thing. He met her eyes and smiled. As much as you could with a regulator in your mouth.

He looked up, and so she followed his eyes. Their bubbles were collecting like mercury beads on the rusty roof of the ship's cabin. She squeezed his hand, feeling a swelling gratitude from the simple gesture. Of just being here with her and letting her experience something wondrous. The colonies of fish were busy bustling through the wreck that had started to become a part of the ecosystem. Growing things clinging to the man-made struc-ture, absorbing it and building a life around its intrusion.

Airmid lost sight of Douglas, remembering the strict instructions to stay together. She saw a nurse shark, tarrying ahead on the sandy bottom. Its dull eyes didn't acknowledge her, but she knew the shark missed nothing. They weren't aggressive unless provoked, so she gave it a wide berth as she let Daniel take the lead.

That's when they heard it. His tank banger was pinging through the water. A hitch of panic seared her chest, but Daniel didn't hurry. One ping, waiting five seconds, another ping. Not an emergency. Rapid-fire pings meant trouble. She slowed her breathing, watching Daniel's fins as he popped up onto the deck of the old ship, or what used to be the deck. There was another gaping hole. Douglas floated weightlessly, hovering over the opening. She watched as he sank, feet bent upward so that he'd land on his knees. He sank not by fins or arm movement, but by controlling his breathing. A pang of envy hit her because she knew she'd have to go in head first. Daniel did the same as Douglas, taking both her hands as he sank down. Easing her with him as she fluttered her fins for an extra boost.

They settled, hovering over the bottom. Their underwater torches helped, but she noticed Douglas had marked what he wanted them to see by leaving a chem-light wedged in a nook of the room. There was a compartment with a lock that had long withered away to pure rust. She watched as Daniel opened the cupboard-like compartment and saw what Douglas had found. Some sort of more modern technology. A red light shining through the murky water. She'd seen one of these, she thought. An underwater locator beacon. They put them on black boxes in aircrafts. They sent out a signal so that someone could be led right to them. It emitted an ultrasonic pulse that could be detected by sonar.

But why would it be on a shipwreck? So that large boats didn't go near it? Maybe. Or perhaps someone put it in here to act as a beacon for a secret meeting place. Most small boats wouldn't have the equipment to pick this up. But search and rescue and the military would. Even commercial shipping crafts. And it wouldn't be that difficult to equip even a personal yacht with such equipment. Maybe it was nothing, but maybe it was something very significant. Douglas took it gently from the cupboard, the hinges giving just a bit on the door. They needed to make sure they put it back how it was.

Daniel held it while Douglas took pictures with his stupidly expensive camera. The serial number had been scratched up, but their computer software would easily decipher what it said. It was screwed into a small board to keep it from rolling with the water current. Airmid stopped him before he put it back, catching a glimpse of something. There was some sort of algae or microorganisms that had started colonizing on the wood board. But there were distinct areas where they didn't attach, like something repelled growth. Daniel brought his light in closer. Nothing. But then he switched on the black light that ran down the handle of the thin torch. The numbers glowed under the light. More pictures. Then Douglas put the beacon back where he found it.

———

Airmid washed off with the outdoor showerhead, glad to be back on shore. The sight of that beacon had chilled her bones. A reminder that she wasn't playing at this. That she wasn't enjoying a holiday with two beautiful men. She made the rinse-off quick, then went to the bedroom to get dressed. Douglas was in the shower inside the cabin. Much to the cursing of Daniel. He opted, instead, to use the freshwater hose outside.

Airmid was wrapped in a sarong, tying it behind her neck like a dress. Other than that, she wore a pair of cotton panties because the sun was brutal overhead and it was a hot day. Her hair whipped around her in a wet tangle as their boat drifted on the mooring line. She tried not to watch the water sluice over Daniel's body, but she couldn't help it. He sprayed inside his shorts and let out a very unmanly squeak. She pressed the back of her hand to her mouth, trying to hold in the laughter.

Daniel narrowed his eyes on her, then one brow went up. She pointed. "Don't. Mac—Millin." Shit. She'd almost called him MacPherson. She went into the cabin of the boat to escape him because he was definitely tempted to turn the hose in her direction. She saw it in the boyish smile that he couldn't suppress. Just as she opened the refrigerator to get a cold drink, Douglas let out a howl and burst from the tiny lav.

"Jesus Christ, there's a spider the size of a cat!" he yelled, just as he tripped over his own feet, shoving Airmid under him and onto the small sofa. She bent backward over the arm, taking Douglas with her as their feet ended up higher than their heads. Daniel bellowed from the stairs as Douglas scurried off her. He pulled her up with him, sputtering. Then he dropped her arm and put both hands over his impressive man parts. Did she look? Hell yes, she did. Every woman who spends any amount of time with a gorgeous man has questions. And hers just got answered about one of the beautiful men. *Bravo, Laird Douglas.* He grabbed a jungle-themed, pastel pillow for better coverage. Jungle ... as in anaconda. She was stopping now.

"I'm sorry, lass. Jesus, I'm so sorry. There's a spider in there—"

Airmid grinned. "The size of a cat. So I heard. I think everyone on Grand Cayman heard you." She was trying so hard. It was when she looked at Badrick that she lost it. She was laughing so hard, she couldn't breathe.

Douglas was walking backward toward his bedroom area, saying, "I don't think it's funny. But as I've got no trousers on, I can hardly form a reputable argument." Douglas looked at Daniel and swallowed audibly.

Daniel watched Airmid laughing. Badrick wasn't helping. He'd come next to her, both sitting on the sofa and bent over their knees in uncontrollable fits of laughter. Daniel had seen the appraisal in Airmid's unguarded gaze. And for God's sake, Douglas had all but penetrated her with that paltry cock of his. He knew it wasn't paltry, but it made him feel better to think it, at any rate.

Douglas made an appearance after he had some bloody trousers on. "Sorry, boss. I just came out in a hurry and tripped." This sent Airmid's giggles careening out of control. He had tripped, cock-first, into his coworker was more like it.

Douglas had the good sense to be completely scarlet. The man never blushed. Daniel exhaled. "For fuck's sake, Douglas. You and spiders." Daniel opened the bathroom door, pulling aside the shower curtain. "It's likely a tiny ... Suffering Jesus! What the fuck is that?" He actually jerked. It was ghastly and bloody huge.

Badrick was finally together enough to come have a look. "Huh. This is a banana spider. Not very toxic, but the bite is painful. They usually don't come indoors. They like to live in the bush or gardens. It must have come in with the supplies." Douglas looked at the fruit bowl and yanked his body away from the counter. Badrick said, "I'll check the rest of the boat. The rental company is going to have to do a full cleaning and extermination."

Douglas said, indignantly, "For what the British Government paid for this goddamn boat, you'd think they'd have checked the shower. Now, who is going to kill the bastard?"

Airmid had immediately googled the banana spider. "It's a

female," Airmid said. "The females are bigger. Holy God, that thing is huge! I vote for the Jamaican being the one to clear it away. But not before I snap a photo for posterity." Then she looked at Douglas, smirking. "I should have been quicker with the camera."

Douglas mumbled, "Cheeky little smart-ass. I'm supposed to be your brother, you little pervert."

———

Badrick's wife had sent dinner. He crisped up the conch fritters in the tiny oven, as they'd softened in the cooler. Fritters and ackee and codfish, the national dish of Jamaica. Airmid helped Badrick in the small galley kitchen, stirring the dish in a large pan in order to reheat it. His wife was very adamant that they not use a microwave, as it would toughen the ingredients. So, she stirred it on low heat, and the smells of the island whirled around them. They ate as they talked, drinking Red Stripe lager and discussing what they'd found on the wreck.

Daniel was busy on the computer. "I had assumed the coordinates from the ship's GPS led to this moor we are tied to, but I could be wrong. They could have tied off on the shipwreck, just southeast of where we are anchored. But what about the numbers?" Daniel asked. "They are coordinates, I'm assuming? Are they to the port where they seized the boat?"

Douglas took the laptop from him. "Not even close. You did go to Cambridge for your graduate degree, didn't you?"

Daniel took the jab. Shrugging, he said, "I was busy with cricket and fast women."

Airmid snorted, not liking the spike of jealousy that went through her. "So, where exactly?"

Douglas pointed out the hatch toward the island. "The coordinates land you right in the middle of that preserve."

Airmid smiled as Daniel said, "Hell, yes."

———

Airmid tossed and turned in the little bunk, wondering why the hell she'd slept in here instead of in the queen bed with Daniel. These were children's bunks, and all she could think about, burrowed in this little nook, was that fucking spider. She wasn't overly silly about spiders or other bugs. But that thing had been as big as a man's hand. The body had been the size of a plum tomato. Full of eggs and ready to make an egg sack, according to Badrick.

Badrick had gently taken a paper plate and a bowl to capture it. Then he'd set the spider adrift, giving her a fighting chance of settling on the island nearby. He assured Airmid that any spider that was on the big islands was also located on this protected island, so they wouldn't be introducing a non-native species. If she survived, she might be a tasty bit of protein for the wildlife.

Airmid felt the absurd urge to dive in after her. *Charlotte's Web* was still one of her favorite childhood books. She couldn't wait until Erin was older so they could read it together. So, Charlotte was adrift and headed for the perils of Blue Iguana Island, but did she have friends still on the boat? The thought made her toes twitch.

She heard the soft, steady breathing of Badrick on the sofa. He'd opted for the living room, not wanting to intrude by climbing onto the top bunk. Still, she felt like she was in a coffin. The air conditioning didn't manage to blow into her little cubby.

When she'd taken her pillow out of the bedroom, Daniel had been reading his father's journal. How sad to think he'd married a woman who had been in love with another man. As if she heard his thoughts, Daniel roused from the bedroom and walked out onto the deck above. She decided to follow him, knowing she wouldn't sleep.

Zero dark thirty, they'd head out on the island. While it was still dark enough to be sneaky, but not pitch black. They decided to embark around half four, an hour before sunrise. That would give them some time. It was only nine o'clock or so, but they'd turned in early to get some sleep. Airmid was jet-lagged, but also wired. She'd hoped the lager would help, but she was still wide awake.

Daniel felt her as she emerged from the cabin. He turned, and she stole his breath. She was so goddamn beautiful. It hurt him, deep in his chest. He looked away, not able to meet her intelligent eyes. She padded on the deck in her bare feet. "Couldn't sleep?" he asked her as he looked out over the clear, starry sky.

She asked softly, "Are you okay?"

His jaw was tight. "I am. Why do you ask?"

"I saw you reading your da's journal. And you just seem ... like you're holding back a tempest."

He exhaled. She had no idea. He'd been reading about the day he was born. "He loved me so much, Airmid. I knew that. I always felt loved. But after finding everything out, one starts to question it all. But even in the privacy of his own diary, there was nothing but"—he took a cleansing breath—"nothing but love. For me and for mum. They became a family. And I loved my papa. I was his little shadow, always. And he never tried to shove me off while he was busy. I just hope he knows how much I loved him. Despite the biology. He saved my mother. I mean, her family could have very well worn her down if he hadn't come and taken her from Manchester. Maybe she'd have gone back to John Mullen, but maybe she'd have just gone and done what they wanted. Made the problem go away."

"I think you'd be surprised what a woman will do to protect what's hers. But you're right. They could have thrown her out, penniless, and who knows what might have happened. Your father was a wonderful man. And he raised you to be the same. I have no doubt whatsoever that he knew you loved him. You aren't the sort to leave that to chance."

"You barely know me," he said. "I can be a repressed jackass when I let my English side take over." The corner of his mouth was twitching.

"Now *that* I can believe. If you were channeling your Irish, you'd be letting all those feelings rip through the room with reckless abandon," Airmid said with a grin. Her voice was low, trying not to wake the others.

Daniel looked at her mouth, mauve in the moonlight. He turned away, saying, "You can't sleep because you're crammed in that cupboard they're calling a bed. Were you waiting to catch poor Douglas unaware in the bath again?"

Airmid choked down a laugh. "Christ, don't get me started again."

He wasn't laughing though. Daniel said, "I suppose he does cut a rather dashing figure. He's in good shape for an aging duke."

"He does at that," she said. And wasn't sure why she'd said it until his eyes darted to hers, brows down. "Although, I prefer dinner and a movie more so than being accosted so early into the relationship. The full-frontal nudity alongside that unholy spider divided my attention."

And she coaxed the first real smile out of him since they'd started this conversation. He looked out over the water and said something so softly, she strained to hear it. "I want her to have loved him."

Airmid's heart squeezed. "He sounds like the sort of man who could only be loved. And she did have two more children with him, so she must have felt something other than friendship."

Daniel said, "I find myself playing over what I saw of their relationship. Was it companionship or were they in love? It makes me question whether there is such a thing. I see my Irish family, and it makes me think maybe there is. Maybe she's just not capable of it. John was this great love, yet she walked away without even giving him a chance. He'd have survived the job loss. Sorcha said he was a good student. That he stayed at the mill, probably waiting for my mother to return. Then he got lung cancer from the poor working conditions of my grandfather's death trap of a mill. But Edith and Michael are wonderful people. They'd have helped them. They'd have loved her. It wouldn't have been a life of privilege, but it would have kept them together and thriving. She just let them take her away. And then she married Robert out of desperation. Maybe she's just too pragmatic to let love get in the way. It all boils down to how someone is wired. I look at her, and I see myself. And it scares me, Airmid."

Airmid ran a hand over his arm. "Has there ever been anyone for you?"

Daniel shook his head and said, "Not really. When I was a lad, sure. Ye think you're in love a hundred times as a lad. You confuse a cockstand for emotion. Affection for love. But since then, no. Just brief affairs. And that's okay. This isn't a life that is cohesive to building a trusting relationship." Airmid understood it. People thought she worked as an interpreter for an oil company. And now she was on the books as an interpreter for a non-profit.

She said, "Aye, I suppose it's not. And I'm not going to lecture you about it. I've had one fling since Tommy died. Purely lust on both sides because after a while, you miss being touched, don't you? Humans aren't meant to be alone. I have Erin, yes. But she's my baby. Mine to love and protect. So, I kept it shallow, never introduced him to my daughter, and then it was done. The itch was scratched, and honestly, it was utterly forgettable. So, no, I'm not going to lecture you on the glory of falling in love. And just because your mother is the pragmatic sort, doesn't mean she didn't love both those men. She's lost them both. I know a little about being left behind. My unsolicited advice is, cut her some slack and forgive her. Life is too short. And keep reading, Daniel. I think there might be a reason she gave you his diary." When she said his real name, soft and secretive, it rolled through him like a song.

They quietly made their way back into the cabin of the ship, tiptoeing past Badrick. When she started to retreat, Daniel took her hand. "Come. The bed is plenty big enough, and I've got my own AC unit."

Airmid said, "Ye really know how to tempt a girl. And you checked it for spiders?"

"Twice. Come, hen. Come to your husband's cool, soft, pest-free bed. You need your sleep." And his soft burr made a prickle of something travel over her skin.

"You really can lay that lowlander accent on when you want something, can't you?" She was grabbing her pillow as they passed the small cubby where the children probably slept.

He let go of her hand, letting her choose, and she did. That bed looked so damned good. He slid between the sheets, sliding off his T-shirt and wearing low-slung shorts. She fought the impulse to stare. And run her hands all over his chest and arms. He was too potent. It was like too many sweets. The constant exposure couldn't be good for her. Yet, she found herself sliding in beside him, the cotton sheets cooled from the AC. The pillows soft and downy. She moaned, sprawling, and all but shoving him off the bed.

Daniel laughed. "No starfishing. You're half my size. You're lucky I don't shave down your portion." But she was already drifting away. He watched her for longer than he should. Something about this felt so right, it had to be wrong. He gently peeled a strand of hair away that was caught on an eyebrow. He leaned over before he thought better of it and kissed her head. "Good night, Airmid."

———

Badrick sipped a cup of good Jamaican coffee and said, "The cameras are off. It's important that you understand that the cartel could have put their own in place. Look for these." He showed them what the brand of camera the conservation initiative was using. "This light should be off. If you see anything with a small, red light burning, it's active. If you see anything other than this particular camera, then you should assume it's not one of the conservationist cameras and that it is delivering live feed to the drug cartel. If they were smart, they'd match the brand, but you are dealing with the scum of the earth, so who knows. Drug runners aren't known for their brains."

Douglas pulled out two black pieces of tech that Airmid didn't recognize. "Signal jammers. Don't turn them on unless I say to do so, or you see the telltale, little red light. It will interfere with our communications equipment. Any photos you take will automatically be dumped into a secured cloud, so don't dally with sending them anywhere. Even if your phone gets smashed or lost, we will have the photos. That said, don't drop your fucking phones. They're stupidly expensive and encrypted. It would raise questions."

Badrick nodded. "I'll be listening. If someone approaches, you are to stay hidden. I'll either get rid of them or move the boat. The island is small. It won't be difficult to find you if I have to move.

There are no tide changes, so you won't be fighting the timeline on that, but the sun comes up at 05:38 today. Get in and get out. Likely, there's nothing to even find."

They dressed in dark clothing, but nothing so obviously militant that they'd set off a red flag if they were detected. Good hiking leggings or trousers and a light jacket to hide their technology. Ball caps and lots of bug repellant. The no-see-ums were ruthless on these uninhabited islands. No pest control in order to protect the wildlife.

They left off the stern of the sailboat, beginning their exploration with a GPS to find the exact coordinates that had been marked on the beacon. They walked slowly and calmly, each of them taking a direction to look for any signs of life—or any indications of live camera feed. The only thing they saw plenty of were whipping tails, scurrying from their light source.

The craggy rocks underfoot were a balancing challenge. Daniel said, "Don't turn a fucking ankle, Douglas. I don't relish the idea of carrying you out of here."

"I am equal parts fit and grace. Worry about yourself, old man," Douglas said with his most pompous demeanor possible.

Airmid snorted. "How much older?"

Daniel said, "I am one year and two months older, and he never lets me forget it. Arsehole. Now shut it and keep looking. We are about six hundred meters from the pin I dropped on the navigation."

They'd left the jutting rock formations and were headed up a small hill covered with thick brush. Airmid saw a variety of creatures flying through her stream of light and was hoping she didn't meet up with any poisonous snakes or spiders. Likely, this place was crawling with them. There was a plateau of sorts before the low-grade hill continued, and she noticed some taller trees had managed to find purchase.

That's when she saw it. Daniel must have seen the same thing. He motioned to stop, putting a hand up. Surprisingly, there was just one. Likely, so that they didn't raise suspicion with the environmental agents who checked the island and tagged animals. The camera was well hidden, and she thanked Daniel silently in her mind. If they'd come after sunrise, they'd have never seen the camera. He was an excellent squad leader, and he was keeping them safe.

# 8

They had about thirty minutes or so to figure out why this place had been marked. They activated both portable signal jammers, so anything within fifteen meters would be ineffective at tracking or recording them. Daniel said, "Look for trip wires or sensors. I don't think they'd be dumb enough to set a mine on a government-run wildlife preserve, but you never know."

They carefully walked to the area with a copse of trees. They started searching for disturbed earth or any sign that something was buried. Airmid said, "That's not nature made. Look at how the rocks are piled. And it is right near the sandy part under the palms."

Daniel took a small e-tool shovel from his pack. Then he started moving the rocks. "Brilliant, lass. Truly." After he'd moved some of the rocks, he put the shovel to use. It didn't go in two inches before he hit something hard and not made of wood or stone. He moved the dirt. "It's the lid of a large pail. Like those plastic pails that hold paint." They used their hands, clearing the dirt away from the lip. He didn't want to break it or flood the inside with sand. He and Douglas inched the lip up and slowly lifted it off.

Douglas mumbled, "Hopefully, this isn't a fucking bomb."

"No, but it is evidence. It's a fucking portable navigation system," Daniel said.

"Can you copy the data and put it back?" Airmid asked.

"I think I can, if it has a USB port," Daniel said.

Douglas said, "Do it fast. Everything. Even if it deletes it. They'll think it was an operator cockup. But we need everything. It could have the next shipment already recorded, or it could have the port of origin. I need my tech guys on this."

"Aye, I've got it," Daniel said, swatting a huge bug from his face. "It's Google earth compatible. But maybe we should take it. If they've deleted something, we might be able to retrieve it."

"If it was wiped, it wouldn't be buried on lizard island. It's better not to take it. Big picture, it may help us seize another shipment before it arrives in Europe."

Airmid looked at the horizon. "Tick tock. I see a glow on the horizon. And I don't have a visual on the other side of the island. Maybe I should go all the way to the top," she said, standing as if to start finishing the climb.

"No, we stay together. We have what we need. And it's about a minute from being done," Daniel said. "If they get anywhere near our boat, that's why we have Badrick there." He felt her bristle at the order to stay put because it was an order. He was squad leader. He said, "It's done. Let's get this covered back up."

They made quick work of replacing the dirt and then piling the boulders back over the pail, putting everything back right where it was. Then they started hiking back out of the bush. They erased their footprints in the sandy patches near the trees by dragging a palm over them, then took the same path down. The sun was starting to come up just as they reached the shore, and their headsets were going off.

Badrick's melodic voice came over the airway. "The sun is up, and we've got a porpoise pod approaching from the west." Which was code for a boat heading toward their location.

They ran to the boat, seeing that Badrick was already untying the boat from the moor line. They used the boat's motor instead of the sails, pulling the boat out of sight as they began changing clothes. The skin-diving gear was hung up to dry, as if they were mere tourists, and the three men started raising the sails and getting them moving without the engine. They had no way of knowing who the boat belonged to, but they needed to look like a bunch of people out for a few days of sailing.

They came around the island, sailing toward Cayman Brac as the boat approached the iguana preserve. They'd unjammed all the cameras. The cartel cameras they'd done portably, and the tech connection Badrick had on the island was reactivating the nature preserve's circuit of cameras that monitored the wildlife.

Daniel sat with the external hard drive, loading everything onto the computer. He asked Douglas, "Will they be able to tell I copied the data? Can they trace the device?"

Douglas replied, "Not our devices, fuck you very much. They would be able to tell something was plugged in and ejected, but why would they check? Someone who's hiding the device in a bucket and penning the coordinates in on a piece of wood is really not equipped to adequately track or detect us. For now, just get that data to my analysts back home."

Airmid came out of the lav wearing her skimpy swimsuit. She stopped when she saw them give her the once-over. "What? The other one is wet. I hate putting on a wetsuit."

She walked up the stairs to the deck, and Daniel watched the subtle sway of a primo set of curvy hips. She wasn't thin in the classic sense. She was curvy and athletic. She was strong, and she took care of herself.

Douglas was laughing. "She was worried about bloody stretch marks and no plastic surgery. She doesn't get it." Daniel fought the urge to put his best mate in a headlock, and he suspected Douglas knew it. "And you have got it bad, old boy. Christ, I've never seen you like this."

Daniel bristled, tensing. "I don't know what you're on about. Get up the fucking steps or get out of my way." And as he charged after Airmid, he heard Douglas give a husky laugh behind him.

He came onto the deck as a yacht passed them far to the northwest, someone waving from the bow. It looked familiar. As did the woman who waved. The blonde from the entourage of Jensen's VIP section.

Airmid was sprawled on the upper deck like a queen, playing her part too well. She waved dismissively, like Aphrodite lying back and being worshiped. Her hair was a thick wave behind her as she reclined on her elbows. She said with a grin, "*Sports Illustrated* Swimsuit Edition ... here I come."

Airmid was trying to channel her inner goddess, but every stupid insecurity she had was trying to rear its ugly head. Douglas was a looker, yes. But it wasn't him who drew her gaze. Daniel, the goddamn Earl of Hawick, was like her own personal kryptonite. He was nine years older than she, and Airmid saw a tiny bit of grey starting at his temples. Fine lines around his eyes. But he was stacked in all the right places. Lean and masculine. Having him sharing a room with her was torture. Now he was walking around the boat with low-slung shorts and no shirt. He was getting a bit of color being in this tropical climate, even after a couple of days. She said, "Do you have sunscreen on your back? You're going to burn that English skin like seared tuna."

Daniel was currently trimming the sail and just grunted. Douglas threw a stray T-shirt at him and said, "She's right. Stop showing off your muscles and put a shirt on at least. You'll be laid up in the hotel room with a bottle of aspirin and aloe instead of doing your job."

The sun was fully up now. The wind pulling her hair around her face as she watched him slide the shirt over his chest. *Fuck me. Stop looking.*

Daniel dismissed the henpecking and said, "While we wait to hear from London, we'll work on getting an invitation to Jensen's party crowd. Once we know what that hard drive holds, we could possibly fly back tomorrow. I know we gave it five days, but we may not need it. You all did well. I think we got something back there. I think it's important. And it's possible Jensen has nothing to do with this business."

Badrick interrupted. "If it's happening in Jamaica, he knows. He may not be directly involved, but he knows the key players. Apollo said they picked up some crew members on the last run. What you don't know is that they found two bodies dumped in the harbor in Kingston. Two men who are still unidentified and of Central American or South American descent. That's why they needed two more crew members. Something happened on the way to that little island off Cayman or while they were in this area, and they found themselves shy two crew members. I suspect they shifted men around and put the two new men in the kitchens to keep them out of the way."

Airmid said, "Yes, they didn't know anything. And they were scared to death. The others were withholding for the same reason, but I feel like the two new guys didn't know shite about what was happening. They needed the money and they agreed to go." Airmid shrugged. "What do you think happened?"

Badrick tilted his head as he steered. "Maybe they asked too many questions? Maybe they tried to steal? Or maybe one man goes to swap out the navigation system, and they got curious for a peek at what he was doing? They are guarding that information so it won't lead back to the port of departure." He shook his head. "As they say, *dead men tell no tales*."

Airmid said, "I think Morgan needs this information now. Can you send a secured message? If she's still in Amsterdam, she can question the detainees about the dead crew members. It might catch them off guard and they could reveal something."

Daniel said, "The Dutch interpreter is pretty good. I'll do it when we get back. It's late afternoon right now. She leaves Amsterdam tomorrow. We've got agents there looking into Jensen as well. Something is off about his wife being in Finland."

"Why do you say that?" Airmid asked.

Daniel said, "Jensen seems like the type who does as he pleases but wouldn't allow his wife the same liberties. Her making a cuckold of him with some other bloke just smells wrong. Like maybe she's not gone for that reason. It's perhaps a cover story, so he seems like some sort of swinger who doesn't mind the ongoing fuck fest. I mean, you've heard the rumors about those parties. But maybe he's hiding her to protect her. Men like him live by a strange code."

Airmid snorted. "Aye. It's the 'Do as I say, not as I do' double standard that makes women want to start stabbing men after the third date."

Douglas couldn't resist. "And how many third dates have you been on since you had wee Erin?"

Her mouth turned up on one side. Airmid said, "Touché, brother dear. Touché."

———

The marina workers did the heavy lifting, per usual when dealing with the wealthy and idle. Airmid slipped back into her Tara skin. The woman who leaned into her husband's strong hands. And he played the part as well. They walked through the resort, his warm palm on the small of her back. Douglas broke away, heading to his suite in the singles wing. He'd had his eye on a drink and an American woman who'd been jilted a week before her wedding.

Daniel stopped by the desk. "If you could send a pair of masseuses to the room in about thirty minutes. And a grog cock-tail and a"—he looked at Airmid—"Tara, love, would you like a Dark 'n' Stormy or something else? A French 75 perhaps?"

She leaned in, playing with the buttons of his shirt. "A Dark 'n' Stormy sounds perfect. And a massage sounds even better." Airmid was shocked at the gesture. More for show, obviously, but damn if she wasn't going to enjoy every minute. She felt the cold presence staring at her from a short distance. Knew the why of it. "But why not just go to the spa, darling?"

Daniel leaned down, nose-to-nose. "Because I don't want to have to walk back to our bed afterward." His lips brushed hers so lightly, it wasn't even a kiss. But her breath hitched and her eyes flared. He was a consummate actor, and she didn't even want to think about the fact that he'd done this with another agent in the Ukraine. Nope. Blocking that thought out completely. She smiled against his lips.

"You are a devil," she said. And they turned to find eyes on them. Light, steely eyes that roamed over her. She gave Jensen a shy smile. The blush on her cheeks from Daniel's attentions not faked. But not for this creepy bastard.

She took Daniel's arm, looking away from the Dutchman's

intense gaze. When they were far enough away, Daniel said, "I meant what I said. You are not to leave my side at that party tonight. Because he will invite us, and I'll kill him rather than see his hands on you."

His jaw was tight, and Airmid knew he meant it. He protected his partners. Put their safety above the mission, which was a modern approach to this sort of work. In the eighties, she may very well have been expected to seduce Jensen. She tried to lighten the mood. "And what if one of the massage therapists is a man?"

He loosened a bit, knowing she was trying to tease him. "Then I suppose it is the lady's choice. God knows I'd prefer a woman's hands on me. Though, stronger hands mean a stronger massage. Hell, maybe I'll flip you for the male masseuse."

She leaned in, her arm wound into his. Her head touched his shoulder. "It's a deal. I hardly care. I've never had a professional massage." He actually stopped dead in his tracks.

He said, "That surprises me. Did I overstep?"

She laughed. "Not at all. It's just something I haven't indulged in on a professional scale. I believe it was a back rub that led to the conception of Erin. A back rub and some failed contraception, that is. And that was the sorry extent of my massage experience."

Daniel suddenly wanted to resurrect the bastard who'd sired that sweet little girl and hadn't bothered to marry her mother. "Well, as sweet as the result was in that particular instance, I think you'll find this a whole different experience."

"I can't wait. And I do adore a well-made Dark 'n' Stormy," she said, letting her fake and very thoughtful husband lead her into their suite.

———

Airmid moaned under the surprisingly firm touch of the petite, middle-aged woman at her back. The two women were sisters, and they had to be some sort of sorceresses. She was embarrassed by just how loud the moan was, and her eyes shot open to find Daniel watching her. A private smile on his lips. Right now, the blanket was covering below his waist, but she watched as the woman slid it aside to reveal one side of his absolutely stunning gluteus muscles. She wasn't going to apologize for looking. He was beautiful. And they were playing a part, weren't they? For all they knew, Jensen had hand-picked these two and they'd report back to him. Happy couple and all that. So, she looked her fill. From his arms and down his ribs, to the powerful hips and ass and his well-defined leg. A small peek of heaven without revealing the whole of him.

The woman at her back took that particular moment to instruct her to flip over onto her back. Her eyes bugged out just a bit, but Daniel saw it. His eyes dared her, as if to say, *turnabout is fair play*.

The woman lifted her towel, as if to aid in the repositioning, and to her surprise, Daniel didn't look. He kept his eyes on hers. Watching her face as her cheeks grew warm. She turned over and the blanket settled above her breasts, then the woman exposed the full side of her body, the blanket barely covering her nipple. The long expanse of abdomen, hip, and leg open to the air. And finally, he ran those eyes over her, and she felt her skin tighten. Her nipple pearled. It was like a caress. His eyes were a darker green, if that were possible, and more intense. Her massage therapist was a master, and she felt the relaxation down to her soul. Like she was drifting. She didn't understand what was happening until Daniel said, "I added a little extra for you. Something I think you'll enjoy."

The woman who'd done his massage left him to his relaxed

state as she took over rubbing Airmid's legs and feet. Her sister brought a large, grooved bowl to the table, full of warm, scented water. She adjusted the table and said, "Hair washing?" Airmid gave a drowsy nod, and the woman started the process of gently washing her hair like she was some sort of queen, then rubbing oil into her scalp, massaging her neck and head, and sending her into a sleep that rivaled death.

———

Daniel couldn't stop watching. The moment Airmid drifted off, he got a thick feeling in his throat. She'd called her daughter twice a day since they'd come here. And he saw the tears she wouldn't let fall. Saw the stress in the lines of her body. Saw the guilt for being away. But she deserved everything good in her life. So did her daughter. And for an hour or so, he wanted to pamper this woman. It wasn't about the bloody mission. It wasn't about playing a part to keep up appearances. It was about her. Airmid. The goddess of healing. But who healed her when she was hurting?

The sisters were done, and he tipped them generously. They offered to leave her table, but he didn't want her rolling off the thing. "I'll get her." And he heard the gravel in his voice. The dangerous emotion that thickened his words. He wanted to give her some modesty, so he kept the blanket over her as he slid one arm under her knees and the other under her shoulders. She woke and looked at him as he lifted her. "Just moving you to the bed, darling. Just let yourself bide awhile in bed. We had a rough night." He whispered against her hair as the women began packing their supplies. He took her out of the sitting area and over to their bed.

Airmid said, "I fell asleep. Sorry."

"Don't be sorry. The point is to relax." He laid her down and adjusted her pillows. Then he kissed her head. "I'm knackered as well. Let's just take an hour off, shall we?" And before he was even done with the sentence, she was drifting off again.

# 9

## HAWICK, SCOTLAND

Brigid Murphy unloaded her youngest children, Declan and Finn Jr., from the child seats as her daughter, Cora, and other son Colin exited from the other passenger side. Cora said, "Mam, I don't know why you won't let me sit in the front. I'm old enough. You put me in the back like a baby."

"You're old enough, my dear, but not tall enough or heavy enough. We've had this conversation. And maybe your da's giant genetics will take over, but not for now. Can ye grab the bag for me? There's a dear. Colin, carry your own bag and get Mammy's pocketbook. There's a good lad."

Cora continued to argue. "Well, if that's the standard, you're a runt. You shouldn't be in the front seat either. You should let Colin drive."

Colin said, "I can't help it if I'm tall and manly like Da. You're both runts. I'm only ten and I'm taller than ye both." And so it continued as they began to disembark.

Davis came rushing down the front stairs of the Hawick manor house, flustered and apologetic. "I'm so sorry, Mrs.

Murphy. Mrs. O'Brien was just in need of an extra pair of hands, and I was on the third floor. Please, let me take your bags. Leave them all right on the front stoop."

Brigid smirked. "Please call me Brigid. You can certainly take my bag so I can get a better handle on this wee fiend." She adjusted Finn Jr. in her arms as Davis took her bag, glancing down at the small boy grabbing her leg. Brigid motioned to Declan, Colin, and Cora and said, "The clingy one is Declan. Cora and Colin are more than capable of carrying their own bags. Just show us the way, love. Thank you." Then she hoisted Declan on her other hip.

Colin approached, chin up. "Da says men carry the heavy stuff for their women. And my mam is a runt, so I should help more than most. So, I've got her other bag. But thank you, sir." He was not ten, but he would be next month. A fact of which his sister continued to remind him. As smart and handsome as his father and as cheeky as his mother.

Davis choked down a laugh that was bubbling to the surface as Brigid sputtered, "I am fun-sized, thank you very much. Remind me to knock your father arseways when I see him next." And they proceeded to walk into the stately manor. Davis was convinced this O'Brien family should take a comedy act on the road. He'd met Brigid on a previous visit, but she hadn't spent more than a few hours with Daniel before heading up to the Highlands with her husband. Davis liked her already. Fun-sized indeed.

They made their way up to the third floor as the children dropped their bags and ran toward the sound of other children. Brigid shook her head. "Sorry about that, Mr. Davis."

"It's just Davis, madam," he said with a warm smile. "And Donna is the housekeeper. Why don't we leave our bags just here, and I'll take you to your sister-in-law? The children have been really enjoying themselves. I can arrange a pony excursion with the groom as well. It has been a blessedly dry few days, so it's a good time for it."

They walked into the nursery, and Declan started wriggling to get down. Finn Jr. was rooting on her blouse. She smiled at Declan's back. "And he's off. I'm dead to him until bedtime," Brigid said affectionately.

Davis's face was so full of warmth and good cheer that it almost made her tear up. He said, "It's been a long time since we've had a full nursery. And even then, it was never this full. I'd hoped to have some bairns in the house by now, but it's not happened for our young ones yet."

"Davis, you're an old softy, aren't you? Yer man Daniel needs a woman. We all see it. He's a good sort. And with a nursery like this, it's almost his duty to get an heir and a spare in the house."

Donna made an appearance, clapping her hands together. Most household staff would be horrified at the prospect of eight visiting children, but these two were over the moon about it. Donna nodded to Brigid. "I've heard so much about you all from our Danny. It's like I already know you. You didn't stay nearly long enough last visit. And please, meet our new addition to the household. This is Constance. She's been a godsend. And this sweet little lassie is Erin. Her mum works with Daniel and is on a work-related trip abroad. They'll be home in a couple days. I hope you'll stay, Mrs. Murphy. I'm afraid I haven't persuaded Mrs. O'Brien to stay on."

Alanna wiped her hands on a disinfecting wipe and stood. "Sorry, I've got watercolor paint all over me. Hi, Brigid." She hugged her sister-in-law. "I wish I could stay, but I need to work a bit before the weekend. I've played hooky as long as I can. We've had so much fun with our new friends, though, haven't we?"

Davey answered the loudest. "Yes, and I've been the oldest.

I'm helping with the little ones. But now Cora and Colin can help. Erin likes ponies, and she doesn't like cold cheese."

Random facts were Davey's specialty. Brigid smiled widely and said, "Thank you, mo chroí. I'll make a note of that. Alanna, my brother has not called me. What's he doing? I need news. You know I hate going without news."

Donna interrupted. "I'll bring up a small bit of something for tea. Dinner is at seven." And she left to go prepare some snacks.

Davis said, "And there's a full bar in the parlor. In case you need a boost." He winked and left behind Donna.

Brigid pooched her bottom lip out. "I want one."

Alanna laughed. "Don't we all want a Davis and Donna? But to answer your question, Aidan is having fun and treating jungle rot between his toes. Apparently, the rainy season has started early. And just for fun, google the banana spider."

Brigid put her hands up. "Nope. I'll do no such thing. The fecking stories Liam and Izzy have shared about jungle life have given me nightmares. I will not google it."

Cora said, "It's ghastly. Look, Mam!" And she shoved her phone under Brigid's nose.

"I said I didn't want to know, you devil child!" And the other kids laughed. "And don't be showing that to the little ones!" She looked at Alanna. "Why did I ever agree to give that child of mine access to the Internet?"

Cora just rolled her eyes. "Ma'am, I'm going to be in ninth year. I was pushing fourteen with no phone. Do you want me to be a social pariah?"

Brigid smirked. "Of course not. But I'm more concerned about you rotting your brain on YouTube."

Cora waved a hand dismissively. "YouTube is old school. It's all about TikTok now. You need to catch up if you are going to monitor your teenager. I could be up to nefarious things, and ye'll be on YouTube waiting for the ads to end."

"No one likes a smart-ass, Cora Murphy," Brigid said. But Alanna was laughing under her hand, and Brigid was well aware that she'd created this wise-ass child in the very image of herself.

---

### BATSUB Headquarters, Belize

Aidan didn't own one single pair of dry clothing at this point. How the devil did Liam live like this? Likely, the sisters of St. Clare Charity Mission had an industrial-size dryer. He, on the other hand, had to wait for one of the paid dryers to free up in the barracks. "Kearsley, if ye jump in line ahead of me for that dryer, I will throttle you to within an inch of yer life."

Kearsley grinned at being caught. "Yes, Major. I wouldn't dream of it. But if it takes much longer, I'm going to be walking around in my skin."

"And then you'd have even more bug bites than you do now. Christ, lad. They seem to have a taste for you."

Kearsley scratched his neck. "They do, don't they? Did you get to call home?"

"I did. And you? How is the baby?" Aidan asked.

"Apparently, she slept for four hours straight. And my wife woke up well rested and had soaked the bedding through because the baby hadn't fed. Who knew that was a thing?"

"Well, you should try to learn. My mother is a midwife. You'd be surprised what gets discussed at the dinner table. But not everyone had my education. Ask questions. Her body is going through a lot. If the feeding schedule is off, or something happens like a cold rush of air, she can start spraying like a garden sprinkler."

Kearsley stopped. "I'm sorry, what? From cold? Like walking outside?"

"Like a draft when she's changing clothes, like a walk through the freezer section of the grocery store, or even hearing someone else's baby crying. It's like walking around with milk grenades on their chest. Be a hero and keep an extra shirt and some pads in your car. It's the little things that are going to matter when you're old and grey."

Kearsley nodded, smiling. And Aidan knew the man was thinking about his wife and how much he missed her. "Thanks, Major. I'm an only child, and my mum died last year. I wish she was here. I could really talk to her, you know?"

"I do. My mam is the best. And what about your da?" Aidan asked.

"He took off when I was seven. Never looked back. I think he lives in Australia, actually. Last I heard, anyway. I started trying to look for him, then I decided I didn't need to know him."

Aidan didn't know about Kearsley's parents. Jesus. "What about yer woman? Does she have both parents?"

His face was transformed. Kearsley said, "Yes, she has both. They are fantastic humans all around. Her dad and I are pretty close, actually. Although, he's a Chelsea man. It was hard to over-look that at first. You know how I feel about Liverpool."

Aidan laughed. "Yes, about the same as I feel about Derry City. So, you're both wrong."

Kearsley gave a snort. "You're one of those rugby diehards, so you don't get a vote anyway."

Aidan's mouth turned up. It was true. He liked a good football match, but rugby was his drug of choice. "Well, then. About the rain. We're going to have to help with sandbags in the morning. They're expecting this rainy season to be worse than last year's rainfall. They need help filling them and stacking them in a storage area in case they need them this season. It should take two or three hours if we work efficiently. A colonel from the Belize Defence Force is visiting tomorrow as well and wanted to host a sort of barbecue picnic tomorrow. The weather is supposed to let up tonight, and it might be our only clear evening. I told Ramirez we'd supply some cold drinks. Sodas and some beer. We've got a two-beer limit that is going to be strictly enforced with our men. I don't need anyone going on the piss while we're being hosted by a high-ranking officer."

Kearsley said, "Fair enough. I'll talk to the other officers about pitching in for some cases of the local Lighthouse lager and Belekin."

Aidan said, "Perfect. Get the Belekin stout. It's gorgeous altogether. And get a variety of local sodas and Coca-Cola products. We've got plenty of water."

He watched as his lieutenant took notes on his phone. "Roger that, Major." He put his phone in his pocket. "I'll go see to it. Don't let anyone jump ahead of me in the dryer line. I wasn't kidding about walking around naked."

---

## Montego Bay, Jamaica

Daniel's eyes never left her. He hated this. He'd posed as a married couple in the Ukraine, but it hadn't been like this. The three of them had enjoyed a nice dinner tonight. And, as expected, they'd received a small notecard with an invitation to the VIP rooms in a secured part of the resort. Fucking Jensen.

Douglas was flirting with a few women, all circling him and eyeing him up like a Sunday roast. Airmid had been by Daniel's side all evening, but as the alcohol flowed, things were starting to get interesting. There were people lounging on the numerous sofas around the large room. Tops came off in the pool area. Then, after a time, so did the bottoms. He could see a woman sandwiched between two men on the steps of the pool. Jensen was walking around like a peacock, a woman half his age on his arm. But he watched Airmid. She was the exotic of the party. Fresh-faced. Thirty, not twenty-two. Fair, not tanned. Her smile was genuine and her laughter was sweet. What the hell had Morgan been thinking, putting her on this assignment?

"You look like a mafia hit man, John. You need to lighten up just a tad," Airmid said under her breath. She kissed him on the cheek. "I'm going to the lav. Hold my drink?"

Daniel took them both and set them on a nearby table. He almost cringed as he noticed the couple on the couch nearest them were getting more than a little handsy in front of a roomful of people. Airmid's face was turning scarlet as she swirled around to walk toward one of the designated powder rooms for the VIP guests. It was down a hallway, so he started following her. She said under her breath, "You are not following me into the lav, so back off."

He did, but only long enough to ensure she wasn't going to argue with him. Daniel gave her three minutes. As he made his way down the hall, he saw her. She was creeping toward the darkened rooms, out of bounds for a polite guest. Snooping, no doubt. And normally, he'd commend the idea, but he wasn't having it. He came behind her, and she sensed him before turning. "Jesus, I am seriously going to throttle you," she snarled.

Daniel got up in her face. "You need to check your hearing. Other than the necessities, you don't leave my side. Are you even paying attention to the orgy that is brewing out there? And there are several drunk men eyeing the hem of your skirt tonight!" He hissed the words and she narrowed her eyes.

She ground out the words in a whisper. "Isn't that the entire, fecking, sodding point of this dress? You are an arrogant, over-bearing—" Daniel didn't give her time to think.

He pressed her wrists against the wall, leaning close to her ear. "Play like you mean it." Then his mouth was on hers. Heat exploded between them. And she knew it was for show, but holy shit. He pressed into her, raising her arms up and putting both wrists in one of his big hands. She whimpered as he pulled her hips tight to his. Daniel moaned as he plundered her mouth. Despite the fact that it was completely unprofessional, she couldn't remember ever being this turned on. He pushed a knee between her thighs and she broke the kiss, gasping.

And like a cold bucket of water, a slimy voice interrupted them. Daniel jerked against her as Jensen said, "But I see they are occupied."

Another male voice rumbled with husky laughter. Daniel turned his head. "Sorry, can I help you?" He released Airmid's wrists, putting her dress to rights. And he looked like he wanted to rip both their spines out from their throats. "Excuse me, you can look at me when we're conversing. Not my wife."

Daniel turned, putting Airmid behind him. Jensen said smoothly, "Oh, but it's your wife I most wanted my friend to meet. Please, come into my private lounge." He whispered to his girlfriend and she nodded. "Rubia will get the group some cock-tails. She'll just be a moment. It's some wonderful reserve rum I have for my special friends. Please, come." Rubia was blonde, and Daniel didn't think she was Caribbean, despite the name. Dutch, perhaps, like Jensen, or Scandinavian.

Daniel took Airmid's hand. Jensen said, "Arturo Rey, these are my new friends, John and Tara MacMillin."

Airmid smiled, despite herself. She said, "King Arthur. Can I take it your parents were big readers?"

Arturo Rey had dead eyes. Predatory eyes. "My father was an

educated man. My mother was a good wife and mother. She was a godly woman, but did not attend a university. Señor Jensen tells me that you are an interpreter for an English charity?"

Airmid smiled. "Yes. It's how I met John, actually. And where is your home, if you don't mind me asking?"

Daniel watched Airmid charm these two men with little effort. Not with polish or manipulation, but because of her easy way. Her lighthearted banter. There was more to her than that. She'd seen a lot in her young life. Depth that men like these could never touch. He found himself wanting to know the many layers of Airmid Roberts.

Arturo answered, "I am originally from Belize. My wife is from Honduras and has property in Belize, as well as other homes, so we travel between both."

This set off Airmid's Spidey senses, but she just smiled. "That's wonderful. I've heard the scuba diving is divine in Belize. John was just teaching me how to dive."

The man smiled thinly. "You'll have to tell him to bring you to Central America. The diving is unmatched."

Jensen's arm candy joined them, passing a drink to everyone. She eyed Daniel like he was dessert. Airmid leaned against him, thanking her for the drink. "I'm afraid this is my last. Rum goes straight to my head."

Jensen raised his glass. "To new friends. Cheers," Jensen said.

They raised their glasses, and Airmid said sweetly to Arturo Rey, "Salud, Señor Rey."

———

Airmid feigned fatigue just as Jensen tried pouring more rum into them. He was openly staring at Airmid's chest and legs, and Daniel was ready to put the wee mongrel on his ass. Douglas had made progress as well. He was busy watching the match on his phone with two guards from Arturo Rey's security detail. The whole thing reeked of cartel money. But Daniel hadn't heard of Arturo Rey. He had to do some digging. The geography was certainly convenient, given Airmid's theory that the boat had come from somewhere on the East Coast of Central America.

They were standing next to Douglas when Jensen and his not-wife arm candy approached them again. Airmid was polite, which was more than he could muster after watching two men eye-fuck his woman all night. Not that she was his woman, but it was the point of it. Rubia sidled up next to him, putting her breasts up against his upper arm. "Do you have to leave so soon? The party will go on until dawn." *Not Scandinavian, German. Interesting.*

Jensen was on the other side, too close to Airmid for Daniel's liking. The bastard said, "Darling Tara, perhaps we could find something more comfortable for you. You could relax with us in my private quarters. Such beauty should not go down with the sun."

Rubia whispered something in Daniel's ear as another groupie took Douglas by the arm. Jensen said, "There is a high-stakes poker game going in another one of the lounges. And the match is on a much bigger screen. Maybe I could show Tara to the sauna?"

Daniel saw the evening as this man saw it. He'd be pressing his intentions on Airmid while Delilah and Rubia were sucking him off and helping Douglas out of a year's pay. But Rubia had surprised him. She had whispered, "Don't leave her." So softly that anyone would assume she was propositioning him. He pulled away from Rubia, taking Airmid by the arm and playing it off as mere flirting. "I have all I need right here."

Jensen wasn't fazed. "Yes, but there's always beauty in a little excess."

Airmid stiffened. "I wonder if Mrs. Jensen would agree.

Doubtful. Now, if your pleasure girls wouldn't mind unhanding my brother and husband, I find myself quite ready to retire."

Jensen gave a husky laugh. "You English are so very prim. I think we've offended you. But no bother. My real reason for coming over is that I'd like to extend an invitation to any one of my resorts in Central America. You would be my guests, of course. And you would want for nothing."

Douglas gave his empty glass to a passerby with a tray. "We will certainly think on it. I love a good exotic holiday. Once we've checked back in with our home and work, maybe we'll take you up on it. I, for one, have found your hospitality to be top-notch." There was an exotic woman, Delilah, who appeared to be of some sort of Latina descent. She'd joined them alongside Rubia, and she put her arm around his neck. Then she pulled his mouth to hers with no care for who was watching. Airmid said, "All right. That's it for tonight. Goodbye, all. Thank you again, Mr. Jensen, and please give Arturo my warm regards."

———

Douglas called just as they were coming into the room. "We heard from our tech people. The glitch we had with our charitable distribution software has found a definitive diagnosis. We can head back tomorrow to regroup. And John, check your room. I think I've had a pest, but I think I've sufficiently repelled any others."

Daniel put an arm in front of Airmid. Then, with no warning, he pulled her to him and buried his face in her hair. "The place may not be secure," he said softly against her neck. And she nodded once, affectionately running a hand over his arm.

Then she walked into the room. "I'm sorry we have to leave tomorrow. Maybe we can have another holiday once we've sorted the distributions for this quarter. I do fancy doing some more scuba diving."

Daniel was surveying the room. "Aye, we'll see. Somewhere a bit more private with a few less swingers." And despite the seriousness of the situation, his mouth turned up in amusement.

Airmid gave a genuine laugh. "Did Rubia scare you? Don't worry, love. I'd protect you. You know I don't share." At that, Daniel tensed, feeling the overwhelming urge to beat that fucking Dutchman with his fists and boots. He pulled Airmid to him, hoping the son of a bitch was watching or listening.

Daniel kissed her, slow and deep, and she was right there with him. He lifted her and pulled her legs around his hips, marching her into the smaller bathroom that he'd been using. He kicked the door shut. He put her down, her back against the door, then turned the shower on. He palmed the back of her head, not sure what the fuck he was thinking kissing her like that. He whispered, "I'm sorry. Fuck, Airmid. I'm sorry. I shouldn't have brought you here." He pressed his forehead to hers. "If one of the bathrooms is bugged, it'll be the other one. He'd likely just do audio, but short of ripping the vanity out and checking for cameras, I don't know. Once the lights are out, I'm going to jam everything within a fifteen-meter radius. Douglas already did it in his room."

He was talking low against her ear now. She shuddered at the close contact and the aftershocks of having her legs wrapped around him. Daniel said again, "I'm sorry. I'm sorry for the hallway. I'm sorry for dragging you in here with my cock pressed against you. I'm sorry we don't have privacy right now, but I am feeling really fucking on edge, so it's probably for the best."

Airmid swallowed hard. "It's okay. It's the job. I understand, and it's okay. It doesn't mean anything."

Daniel weaved his fingers in her hair, then he tugged so that she couldn't look away. He met her eyes and she saw the heat. He saw it too. Saw her pink cheeks and her flushed mouth. "You can take a shower. I'll keep my eyes averted. After a bit, we'll go out and go to bed. Once I've jammed the technology, you'll feel safe to rest, I think." But he wouldn't. He had to get her out of here.

The smell of Airmid in the shower was something uniquely torturous. She rinsed out the remnants of her own skin and beauty products, replacing them with his body soap and shampoo. And it was as if their two scents merged, like they would if he and Airmid were lovers. Like she'd smell if he'd finished what he started. Fucked her up against that shower wall until she was too limp to walk. Daniel shook himself, willing his cock to stand down. To quit aching for her.

After a bit, he went to her bathroom and got an extra towel and pajamas so she could change, while he took the quickest cold shower of his bloody life.

Once the lights were out, Daniel went to the camera bag where the portable signal jammer was kept. After a minute, he turned on his bedside lamp, then closed the door. He swept the room, and that's when he found it. Someone had been in the safe. His small laptop was encrypted, and other electronics were camouflaged to look like camera equipment and other rich-boy electronics. But someone had looked. He found a microphone in the USB port at the base of the lamp. And in the ceiling fan, there was a micro-camera. He should turn the jammer off. Play like nothing was wrong. But he'd be damned if he'd let that motherfucker spy on them all night. The randy piece of shit.

Daniel climbed in bed next to Airmid, taking a decorative pillow off the bed and dumping it over the top of the lamp base, muffling everything in case they had a jammer failure. He said, "What I don't know is why." And she understood. Was this a matter of him watching them for some sort of perverse pleasure? Or had something tipped him off? But then, why would he bug

Douglas's room? Daniel didn't want to go to sleep. Didn't want to stop watching over her.

Airmid took his wrist and pulled him down. She said, "Stop thinking so much. It's late. Just turn the light off and rest."

Daniel reached over and clicked off the lamp. Then he let her pull him down onto the bed beside her. He positioned himself closer tonight. Flush against her like he hadn't dared before. Not to seduce her. Not to take care of the pounding arousal that coursed through him. But to feel the fact of her. To know that she was safe.

The room was glowing with the predawn when he woke, watching as a bit of light streamed through the window treatments. She was so bonnie. Thick, wavy hair spilled over the pillow. Daniel rose from bed and called room service. He wanted coffee, and he wanted to spend the morning watching Airmid, lying in sweet repose with the morning light on her hair.

Daniel couldn't do this again. He couldn't let her go to Central America. His life meant nothing in the grand scheme of things. But those drug cartels were ruthless. Run by sociopaths. He thought of Arturo Rey's dead eyes. Of what a man like him might do to someone like Airmid. She was a mother. He would not orphan that little girl for a fucking mission.

The room service texted him, as he'd requested. He didn't want to wake her. He tipped the staff generously and brought the tray in himself. Then he poured some coffee. It wasn't even six o'clock, and they'd had a late night. A primal part of him liked watching over her like some sort of guardian. Liked that she felt safe enough with him to sleep so soundly.

Daniel read another passage of his father's journal, and it warmed his heart in a way that nothing ever had. He'd written about the first time Daniel had walked unassisted. Four steps. And his father's pride was evident in the writing.

*"Molly came running into the room, and before I thought better of it, I pulled her into my arms. She was so stunned to see our little lad on two feet, his chubby thighs making short work of the stretch between the chair and the sofa. She put her hands on her cheeks and smiled so widely. It was like the sun had finally come up after a long, dismal rain. I know she doesn't love me. Not the way that a woman should love her husband. But she hugged me back. She squeezed my shoulders and beamed up at me with that smile. And it was enough."*

Daniel stood, distancing himself a bit from the words. They were sweet. But they hurt as well. The son in him loved the words. The man in him ached for his father. Wanted more for him than to live in the shadow of another man's memory. *I wish you were here, Da. I could really use you right now.*

Airmid stirred, and Daniel's heart thumped in his chest as he watched her extend an arm to his side of the bed. Reaching for him. He poured a cup of coffee for her and she sat up a bit. She saw his e-reader, where he'd scanned his father's diary, and her eyes met his. Something like compassion in them. He put the coffee on her nightstand, and she placed her hand over his. "Are you okay?"

Airmid looked at the raw emotion in Daniel's eyes and it broke her heart. She said, "It's okay if you're not."

Daniel didn't give himself time to reconsider. He leaned into her and covered her mouth. She rose to his mouth, arching her neck. He moaned, taking her deeper. He rolled onto the bed, pulling her astride him. He kissed her neck, her collarbone, the cap of her shoulders as he pulled the neck of her pajamas aside. He was hard within seconds, tucked against that sweet spot between her thighs. He ran his hands up her ribs, sliding her top over her head. Then he had her on her back. "I need you. Fucking hell, I'm mad with it. Stop this, woman, because I won't."

But Airmid ran her fingers into his thick hair, guiding his

hungry mouth to her breast. She bowed off the bed as he tasted her nipple, then moved to the other side. Some part of him heard a couple of text messages come in, but he didn't care if it was the fucking prime minister. Not until it was followed up with a loud knock. He cursed, resting his head between her breasts. She was breathing hard, and he thought he heard her let out a little whimper. Too right. He was going to actually murder his best mate.

"Wait a minute!" he snapped. Airmid inched out from under him, grabbing her pajama top and retreating to the bathroom. He yanked the door open so fast, Douglas was still standing there with his fist in the air, primed for another go. "It is half six. What the fuck do you want?"

Douglas reared back, "And what the fuck is your problem this —" And he saw what Daniel wouldn't have been able to hide with three pairs of trousers and four cold showers. His cock likely looked as murderous as he felt, stabbing out of his shorts. Douglas had the gall to look irritated. He narrowed his eyes on Daniel. He came in, obviously looking for Airmid. He turned. "What the fuck are you playing at, John?" He said the name like a curse. As if to remind him this was a job. That Airmid wasn't his wife. That he was a piece of shit for making a move on her. And Daniel understood the outrage.

He ran his hands through his hair. "Fuck me," he said. He shook himself. "She's in the lav. I need ... I need a minute."

Airmid came out, obviously having splashed cold water on her face. "What's amiss?"

Douglas said more gently, "We have an appointment at nine. Flight leaves at one. Best get yourself packed. I called our driver."

# 10

## KINGSTON, JAMAICA

Daniel was ready to have it out with Douglas. For some reason, he'd taken the big brother thing to heart and was set on keeping himself, body and soul, between Airmid and him. At least, that's what he thought. Maybe he was reading this wrong. Maybe Douglas fancied her. And how pissed would Morgan be if her two agents came to blows over a third. Morgan was just as protective over Airmid. He needed to take the unwanted advice from Douglas and distance himself from her. Daniel had been two minutes from pushing inside her when that knock had come.

Daniel looked behind them for the tenth time as they drove to the other side of the island. Apollo said, "No one is following us. This isn't my first rodeo, as they say." They were going to look at the autopsy results and the personal belongings that had been found on the bodies in the Kingston Harbor.

Apollo said, "The autopsy results say the cause of death was blunt force trauma to the head for the first man, followed by a bullet to the temple. The second male's cause of death was a gunshot wound to the back of the head. They were both ditched postmortem. I have their personal effects. The bodies are due to be cremated tomorrow, as they were found two weeks ago and the decomposition is significant. I'm afraid they're rather a mess. Dumped in the harbor and feasted on for a day at least. But not enough to conceal how they died." He turned down the drive to his home. "I'd like you to analyze the personal effects. See if you can get any information from the labels or style. I just got access to everything yesterday."

Daniel said, "It's slightly ridiculous that they allowed a foreigner to gain access to evidence in a double homicide."

"I work for the embassy, as far as they are concerned. And unfortunately, money talks. It cost me a thousand quid. I trust the coroner though. He's good. So, any information we get from him is solid. Unless you think you need to see the bodies?"

Daniel shook his head. "Not necessary. I'm not a doctor. Have our team look at the report today, before they are cremated, in case they have questions that need to be answered."

Apollo said, "Already done." He helped Airmid out of the car, and Daniel wanted to shove the bastard into the bushes. What the fuck was wrong with him? Unspent lust. That's what was wrong with him. Apollo said, "Madam Tara, please lead the way and show me your genius."

———

Airmid took several pictures of the clothing and shoes. One man had been wearing a ring, so she took detailed photos of it before leaving the garage and taking in some fresh air. Daniel came next to her just as she was getting her bearings again. "Christ, that smells."

Daniel nodded grimly. "Aye, and the bodies must be something altogether more ghastly. They've been in the cooler for almost two weeks. Time to let the old chaps return to ashes."

Airmid smiled at that. "It was from ashes you were created, and to ashes you shall return." She grinned. "Or something like that."

He addressed the elephant in the room directly. "I'm sorry," he said softly. "I'm a prat of the first order, and you should have slapped me."

Her mouth lifted in a contrived smile. He regretted it. And didn't that just burn a hole in her pride. "You were hurting. And this has been stressful on all of us. All that public groping stirs the body where the mind doesn't wish to go. I get it. Let's just chalk it up to the contact high we got from Jensen's orgy and forget it happened."

"Is that what you want?" he asked.

Airmid said, "It's what you want. And it's what is wise. I have a child. I need this life to work for me. Your regret is unnecessary. We're on the same page."

He chuffed a bitter laugh and she narrowed her eyes, finally looking at him. Daniel said, "You think I regret it? That I wished I hadn't kissed you? Had my mouth all over you?"

She sucked in a breath, closing her eyes. "It doesn't matter. We have a job to do. And I need to go see my little girl." Airmid looked at the pad of paper in her hand. "I need Douglas to look over these clothing items. They're good quality. Not the night market type of knock-offs. And this ring is expensive. Fourteen carat gold and some sort of semi-precious stone. Maybe one of the quartzes? I need the lab to look at it. Do you think they'd release it?"

"Not likely, but I can talk to Apollo. He may have someone here who can take a look. A geologist would be our best bet. A local jeweler might talk."

Airmid nodded absently. "What did these guys do or

witness to make someone kill them? And who did the killing? If we can threaten to extradite from the Netherlands on murder charges, either to the Caymans or Jamaica, maybe we can get someone to talk. In Jamaica, the penalty for murder is death by hanging. We need to use that. The Cayman's are part of the UK territories. No death penalty. We need to assure the detainees in Amsterdam that we know those men were killed in Jamaica, and that they are going to hang. They may talk just to make sure we know they weren't in Jamaican waters when the men died."

Daniel said, "It's a good tactic. I'll contact Morgan before we leave for the airport. She's going back into the interrogations with the new information. I have a feeling that by the time we land in Edinburgh, we are going to know where that boat left from. That will decide where we end up next." He and Douglas because Airmid was going nowhere near Central America. He'd find a local interpreter. He was a rotter of the first order for making a move on her. She was a guest in his house. She was on his team. *Fuck!* "I think we're done here. I'll tell Apollo to get us to the airport right after I call the office."

---

## Hawick, Scotland

Airmid dropped her bags and ran to her daughter. It wasn't until she got her in her arms that the tears started. She'd learned how to compartmentalize her emotions during her time in the army. But now that she felt Erin's soft curls on her face, she couldn't stop. She smelled her, soaking in every childhood smell that was so unique to her Erin. She kissed her head, her face, her nose, her eyes. "Mammy, you're getting my face wet."

They were sprawled at the base of the stairs, oblivious to

everyone around them. "I know, boo. I'm sorry. I just missed you somethin' fierce. So much. Did you miss me? Did you have fun?"

She looked up at the teary face of an unfamiliar woman. Constance was standing next to a petite woman who looked maybe a few years older than Airmid. And a child in her early teens who was so beautiful, she didn't seem human. *Fae.* That's what she made her think of. Some sort of Celtic fae. Dark, wild hair and soulful eyes. Ancient eyes. "Who are your new friends, love?"

Daniel stepped forward, hugging his cousin. "Airmid, this is my cousin Brigid Murphy. Another from the O'Brien side of the family." His voice was hoarse, and his cousin looked at him with knowing eyes.

Then she looked at Airmid. Brigid said, "Alanna had to go back, so we thought we'd send the next wave of children to help Constance keep the lass entertained. It's so good to finally meet some of Daniel's friends."

"I'm more of a colleague, but it's wonderful to meet you too. It's so nice of you to come and play with Erin." She looked at the older child. Cora stepped forward.

"I'm Cora. It was my pleasure. She's a good girl. And she doesn't take any stuff from the lads. She can hold her own. That's her Irish blood, I think."

Airmid's face beamed with pride and love, and it damn near broke Daniel. He thought about her words. *It's what you want. And it's what is wise. I have a child. I need this life to work for me. Your regret is unnecessary.* Was it what he wanted? He wasn't so sure. But it was wise to stay away from her. His protective instincts when it came to Airmid were interfering with his judgment. It was more than the squad leader watching out for his team. He'd let it get personal. He'd been ready to gut that fucking Jensen and throw him to the sharks.

Davis and Donna came to join them, Daniel bowing to receive a kiss on the head from Donna. "It's good to see you home, Danny. Let's get your bags up to your room and let poor Airmid spend some time with the lassie."

Airmid said quickly, "I'm going to go home, but thank you. I want to give Constance a break, and I've imposed enough." She wouldn't meet Daniel's eyes, but he would not be dismissed from the conversation.

Daniel said, "I need you here, Airmid. And Cora and the boys have just gotten here. I'll send Constance home for a paid break, and we can all pitch in to care for the bairns."

"She's my responsibility. I don't have to stay," she said.

Brigid said gently, "Daniel, maybe she's ready to sleep in her own bed. Surely your charity work can wait a day or two?"

Daniel's eyes glittered with all sorts of things Airmid didn't want to deal with. She said, "Yes, just a day or two. I slept on the plane. We'll be back in a couple days. Until then, Douglas or Morgan can brief me through the regular channels." And with that, she turned toward Constance. "Thank you, dear. You've earned a break. I'm just going to take her up and pack her toys."

To her surprise, Erin said, "I just need my panda and my dolly. We can come back for my toys. Maybe Declan and baby Finn would like to play with them." She turned toward Cora. "Will you be here when I come back?"

Cora smiled. "I don't know. We'll have to discuss it. But I'll try, okay?"

Erin's mouth turned down. "I want to play with her, Mam. I don't want to go if she's going to leave." Airmid closed her eyes, finding her patience. Daniel's eyes held triumph, and she was close to violence. Brigid took Cora's hand and said, "Let's go see if the groom needs help brushing the horses before lunch."

Daniel didn't even pretend they weren't going to have it out.

He walked into his office and waited. He heard Constance offer to take Erin, and then Airmid was there, slamming his office door. She pointed at him. "Wipe that smug look off your face before I knock ye arseways over that desk!"

He felt himself getting hard. For fuck's sake, she was brilliantly pissed. He stalked toward her. "Do your worst, lass. I've got it coming, no doubt."

"I do not need to remain here during this break in travel. We don't even know where we are headed, yet. I am not obligated to stay here."

"Apparently, Erin thinks otherwise. I have ponies and Cora. You don't stand a chance, and you bloody well know it," Daniel said.

She actually ground her teeth and hissed at him. He got closer. "And I do not regret kissing you for one moment. I loved every goddamn minute of it. It's all I can think about in my stiller moments. What would have happened if that sodding partner of mine hadn't interrupted us? Because I didn't get nearly enough. And maybe that makes me unprofessional and the worst squad leader to ever draw breath, but all I can think about is slipping my tongue deep between your thighs. Then fucking you senseless." He'd walked toward her until her back was to the door she'd slammed. "So, yes. I'm sorry for being an unrepentant rotter. The fact still remains that you are needed here. We do know where we're going. Morgan sent the secured message while you were sleeping in the car. Douglas and I leave for Belize in four days. You will work remotely from here because my home has been secured and you have childcare here."

She reared back like he'd slapped her. She shoved him away. "You are not benching me. Ye can piss off, MacPherson. You will not bench me because you're letting your cock distract you."

His jaw was tight and his eyes burned. "That is not why I'm

leaving you here. You have a child, Airmid. And you are not a field agent. I should have never involved you in this. Jensen and Rey were both drawn to you like flies to honey. Do you know what men like them do to women who spurn their advances?"

Airmid said, "You need a Spanish linguist. Morgan will not let this stand. You don't have the final say any more than you did when we started this mission. I'm going, Daniel. Because you aren't going to want to explain to our boss why you don't want me to go. Unlike you or Douglas, I have been to Belize. I know the culture and the dialect. I've done training in that environment. You need me, and I will be on that plane if I have to get you benched." She poked him in the chest. "I think Douglas and I could get by just brilliantly as man and wife." And the tick she saw in his face said she'd hit her mark.

The intercom sounded just as Daniel started to do something really stupid. "Danny, your CEO, Mrs. Morgan, has just arrived." It was laughable. As if he could ever see Annabeth Morgan as a CEO. She was born for this work. Unlike Airmid, who was too good. Too transparent. The woman made him crazy.

Airmid grinned. "Perfect timing," she purred. Then she turned and opened the door.

———

Brigid watched her cousin brood around the house for the better part of the day. They went in and out of meetings about God knew what. Another man who was introduced as Andrew Douglas, the Duke of Roxburghe, arrived just after lunch.

Right now, Daniel was getting a cold drink out of the subzero while she put some biscuits on a tray for the children. Cora was occupied with dressing Donna up with a metric ton of eyeshadow. Some bloody Internet tutorial was likely to blame. Erin was helping, and Colin was playing football in the yard with Davis and the groom.

"I finally got Declan and Finn Jr. down for a nap," Brigid said. "It's just like at home. Cousins are endless fun. Finn Jr. likely assumes Erin is one of your brood and adopted her."

Daniel grunted a reply. She put the tin of biscuits back in the press and said, "So, you had a fight. Apologize. Because I can guarantee it was your fault."

Daniel furrowed his brow. "What happened to family loyalty?"

"Sisters before misters, Danny. It's science, or we'd have never survived this long. Your Mullen temper likely got the best of you. And your Mullen libido, as the two of you are like two steaming tea kettles."

He rubbed a palm over his face. "Brigid, must you be so blunt?"

"Yes, I must. I am my mother's daughter. So, you've stepped in it somehow. And now she's staying despite her reservations. Don't get all fat-chested about it, or she'll likely give you a kick up the arse and leave in the middle of the night."

"Oh, she most definitely wants to do that," he said.

Brigid walked by with a tray of biscuits. "Time to kiss a little ass, *deartháir mo chroí*."

———

The meeting went on until well past teatime. Brigid brought Erin in to see Airmid for a short visit, and Daniel heard them speaking in the Irish. When Brigid left with the child, he asked Airmid, "What is *jarhur* in Irish?"

Airmid made him repeat it. "Can you give me context because I'm missing something."

"Jarhur mo kree," he said awkwardly.

She smiled. *"Deartháir mo chroí?"* she asked. He nodded, his ears turning pink. "It means brother of my heart. It can be said to a beloved brother, or to someone who is so dear that they are like a brother. A brother of the heart, if not by blood."

Airmid watched the emotion flicker over his face. And for the first time since they'd been standing in Apollo's garden in Jamaica, she softened toward him. "It's a term of great affection. It's not said lightly." He just nodded again, and she wondered if it was because he was too choked up to speak. She turned toward Morgan. "So, the names stay the same for the trip west, I assume?"

Daniel had already gone at Morgan for not pulling Airmid from the case. She and Airmid were a united front. Even Douglas hadn't taken his side on the matter. Morgan stood. "I'm knackered. I took the red-eye from the Netherlands, just like you. Time for everyone to rest up. It's game time in four days. You'll start in Belize City and work your way toward the southwest border with Guatemala. The route from Columbia likely traveled by plane into El Salvador or Honduras. They loaded the goods in Punta Gorda, not Belize City. Likely to avoid the customs agents and defence forces. Punta Gorda is a coastal fishing port. They could easily load a fishing boat at night and meet the yacht just offshore. They'd have traveled with extra petrol and stopped in Abaco and probably some remote part of Canada in order to make the journey. They must have either gone to remote fueling stations, or they have someone in their pocket at those ports."

Daniel said, "I should know more about Arturo Rey by tomorrow. They are digging into his possible aliases and any family connections."

Douglas said, "Check the wife's family. She's from Honduras. He's from Belize. He could be lying, but arrogant men rarely feel the need to lie about small things." He stood. "Good night, Airmid. Excellent work. This is my first time in the field as well, and I am glad you're with us." He gave Daniel a pointed look. "Good night, Danny. Try not to step on your dick again before tomorrow's meeting." Morgan actually spit her water out mid-sip. Douglas just winked at Airmid and saw himself to the door. Morgan left right behind him.

Daniel said, "Donna has made some sort of pasta. She thought it would go over better with the five bairns."

Airmid stood. "I'll get Erin washed up and be down by half six."

He paused, then said, "It wasn't my cock that was causing the problem, Airmid. Despite my rather crude description of what I'd like to do to you."

She lifted her chin, not saying anything. He continued. "It was my heart. You have Erin. My siblings could both step in as my heirs. My life doesn't have any particular value. But yours does. Douglas and I are both childless. No wives. We'd be mourned, but we wouldn't orphan anyone. The way that child lights up when she sees you … it wakes me up at night, thinking about her losing another parent."

Airmid said, "I never signed up for this, you know. I was assigned to this job. But I will see it through. I'll do it for Erin. So that she can live in a world that has a few less drugs and rid the planet of the people who infect our homes with them. I will see this through because if you do come across anyone from Jamaica, it will be suspicious if I'm not with you."

He knew she was right. Before she walked out, she said, "And I don't regret it either. It was nice, MacPherson. It felt good to be touched. To be wanted. Even if it was a few stolen moments."

———

Daniel watched across the table as his houseguests bantered. How long had it been since this table had been full? He'd insisted that Davis and Donna eat with them. This wasn't Downton Abbey, for God's sake. They were family. Davis had Declan on his knee, and Erin was currently standing on her chair, giving a passionate dissertation on the merits of putting bubbles in her little kiddie pool. Airmid said, "Love, sit down. You must use your manners."

Daniel put a hand on her wrist. "Let her go. She's excited."

Airmid smiled, looking at her daughter. Erin sat, but Colin kept her excitement for the topic going. Colin said, "Then you won't have to take a bath later. It's brilliant, Mam."

Daniel looked at Donna, and her face was beaming. She sat opposite Airmid, at Brigid's insistence. Donna had Finn Jr. cradled in her arms and said, "It's been ages since we've had a full table. You'll have to invite more family to stay. We can always call Constance. With what you're paying her, she's the best-paid nanny in the county."

Airmid cocked her head. "That surprises me. I thought the government's reimbursement rate was pretty standard."

Daniel smiled. "Yes, maybe for England. I think the wages in Scotland might be a bit lower." A lie. A completely shameless lie. He was not going to tell Airmid he was supplementing the lass's wages. And Constance deserved it. If he had his own children, he'd be lucky to have such a good childminder. He dared a glance at Donna, whose eyes held an apology. She'd slipped and she knew it.

Brigid said, "Erin, have you heard of s'mores?"

The girl looked confused. "What is a shmoor?"

Colin answered, "S'more. And it's so good and a bit of good craic. We need a fire though. Mam, they aren't real s'mores if there's no fire to torch the marshmallows."

Brigid smirked. "Aye, so I'm told. Davis has taken care of it.

Now clean those vegetables off your plate or there will be zero craic after supper."

The children ate their broccoli with gusto, then helped Donna clear the table. Daniel watched Erin as she followed Cora around like a puppy. But when it came time to go back in the garden, the little girl was watching Davis carrying little Declan. She turned with her arms up to Daniel and said, "Carry me, Mr. Danny?" He didn't hesitate. The child needed to be held.

Airmid said, "I can take her."

"Aye, but she didn't ask you, now did she? Right now, I'm her favorite. Remember. I've provided ponies and an endless supply of cousins. Don't go trying to steal my thunder."

Erin settled against his hip and put her head on his shoulder. He patted her back as they walked into the back garden. The sun was low and pink on the horizon, giving the gorgeous gardens an ethereal glow. It was alive with bumblebees and butterflies.

"Your garden is beautiful, MacPherson. I'll give you that." She walked beside him, and she tried not to think about why her daughter had sought comfort from a man she barely knew. She was so used to doing everything alone, she didn't really think about how much Erin was missing in a typical life as a child. A father. Maybe some siblings. She was normally cared for by a pensioner in Airmid's neighborhood, and the old man wasn't strong and healthy like these men.

They settled around a clearing. There was a fire pit and several chairs, and there were blankets folded across the backs of the chairs for them to sit and cuddle. Daniel thought Erin would join the children, but she didn't. She settled on his knee instead. Airmid watched as he adjusted, letting her get comfortable. Declan noticed as well because he toddled over and sat on Daniel's other knee. Brigid laughed and said to Airmid, "He's a baby magnet. They love him." She motioned with her chin to Finn Jr. "If this one was awake, he'd be right in the middle."

Airmid smiled as she watched him toy with Declan's shoulder-length hair. One of the older boys had black hair like his sister. Only Declan and Finn Jr. had something close to Brigid's coloring. "Can I assume your husband has the raven hair?"

Brigid nodded. "Yes, it's long. Down past his shoulders. He looks like a barbarian when he wakes up in the morning. It's rare that two a generation get that particular coloring, but Colin's hair started going dark at about five years old, and we thought his eyes were going to be blue and green, but they got darker and darker every year. It's hard to pin those eyes down to one particular color. He is a handsome little devil, though."

Cora interrupted. "Da's side of the family goes back to the ancient Picts and the dark Celts of Ireland. He can hear the old ones. Like me."

The hair stood up on Airmid's arms. She looked at Brigid, but there was no hint that the child was kidding. Cora continued. "It's okay if you don't believe in that sort of thing. Many don't. But I've helped the Garda and the Coast Guard with some cases. It's my weight to carry. The knowing." She put a marshmallow on her stick. "But I don't mind it. It's just another way to help. To do my duty. Like the doctors and nurses or first responders in my family. It's like my auntie Branna says, 'If you can help, you should.'"

Airmid cleared her throat. "I do believe you, Cora. And I think you are extraordinary."

Cora just put a s'more together with a smile. Then she handed it to Erin. "This is a s'more. Marshmallow, chocolate, and graham cracker biscuits. It's messy and warm, so have a care."

———

Daniel called his mother, and she answered her cell after two rings. "Danny, love. How is my lad?"

Daniel said, "I'm grand, Mum. I have a lot of visitors, actually. The nursery is full."

His mother paused, then asked. "Is it John's kin? His great nieces and nephews?"

"Mostly, yes. A revolving door of them. And a coworker has been staying with her daughter. We are working a lot and she needed childcare. I hired a local girl, like Papa taught me."

He heard her sniffle. "That's good, love. How is work? Well, I suppose I can't ask that, can I?" She was the only one who knew because his father refused to keep it from her when he'd brought their son into British Intelligence.

"It's going well, Mum. I can't say any more. You know the drill," he said. "I've been reading Papa's journal."

Molly said, "I'm glad. He really was completely in love with you, Danny. He loved his lad from the start. From the first time you moved in my belly, he loved you." She laughed on a sob. "He used to read to you at night, before you were born. Arthurian legends, Nordic myths, even spy novels. It was so silly, really. But things were ... tense with me. I didn't mean for them to be, but they were. But I think we became a real family when I started showing. He'd get up at midnight to make a milkshake for me. I craved them with all three of you."

Daniel's breath hitched. She so rarely talked about the time when she was first married. "He loved you, Mum. I hope you know that."

She said softly, "I do know that, Danny. And I loved him."

He sighed, suddenly wanting to believe that more than anything. "I know, Mum."

Molly said, "Do you? I hope that's true. I think you needed to hear it from both of us. I hope the journals helped. And maybe someday I'll read them too. Now, it's time for an old woman to go to bed. Be careful, my sweet boy."

———

He read later than he should have, soaking in all the details about his father's life. By the time he was three quarters through, his father wrote about something that made his throat seize— the desire for more children. He never spoke a word about wanting some natural children of his own. It was more about having a full house. Having little ones for Daniel to play with. Daniel thought about Erin, an only child with no father to tuck her in at night. Airmid was a wonderful mother, but it must be exhausting doing it all alone. He read the final entry before he retired.

*"I kissed my wife today. And for once, I didn't hold back. I didn't restrain myself. I laid myself bare before her, the desire in my eyes. I was scared, but I am tired of pretending. So, I decided to ask the question, hoping I could live with the answer. And to my surprise, she kissed me back. And for the first time in six years, I felt wanted."*

Daniel walked out the double doors, needing fresh air. His heart was like a thick lump in his chest. His throat ached. For six years, his parents had lived as friends. His father had shown such restraint. Such tenderness. He felt the hot sting of tears, but he just couldn't open that wound. He missed his papa like a missing appendage. After he'd found out about John Mullen, he'd been so angry with his mother. For the betrayal of one man, and the imprisonment of another. He'd been sad for John and for the whole family. The kind and loving grandparents in Belfast who had never known they had a little piece of their son who had survived him.

But he'd been equally distraught that his mother had married his father, even though she'd loved someone else. The thought that she'd settled for his papa out of desperation hurt him in such a deep way. And what of Daniel's siblings? Molly hadn't wanted to tell them, but he'd insisted. Tell one, tell all. Even if it meant that they looked at Daniel through an altered lens. His mother had underestimated them, maybe. And Daniel felt there were enough secrets in his life. This one wasn't going to be one of them.

Eventually, though, his mother had succumbed to his father's irrepressible charm and wit. Robert MacPherson had been a dashing, intelligent man. Handsome like Gregory. And he'd been funny. Truly funny. Daniel noticed that his cheeks were wet, and those tears that he'd kept in for so long were not going to be denied.

A voice came from behind him. "I saw you from the window. I hoped you'd like some company," Airmid said.

Daniel couldn't look at her. "I'm afraid I'm not very good company right now."

He felt her hand on his arm, and he shuddered. "You've been reading your da's journal. I can always tell when your wounds have been opened. You must have loved him a great deal."

"I did. I just ... I was so afraid that she never returned his affections. Never truly loved him. I think it took her a long time to see what was right in front of her. I feel for John Mullen and the whole family. It's such a betrayal. But I feel for my papa as well." He wiped a stray tear roughly. "It's stupid, really. He's been gone for years. But reading his diary, man-to-man, I see him with clearer vision, through the eyes of an adult. And I just wanted to know that he didn't spend his whole life with a woman who never truly returned his love. He deserved better."

"And after what you read tonight, what do you think?" Airmid asked.

"I think maybe she did love him. That perhaps a sort of passion did grow between them. And I'm so glad for them. I didn't want to be the reason he never had love. I didn't want to be the reason she was never able to be with the man she loved."

Airmid turned him and put her hands on his face. "You were undoubtedly the best thing that ever happened to your parents. I was scared and alone when I had Erin. I didn't even have anyone in the delivery room with me. I love my parents, but they were too squeamish and a bit old fashioned for all that. They helped a lot afterward, but being pregnant out of wedlock, then having Tommy not marry me, it was stressful on them. My father wanted to kill Tommy. My mother was very cool toward him. Then he was gone, and everyone was just stunned.

"It wasn't the magical time it should have been. But in the still moments, I'd feel her move in my belly. I'd talk to her and wrap my arms around her and tell her that we'd be just fine. That we'd be a small family, but so happy. I never once felt anything but love and gratitude for her, and I'll bet your mother can say the same. You were a miracle, Danny MacPherson. You still are. And if your papa is looking down on you, he'd be so proud of you. And if he could speak, I think he'd tell you to forgive your mother, and that he was so grateful that he had such a beautiful life."

Daniel pulled her to him, and she went willingly to his mouth. He said against her mouth, "I need you. I'm sorry, but I need this."

Airmid said, "Stop apologizing and kiss me. Deeper, Danny. I need all of you." He groaned. Hearing her speak his true name. The name only those closest to him used. They kissed like they were starving, frantic and urgent. That's when they heard it through the open window. A child's cries.

He distanced himself. "I hear Erin." He kissed her forehead. "It's okay, I'll come with you."

Airmid's head was fuzzy, but she rushed back into the house and jogged up the stairs with Daniel behind her. Brigid was just coming out of her room to see to the child when she saw them appear up the stairway. "I've got it, Brigid, but thank you," Airmid said, going to the open door. Erin had her own bed in the nursery, but she'd wanted to sleep with her mother. Something Airmid never minded. She said, "How is my girl? Did you wake up?"

Erin was rubbing her eyes. "Mammy, where were you?"

"Just getting a drink of water, love. And I ran into Mr. MacPherson," Airmid said gently.

Erin tried to see to the doorway, so Daniel walked to the side table and turned the light on. Erin asked, "Do ye ever have bad dreams, Mr. Danny?"

He sat on the cushioned bedroom chair and smiled. Daniel said, "I do. Sometimes, I remember them. Sometimes, I don't. Did you have a bad dream?"

She just nodded. "I dreamed someone stole all my toys!" Daniel suppressed a grin.

He said, "That's terrible. Who would do such a horrible thing? It's a good thing the dream wasn't real. It was just a silly movie that plays in your head while you are sleeping. Right?"

Erin thought about it. "Yes, because I can see some of my toys over there!" She smiled, suddenly relieved.

Daniel smirked, meeting Airmid's eyes. "Well, my dear girl. As nightmares go, it could have been much worse. Do you think you can sleep now?"

"I need another story," Erin said with dramatic flair.

Airmid narrowed her eyes. "I gave you three stories a couple hours ago."

Erin said, "I want Danny to read a story to me. I like how he talks."

Daniel winked at Airmid, as if to say, *See, I'm her favorite.* Airmid climbed in bed beside her daughter, curling around her like a warm blanket. Daniel said, "Well, Erin, I think I can manage a good story. Do you mind if I tell you one that you might not have heard?" Erin nodded excitedly, and Daniel said, "When I was a lad, my Scottish grandmother would tell me the story of Robin Redbreast and his marriage to a wren. Unlike my grandda, who was from here in Hawick, my granny was from the Highlands. I can't do the Scots dialect as well as she could, so I'm afraid I'll have to give you the weak version." He said this for Airmid's benefit, more than Erin's. "I'll try though. It was my very favorite."

And he began. "There was an auld grey pussycat. And she gaed away down by the waterside, and there she saw a wee Robin Redbreast happin' on a brier ..." He laid the Scottish accent on thick, remembering his school days and the young lads who weren't raised with an English mother. It absolutely delighted Erin, and he watched Airmid try to stifle her own giggles. That's when he decided that making these two women smile was likely the best feeling he'd ever experienced.

———

Daniel told two more stories as he watched the two Roberts women drift off to sleep. He rose from the chair, standing above them. His heart squeezed at the picture they made. Airmid was a good mother. That was so important in life. He'd had a great set of parents, despite the differences with his mum. He leaned over them and kissed Airmid on the temple. Then he kissed the child's forehead, so peaceful now.

He'd left the door open, and he was surprised to find that Cora was there. He slipped out the door with her, not wanting to wake little Erin. When he shut the door, he turned on a hall lamp so he could see Cora better. "Hello, love. What has you awake? Were we too loud?"

Cora said, "Sometimes Da makes me some warm milk. Something about a chemical in it helping you sleep. The same one that's in turkey."

He smiled. "Tryptophan, I believe. Yes, I'll join you. I could use a bit myself."

They walked down the stairways and landed on the first floor. "Are you hungry, or just the milk?" Daniel asked over his shoulder.

"Just the milk, thank you," Cora said. "Colin kicks, but Mam wants us in the same room in case he gets scared. Not that he'd ever admit it."

"Well, if you want your own room, just let me know. We have some spares," Daniel said. "This house is too big for me, but it's our family estate, so it's kind of my responsibility."

"Yes, Mam said you are an earl. That's grand, I suppose. And you've got rooms for visitors. It's like an inn, but better food."

Daniel's mouth turned up at that. "I'll tell Donna you approve. She's been with us a long time."

"You mean when your da was earl?" she asked. Her eyes were gentle ... and old before their time. "I'm sorry he's gone. You were still young when he died. Younger than my mam."

"I was. I miss him very much," Daniel said as he warmed the milk on the stove.

"He misses you too, *col ceathrair*," Cora said. At Daniel's puzzled look she said, "It means dear cousin. You don't have the Irish, I suppose. You wouldn't have learned it. Did ye learn any Scottish Gaelic?"

"Just a few juicy curses that I won't repeat," Daniel said as he poured the milk. "And how do you know my papa misses me?"

She gave him a thoughtful look, weighing something. "Because he told me."

Daniel knew all about Cora's gifts, but he'd never been on the receiving end. The hair stood up on his neck. "Did he say anything else?"

She nodded, sipping her milk. "I don't know what it means, but yes, he did. He said it was enough and that he died a happy man."

Daniel choked down a sob. Cora said, "I'm sorry. I didn't mean to make you sad. It's just, I feel like people come to me for a reason. But that wasn't the thing I didn't understand. He said ... he said to fake left."

That caused more hair to stand up on Daniel's arms. He'd played football in his younger years. And his papa was convinced that every player expected the other guy to go left. Probably because most were right-side dominant and automatically felt stronger blocking to the right. So, the running joke was that he should always fake left, then go right to get around the player. It became his advice for everything from dealing with an angry woman to managing an idiot coworker. It became a private joke, long after his football days.

"Fake left, yes. I understand. I mean, I don't know why, but I get the reference. Thank you, Cora. Staying in an old house like this must stir things up a bit."

She just smiled. "It's usually when something is important. He wanted you to know that, and I was here. I'm glad for both of you. I think he's at peace."

"I think so too," Daniel said. He'd always thought so.

Cora finished her milk, then took her cup to the sink. "I like Airmid and Erin. I think you do as well."

"I do, actually. It's good to like the people you work with," he hedged.

Cora said, "If you say so, Danny." And the infernal child left without a backward glance.

# 11

Airmid woke to her sweaty little girl curled up next to her like a hot coal. Her father had been that way. Radiating a heat of his own that had her curling next to him on cold nights. She touched her daughter's face, smoothing the damp curls off her forehead. Curls like her father's fair hair. Then she looked at the chair where MacPherson had sat next to their bed, delighting Erin with tales from his Scottish grandmother.

Would Tommy have been in their lives once she'd given birth? Really been there? She tried not to think about the fact that he'd never defied his parents and just married her. He'd talked about it. Not in the form of any real proposal, but in less committed terms. *"My parents will come around when the child is born, then it'll be easier."* And deep down, she knew that if he'd been serious, he'd have done it without their approval. Would have made sure that Erin's future was secure. All the benefits of a child whose father served in the military. She'd had to submit to a DNA test when the custody hearing had happened. Erin was, in the eyes of the law, Tommy's child. But what did it matter, eight months after his death? Erin had been only a few months old when the court ruled in Airmid's favor.

Airmid allowed visitations with her paternal grandparents. They had taken Erin out for ice cream or to the cinema a few times. Short bursts just to check the box. Never overnight. Never more than three hours. And she was glad. The judge had requested she consider letting them be a part of Erin's life but hadn't required it. And she hadn't really seen any reason to fight them on it. The more people who love Erin, the better. The fact that they'd never given a dime of support didn't matter. It was money. They could go hang if they thought she'd ever ask them for anything. But to deny them the biannual trip to the ice cream parlor and occasional Disney movie seemed petty.

As if summoned from the darkest depths of hell, Airmid's phone rang. She saw the caller ID and answered, "Yes, Theadora?"

Her old lover's mother was a real piece of work, so she couldn't muster politeness. "Where the bloody hell is my granddaughter?"

Airmid sat up, not wanting to wake Erin with this woman's screeching. "Well, she's asleep next to me. Can I ask why you're calling at six in the morning on Saturday?"

"You aren't at home. She's usually with the childminder during the week, and I've called the house phone repeatedly. I asked where the hell you are? Why didn't you tell us you were leaving town?"

Airmid walked out into the hallway. "Let's start there, shall we? Mind yer tone, or I will ring off without answering any of your questions. I don't have to tell you if I'm out of town. I don't owe you anything, and you have no right to anything with regard to Erin. My daughter is with me and safe. I am on a business trip, and my employer has provided an on-site nanny. Despite what you might think, I am gainfully employed and have excellent support and benefits. Now, I haven't even had my coffee. What is it you need?"

The woman's voice was venomous. "I told Tommy you were no good. Papist trash and a whore. God knows how many of his men had you before him."

"Goodbye, Theodora. I'll give Erin your love," she said. And Airmid rang off. It rang again and she declined the call. After three cycles and one message she wasn't going to read, she blocked the caller. She couldn't very well turn her phone off.

She looked up to find Daniel watching her. "Sorry if I woke you," she said.

"Was that Erin's grandmother?" he asked, his face darkened with anger.

She sighed. "Yes, it was. Apparently, she rang the house phone this week and no one answered."

"And was she uncivil to you?" he asked.

Airmid let out a bitter laugh. "Besides the usual calling me Irish trash and a whore and attacking my chosen faith? No, she was grand."

If it was possible, his face darkened even more. She softened because it made her feel kind of squishy that he was so offended on her behalf. "I've let those insults roll off for a long time, MacPherson."

He walked closer to her, leaning in. "I prefer it when you call me Danny."

She swayed, smelling him. Feeling his heat. "Yes, well, the old cow has me in a prickly mood. So, MacPherson it is, for now."

He pressed her up against the door. "What can I do to take the edge off, Airmid? Name your price."

She leaned up to his face and said, "Food and caffeine."

He grumbled with husky laughter. "Your wish is my command, my liege."

Constance chose that time to come to the front door, and Airmid heard the intercom squawk from the second floor. Daniel brushed her lips so swiftly, she barely felt it. Then he jogged downstairs to give Davis instructions. She threw on a robe and brushed her teeth in the third-story bathroom before meeting Constance on the stairs. "She's still asleep. If you want to just stay close in case she wakes? She had a nightmare last night." Airmid thanked the woman before heading down to the ground floor, in search of sustenance.

Daniel looked up as Airmid walked into the kitchen. "Breakfast is informal this morning. I decided to let everyone sleep in. And I told Morgan and Douglas to come at teatime."

She raised her brows. "Well, that's a surprise. It's good, I suppose. They've both been traveling."

He tilted his head. "I thought you and I could take a ride today. The kids have been enjoying my stables, but you haven't had the chance. What do you think about a morning ride. Just you and me?"

She blushed. She actually felt herself blushing as Donna dug around in the press and pretended not to be listening. "I'd like that."

"That's grand. Now, here's your caffeine. Cappuccino, no sugar, if I remember correctly. Go get dressed. Something warm and boots are better. I'll pack a hamper for us."

"Let the girl get a bite in before you go, Danny. Don't rush her. You'll have her all to yourself in no time."

Now it was Daniel's turn to blush. He felt his ears reddening. "Yes, madam."

Airmid smiled as Donna slid a bit of jam and cream in front of her, followed by a tray of pastries for her to choose from. Daniel watched her with an almost predatory gaze. He was already dressed. She made idle chat with Donna about what her daughter liked to eat, then she grabbed her coffee and headed upstairs. Anxious and nervous to be taking an extended day ride with Daniel.

His intent was clear. He wanted to get her away from all the distractions. To steal some time when they weren't on the job. A morning just for them. At least, that's what it felt like. Like something private and ripe with possibility. And if it was just two friends going out for a ride, she'd be content with that. Content with this span of time she had with Daniel. Because after this, she'd go back to her analyst work.

Airmid never asked to be a field agent. The money going into her bank account right now was going to pay the loan off that she'd taken in order to fight for sole custody of her daughter. After that, she'd be comfortable. Erin would be starting school in another year, and she'd have significantly fewer childcare expenses. Maybe she'd be able to afford to buy her own home rather than leasing.

She gathered a jumper and some warm jeans. Her boots were stowed in a coatroom off the front entrance of the house. She changed in the bathroom, running a brush through her hair one more time before going back downstairs. Daniel had her boots in one hand and her coat in the other, smiling as she came down the stairs. Her heart thumped in her chest as she did up her laces. She was not going to read more into this than Daniel wanting a ride and offering a distraction for her. He'd overheard at least part of that awful phone conversation. "I'm ready, MacPherson. Show me this big estate of yours."

———

Daniel watched Airmid riding alongside him, unable to hide his admiration. She was comfortable on a horse. Erin had been new to riding, more or less, but Airmid had taken dressage in Northern Ireland when she was a girl. Just for a couple years, but riding a horse was like riding a bike. You fell back into it pretty quickly.

He took her along the bridle path to the wooded area that ran along his estate and the neighboring one. They shared the trails, but the new owners didn't have any horses. It was cloudy and cool, but the mist was dispersing from the rolling grass, and as they headed into the woods, the birds and wild things greeted them.

Airmid's smile was a light all its own. "I think this must be where the little people roam. Did the children come this far?"

Daniel said, "No, they stayed near the barn. Maybe we can come back with Erin. She could ride in front of me. I've done it with wee Isla before."

"Why do you think your siblings haven't settled down and bred like your Irish side of the family?" Airmid asked. "I'm assuming you never did because of the job. But for all three of you to be in your thirties, or almost thirty, and never had a serious partner, it seems strange."

Daniel casually lifted one shoulder. Not offended by the question in the least. He'd asked himself the very same thing. "I suppose it is strange. And you're right, about me at least. It's not a job you can just talk about on your first date. And at what point do you come clean—if ever? And if you never do, then what does that say about your relationship? It's why I've kept my entanglements more short-term and superficial. My father was married before he was recruited by MI-6. My mother was part of the process. He wouldn't have done it without her blessing. I was recruited right out of university. I didn't even finish graduate school."

"Same," Airmid said. "I couldn't have afforded graduate school anyway. I did six years in the army, then got pregnant partway through my degree. I was using my military benefits, and I got scholarships to assist with childcare and other bills. My parents helped as well because I was still in Northern Ireland. When I was approached by the agency, it was like a godsend. A well-paying job and no student debt." She paused. "Listen, I really want to work this case. I'm committed until it's over. But after this, I'm okay returning to my position as an analyst. It's better for my family situation. Erin needs me. And after this job, my debts will be paid. I was just thinking about what it would be like to not have to lease a house. Maybe, once Erin is in school, I could buy something. But this international jet-setting isn't going to be sustainable for me. I hope you understand that."

He'd expected as much. Was glad of it, actually. Having Airmid Roberts in harm's way was doing things to him. Things he couldn't put into words. Daniel met her eyes. "I do understand. I think you are a natural at the undercover work, Airmid. But I also think you are an amazing mother. The best of mothers. And if you had to choose, I can see where Erin would win any day of the week. She's rather wonderful."

Airmid's eyes burned with emotion. "I'm glad you understand. Oh!" She held her palms out, turned up toward the sky.

Daniel heard the misting rain starting to tap the fresh, green leaves overhead. "I suppose it was too much to hope for that we wouldn't get any rain. There's a little cottage up ahead. It's not much, but it's dry." He urged his mount to speed up, and Airmid followed him. The rain started coming down harder, and he heard her laughing behind him. A beautiful sound.

Airmid saw the structure ahead. A small cottage that likely hadn't had anyone living in it since the witch tried to snare Hansel and Gretel. Daniel slid off his horse, tying the black Friesian to the post. He helped her off her grey Eriskay Pony. He tied them off under an overhang, probably meant for a carriage.

Then he dug in his pocket for the key to the front door. The rain was really coming down now, and he urged her into the compact building. Then he ran back out for the picnic hamper and another saddlebag. It was dark, and she wondered if the place even had electricity.

Daniel came in the front door just as a drip started in the corner. He scooted a pail under the leak in the roof. "Sorry, it hasn't been occupied for probably thirty years. The groundskeeper used to live out here when my grandparents lived here, and my father let him retire and stay, even after he hired a local lad to do the work." He shook his coat out and placed it over an old, wooden chair, so she inched out of hers. "I replaced the lightbulbs about a year ago, so keep your fingers crossed."

He switched on two wall sconces, and finally an overhead light. It was a bit worn and dated, but surprisingly, it was furnished. "My sister used to use this as a writing cottage when she lived here. Then she got her own flat. Now she is planning a trip to Inisheer to my island house because she wants a change of scenery. Still, Donna keeps it up in case she wants to use it. It's rough, I know. And apparently, I need to get a roofer out here about that leak."

Airmid was just smiling. She walked around the small house. There were two tiny bedrooms and one small bathroom and water closet. She watched as Daniel lit a fire in the hearth, methodically stacking the small slivers of wood and using matches from a container on the wooden mantle. It was a pretty cottage. Old and rough from lack of daily use, but good bones and a sense of a different time. A time when a villager's son would find work at the earl's estate and be lucky enough to have a roof over his head in the bargain. He might have brought a wife and maybe a child or two to live in the wooded part of the estate.

Daniel took a towel from the lav, well-worn and clean. And

she was surprised as he tenderly started drying the dripping ends of her hair. He grabbed an old blanket from the chest in one of the bedrooms. It smelled like cedar and something a little damp, but not unpleasant. He draped it over her shoulders. "Sit, and I'll put the kettle on."

She stared at the fire, just content to be quiet. To be at peace while he boiled water for tea. "Do you come out here often?"

He smiled as he worked. "No, not really. I don't even get out for a ride as much as I'd like. But it's here. It's always been here. By the time I was an old enough lad to remember, the man who lived here was pretty old. I'd take him biscuits or bread when Donna was baking. Or check on him and his wife if someone was feeling poorly. They died ten days apart. It was like, once she was gone, he couldn't bear to stay. I came out every day, and he'd just say, 'Don't worry over me, lad. I'll be with my girl soon enough. And don't be sad. We'll be dancing among the stars.'"

Daniel said the words with a Scottish burr, as if channeling the old man. It made her want to cry. "That's beautiful. It sounds like this house was full of love."

"It was. They never had children. I think they couldn't have them. Sad, because I believe they would have been really good parents. They were like another pair of grandparents to me. Maybe it was God's way of replacing the ones I didn't care to know and the ones I never knew I had. I mean, most lads got two sets, and I just had the one pair."

"And were they good grandparents? I think your gran was the storyteller. Was your grandda a good sort?"

"Oh, yes. The very best of fathers and grandfathers. Some days, I sense that I can feel him. He had an estate in England as well as this one. He was English and Scottish. His father held the title, but his mother was full-blooded English. They spent most of their time there. It was a bit warmer and closer to good doctors.

My father's side of the family was a close-knit group. They're good people. I have some cousins here and there on both sides of the border." Daniel put some tea down in front of her. "I'm afraid I'm all out of fresh milk."

Airmid accepted it and thanked him. "I wish Erin had two sets of good grandparents. My parents are very good people. They both still work. They're closer to my brother, more due to geography than anything, but they are good parents to me. As you heard today, Erin is better off without the other set. I let them see her when they ask. Just a couple hours once or twice a year. Just long enough to ease their conscience, buy her ice cream and a toy, and insult me on the way back out the door.

"And to this day, I never understood why. I mean, Tommy said I had to give them time. But not warming up to someone is not the same as outright hostility. I know now that Tommy had a girl at home. One from his teenage years. He broke it off with her before me. I mean, before we got together. We were friends, and I think he had feelings for me. He did the right thing and broke it off with the girl. He said he'd stayed with her because of family expectations, but they'd grown apart. Their families had been friends for years. They were already picking out china patterns and pressuring Tommy to propose by the time he was twenty.

"We were together for a year when I got out of the military and started going to school. But apparently, they never stopped campaigning for him to get back with his ex. I was in Belfast, and he'd take the ferry over to see me when he had leave instead of going home. They hated me for it. And I think part of me knew he was hiding. Hiding from them and also hiding our relationship from them. Then I got pregnant, even though we used protection. I was six months along when he died. They wouldn't even let me come to the funeral. 'No one outside the immediate family knew he had some Irish floozy knocked-up over the water,'" she said bitterly.

Daniel caught her chin. "Don't ever call yourself that, even in jest. My mother got pregnant out of wedlock, too. And her parents had the same sort of prejudices that Tommy's parents did. Fuck them both. You are too good for the lot of them, and they are extremely lucky that you let them anywhere near Erin. And you should stop if they are saying any of those vile things in front of her."

"They've been warned, but it's only a matter of time," Airmid said. "I'm a little worried, to be honest. That phone call was odd. She was a bit manic. Like she was afraid I'd run off without telling them. I don't trust her or that horrible bastard she's married to. She was so rude, I hung up before I found out what she wanted."

"Well, don't think about it anymore. Let's just forget about the past for a bit." Daniel stood from his chair, squatting in front of her. "Just be here with me, love. Let's pretend it's that simple."

Airmid palmed both sides of his face. And for once, the passion wasn't frantic or edgy. It rose slowly, like a magic spell that breathed life into the little cottage. She bent and kissed him, soft and sweet.

Daniel almost fell over with the force of the longing in his chest. He leaned his forehead against her and couldn't seem to find any words. Straining toward her both with his mind and his body. He stood, taking Airmid with him. He threaded his hands in her hair and kissed her until neither of them could stop from trembling. She croaked his name, "Danny."

He pulled her tighter to him, the sound of his name on her lips like gasoline on glowing embers. The flames licked between them. "I need you, Airmid. I need you so much, I can barely stand the wanting."

Airmid fumbled with the hem of his wool jumper, and he let

her slide it over his head. Then his T-shirt was next. While he yanked off his shirt, she feathered kisses over his chest. He pulled her sweater over her head, the breath shooting out of him at the sight of her in only a bra and jeans. She was curvy and lushly figured, but he felt the strength beneath. The athletic power of her body.

Daniel wanted to touch every inch of her. Getting the wet jeans off wasn't as easy. He took his time, dropping to his knees as he kissed her breasts and stomach. He mumbled lovers' words against her skin. Words like beautiful and perfect. "You're so soft. Like silk." He looked up at her as he nibbled just above her panties. "Will you let me have all of you, Airmid? Let me see you and taste you?" She nodded as he closed his mouth over the thin fabric of her panties. She gasped, throwing her head back as he started to peel her panties off and nibble her hip bones. He palmed her ass as he teased her with his small bites.

Then he was on his feet, lifting her and wrapping her legs around his waist. He unhooked her bra and threw it over his head as he started his attentive exploration of both breasts, licking and tasting her nipples. He dipped a hand under her ass to the sweet, slick spot between her thighs. He moaned against her breast, then met her eyes. "You are deliciously wet, Agent Roberts."

She was panting, rubbing against the seam of his jeans. Against the hard ridge of his arousal. "Danny," she whimpered. He was gentle as he spread her out on the small bed. Then he knelt on the floor and hooked both legs over his arms. He gave a not-so-gentle yank as he pulled her to the edge of the bed.

"I've wanted to do this for weeks," he said, and he slid his tongue through her sex, then inside her as she arched off the bed. He held her hips down as he settled into his task. Learning her. What she liked. What made her thrash her head back and forth. She wasn't quiet, and he was suddenly glad they'd waited until they were out in the forest to do this for the first time. He wanted her unhinged. She screamed when she came, bucking against his mouth. He let her ride it to completion, then he stood above her, getting out of his own wet jeans.

Before Daniel could think about mounting her properly, she was up and palming him, her mouth gliding over his thick head. "Fuck! Airmid. I'm not going to last if you do that."

But she sank onto his cock, taking him deep. Then she said, "I'm on the pill." And that's all he needed to hear before abandoning any ideas about stopping this so he could retrieve the condom out of his wallet. She reclined on her back, lust and tenderness warring in her eyes. He came over her, spreading her thighs with his hips.

Daniel gazed deep into her eyes as he worked himself against her core. Then he pushed in, watching every nuance of her facial expression. He stilled, just savoring the joining. Unhurried. Letting her adjust. He knew it had been a while for her. She'd only had one lover since Erin was born. Out of loneliness, no doubt. The need for a connection. *It was nice feeling wanted. Being touched.*

He leaned on one arm, exploring her face and hairline with his fingertips. He brushed a soft kiss over her mouth as he moved, gliding back and then in again. She whimpered under his slow, deep thrusts. She closed her eyes and he cupped her chin. "Let me see you." He felt the tightening of her womb as her eyes begged him for something. For mercy, maybe?

Daniel knew this was a bad idea. Unprofessional and unwise. But he couldn't help himself. Couldn't turn away from this connection. Something he'd never felt with another woman. Her hips moved with his, her body gripping him. "I want to come inside you. Do you want that? Do you want to be filled with me, Airmid?"

She arched and exploded, her voice keening as she climaxed.

He yelled out a juicy curse as he went over the edge with her. Airmid gripped his cock so hard that he saw stars as she pulsed around him. He pulled her hips off the mattress, diving into her until they were both wild. A rawness and truth he'd never felt before.

———

They curled up in blankets in front of the fire, nibbling on snacks from the hamper and drinking bottled water. And when they'd warmed a bit, Daniel stretched out on a blanket and pillows in front of the fire. "Come to me, love. Take what you need."

Airmid sank onto his cock and moaned as she arched and strained above him. He slid a finger between them, feeling her slick, swollen flesh. She started to climb, and he raised up to take a nipple in his mouth as he palmed the back of her neck with his other hand. Daniel felt a release of slickness as she shuddered above him. He watched her come apart, and it was so beautiful, it nearly stopped his heart.

They drifted off for a time, then he woke with the need for her strong in his blood. He flipped her on her stomach and pulled her hips off the blanket as he impaled her with one thrust. He rode her hard, wanting to mark her in some way. To dominate and take her, rough and fast. He came in a white-hot flash of pleasure as he watched her face, turned to the side and against the blanket, as she smiled a wicked smile. Enjoying the claiming.

———

It was time to start back, so Daniel used some of the warm water from the kettle to gently wash her between the thighs. He liked that she was full of him. That he'd spilled in her three times. But he'd also made a mess of her, and she did have to dress and sit on a horse. He was slow as he swept her swollen flesh with the cloth. Airmid smirked. "If ye get me goin' again, Daniel MacPherson, I won't be responsible for you being late to yer own meeting." And that sweet Irish lilt just revved his engine enough to where he considered going for a fourth round.

They would leave for Belize in two days. While she was here, she was sharing a room with her daughter. This was likely all he'd get of her until they landed in Central America. He was staring so hard at her that she actually laughed. She said, "Time to go, Danny. Leash the beast."

He settled over her, now wearing jeans. She was under him, completely fucking naked. He kissed her in drugging sweeps and tugs. "I can't stop wanting you. I can't turn it off. We may need to go back to work, but just know that I am completely distracted by thoughts of what it felt like to be inside you."

She ran a hand from his temple to his cheek. "I don't want the bubble to break. This was beautiful."

He closed his eyes, bending to brush her mouth. He said, "It was beautiful. And whatever this is, it's not over."

―――――

They rode home in comfortable silence, only talking occasionally. The rain had stopped, and despite the damp clothing, it was a delightful ride. The wet, bright foliage and full, swaying trees were hypnotic. They came out of the woods, finding that the sun was peeking out of the clouds.

Airmid wasn't going to let herself fret over this turn in their relationship. Her only serious relationship in her life had left her gutted and fighting for her child. She wasn't going to overthink this thing with Daniel. He was smart and handsome and he was a giving person, but not in any way that begged obligation. He helped because he could.

She finally broached a subject she'd been wanting to discuss. "I checked the reimbursement rates for government employees. Morgan hedged a bit, but what I found out was that it capped at ten hours per day, and it is half what Constance is being paid."

He looked at her, chin up. "It's taken care of, Airmid. And Erin is safe and cared for. She's got three or four people at her disposal when you're away. The details don't matter."

"They do if you are the one paying the difference. Why do you think it's your responsibility, Danny?" She wasn't angry. She wanted to know.

He just kept urging the horse at a slow pace. "This village loses young people every year. They leave for better jobs. Better pay. You make cracks at my expense about being a part of the peerage. But I take it seriously. I might not do things publicly. I can't, obviously. But a hundred years ago, it would have been my job to make sure to hire within the ranks of my own villagers. Their welfare would partially fall to me. Constance is a good lass, and you needed this. It works out for everyone. I'm not a rich man compared to some, but I could do this for the team. I could help. Why wouldn't I?"

"I should pay you back," she said. Her pride was taking a hit, despite his logical argument. "I make an adequate living. Enough to pay you back."

"No, what you should do is pay off those legal fees and start saving for a house. You didn't ask for this assignment. And you shouldn't have to go in the hole because we dragged you onto our team with no warning."

"Danny—" she said, but he cut her off.

"If you buy a house, get in the black, and feel compelled in five years' time, you can pay me back. I won't take a dime before all of those things are done. And if you say you want to pay interest, I will slap that horse's arse and let him buck you off into the mud."

She'd just been about to offer that very thing, damn him. Airmid tightened her body, lips closed and thin. "I've never needed taking care of, and it's not your job."

Daniel ignored her because he couldn't say what he wanted to say. It *was* his job. Deep in his gut, he was drawn to her. And he wasn't sure she was ready to hear everything he was feeling. He wasn't sure he could even process it. "If we speed up, we can get back and get freshened up before Morgan and Douglas sense what we've been doing all day." He raked his eyes over her. "You look like you've been thoroughly plundered, My Lady."

And she laughed because he changed his voice to sound like some uptight earl from a romance novel. "Aye, I have, My Lord. Thoroughly." His look seared her to her bones. It was intense. So, she urged her pony into a trot, leaving him behind her. She said over her shoulder, "Stop looking at my ass, Danny."

He said one word. "No."

# 12

## BATSUB HEADQUARTERS, BELIZE

Aidan finished moving his cot and gear to the main barracks. The rain continued, and now the officers' huts were under three inches of water. Enough to make them unusable and unsafe. They'd cut the electricity just as he'd been moving the last of his gear. The water had been coming under the door as they folded the cots and rolled them up to the barracks that housed the rest of his men. No bother, really. Other than the fact that he'd liked his private shower and water closet. He turned toward his new friend and comrade. "Ramirez, I distinctly ordered no rain."

Ramirez laughed, low and deep. "I'll tell The Boss." And he pointed at the sky, as if he had a direct line to the Almighty. His English was passable. Better than Aidan's Spanish, to be sure.

Aidan asked, "How will the villages get on?"

Ramirez grunted. "The people of the rivers and forests know what to do. The bad time comes when the cities flood. Too many people. Too many ... *basura*."

Aidan didn't know that word. He took out his phone.

"Garbage. Yes, I understand. That would be *problemático*." One word he had learned. How to relay that something was going to be a potential shit show.

Kearsley came into the barracks. "Everyone is moved. The lieutenant colonel from the Royal Dragoons is in the cottage straight above us. Sorry. I tried to get you in there as well, but it's too tight."

Aidan shrugged. "I'd rather be here with my men. Privileges of rank and all that. He's earned a little peace and quiet." And he had. Aidan had known him peripherally in Afghanistan. "Where is the extra linen? I'm going to change this out since we've had it in the damp. Then I want the squad leaders in the mess hall at 14:00. We need to go over some contingency plans. Did comm get the Wi-Fi up and running again?"

"No, sir. Sorry. They're still working with the local lads. I was supposed to call the wife tonight. The baby had a checkup." His cheeks turned pink.

"Don't be embarrassed about checking on your girls, lieutenant. If this goes on too long, we'll figure out a way to at least get messages to everyone. If I can get Alanna on the satellite phone, she can put out a message to all of the spouses and parents." Some of his men weren't married, but they had mums at home.

Kearsley's face showed relief. "The linen is in that storage press. I'll go tell the squad leaders about the meeting."

He walked away, and Aidan noticed Ramirez was watching the exchange. "He's got a new baby at home. And a pretty wife." He winked at the man and Ramirez smiled.

Ramirez said, "Your men have *el respeto*. They like you. But I think they are a little afraid, too. This is good."

"Yes, well, Irishmen are known for their hot temper. *El mal genio?* Is that right?" He could tell his friend understood. "And we are bueno with the ladies." Ramirez laughed.

"The men have talked about your *sposa*. A beauty," Ramirez said. Cheeky bastard. Aidan took out his phone and found a nice wholesome picture of his wife. No need to exploit his woman to prove a point. She was holding little Isla.

Ramirez's eyes actually bugged out of his head. "La rubia," he said. "With eyes like emeralds. They are right. You are a lucky man." Then he took his phone out of his pocket. He showed Aidan his wife, and it warmed Aidan to see the pride. Ramirez was only in his late twenties. His wife looked about twenty-five and pretty as a picture. She had long, dark hair and big eyes the color of chestnuts. She had thick, sooty lashes and a lovely smile. Her skin was like rich, dark honey, perfectly youthful and unlined. She had her hand on a swollen belly.

"She's a beauty, to be sure. You're expecting a child, then?" he asked. "Is she safe from the flooding?"

"Yes, she's with my madre in the high country. She is safe. There is a clinic nearby, for when the baby comes. Then we will move closer to the base. They said maybe we'll be at Price Barracks."

Aidan said, "That's a big move. It's an old British base. Is she happy about it?" Aidan knew the closest Belize Defence Force base to them right now was Fairweather in Punta Gorda. They did their jungle training in the Machaca Forest Reserve, which was only twenty minutes away. "You can't get Fairweather?"

Ramirez shrugged. "It depends. I am up for a promotion in rank. If I get it, then it will be the bigger base, I think," he said. "It is good work." The men kept talking, stumbling their way through their stories about their time in the military, how they met their wives, and what it was like to have pushy peahens for sisters and mothers. Before Aidan knew it, it was almost time for his meeting. "It was good talking to you, mo cara."

"What is this? Mo cara?" Ramirez asked. "It is English?"

Aidan said, "It's Irish. It means my friend. Amigo."

Ramirez said, "Si, amigo. A good talk."

————

### Hawick, Scotland

Morgan got right down to it. "The analysts didn't come back with a whole lot on Arturo Rey's family. And it's Reyes, not Rey. He dropped the end to sound more like a knight than a devil. What a wanker. Regardless, they didn't find anything of note until the search branched out to the wife's connections. Maiden name of Escobar. Alessa Escobar is a cartel princess. Her father's name is Cadmael. It's a Mayan name. It means war chief, and it is fitting. He's second in command of the Escobar drug cartel in Honduras.

"It's likely that the drugs are flying into Honduras from Columbia. The illegal airstrips in the jungle areas allow them to transport the product by land. They are likely crossing briefly into Guatemala and coming through the less-monitored Western border, through the forest reserve. Or the Southern border, closer to Punta Gorda. They may vary the route. If they're smart, they are doing just that. They'd load small boats and take the product offshore to transfer to the large boats. It would have to be a big enough boat to make the trip. They switch the navigation system in the resort areas of the Caribbean, then head north. The yacht they seized in Amsterdam had extra fuel stored on the lowest deck, but they still would need to stop somewhere on the Eastern Seaboard or Canada to fuel up. Somewhere remote enough that they'd just look like jet-setters."

"What about the captain of the boat?" Daniel asked. "He was

of mixed race, wasn't he? Some sort of Anglo-European and an unknown country of origin in Central America. Did you apply the appropriate pressure with regard to extradition to Jamaica?"

Morgan smirked. "I'm getting to that, MacPherson. Hold your water." She shuffled through her file, handing them transcripts from their interviews. "The countries of origin for the crew were Belizean and Honduran. The captain was stubborn, however. He would not give a name. Our interpreter has his suspicions though. He feels that the man was definitely following their conversations."

Daniel's brows rose. "You mean in Dutch?"

She smiled. "Aye. He was telegraphing signs of listening. He may be bilingual. Airmid, I want you to look over his interviews. I have the video. See if you can pick up the dialect. As for the other crew members, only one gave any information. Better hanged by Jamaicans than tortured by the Escobar cartel, apparently. The only information he gave us is what we already knew. He boarded off the coast of Punta Gorda. It's his second trip. They didn't tell the crew much. He said a man came aboard in Jamaica. He's a middle-aged, older, Spanish-speaking man. According to him, they went offshore, lined the crew up on the deck, and executed the two men. Evidently, that's what they got for snooping. They were caught going through the hard-copy navigation maps that we assume were burned to ash before the boat came into port. Apparently, that is standard procedure every time they stopped. It gives us a direction, at least. I think the men may have been undercover."

Douglas had been uncharacteristically quiet until now. "Jesus, Morgan. Why do you say that?"

She sighed, and they all knew she was weighing whether they needed to know. "There are two members of the ... clandestine community who have not checked in. They may or may not have been"—she did air quotes and continued—"*Spanish immigrants* assigned to an undisclosed nation in Central America. The DNA is being sent to their country of origin so they can confirm if it is them. And it's looking very likely. That's all I can tell you for now."

Daniel stood, running his hand through his hair. His eyes darted to Airmid's, then to Morgan. Morgan said, "I'm thinking the same thing. Airmid, you weren't trained as a field agent."

Her back went ramrod straight. "Fuck that for a laugh. You aren't sending these two louts into harm's way without an interpreter. No fecking way. And if they show up with someone else who also just happens to speak Spanish, and they run into anyone we met in Jamaica, you may as well paint a sign on their foreheads. No, Morgan." She looked at Daniel. His jaw was tight. He was going to try to fight her on this. "No. Fecking. Way. That is the end of it. We see this one case through, and I will gladly go back to being the geek on the headset. But you are not benching me right in the middle of a case. It will compromise them." She dared the three of them to argue with her. They all knew she was right.

But it was Douglas who came to her defense. "We need her. It would be foolish to change up the team. She can do this. Any other hang-ups about her going need to be shut down."

The look Daniel gave Douglas dropped the temperature in the room by ten degrees.

————

Morgan left after the briefing, and Airmid went up to the nursery to see her daughter before dinner. They still had work to do, but they didn't need Morgan for that part of it. When they were out of the area, Daniel rounded on Douglas. "What the hell was that, Douglas? I thought you'd have my back on this. Are you trying to get her killed?"

"You've had reservations from the start, but she proved herself in Jamaica. We have to finish this mission, Danny. You are letting your cock do the thinking right now." He hissed the words, not wanting anyone to hear. But he was pissed. He knew. Damn him, he knew.

Daniel's face shifted. That's when Douglas saw it. "It's not your cock that's the problem, is it? You're in love with her."

Daniel turned toward the hearth. "Fuck you, Douglas. You're worse than my mother."

Douglas mumbled. "Of course you're in love with her. She's the real deal. But it doesn't matter, Danny. You have to see that. This could make her career. If she bows out in the middle of a mission, it won't look good for anyone. And we do need her. You saw the way Jensen and Rey were around her."

Daniel turned around and pointed at him like he held a dagger. "That is precisely why we shouldn't take her. They'd torture us if we were caught, but they'd do worse to her. And they'd make us watch. They'd break us both with it. I can't do this! You are both new to fieldwork. I can't lose one of you."

Douglas walked up to him, inches apart. Uncowed by his aggression. He palmed his shoulder. "So, then we don't get caught. You've been at this for fifteen years, Danny. You can do this, and you can keep us safe. I trust you and so does Airmid."

They sat at the table, Douglas having poured them both a stiff drink. Douglas said, "I think Jensen is involved. I don't know how, but I still think it. If his entourage makes an appearance, I'm going to try a different tactic."

"What is that?" Daniel asked, feeling defeated and a little ashamed.

"Rubia. Obviously, a nickname due to the hair. We'll start there. I want a name," he said.

"You speak fluent German. Try that angle. See if you pick up any indicators of where she's from. She could be Belgian."

Douglas shrugged. "Maybe, but I'd need to hear it in her native tongue. How competent is Airmid in Germanic language?"

Airmid came in behind them. "Not very. If she's Belgian, it may be a Flemish form of Dutch, but it depends on where in Belgium you're talking about. The accent sounded German though. Specifically, Bavarian. I'm not fluent, but I get by. I think your first instinct is correct, though, brother dear. I think you should focus on her if the opportunity presents itself. She warned Danny not to let them separate me from you. Getting close to her is a good move."

Douglas narrowed his eyes. "Are you suggesting I whore myself out for information because I do not take sloppy seconds from a man like Jensen. And for all we know, he and old King Arthur have tag-teamed her." He shuddered. "Though, she is gorgeous. I won't say it wouldn't be tempting."

Airmid said, "Play hard to get. Women like her are used to being worshiped. Tell her you have a woman at home."

Douglas snorted. "I wish."

"You could have your pick, Douglas. Modesty doesn't suit you," Daniel said.

"Yes, well, you have managed to fall under the radar with the peerage. You try, never knowing if someone is after your title and your inheritance," he said.

Airmid's face softened. She said, "That's rotten. I never really thought about it. No one's after my money. They just want in my knickers. Until they find out I have a child. Then it's, 'Oh, my. Look at the time!' Then they head for the closest exit." She laughed at her own comment until she felt Daniel stiffen. She gave him a look that said *present company excluded*, but she was afraid the damage was already done.

Douglas missed the back and forth. "Well, if we all end up single, Danny has spare rooms. We can live it out with Davis and Donna. As for Rubia, I think the best way to go at this is by staying a night or two in Jensen's resort. Then we head inland to the resort in the forest area outside of Punta Gorda. Morgan has been in contact with our colleague in Central America. We'll have access to an off-road vehicle, and the bloke will pose as our excursion guide. Lots of ground to cover. And bring your wellies. The rain has been heavy for the beginning of the season. Our flight leaves tomorrow evening. I'll see you at noon." He got out of his chair, grabbing his blazer. "Time to put the masks back in place. Tara, John, good night."

———————

Douglas left them alone, and Daniel could hear the stirring of all the other people in the house. Airmid was a hum in his blood. A prickle in his skin. She turned, intent to rip into him plainly on her face. And he had to give her credit. She'd saved her ire for a time when they were alone. Daniel said, "Just hold that thought a little longer and follow me."

She thought he'd leave out the door, but he didn't. He closed the ornately trimmed door to his expansive office and private library. Then she watched as he went to a painting that was nestled on the wall between two bookshelves. He fingered the edge of the thick frame, and she heard a small click. He then opened the frame like a book cover and she saw a panel. "Come, let me show you. Although, it would be Donna or Davis using this place while we are gone, and they already know the how of it."

He pushed in a four-digit code. Airmid was too stunned to say anything. Was it a safe? "One, zero, six, six?"

Daniel smirked. "The Battle of Hastings. My father was a

history nut." He pressed enter, and she heard a sort of hiss as the shelf shifted. He pushed and it opened. "It's a panic room. I'm sure you've heard of the concept. You can only lock it from the inside with the same code—a code, I'll have you know, that has only been known by five people."

"Your parents, yourself, Davis, and Donna, I assume?" Airmid said as she walked into the chamber with awe. "I'm sorry, Daniel, but it's pretty unfair of you to show me this now when I am trying to stay angry with you. You have a library with a ladder and a secret passage. You are clicking off some of my inner fourteen-year-old's bucket list."

He smiled and pushed the buttons, causing the door to click back into place. "It's not one of those airtight spaces. He just wanted to ensure that no light pierced the crevices and leaked into the office. It's well ventilated. The place is old enough to where it has a few hidden passages."

"It's likely a priest hole. We Celts were e're hiding our priests. Or a weapons stash," she said, laying on her thickest Irish accent. Her mood was improving by the second.

"I'm showing you this because I want you to know that Erin is safe. And Davis is a dead shot. I don't have any reason to ever think anything would happen here, but my father was very cautious. He was an agent during the end of the Cold War and during the troubles that still raged in the nineties. So, he had this space converted." She looked at the two cots and a shelf full of water and military rations. He pulled open the door to a file cabinet. "There are two phones in here at all times. But all you'd need to really do is push this button." There was a blue button on the interior panel that said *Police*. "And the rations are circulated to the bin once they expire."

She pointed. "What's up there?" A shallow staircase made of stone led to another floor.

"Lead the way," he said, and she started to climb. It was another level, with a door that appeared to be sealed off.

"Does this door work?" Airmid asked.

"It's caulked shut, but it wouldn't be hard to get through with a knife or box cutter if you really had a mind to check it out. There's likely a well-established colony of spiders and rodents in residence. Under this set of stairs is another narrow passage that leads to the butler pantry. I think the servants used it back in the day. You know, like the backstage of the house."

Airmid tilted her head. "How old is this house?"

"One hundred eighty-two years young. Converted for modern amenities over the years. The groundskeeper's cottage is about a hundred ten."

She thought about the time they'd spent there, tangled in his arms. Then she looked at the sort of loft area she stood in now. There was a pallet on the floor, some toys that appeared well cared for. "Donna keeps it up, I see."

Daniel nodded. "Yes," he said. "More out of habit and maybe out of respect. He wanted to have a space for the kids if we ended up using it. Somewhere we'd feel safe and be distracted. It would seem like he was the paranoid type, but he really wasn't. He was thorough. He thought of all scenarios. And he used this space because it was here. Forgotten. I didn't know about it until I was nineteen years old. When he figured I was old enough to keep the secret and not be drinking beer in here with my mates like a dolt." Daniel heard her soft laugh.

He looked at her, and she seemed to be weighing something. She said, "You can't try to interfere with my job because we slept together. You have to keep whatever this is between us outside of our working relationship."

Daniel narrowed his eyes. "Aye, lovers pretending to be lovers. And my argument is sound. I made it before we came together, and you well know it. Now, I have to look at photos of two dead government agents and then ride into the melee with you on my arm. I hate it. Maybe this is another instance where you were *scratching the itch*, as you put it. But I'm not wired like that. At least, not when it comes to you."

She punched his chest. "Do you think it's any easier for me, Danny? Do you know what it's like to lose someone on the job? Because I do. My shields are there for a reason. They aren't about you. They're about me protecting myself and Erin."

He envied her. He had no such shields to protect himself from her. He moved close, running his hand along her neck. Sweeping his thumb along her jaw. "Forgive me, Airmid. And if you need the shields to stay in place, then so be it. I'm enough of a pathetic sod to keep coming to you anyway."

Her throat choked down some sort of noise. The only sign of her internal battle. Her eyes never left his. She wasn't the sort to shy away from the hard stuff. He bent his head to kiss her. Daniel said again, against her mouth, "Forgive me and just let me in for a while." She lifted her mouth to meet his, her body trembling. They undressed in silence, trading kisses as they went. Where their time in the cabin was raw, edged with unspent lust, this was different. He'd shown her this place as a gesture. Or maybe a peace offering. Or maybe because they couldn't be heard if they argued, which was an amusing thought. He guided her back to the mattresses on the floor, the smell of fresh linen permeating the enclosed space. He didn't take her right away. He ran his hands over her, feathering her skin with kisses. "You are so beautiful."

She felt beautiful when he looked at her. No one had ever made her feel so beautiful. Daniel ran his mouth over the curve of her waist, making approving noises as he explored her curves. He closed a mouth over her nipple as he finally placed his big palm between her thighs. He moaned when he felt her wetness. "Airmid, you're going to be the death of me." Daniel licked his fingers, and she arched off the mattress as she stared at him between her thighs. She'd left a small strip after her Brazilian waxing, and his eyes devoured her. Then he met her gaze and ran the tip of his tongue along the seam of her sex.

Airmid's chest was pumping, noises coming from her as she watched him slide a thumb inside her, parting her flesh with his palm. He found a rhythm as he watched her. So attentive to her reactions. Knowing right where to stay and not to stop doing exactly what he was doing. She wanted his length, stretching her, but she couldn't ask. Couldn't look away as her hips rocked against his mouth. She came from deep inside, long, rolling crests that seemed to have no end. She didn't want the connection to end, holding tight to the contact. To him. She gasped as she rolled into a back-bending climax, one that had her moaning his name. He moved above her and slipped inside her with one thrust. She gripped his length, trembling under him.

Daniel watched his lover as she succumbed to some sort of double climax. She was flushed, her nipples like berries. Her sex on fire. He cupped her head in his hands as he moved in her. Felt her, chest-to-chest, as her heart raced out of control. Her eyes begged him. Always begging for something she wouldn't name. *Mercy*, he thought. But he wouldn't give it. Wouldn't hide the emotion that was on his face. It's what she wanted. To enjoy the physical while keeping the souls separate. But it was too late for him. It had been too late the first time he'd touched her.

# 13

Airmid held her daughter as the stress of the day slowly leaked out of her. Erin was groggy, but she said, "Mammy, sing."

Airmid knew she wasn't a particularly gifted singer, but Erin liked her voice just fine. She started to hum, swaying with her precious parcel draped around her like a baby monkey.

Daniel walked by the open door of Airmid's guest suite and had to stop. She had the child draped over herself, and she was singing to the girl. The sweet way that mothers did, whether they were musically inclined or not. *"I know I'll often stop and think about them, in my life, I love you more ..."*

His mother and his grandmother sang to him until he was about ten, when he thought he was too old for such things. But he'd linger by the nursery door, listening to his mother singing to Gregory and Elizabeth. His papa would tell stories, but it was the women who sang. His heart was heavy in his chest and filled with such longing. He wasn't sure what it was about this situation that provoked the painful feelings. Missing his grandmother? Missing simpler days? Or was it about seeing the way Airmid was with her little girl?

Daniel walked away, knowing he should give them privacy. She was saying goodbye to the lass before they left tomorrow, and he shouldn't intrude. He'd stolen his own time with her, and he'd been thinking about it ever since. He started down the stairs, humming along to the melancholy Beatles song.

A voice came from the doorway, "Danny, are you busy?"

He turned to see Airmid with the child on her hip. His heart pressed against his ribs. "Not at all. What does Princess Erin need of me?" he asked, smiling as the child's hopeful eyes met his. He walked back toward the bedroom, and Erin put her arms out as if she wanted him to take her. Airmid's brows shot up, and he gave her an apologetic look. He knew Airmid was wary of bringing men around her daughter. Didn't want her getting invested in some bloke who wasn't going to be around in a month. But as Erin put her arms around his neck, his papa's face flashed before him. He'd held all three children like this. And Daniel had never felt less loved than the other two. Why was he thinking about that right now?

Daniel asked, "What's it to be? A story?" And they all three walked back into the bedroom so he could tuck this little family into bed. He kissed both of them on the forehead before he sat on the old chair, and the look on Airmid's face wasn't contentment. He couldn't read it. It wasn't fear, exactly. It was apprehension. For as much trust as there was between them, she was more wary of trusting someone with her daughter. But she had stopped him, hadn't she? He'd been silently retreating and Airmid had called him back. So maybe—just maybe—something was happening here. Something that scared the hell out of him, too.

The child's voice was tired and sweet. "I want to hear about Robin Redbreast."

———

They enjoyed a big breakfast together. All the children and adults in the house gathered in the dining room for another family meal. Now, Daniel watched Airmid saying goodbye to her daughter, and it was like a punch in the gut. Brigid was uncharacteristically quiet. Erin walked toward Cora and took her hand. The Murphys couldn't stay past tomorrow, but he was glad they were here. Brigid looked up at him. "Are you sure everything is okay? It seems a bit grim for a non-profit conference. Do you need me to stay? I can try to work something out with the kids' school."

Daniel smiled, trying to brush off her concern. "No, love. Erin will be spoiled rotten, no doubt. Constance has some excursions planned. I think Airmid is just worried about two trips so close together. We've been working a lot."

Brigid said, "Okay, if you're sure. Just check in with Mam. She's had a rash of deliveries close together or she'd probably be visiting as well. You should come to Ireland. Bring Erin and Airmid. We'll have a real piss-up when my brother gets home. Aidan, I mean. Liam will be gone for another three months at least."

He put his arm around her. "I might just do that. And I'll take the ferry over to check on the island house."

"Now you're talking. We'll stir up some good craic, and there are plenty of little ones to keep Erin happy." He gave her a sideways look because Brigid was not subtle. Ever.

Daniel grinned. "We'll see." He hugged her properly, then moved to Erin. He got down on one knee. "Where we're going, they like to carve things out of the wood that grows in the jungle. Can I bring you a dolphin or a turtle?"

Erin said, "I like sharks!"

The corner of his mouth twitched. "Of course you do. I will try to find a shark. And if I can't find that, I will look for something else you might like."

Erin did the oddest thing. She touched his stubbly cheek. Normally, he was clean-shaven, but he'd done the scruffy beard for this mission. She smiled. "I'll miss you, Mr. Danny. When ye come home, can you tell me some more stories?" Then she hugged him around the neck.

He was startled at first, then he put a palm on her back and returned the hug. She was so small. Her bouncy curls and pretty, golden eyes were so precious. But she was fierce like her mum. The type of girl who liked sharks better than dolphins. "I'll think of some more. Maybe I'll call my sister and ask her. She was always one for stories."

He stood, hugging his two nephews in turn and kissing little Declan on the head. Cora hugged him last. Cora said, "Be careful, cousin." And the hair stood up on his neck when she mumbled, *"Fake left."*

# 14

## BELIZE CITY, BELIZE

I t took them ten minutes to find the contact who would aid them during their time in Central America. The man looked to be about sixty and had failed to use sunscreen for the better part of his life. "Harry Stirling, pleasure to meet you all. Let's get you out of this chaos, shall we?"

There were no posh beach resorts in Belize City. Jensen's playground for the wealthy was located on one of the cayes offshore. They'd take a private ferryboat there in about two hours. Harry drove to an urban area where he parked next to a block of flats. "Just up here. Myself and two other ... expats," he said slowly. Meaning, two more agents. "We have the west wing of the fourth floor to ourselves. Perfectly secure."

They walked up four floors of a mildly sweaty stairwell and into Harry's flat. The place was nicer than Daniel had been expecting. Harry handed the three of them bottles of cold water. "Don't drink the water. Even at the resorts. Don't even brush your teeth with the water. Don't trust ice cubes you didn't make yourself. Now, we're pressed for time."

Harry opened a bag of crisps and a bag of some sort of biscuits. "Get your blood sugar up and stay hydrated. Once you get onto the resort, assume you are being watched and assume your room is bugged. Don't use the Wi-Fi or the phone in the room. Jensen could be in deep with the Escobar drug cartel. Not directly, perhaps, but he's tight enough that there's no way his hands aren't dirty. We've actually monitored the private island where his resort is located, thinking maybe the drugs were leaving Belize from there. But that's not the case. You won't find the name on any map, but he named it Ingrit's Caye, after his wife. Ironic considering what a fucking man-whore the bloke is."

Douglas snorted and Harry continued. "Your theory about Punta Gorda is solid. It's close enough to the border to where it would be easier to move the product. We've checked the petrol sales in the country, and there's a petrol station just inland from Punta Gorda that has had abnormally high sales of the type of fuel you'd need for a transatlantic voyage on a large vessel. The boat they seized in Amsterdam was diesel, so it lines up. As for the private caye, the ferry runs back and forth four times a day. Best to get out on the first voyage of the day on Thursday. That gives you two nights to gather anything you can. The real game starts once you are inland.

"My partner, Antony, will be your guide. His father was an agent during the time when this was British Honduras and then after. His mother is Belizean, so Antony is a local as far as anyone is concerned. He's lived back and forth between the UK quite a bit as a youth, and he's been here for the last five years. He's the best, so you are in good hands.

"The resort you'll be going to is surrounded by a river on one side and a cacao farm on the other. Go farther west, and you hit the forest reserve, which borders Guatemala. Be careful. Don't wander out without Antony. Do not trust the police. They aren't all dirty, but I beg you to take that seriously. The cartels in Central America, as well as Columbia, have a very far reach and very deep pockets. This is a dangerous play garden you've stepped into."

Harry handed Daniel a burner phone. "Use that only in an extreme emergency. I don't have a large cavalry to come to your aid. Other than Antony, there's me and another named Justin, who is barely off his mother's teet. He's currently recovering from appendicitis, so he's out of commission."

He held up a photograph. "My neighbors, Justin and Antony. I took this photo a week ago, so it's current. Look carefully. I will never send anyone other than these two. If it is anyone else, they aren't mine. And watch the fucking honeytraps."

Harry took a sip of water, then unrolled a map. "The GPS is spotty in the bush unless your equipment is very high tech. This map is going to be your best friend. It is current with logging roads and dirt roads through the parklands up to date. Take photos of it on your phones, put one in each of your day packs. Fold it up tight, have it in a plastic bag, and keep it on you from the time you get back to the mainland until you are back in England. And I mean each of you. I've got three here all ready to go. This will be your lifeline if you ever get separated for some ungodly known reason. But don't. Stay together and stay with Antony if you leave the resort." As if he needed to repeat it, but Daniel was going to cut the guy some slack. He didn't like having novice jungle trekkers loose in his territory. "I'll be watching the activity in the city, and I'll reach out to Antony if there's anything you need to know. We've worked out a cypher that I have no intention of teaching you. Do you have any questions?"

"Yes," Douglas said. "Jensen has a sidepiece named Rubia. Do we have any information on her?"

Harry didn't make eye contact when he said, "Ah, yes. Tall,

blonde, with D cups? She's fairly new to the entourage. We haven't been able to get close to her. She travels to Jamaica with him, and she has not returned to the EU since the time she's appeared with him. They could be lovers, but I can't confirm it. She hangs all over him, but you know how Jensen is. It is invite-only to his little orgies. Good luck with that. Don't let your *wife* out of your sight. The idea of body autonomy and consent is a bit looser with this crowd." Harry stood. "Let's get you to the ferry dock. I don't want to leave your bags in my boot any longer than necessary. The theft in the city is pretty bad."

Daniel stood, offering a hand to the man. "I'll expect to see Antony on the ferry dock in two days. We'll be on the first boat out."

---

### Ingrit's Caye, Belize

Airmid smiled at the woman who was working the desk at the very posh resort. Opulent, with mosaic tiles and clay pots with exotic trees decorating the lobby. They were only here for two nights. A nod of acknowledgement to the Dutchman who made her skin crawl. They needed information, and so they'd accepted his offer of accommodation. No doubt, someone would contact him directly. He'd find out in Jamaica, perhaps. Would he show up here before they left? They could only spare the two days. Then they'd go into the bush, where an eco-resort with huts and the ultimate green space awaited them. Located between one of the national reserves and Punta Gorda.

Daniel came behind her, putting a hand at the small of her back. Her skin sizzled at the contact through her thin, silk top. This time, Douglas was assigned a room much closer to them, which was good. They didn't like being so far away from him in the Jamaican resort.

Douglas and Daniel were rich-boy chic. Linen and cotton from big designers. And if she wasn't mistaken, Douglas was wearing a pair of Louboutin, tan, suede boat shoes. Easily nine hundred quid. Daniel had upgraded her shoes as well, having them shipped to Hawick on the company dime. She had a Flora Bella raffia handbag and a pair of Tory Burch sandals that, combined, could pay her power bill for two months. She'd been careful not to take advantage, only getting enough clothing to make an appearance for three or four days at a time. But if she showed up here in her Birkenstock knock-offs and a pair of sale-rack shorts from Fenwick's, she'd likely get less of a reaction from the men they were trying to investigate. *Swine.*

They were led to their rooms, walking past the playground for the wealthy. Swimming pools that looked like they'd come from Mount Olympus. Designed for opulence. The gentleman carrying their bags was handsomely tipped and sent on his way. Once the door closed, Daniel said, "Another rough day at the office."

Airmid looked around the suite, knowing it was likely bugged. It was also chosen to show her that Jensen could offer her something of the sweet life. Daniel was well off, but this suite was about five thousand pounds a night. She removed her shoes, glancing at Daniel. They'd discussed this. Knowing the room was likely bugged at best, and cameras weren't out of the question. Daniel was going to use the signal jammer sparingly. And it wasn't foolproof. If the equipment was permanent and hard-wired, it might not work. So, they were going to pretend they didn't know goddamn well that someone was likely monitoring them. Airmid unbuttoned her pants. "I want to get out of these clothes and lie down."

Daniel's eyes roamed over her as she stripped down to a

camisole and panties. She slid between the sheets of the obscenely big bed. He stripped down to his boxer briefs, darkening the blinds and turning off the lights. It was daylight, but it bathed them in a dusky light. Suddenly, a nap seemed like a grand idea. He moved to the center of the bed and pulled Airmid to him. He brought her back to his chest, her curvy ass making his cock stir. He grazed his teeth on her shoulder, rubbing a thumb on her belly. She sighed, settling into him. And to his surprise, they both slept.

———————

Airmid woke in a cocoon of heat and warm skin. He smelled so good that it made her body stir with arousal. He sensed her as she was released from sleep. His hands started to roam, and she felt her nipples harden. She ached between her thighs. Then it hit her. She stiffened, and it seemed to bring him completely awake as well. They were likely being watched. If not with cameras, then certainly with audio surveillance.

Daniel whispered against the shell of her ear, "Sorry." He squeezed her tighter, as if in apology for getting her juiced up. It didn't remotely help the situation. She groaned, in actual pain from the desire. His laughter rumbled against her back. Then he said, "Hold very still and be silent." His tone was low and with a hint of command. He cupped her between her thighs and she jerked. His voice was a husky burr against her neck. "I said, be still. Still and silent, or I'll stop."

Airmid gritted her teeth. He was teasing her, and she wanted to give him a smack. "You are the devil," she murmured. His motions were so smooth, he didn't even stir the blanket. He slid her panties aside with his fingers and glided them along her slippery cleft. Her heart was pounding as he reminded her not to move. To just endure it. Surrender in silence. It just forced her to focus on the contact. On the feel of him flicking the top of her sex.

She put the edge of the blanket between her teeth as he pulled her tight against his hips. His hard length nestled against her ass as he pinned her hips. He dipped inside her while he used the palm of his hand to rub the top of her sex. His other hand was over her heart, feeling the rising frenzy in her body. "When I get you out of this fucking city, I'm going to roger you senseless. And you will be allowed to scream when you come."

Airmid bit down hard on the blanket as she shuddered against him. She felt her body contract around his long finger as he kept the climax going. And she thought the lack of movement, the inability to moan and whimper under him, was going to kill her. But it was erotic as hell. Being forced to endure his ministrations in stasis. She finally settled, and he held her. Kissed her neck and shoulder. It had been hot and frustrating and so fucking dominant that she wanted him to press her into the mattress and take her from behind. He was going to pay for this. When they got out of this resort, it was him who would be screaming for her.

Daniel's phone pinged. "Douglas is coming over in fifteen. Time to rise." He kissed her temple.

She turned in his arms and said against his mouth, "Payback is going to be so sweet."

———

Airmid laughed as Daniel corralled his cock into submission by pinning it against his waistband. He gave her a chiding look, even though it was his own fault. She quickly dressed in a casual but stylish day outfit. Fifteen minutes on the dot, Douglas was at the door. "How was your nap, John? Tara looks well rested, but you certainly don't."

The fucker knew. They'd been friends since they were lads. "Yes, well, that jet lag can be a bit of an ogre. Nothing a drink won't solve."

They made their way through the resort, heading for the main lounge that overlooked the pool. It was raining hard, the intermittent shower coming in by force. Daniel stood behind Airmid as she slid onto a carved barstool. The bartender came to her immediately, his eyes appreciative. His nameplate said *Pietro*.

Airmid opened the small cocktail menu, looking over the selections. She said, "I like the Jungle Remedy, but I'm not much for vodka." She said it in Spanish, and the man's eyes lit up. He recommended substituting the local white rum for the vodka and went about making it for her.

Pietro smiled as he said in English, "And for the gentlemen?"

Douglas said, "A pint of Belikin Premium."

Daniel looked at the sparkling bottles behind the beautiful, mahogany bar. "Two fingers of your Flor de Caña 18 Year. One ice cube."

The man smiled approvingly. "Very nice, sir. Straight from Nicaragua. Very smooth." Once he'd prepared their three drinks, he looked at the computer in front of him. "Your drinks are to be charged to your room, I see."

Daniel hated this. "You can charge the two drinks to the room, but I will buy my wife's drink. Thank you, Pietro." And he slid cash to the man. "Keep the change."

The bartender was speechless at first, but Daniel saw the wedding ring on his finger. Pietro said, "Yes, sir. I understand."

They made idle chitchat with the man, learning that he lived in a village outside the city. He'd worked at the resort for eight years and had two children. They were finishing their drinks when one of the women from the desk approached. "Good afternoon, señors and señora. Your friend Señor Jensen would like to invite you to dine in his private wing tomorrow evening after he arrives. Around six o'clock? It will be a small group, and you would be his honored guests."

Daniel started mumbling something, and Airmid kicked him discreetly under the bar. She said, "That would be grand. Thank you."

The woman left, and they turned to see the bartender watching them. "This is a big honor, Señor MacMillin." Pietro wiped down the table and leaned in. "Be careful," he said so softly, Daniel almost missed it.

———

Daniel and Douglas took Airmid diving, staying on either side of her as she regained her confidence in the water. They headed back to the resort and to their rooms in order to shower and dress for dinner. There was no "town" as it was a private island, so Daniel spoke with the concierge about dinner for three. Afterward, Douglas pulled him aside. Douglas said, "I'm going to spend a little more time with Pietro."

Daniel met Douglas's eyes. "Good idea. Truth be told, the pub fare looks better. I suppose we have to keep up appearances though."

"Dating on the company dime. Shameful," Douglas said, giving him a nudge and Airmid a wink. Then they went to their rooms. Daniel had run clear tape over the top of the door, which was still in place. When they entered the room, he stripped without a second thought. If someone was watching them, let them kiss his big bollocks. Airmid, however, said something about rinsing her suit out in the shower and waited until she was safely behind the shower wall before stripping and washing.

Daniel really couldn't wait to get out of here. It was necessary not to snub an offer from Jensen because they were trying to link him to the drug money. But they could get nothing else accomplished here on this island. And more importantly, when there was a good chance that the room was bugged. The real intelligence-gathering wouldn't happen in this room, so they suffered the indignity of potentially being watched. And he had to admit, making Airmid come against his hand without a whimper had been complete and utter heaven.

Airmid was assertive and self-confident. Even a bit aggressive. To feel her submit to him had been delicious for both of them. He had no doubt that he'd pay for it later, and he couldn't wait. His cock was stirring just thinking about it. Daniel considered going into the second bathroom, but his body drew him in another direction. He walked into the large master bathroom, and the steam rose from the shower. He stepped in and Airmid squeaked.

"I thought you could use someone to wash your back," he said with a devilish smile. Then she shocked the hell out of him by grabbing his cock and stroking him. He hissed. "Fucking hell, woman." Airmid pressed him against the shower wall, and they were as hidden as they were going to get, both in sound and sight. He'd actually checked the shower to make sure it was clear. No way was anyone spying on his woman in the shower. His woman ... yes. She sank to her knees and he cursed because she was not messing around. She took him deep in her mouth and he understood. She was right. Payback was going to be very sweet.

———

Daniel was trying to concentrate on the absolutely delectable meal in front of him, but he couldn't stop the slide show of images going through his mind. He looked at Airmid's mouth, and she gave him a wicked grin. She knew exactly what she'd done to him. She'd ruined him for any other woman. Forever.

The server came to their side and spoke. "Your dinner is complementary tonight, and we'd love to offer you a bottle of wine from our private selection."

Daniel knew this was part of the job, but he didn't like it. Airmid surprised him and the server when she said, "I think not, but we do appreciate it. And please, bring the bill to me. I'll pay for my own meal and that of my husband."

The server appeared confused. "Whatever the señora wishes."

Daniel smirked. "Tara, dear, I think you've baffled the poor child." Because the woman couldn't have been more than twenty.

"The arrogance of that man is endless. He thinks everything is for sale, and I'm not. Though, given the decadence of that orgy, maybe it's you he fancies."

Daniel laughed. "I've respectfully thwarted an interested male on more than one occasion. I assure you, he wasn't interested in me."

Airmid's eyes sparkled. "Do tell."

"A gentleman never talks," he said, taking a sip of his water. "I just gently informed him that despite my polished good looks, I was straight as an arrow." Airmid choked on her own water, eyes lit with mirth.

"Could I interest either of you in dessert?" the server asked sweetly.

Airmid couldn't resist. It was just right there like an open door. "No thank you. I had a decadent dessert about two hours ago, and I am just still so satisfied."

If the woman caught on, her face didn't show it. Daniel's face was actually pink. He gave her a look that said, *Behave.*

They made it an early night, and neither felt compelled to lure the other into a dark corner. They retired to the large bed like a well-established habit. Daniel was reading his father's journal, and Airmid was reading Elizabeth's latest novel. He'd hesitated to bring the journal, as it tied him to his private life. But Airmid was carrying it on her at all times. It wasn't the actual journal but a scanned pdf loaded into his e-reader like any other book. Davis had scanned it for him, and his sister had walked him through the rest. He'd even given it a fake book cover and title. Airmid was also carrying what she could fit of their electronics that couldn't be disguised as camera equipment.

Daniel had no doubt they were being watched, and he wasn't sure why. Did Jensen spy on everyone, or did he suspect something? He had no reason to, but Daniel still couldn't shake the feeling. No one had entered the room. He knew this. He had more than one way of detecting it. As they huddled in together, Daniel felt a sense of peace with Airmid next to him. And it had nothing to do with her being his fake wife. It had to do with her.

He read his father's second journal, and the mood was lighter. His papa was courting Molly Price MacPherson like a lad. They'd been married for years, and he finally felt free to shower his wife with the affections of a man in love. It was sad and sweet but sort of uplifting. He was toward the end of the second installment when it started to get rather private. Something stopped him in his tracks.

*"I know that someday, Daniel will find out about John Mullen and the circumstances of my marriage to Molly. It scares me, but I also know that it is an inevitability. I just want him to be mine while I live. I don't want to share him with another man. And for that, I am ashamed. I understand why Molly did what she did. It was her choice, but I am complicit. He was likely a good man, otherwise my Molly would not have loved him so deeply. But this family is mine to care for, and I am afraid I cannot see a way to let this secret out without breaking my family apart. As our relationship grows, I am certain Daniel will*

*understand someday that he was in a loving home. And despite the origins of this family, it is a blissfully happy one.*

*"Last night, I made love to my wife for the first time. It had been so long for the both of us, it was almost like the first time. Molly was not shy, as I'd expected. She loved me as an equal. It was tender and wonderful. Maybe not with the consuming passion of first love, but she loved me completely. And as we finally consummated our marriage vows, flesh of my flesh, it was the most beautiful moment of my life. I felt loved and wanted, and I left no doubt that I loved and worshiped her as well. Maybe someday, our sweet Daniel will have a brother or sister. He is my heir. He will someday inherit my title. That will never change. But I know the love of a big family, and I'd like for my son to understand the joy of brothers or sisters or even both. At this moment, I feel like our lives are just beginning. I feel reborn."*

Daniel couldn't keep it together, especially lying next to Airmid. Pretending to have everything his father spoke of, but actually having none of it for himself. He got up silently and said, "I just need some air."

His voice was hoarse, and Airmid just said, "Whatever you need."

He opened the sliding door to their private cabana, feeling the ocean air sweep over his bare chest. He walked toward the water, just needing to feel the sand under his feet. He took deep, cleansing breaths, watching the moonlight ripple in the warm, sparkling water. That's when he heard them. Douglas was sitting on a lounger on the beach, and there was a woman with him. He jolted. A German woman. *Rubia.*

He heard Douglas say, "But your English is so much better than my Deutsch, fräulein."

She laughed like a girl. Daniel wondered if she had come ahead of Jensen, or if he was already here. *Interesting.* She said in accented English, "You should come to dinner with your sister and her husband. The invitation was for all of you."

Douglas said, "Aye, well those party guests seem to include a great many couples. I'm not much for being a third wheel."

"Then you can be my guest," she said.

Douglas said, "I don't know what games you and your lover like to play, but he seems the possessive sort. And if he isn't, then I am. I'm not overly fond of sharing."

He heard some stirring, like someone was standing. Rubia said, "I am not his possession. I am no man's possession. Come if you like, or don't. I am sure I will survive your absence if you find your entertainment elsewhere."

Daniel had found a place shrouded by a tree. He watched as Douglas stood swiftly, taking Rubia by the wrist. He said something unintelligible in German, then he kissed the hell out of the woman without hesitation. Now Daniel felt a little like a pervert, but he couldn't move now. Douglas said huskily, "Gute nacht. And Rubia is not a German name. It's a pet name from some lecher. Give me your real name if you want me to escort you tomorrow night."

*Bingo.* Goddamn, Douglas was a natural at this. She said, "It's Freya. But don't call me that at the party. It will cause ... speculation. Something I don't need right now. You are right. Despite my feelings on the matter, Karl is possessive. He thinks to add me to his collection."

Douglas said, "And why do you let him believe he has? Anyone would make the assumption."

"I am not his lover. I am his events coordinator. And, like all men, he enjoys the illusion of virility. As do some of his more important guests. But I am no man's whore, Herr Ruthford. He must be managed at times, but I do manage him. As for why, I have my reasons. Don't concern yourself, Englishman," she said sweetly.

"I'm a Scot, I'll thank you," he said indignantly.

Rubia said, "Well, Douglas of the Scots. I will see you tomorrow. *Auf Wiedersehen.*"

# 15
## BATSUB HEADQUARTERS, BELIZE

Aidan ended the call with his wife and parents. They'd had a small break from the rain in the afternoon. But it hadn't lasted. The base was secure, but there was a village that was in danger of flooding. They may very well be doing humanitarian work for the next couple days.

The rain started and he tilted his face up, thinking of home. It rained a lot in Ireland, but without the stifling heat that came with this climate. He thought of Liam, who relished his time in this lush, unending sea of green. Vibrant and so full of life. There was a beauty to it. Despite the poverty he'd seen in the villages, and the crime he knew to be in the cities, the people seemed happy. Seemed just like him. Several generations living near or with each other. Large meals and lots of children. He'd like to bring his children here one day, to let them meet his new friend Ramirez and his family. Or, to visit St. Clare's and help the mission with their security and their school. Alanna could offer supplemental counseling services.

Aidan shook himself, understanding that his mind needed to be here right now. On this mission. He was getting wet. Or more wet, in any case. He hadn't been truly dry since he'd gotten off the plane. Sweat, rain, and mud sinking into his very essence. He went into the barracks, smiling at the younger soldiers who were trying to sell his lieutenant on the joys of playing Minecraft on their phones. "My seven-year-old plays that game, for God's sake."

Corporal Cunningham said, "It's a good game, sir."

"Do you want some Monster Munch and a juice box before your nap?" Aidan asked.

The lad's brows went up in hopeful expectation. "Do you have Monster Munch?"

———

### Doolin, Co. Clare, Ireland

Alanna always felt better after she and the children were able to speak with Aidan. Only the adults had spoken with him this morning, as the kids were sleeping. She, Sorcha, and Sean had woken up at the buttcrack of dawn to do it, but it was worth it. Sorcha slid a cup of coffee in front of her. "It's good to have you here, love. You and the children. You know how I love a full house. We haven't had a chance to talk though. How are you?"

Alanna took a sip, smiling over the rim of her cup. "Well, now that you mention a full house, I'm surprised at how restrained you've been. Brigid and Cora got in late last night. No one's spilled the tea about what exactly has been going on with Daniel."

Sorcha actually launched herself around the counter, and at nine stone, almost knocked her beloved straight on his ass. "What! Tell me everything. Who is the child he has staying there? Why did he go and hire a nanny for an employee? And why are they all staying in one house? What is she like? Did the children get on with the little one? Was his mother, Molly, there?"

Before she could ask any more questions, her husband's large arms came around her. One across her chest, and one putting a hand over her mouth. Her face scrunched into something akin to a miniature wolverine.

Sean said, "Let's just start with how the lad is doing. Then take them one at a time." And he was laughing at the struggle his wife was putting up. "She's still strong when she's got her blood up." He removed the hand just long enough to kiss her, then he released her and ran for dear life. She threw a scone like a trained sniper, clipping his ear before he stopped, picked it off the floor, and took a bite out of it.

"That man! I'll box his ears!" Sorcha said, red-faced and panting. Alanna was laughing so hard that she couldn't even stand anymore. Sorcha bent down and shook her by the shoulders. "I need news, lass."

"What in the bloody hell are you doing to my sister-in-law?" The voice came from behind them, near the back door. Brigid was standing there, baffled, with her hands on her hips. "Stop mucking about. I've got news about Danny."

Given her ability to give more up-to-date news, Sorcha abandoned Alanna and sat, face toward Brigid, with expectation in her eyes. Sean yelled from the other room, "Yer a bunch of nosey peahens!"

"Shut your gob, you thick-headed lout!" But Sorcha was barely holding in her own laughter. She turned back to Brigid. "Tell me everything."

———

Alanna screamed, "Shut up! He didn't!"

Brigid's look was deliciously devious. "He did. He read to both of them until the little girl fell asleep. She'd had a nightmare. And they both call him Danny, not Daniel or MacPherson like you said she did in the beginning. And Cora said he kissed them both on the head before she alerted him to her presence."

The woman sounded like she was narrating a mystery novel. "She came into the room just as he was leaving. Then he and Cora went to have some warm milk and talk for a bit. You should see how he looks at Airmid. And THEN! Jaysus, I just about died when he took the morning off with her and they rode the entire estate. And then it rained, and they didn't come back for quite a long while. And when they did, I swear the lass looked addled. Like rain-soaked sex addled. It was"—she slapped the counter and squealed—"it was like watching my brothers dance around their women in the beginning. He's got it bad. I know it!"

Sorcha stood, leaving them without a word. They looked at each other, then followed. "Mam, what are you doin'?" Brigid asked, following her into her bedroom. She already had her suitcase open on the bed. She started opening drawers. "This is going to take a professional. Someone's got to seal this deal before he or she makes a cock-up of the whole thing!"

Brigid and Alanna were laughing so hard, Sean finally came into the room. He took one look at Sorcha and threw his hands up. "Jesus wept, woman. Stay out of it."

Sorcha snorted. "I've got five sons, a daughter, and a nephew married. Don't tell me my business, Sean O'Brien. Just get on that wee phone of yours and get me to Scotland."

———

**Ingrit's Caye, Belize**

"You can come out from behind that bloody tree, now, you wanker," Douglas said.

Daniel approached and they walked closer to the water, where the sounds of the sea might camouflage their little chat. He said lowly, "I hadn't come out here to bear witness to your seduction skills, but well done. How did you find the German tart?"

"She's actually not a tart, despite the show she puts on. And I didn't. She approached me. I'm not sure who the hell she is, but she's more than she appears. I'm wondering if she's more involved in this than we thought. Perhaps not a pleasure girl, as Airmid so creatively put it. I can't speculate. I'll just stay with her tomorrow."

"Perhaps she is more. Good work," Daniel said. "And be careful."

"Honeytraps were well covered in our training, but thanks," Douglas said. "What brought you from your nice, soft bed?"

Daniel looked over the water, pausing before he said, "Ghosts." He raised his hands. "More rain. Great. Time to head to bed."

He went back to his cabana, finding that Airmid had waited up for him. She asked softly, "Are you okay?"

Daniel just slid in next to her, and she took his shoulders in her arms. He laid his head on her chest, and she ran her nails along his scalp. This is what he needed. She was what he needed. He should have never brought that damn journal. He needed his head in the game at all times. He needed to protect his best friend and the woman he was quickly falling in love with. She may be able to keep her distance from him emotionally, but it didn't affect how his own heart recognized her as his true mate. The type of soul bond that the O'Briens spoke about. He smelled her skin, drifting into a relaxed and contented state, and he felt like he was home.

———

Douglas smirked at Daniel as they watched Airmid murder the large, local-style breakfast. Fry Jacks, beans, thick pork sausages, jams and honey, eggs, and a huge array of tropical fruit. She looked up from her feast. "What? It's good. Am I supposed to act like I don't eat?"

Daniel reared back and said, "Absolutely not. You're just so—"

Douglas interjected, "Enthusiastic."

"Adorable," Daniel offered.

Airmid looked at Douglas. "See, brother. I'm adorable."

Douglas raised a brow. "Yes, and young. Young enough to burn it off just by breathing. I'm going to be in my jowly phase before you know it."

One side of Airmid's mouth turned up. She said very lowly, "You forget, darlin'. I've seen you bare-assed as a babe. You're most certainly not headed into your jowly phase."

Daniel stiffened, narrowing his eyes at Douglas. The Scotsman just gave a husky laugh. "Watch out, Tara love. Old John's probably closer than myself to the jowly phase."

Daniel picked up a cube of mango and beaned it at his best friend. Then the mood at the table shifted as Rubia, a.k.a. Freya, came to their table. She ran a hand across the top of his shoulder. "Guten morgen, everyone. How did you sleep?" Rubia asked with a smile. "Mr. and Mrs. MacMillin? Is that correct?"

Airmid smiled at the woman, despite her reservations. And despite the fact that she looked at Airmid's two partners like she was planning a threesome. She understood completely, but she didn't like it. She said, in passable German, "Good morning, Rubia. Please call me Tara." Then proceeded to ask her what parts of the island were accessible to guests. She had a mind to take a walk.

Rubia said in English, "Karl told me you had a gift for languages. Very good, Tara. The island in its entirety, to answer your question. There are walking paths, but there are also motorized carts. All the Americans call them golf carts, I believe. How would you feel about a private tour? I am free today." Airmid watched as her hand rubbed up and onto Douglas's neck. Interesting. Apparently, Danny was right. Her brother from another mother had made some progress. "There's a beautiful, private cove I would love to show you."

Douglas narrowed his eyes. "Don't you have to check in?"

Her face tightened, and she actually removed her hand from his back. "Mr. Jensen doesn't arrive until the afternoon. And no, I don't have to check in. It's so nice of you to worry."

Airmid gave Douglas a look that said, *You are being a jackass. You are supposed to be kissing her ass.* Airmid said, "We would love that, Rubia. Truly. Can you give us until half eight?"

"Yes, that is perfect. Better to get out before the rain starts again. We'll only get a brief respite. The tropical storm comes to shore in three or four days. There's already some flooding on the mainland."

———

Airmid stripped off her shorts and top, and Daniel noticed that she'd opted for her personal swimsuit this time. An athletic brand with significantly more coverage. Despite her efforts, she was just as appealing. Airmid didn't need to show skin to cause a stir in the room. And he was surprised when Jensen's arm candy, Rubia, was in an even more conservative suit.

The rocky, little cove was sprinkled with urchin and mollusks and plants peeking out of crevices. The sky was not the tropical blue they'd enjoyed in Jamaica. A storm was coming. Was almost here, in fact. They'd come at the beginning of the rainy season, and the tropical storms had started early. Tropical Storm Azriel was due to hit landfall in two days. Daniel saw the bands of weather in the distance. Showers that would just keep coming, followed by bone-bending wind. Jesus. The timing wasn't lost on him. He was glad they'd be off the beach when it happened, at least.

The women were ganging up on Douglas, attempting to dunk him. He was strong though. He currently had a palm on Airmid's forehead that guaranteed she couldn't reach him, and his other arm around Rubia's waist. But Airmid was tough, and she used his weight against him. She dunked under the water, and he saw right when she swept the leg. Rubia grabbed his flying foot and pushed up at the ankle, suspending his leg just as a wave came over his face. Daniel couldn't help it. He barked out a laugh so loud and boisterous that Airmid's face lit from within. She crooked her finger at him and he went, by God. Because he couldn't think of a better way to die than pinned under Airmid Roberts.

---

Daniel was worried. Douglas might be playing a role, but men often let their cocks lead them astray. Contrived, seductive Rubia was something he could have resisted. Played the game. But she was different away from the den of vipers she kept company with. He sighed. "I know you, Douglas. You've got a thing for rescuing females. Be careful. Don't let your guard down." They were back on the private beach, standing in the surf and talking low.

Douglas snorted a bitter laugh. "Hello there, Pot. I'm Kettle."

"It's not the same and you know it. And Air—Tara doesn't need anyone. I'm not a knight in shining armor. I'm a pathetic sap who's likely going to get sent on my way someday. So, don't compare the two. And don't unnecessarily provoke the beast tonight. For all you know, she's trying to make him jealous. He seems to share his affections with that Delilah woman, and maybe she's just using you to push his buttons. We don't need that kind of trouble."

"And I'm using her. So, no problems here. I know what I'm doing. So, I'll give you the same lecture. Our Tara"—he emphasized the name—"she can take care of herself. Dim down the jealous husband vibe a tad. Now, I need a shower before dinner tonight."

————

The rain was coming down like mad as they enjoyed the balmy ambience of extensive covered patio areas. The interior of the house was opened as well. Jensen walked in and greeted them like a man who thought he was royalty. But Daniel felt the tension between them as he shook the man's hand.

He was surprised to see Arturo Rey, or Reyes, as they now knew, swaggering with his personal guards never far from his back. The woman they'd met in Jamaica, Delilah, was on his arm. She looked resigned, but not thrilled. She was a lovely, regal woman with light-brown skin and large, dark eyes. Her hair cascading down her back in silk waves. Black as night.

Jensen shook hands with Douglas, and it was awkward. His grin said he didn't care that Rubia had shown up on the Scotsman's arm. Maybe even implying he was allowing or encouraging it. *I'm no man's whore.* What was her deal? Was she a pretty face to the business end? Another European connection? Daniel accepted a drink Rubia had recommended named The Modern. Raspberries garnished the martini-style drink. Rum, rose syrup, some juices. It was actually less sweet than a lot of the tropical drinks on hand. He lifted the drink and said, "Thank you, Rubia. It's grand."

Dinner was a formal affair. Jensen kept Arturo at his side with Delilah next to him. There was, as much as Airmid could determine, some sort of underling to the Minister of Defence. A very interesting addition that told Daniel all he needed to know about the drug trade in Belize. The man had no companion. That could infer a few things as well because the man had a wedding ring on his hand. He either hoped to score a sidepiece tonight, or he didn't want his wife anywhere near these people. Maybe both.

Likely, the entire government wasn't corrupt, but you had to know where to have an *in* when it came to important people turning a blind eye. The other couple appeared to be from the Netherlands, like Jensen. Or maybe the Netherland Antilles off the coast of South America. Airmid was going to engage them in conversation and would be able to tell.

Airmid looked down at the first course, the starter, and tilted her head a bit. She was very adventurous with food, but she was having an issue identifying what this was. She noticed Jensen staring. He smiled and she said, "Well, now. Is it conch?"

He laughed and said, "Bravo, Mrs. MacMillin. Conch is prepared many ways in this part of the world, but my chef has perfected my favorite. It is similar to the flavors of ceviche, but a bit more refined and like a salad."

"I'm sure it is wonderful," she said graciously. She took a bite and put her hand in front of her mouth. Nodding, she said, "It's gorgeous."

Airmid spoke with the couple next to her, and they were indeed from Curacao, not the Netherlands. They'd moved there ten years ago, and the husband was exploring a resort partnership with Jensen in Bonaire or Curacao, depending on what the realtor came up with. She suspected this was how Jensen kept his finger on the pulse of his home state. Territory islands with connections to the wealthy on both sides of the Atlantic.

She started when the woman to her left nudged her. Apparently, Arturo Reyes was speaking to her. "I'm sorry, señor. Woolgathering."

Daniel wanted to stab Reyes in both eye sockets as his gaze dipped to Tara's chest. They were speaking in Spanish, so Daniel couldn't follow at the speed they were talking. It was Rubia who dipped her head near his ear. "He is honored to have you in his home. He wants to know where you are staying."

He hoped she remembered the lie, and as he heard her answer, Daniel realized that she had. Double reservations. The others would be canceled when they didn't show. He didn't need to know that, however. They were assured this new eco-tourism resort was new and off their radar. Arturo smiled, and it was positively reptilian.

"You must allow my guards to escort you. This is a beautiful country, but it can be dangerous." He said this in English to Daniel. Delilah's eyes widened just a bit, but he saw it. She looked around very carefully, then gave one back and forth of her head. So discreetly, as she tilted her head like she was scratching her brow. But he saw it. He'd had no intention of accepting, but it was interesting that this lovely woman, entrenched in this group, would take the risk of warning him.

Daniel said, "It's already taken care of, señor, but thank you. My foundation provides security and transportation." He politely requested that the server refill Airmid's water glass from the

sparkling water provided to the guests. It interrupted the conversation enough to cause Arturo to take his attention elsewhere.
When Daniel looked up, Delilah was looking at him again. No
head motions, but it was in the eyes. Relief. Approval. What the
hell was going on with this woman? Was she trapped in this situation? He looked at her with fresh eyes. Twentysomething, lovely,
and unlike Rubia, who could go with more freedom, Delilah was
rarely out of reach.

He looked at Airmid, not much older than the two women,
and wondered what these men might do to her if they had her
isolated and alone. Jensen pretended to be a gentleman, but he
was a bloody pervert and too rich to be honest. The company he
kept spoke volumes. A top-tier drug dealer and a politician. Why
were they here? It couldn't just be Airmid.

This wasn't a sex party. This was dinner with some key
players present. If he was able to get his claws into Daniel's *non-
profit*, which had the appearances of a legitimate organization,
what would he do with it? Launder drug money? The thought had
occurred to him with the couple living in Curacao. There was a
strategy here at this table, and Daniel wasn't sure how to get the
bigger picture before they left. He looked at Douglas and
wondered if it would be him who uncovered this. Jensen was so
busy eye-fucking his pretend wife across the table, he didn't even
seem to care about Rubia. Thank God. He didn't need some sort of
lovers' spat screwing this whole thing up.

———

Airmid looked out at the night, drenched in consistently heavy
rain. She smacked a mosquito from her arm. Daniel said, "We
should go in. You're right under the light, and they seem to find
you as delicious as I do."

They couldn't discuss the dinner. If the room was bugged—and he didn't doubt it was—they needed to appear as if nothing was wrong. Airmid said, "The meal was gorgeous. It's rare I indulge in lobster." She didn't elaborate, but he could figure out why. Dinner for two at their house was likely more Erin friendly. He saw the sadness on her face and knew she was thinking of the little girl. "Soon enough, love."

Once they got out of here in the morning and onto the mainland, she'd be free to call home. Or at least, his home. Airmid curled in bed with him, facing him in the dim lighting. He kissed her softly, then whispered in her ear, "And soon, we'll be free to make love, my darling Airmid." He put his forehead to hers and saw the tears misting in her eyes.

––––––––

**Hawick, Scotland**

Davis took Sorcha's bag out of the boot, smiling so warmly as he directed her toward the house. "I've set you up in a guest room on the second floor. Wee Erin and the nanny are occupying the third floor."

Sorcha crinkled her brow and said, "Brigid said she was sleeping with her mam. Is she alone in the room, now?"

Davis shook his head. "She's in the nursery now, and there is an adjoining servants' chamber where Constance sleeps. She's always available. The child has been quite used to the bustle of a full house though. I'm afraid she's finding us rather sedate for her taste."

Sorcha didn't doubt it. First, Alanna had come with her children, then Brigid. "Well, I've got several grandchildren under my belt. I'll see if I can help Constance keep the lass entertained."

Donna greeted them at the front door. "Mrs. O'Brien. It's good to see you again. You really shouldn't have stayed away so long."

Sorcha had only visited once, when Aidan was stationed in England. She'd never stayed the night. It felt strange to be in the home of the man who had raised Daniel. The man who had claimed him instead of her brother. Love made you do strange things though. And she'd met enough unwed mothers to sympathize with the fear and desperation. She wasn't sure she'd ever forgive Molly Price—or Molly MacPherson in this case—but she wouldn't blame the man who had loved Daniel like his own. The call had been Molly's to make, and she'd chosen to leave John in her past. Making Daniel an earl.

She'd met Daniel when he found her in Belfast. Had fainted at the sight of him. Sorcha had barely remembered most of the exchange. She'd thought he'd held some sort of title with the British peerage. A barony or something. She'd never paid much mind to the aristocracy, being from Northern Ireland. But once Aidan had spoken more in depth with Daniel, they'd all been shocked out of their knickers to find that he was an honest to goodness earl. Not one of the big, prestigious earldoms. Daniel kept a low profile. He'd actually passed on a seat with the Lords of Parliament, only appearing and voting if it was unavoidable. He didn't want anything to do with the political side of things, maybe.

When he'd found out about his parentage, Daniel had actually told his siblings. Wanting both of them to understand that he'd be more than willing to pass the title on to one of them, as he was not blood related to the deceased Earl of Hawick. But they'd declined. Hadn't wanted the responsibility. And she wondered, too, if they hadn't wanted to take one more thing from Daniel. After all, Robert MacPherson had named Daniel his heir to the title and the unentailed estate.

Sorcha smiled as she looked around. "These old manor homes are so beautiful. I'm glad to see Daniel so happy and prosperous."

Donna said, "He is that, Mrs. O'Brien. He's been a good employer, and he takes care of the surrounding tenants where he can. It's why he hired Constance from the neighboring village, like the old ways. He wants to provide as many jobs as he can manage."

"Donna, you must call me Sorcha. Please, I insist," Sorcha said. She turned toward Davis. "I'll get settled and stay out of your way. I just came to help with the child. Daniel was good to do this for his colleague. And I've been told I have a way with the little ones."

"I can imagine you do," Davis said. "Your grandchildren are an absolute delight." He walked up the stairs, carrying her small bag. "And Cora is the oldest, I hear. She's rather wonderful."

"Yes, she is. She was my first. The only daughter of my only daughter. We have an uncommon number of boys on the O'Brien side. Now, I mean it, Davis. Don't bother about me. I don't want to add any more to your duties. You should have let me hire a car."

"I wouldn't hear of it. You are family, Mrs. O'Brien. Our Danny's aunt. We are informal here though. I hope you don't mind us all having dinner together. Donna has prepared a very large vat of stew with the spring vegetables and a rather marvelous rhubarb crumble."

Sorcha walked into her room, turning to him. "That sounds absolutely perfect. Now, show me the child." She couldn't keep the excitement from her face.

Davis grinned and narrowed his eyes. "If I didn't know better, Mrs. O'Brien, I'd swear you had an agenda."

Sorcha looked unrepentant at the lie. "Me? Perish the thought."

As they walked up to the third floor, Davis said, "We adore Miss Erin. And her mother is a wonderful, kind, beautiful woman.

From the North, like yourself. Our Danny is very doting on them both." He was glancing at her from the corner of his eye, not hiding the smirk.

Sorcha said, "If I didn't know better, Davis, I'd swear it was you who was up to something." Then they both laughed as coconspirators, walking down the hall to the manor nursery.

# 16

## INGRIT'S CAYE, BELIZE

The sun wasn't even fully up when they headed to the ferry dock. Airmid was uncharacteristically quiet. "What is it, love?" Daniel asked. "You're pale and quiet."

Airmid looked around. "I checked my private email on our secured device. I will tell you when we're back on the mainland."

"Okay, fair enough. Whatever it is, we'll sort it out," Daniel said. Taking her hand, he gave it a squeeze. She cracked her neck, nervous and out of sorts despite the weak smile she gave him.

They rode to the mainland in silence, the early morning leaving them all with too little sleep. They'd exited the private dinner after the digestif. Airmid asked him and Douglas, "What was that drink at the end?"

Douglas answered, "It's a digestif, similar to an aperitif, but at the end instead of the beginning. Some drink cognac or some other type of brandy. That one was a Spanish liqueur called Pacharán. It's made from the berries of the Prunus Spinosa, also known as the blackthorn. The berries are called sloes. The British use them to make sloe gin, which is the inferior of the two liqueurs. The Spaniards take the win in this instance." Airmid and Daniel both just stared at him. He said, "What? I know my spirits." He shrugged. "I like to know how things are made."

That was why he'd been such a good analyst. Attention to detail and a steel-trap memory. Although, the way he'd worked that table last night, Douglas was a natural at fieldwork. Daniel smirked. "Remind me of all that when it's time for your birthday."

Douglas smiled. "You can count on it, brother."

———————

They made their way to Harry's flat, knowing his colleague Antony lived next door. Antony would be the one driving them through the bush and to the resort. He'd be staying on-site as well, and Daniel was eager to get underway.

They knocked on the apartment next to Harry's, and a younger man answered. "You must be Tara and John?" Even this trusted man didn't know their real names. Didn't want to know them. "And Douglas Ruthford. So good to see you made it back from Ingrit's in one piece. Please, come in."

That's when Airmid finally spoke. "I need to make a phone call. It will be brief, but it can't be helped. I have to call our boss in Edinburgh." That's all she said, and she disappeared into the guest lav.

Daniel looked at Douglas. "I have no idea."

Antony said, "Let's just have a look at the map, and I'll show you the routes we will take through the forest." They could hear Airmid's frantic whispering, and Daniel was ready to barge into the space and demand to know what was going on.

Antony was showing Douglas the routes from the southern and western borders of Guatemala. "My suspicion has always been that they were breaking up shipments from Columbia into two locations. From Guatemala, they go through both Belize and Honduras. The Escobar drug cartel has a foothold in both countries. There's a war going on over territory, which is why they've moved up to these areas. They are smaller than the cartels shipping out of Venezuela and Brazil. They transport through the Caribbean, and we think they are entering Europe through the Netherlands and Belgium. The Brazilian and Venezuelan shipments are entering mostly through Spain and Portugal, but there is crossover sometimes. That's where the conflicts happen. This isn't even taking into account what is traveling into the United States via Mexico. The shipment they intercepted in the Netherlands was small, comparatively. And there are some European distributors who want their product."

"How do you know this?" Douglas asked, narrowing his eyes.

Antony said, "I have informants. And no, I'm not going to tell you who they are. Just a concerned citizen, as they say."

"But this person's testimony isn't enough. Or they won't go public with it?" Daniel prodded.

Airmid came out of the bathroom, and Daniel could tell she'd been crying. "Tara," he said softly. "What is it?"

Airmid said, "It's nothing. I have it handled. What did I miss?"

————

They took the Southern Highway to the entrance road that led to the Agua Caliente Luha Wildlife Sanctuary. There was a crossroads with the Western Highway that would take you into Guatemala, which wasn't what they wanted.

After leaving the main highway at a town called Dump, things got interesting as they drove to a remote area between San Antonio and a tiny village called Crique Jute. Not off road so much as very rural and surrounded by the forest.

When they arrived at the resort, Daniel noted that Airmid had said exactly twelve words during the entire hour-long drive. Her face did seem to lighten when she saw the resort. Private, hut-like cottages that were on stilts. Good for flooding, no doubt. And it was certainly coming down. If this had been a real honeymoon, he'd have wanted a refund. He thought briefly about his cousin Aidan. Training in this muck must be murder. Luckily, they had paved pathways to the large main building that housed the check-in, as well as the spa and a farm-to-table restaurant.

"If they don't have at least four dishes that involve chocolate on the menu, I'm leaving and throwing my lot in with Jensen." Airmid didn't say it with a smile. She said it like she was at her wits end and needed to find some love and succor in a plate of mole.

Antony said, "Oh yes, Señora Tara. You will find the menu to be very local and very delicious. The blue tilapia is *muy bueno*."

Daniel said, "I'm starved as well. Let's get settled in the rooms and then see what they have for a late lunch."

They checked in with a young woman who was delighted to have three of her new cottages rented. They'd opened a couple of months ago, but the early rain and tropical storm warning had caused a rash of cancellations. All the better for them.

When they got into the private dwelling, Daniel removed his shirt, wanting to let it dry. Airmid just sat at the small table and stared out the window. That's when the tears started. He knelt in front of her. "You can let go, now. It's just me," he said softly. He didn't know what was wrong, but Airmid was tough. She didn't break down for no reason. And he had to give her the respect of letting her decide to tell him. Not push. She put her forehead on his shoulder, and he pulled her close. "I'm here for you, love. Come what may." So, she told him.

"They finally went to the neighbor's house. The ones who

have been watering my plants. When Mrs. Doyle refused to let them inside my house, they demanded to know where I had run off to with their granddaughter. She told them to sod off."

Daniel laughed. "I already love Mrs. Doyle."

Airmid smiled weakly. "Aye, she's a good sort. By the end of the day yesterday, a bailiff showed up with a summons from family court. They refused it, of course. I mean, they aren't living with me. They gave the man my cell phone, but as you know, no one is answering that phone. So, I had to call Morgan and have her intervene on my behalf. I mean, I don't have any family in England. My mam and da can't just leave their jobs and handle this, and the bottom line is that they need to serve me, not my neighbor. I'm her mother. Because there's no doubt this is about Erin."

"You said that they were barely involved. What do you think prompted this?" Daniel asked.

She wiped her face with her palms. "I don't know. I've never kept them from her. I have been very accommodating when they actually show an interest. I'm not exaggerating when I tell you that it's maybe two or three times a year for an afternoon. She barely knows them. It's so forced, but I just thought it was important for her to know her father's family."

Daniel thought about it. "Sometimes it is. And sometimes, family doesn't need access. I'm so grateful for the O'Briens. And I'm grateful for my MacPherson relations. My mother's family was barely around. I mean, you know the story. They always favored my younger siblings because they knew I was the result of an indiscretion. I didn't understand when I was little, and my mother barely spoke to them because of the way they behaved when they did come around. Now I know, and honestly, they can go rot. I do the bare minimum for my mother and siblings. If the judge didn't order you to do visitations, then I'd think long and hard about exposing her to them. She's going to get old enough to understand that they treat her differently. And you know they won't keep their holes shut about how they feel about you."

"I know. Luckily, Tommy was an only child. There aren't cousins or aunts and uncles. No close ones, anyway. And you're right. Unfortunately, it looks like I'm going to need a lawyer again." She raised a fist and pumped it in the air. "Thank God for overtime, am I right?" It was meant to be a joke, but Daniel wasn't smiling.

"I have a good solicitor in the family. I'd like to help if you'll allow it. He's licensed to practice in the UK and Ireland. He's very good. He's related to the O'Briens. Nolan Carrington is his name."

She rubbed her face. "My attorney from last time was in the North. I think I'd like his name. Is he expensive?" She shook herself. "You know what, don't answer that. If he's good enough for the Earl of Hawick, I'll sell a kidney if I have to."

"You'll likely get the family discount," Daniel said.

She took in his face, considering his words. "I'm not family."

He pulled her closer to him, not daring to say what was on his mind. They were on the job, and he wasn't going to cloud her brain anymore. "I'll call him when we get back. As for the two asshole grandparents, they have no rights to any information right now. And you are out of the country. The judge isn't going to penalize you because you have a job. Erin is well cared for. I just got an email while we were at Antony's flat. My aunt Sorcha is visiting. The midwife I told you about. She was likely beside herself with envy that Brigid and Alanna got their hands on a new bairn and she was left out. Davis and Donna adore her, so Erin is officially the most spoiled little princess in the entirety of the United Kingdom."

Airmid stifled a sob, and he held her closer. He said, "I'm here, love. Whether you ask or not. Whether you push me away or not. Come what may." And he meant every word.

Airmid sank into Daniel's body, afraid to take what he offered. He was a powerful man. And when he cared, he held nothing back. It's why a titled, important man had chosen to serve the Crown in this way. Why there was a costly nanny watching her daughter right now in an obscenely beautiful manor house. The Devon grandparents-from-hell had fought and lost once already, so she wondered what was driving all of this. What the hell were they thinking, serving her with a summons to family court? She wasn't sure she wanted to know, but one thing was for certain. She'd sell her soul to the devil before she'd part with Erin.

# 17

## HAWICK, SCOTLAND

Sorcha smiled at the small child as the groom led her around the lovely pasture. Sorcha was on her own horse, something for which she had her daughters-in-law to thank. Izzy had gotten her up on a horse in Arizona, after not riding for over a decade. Even back then, it had been short family trail rides just to appease her only daughter. Izzy's grandfather had been the one to teach her about the western saddle. Maureen, Seany's beautiful bride, was a horse enthusiast and riding instructor. She'd led them along the paths of the Connemara National Park. A thanks for some favors that the O'Brien clan had done for the therapeutic riding center.

She felt blessed to have such a large family and to see all of her children married and happy. Even her extended children, like Josh and Tadgh. All with loving mates and strong unions. Then there was Daniel. The nephew she'd never known she had until nearly five years ago. She watched the beautiful child smiling over the top of the pony's head, patting the beast on the head like a doting mother.

Sorcha said, "Ye've got a way with the ponies, Erin. You'll have to visit more often or he'll likely miss you."

"He's a girl," Erin said confidently.

Sorcha looked at the groom and he just shrugged. "It's the neighbor's Shetland. And apparently, Napoleon has been renamed. Erin, love, tell Ms. O'Brien what you've named your wee pony."

Erin patted his soft, cream-colored neck. "Her name is Tinker-bell. She's a fairy horse."

"Tinkerbell, is it? Well, that's much nicer than Napoleon. He was an old devil. Tinkerbell is quite perfect altogether."

Erin smiled. "You talk like my mammy. Not like my child-minder at home or my grandmother."

"Do you see your grandmother very often?" Sorcha asked, treading softly.

"No, she and my grandfather don't come to see me much. I only remember a couple of times. We went for ice lollies. I don't like my grandmother. She's mean to Mammy."

Sorcha froze, looking at the groom. "Really, I'm sorry to hear that. I'm sure your mammy doesn't deserve that. She's a good sort if she made you."

"I don't like them," Erin said again. "My granny in Ireland is a nice granny. And my uncle and my grandda. My other grandfather smacked me for calling him Grandda. He said I sounded like a paypus."

The groom stiffened, his face going murderous. Sorcha said calmly, "He struck you? Because you sounded like a papist?" Erin just nodded. "Where did he hit you, love? Did you tell your mam?"

"No, they said not to tell her, so I didn't. I didn't want to make my mam sad. They're mean to her, and I don't want him to hit her. He hit me here," she said, pointing to the spot on her head behind her ear. That son of a bitch was going to pay if Sorcha had to drive over Hadrian's Wall and repay that cuff behind the ear herself.

———

### Jacinto Ville, Belize

Aidan yelled over the din of rain and wind. "The college students have arrived. Let's get everyone in the trucks and move to the next village! The primary school in San Filipe is being made into a shelter!" Kearsley gave him a thumbs-up, walking to the group of soldiers. Ramirez did the same with his team.

They had two large trucks and two Jeeps. The sandbags were running low, but they didn't have time to get more. Hopefully, they had some in San Filipe. The college kids from the local Bible College had secured their belongings in one dormitory and were starting to take stranded families to the other dorm. A few professors were driving two school buses, but with this mud, Aidan didn't like it. It was so damn slippery without four-wheel drive. There was no help for it though. He hoped the road was intact by the time they loaded everyone and went on their way.

The storm was almost here, and they'd been slammed with bands of weather for a full twelve hours. Creeks and rivers were swelling. Reservoirs were full. And the coast was getting ready to get slammed hard. The Belize military was handling the coastal cities, so the Belizean Army had asked the British command if they could aid their local forces with helping the surrounding villages. Of course they would. It wasn't even a question. They could train in this, but what better training than having boots on the ground in the middle of this downpour? Weather always affected the mission.

Aidan hopped into the passenger seat of the large truck,

looking at Ramirez. "Just a wee bit of rain, eh?" And the men laughed as they headed for San Filipe.

———

Daniel had insisted Airmid try to sleep. They'd been up late, and he needed her freshly rested. This weather was going to offer a bit of camouflage, but it was also going to make traveling the bush a nightmare. He showered, cursing Antony for not servicing the AC in his H3. The outside of the vehicle was painted with Antony's cover occupation—Belizean Jungle Tours and Adventures. And if Daniel had been a paying customer, he'd have demanded a refund for the subpar air conditioning.

He soaped his body mindlessly, running a hand over his stubble. His hair was as long as he'd ever kept it. Curling over his ears and around his collar. All of this time in the sun was bringing out some coppery highlights, which would no doubt horrify his maternal grandparents. Too much like their daughter's indiscretion, no doubt. Both of his parents had rich, brown hair. The red came from the Mullen side, from his biological father.

They'd finally been able to call home, and he thought perhaps it had made Airmid feel better to see her daughter's face. Davis hadn't heard anything about a summons, which meant the lass's grandparents didn't know where she was. Good. They had no right to the information. He'd even been able to speak with his aunt Sorcha, who had briefly told him about their ride. She hadn't said anything else but mentioned that she needed to speak more when they arrived home. When she'd heard that the grandparents were on the warpath, she'd advised Daniel that she'd be staying the week. Surprising, but he knew his aunt. She was protective of her family, and obviously, she considered Erin an extension of that obligation. They all did. Davis was ready to go on a rampage himself. Erin was in good hands.

Daniel toweled off, walking into the bedroom to see that Airmid was trying and failing to doze off. She was in cotton shorts and a tank top. Not the normal finery she'd wear while in the company of Jensen and his entourage. It was intimate, seeing her like this. Wearing something she'd wear in the privacy of her own home. No makeup and her hair in a flouncy bun on the top of her head.

His cock stirred at the sight of her. Airmid's eyes roamed over his body, seeing what she did to him. He threw the towel on a nearby chair and went to her, hissing under his breath as she arched on the bed. She wasn't shy with him. She was comfortable with herself and her own desire. But her eyes held a hint of vulnerability that just fucking slayed him.

Daniel came over her, nestling between her thighs as he kissed her. He mumbled to her, easing her. Seducing her with his words. "I want to feel you. I need inside you," he mumbled against her mouth. He slid her shirt over her head, and her soft, supple breasts pressed against him. He worshiped her body then. Slow and deliberate. First with his mouth. Then with his hard length. He shuddered as he said her name.

Airmid was so lost in the feel of Daniel, she had to bite her lip to keep from weeping. The way he loved her body. The way he looked at her. The friend he was to her, even far away from a bed. She ran her thumb over his mouth, replacing it with her lips as he rocked his powerful hips inside her. He moaned as he let go, and she watched him. Greedy for this connection and this escape.

Daniel shattered as he felt Airmid's climax join with his own. He pushed her leg up with his knee as he deepened his strokes, feeling himself fall into the abyss that was Airmid. A woman, after all these years, who might be his salvation or his undoing. He wondered if he'd ever be anything more to her than this beautiful escape. *I'm not family,* she'd said. And she was right. They were work partners. And once the necessity of their sleeping arrangements was over, would she just return to England and end the affair? He couldn't think of it. He just held her afterward, not wanting to ask questions that he might not like the answers to.

————

Airmid felt Daniel drift off in her arms. She couldn't settle. The thought of going back to court and dealing with Tommy's parents had her rattled. Not because she thought they could take her. Airmid would indeed run with her before she'd let that happen. It was more the idea of watching Erin's grandfather glare at her. He looked just like Tommy. Add twenty years of wrinkles and peppered hair, and it was Tommy.

She looked back on the relationship that had thus far defined her life. She'd loved him. She really had. And he her. But he'd been too weak to tell his parents to sod off and marry her outright. Not that she'd needed him to marry her, but it was certainly a topic of conversations most days with Tommy. Because deep down, he'd had to keep convincing himself that it was the right thing to do. And in hindsight, she wouldn't have wanted him to marry her because of a broken condom. Airmid deserved more. So did Erin. And honestly, so did Tommy. His death had scarred her so deeply, as had the custody battle afterward. Now she was going to have to do it all again.

This thing with Daniel was so wonderful. But she was letting it distract her. Airmid needed to get this job over with and get home to her baby girl. And even as she thought it, it seemed like a betrayal to Daniel. A good man who had done nothing but help her. She thought about those two agents they'd found floating in the harbor in Jamaica. Dead by the same horrible bastards who were funneling drugs into Europe. Into Erin's home. Drugs that killed people every day in Britain.

*Two dead agents.* The thought made her blood run cold. She'd buried one lover. Airmid couldn't think about something happening to Danny. Especially as Erin was starting to get attached to him. Why couldn't she fall for a solicitor or a chef? A million other types of men, rather than someone who was running toward danger. She closed her eyes, trying to quell the panic. Airmid just needed to end this. Then she could go back to her nice, quiet life. She was a good analyst, and this deceit and intrigue was never going to fit into her life. The thought made her throat tighten and the tears prick her eyes.

———

Daniel and Airmid walked to the dining hall, and they were assaulted by the smells that poured out the doors. The rain was so heavy, it was like a constant hum. A part of the landscape as much as the trees and the sky. His waterproof hiking books were caked with mud, and he put them next to Airmid's ankle-height Wellingtons. He wondered what Douglas was wearing, as the man was the biggest shoe whore he knew.

They joined Antony and Douglas at a large table along the left wall. The room was in Antony's name, under his tour business account. So, even if Jensen tried to find them, he'd have to work for it. The cuisine of the evening was grilled, stuffed blue tilapia, chicken mole, some sort of ceviche, and cow foot stew. Something they'd found on the ship that was seized in Amsterdam. He'd pass on the cow foot, but he noticed Antony was thoroughly enjoying his. He was also flirting with Airmid. He was young and handsome, and it made Daniel want to slash his tires and head out tomorrow without him. Which was ridiculous. He knew this.

Daniel said, "I noticed you live alone, Antony. No wife or kids?"

Douglas was trying to hide a smirk and failing. Antony was oblivious. "No, not yet. Just busy with the tour company, as you know. It makes it difficult to settle down."

And he couldn't fault the lad for that. Daniel said, "Yes, quite. I don't suppose they've got a mechanic in close proximity who can look at the air conditioning in your vehicle."

"It will hardly matter. You'll be following me in another vehicle, which your non-profit funded. I thought they'd have told you. It's a little smaller and much newer. I'll explain better when we are on our way."

And wasn't that the best news he'd heard today. He raised a glass of some sort of fresh juice. "Cheers to that, mate. I can't wait to see all that you have to show us."

———

## Lubaantun Archaeological Reserve

They parked in a dirt lot on the outskirts of the reserve a couple hours after sunrise. Airmid talked Antony into showing her the Mayan ruins before they got down to business, regardless of the torrential rain and high winds. Tropical Storm Azriel had officially arrived. The first big one of the season and a rotting bastard for the poor timing. They wore hooded rain Macs in the neutral, green hues of the jungle, varying shades of blue-and-brown trousers, and tried, in all their discreetly camouflaged glory, to look like tourists. Antony said, "The rain doesn't bother you?"

They all three laughed. "Scots and Irish are used to a bit of rain. It's the bugs I could do without," Douglas said. "At least I haven't seen another one of those bloody banana spiders."

Antony gave him a side glance. "The Caribbean banana spider has nothing on the creatures that roam this forest. Be careful, my friend."

Airmid was ignoring them though. She was looking up to the top of the pyramid. You could only climb one, as the others were having the stairs stabilized. She started humming the *Rocky* anthem, slowly making her way up the extremely steep stairs. When she reached the top, she raised her arms over her head, doing the little Rocky Balboa victory dance.

Douglas yelled up to her, "Be careful. They likely sacrificed a couple virgins up there."

Airmid smiled. "Good thing that hasn't been an issue for about twelve years!" Then she shook her head. "Stop doing the math in your heads, you perverts!"

Douglas laughed. "Seventeen, eh? Well, now. I've got you beat on something at least."

She was making her way down. "My eighteenth birthday, thank you. Started adulthood off with a bang."

Daniel just rubbed his eyes. "That was a really bad joke, Tara. I thought the Irish were supposed to be funny." Airmid gave him a smack.

"Yes, John, they are. Hilarious. Good craic. Game for a laugh. Unlike our stuffy neighbors over the water. Now, what is the plan?"

Antony said, "I have permission to leave the 4Runner. We depart in the H3, despite the lack of climate control. A satellite maps program has pulled up an illegal airstrip just over the border into Guatemala. We think the most likely scenario is that they are bringing the product overland through the Columbia

Forest Reserve. Coming out near one of the villages where they can take the highway to Punta Gorda at night. If they loaded a couple of small fishing boats outside the main village, they could meet the ship with little detection. None of the locals would dare to inform. It's a death sentence. Even the police turn a blind eye a lot of the time.

"This storm will likely blow north within the next ten hours. They could move the product out of the forest tonight. If they're smart—and they usually are—they flew it in before the storm hit the coast. Then they'll use this rain to cover their tracks through the forest today. Have it ready to go onto the main highway right before sunset. Right now, the defence forces and police are dealing with flooded villages. It's the perfect time to slip past them, as long as they don't come across a washed-out road."

Daniel thought it was a good plan, but he didn't like having two inexperienced agents with him. Two people he loved. Roxburghe was his best mate. He'd known Andrew Douglas, the Duke of Roxburghe, since he was nineteen and mixing with the neighboring aristocracy. His father had thought it important. He'd been bored to tears until he'd met the future duke. Around the same age and in possession of a filched bottle of eighteen-year-old Scotch whisky. They were holed up in the cellar of his family's large estate, bonding the way young lads did. Discussing the MILFs in attendance and getting piss drunk.

There had been a viscount in attendance who had a stunning, thirtysomething wife from somewhere in Northern France. She'd recently given birth, and the dress she'd worn had displayed her hard-earned assets in all their postpartum glory. Sick little bastards, admittedly, but they'd both ogled her breasts enough to make it awkward. It was Daniel's papa who had eventually found them. Instead of scolding them, he'd just taken a seat on a large barrel and put his palm out for the bottle. *You've found your uncle's private stash, I see.*

The Duke of Roxburghe, at the time, had been Douglas's uncle from his mother's side. His father was Laird Douglas, titled in his own right, but the uncle would be the one to hand down the more prestigious title. The mean bastard was dying and had no heir. Likely, his wife couldn't bear to let him bed her.

Daniel glanced at Douglas, over ten years later. His oldest and most loyal friend. A look passed between them. Daniel's eyes touched on Airmid, then back to him. Douglas just nodded. A promise between them.

————

They were outfitted with portable GPS trackers in their shoes, underneath the orthotic inserts. They were the best waterproof, discreet units you could buy. Phones or watches would likely be disposed of if one or all of them were captured, but the shoe sole might just go unnoticed. Antony took them into the forest, and there was a shocking amount of rain coming down off the hills and debris littering the road.

Antony said, "The first heavy rain is the worst for bringing down the dead foliage and branches from the colder season. Not that it ever really gets cold. Not like your home." He went around a pile of mud and rocks. "This should be able to get us over anything short of a large tree. I have a winch if we need to clear a tree from the road though. It's attached at the back. At least the rain has eased."

It had, in fact, started to ease. It was wet and muddy, but the visibility was much better. The worst of Tropical Storm Azriel had passed, giving way to a misting rain. They drove the major roads through the park, not finding anything. Antony got a message just before teatime. "I have intelligence from the air. We have several vehicles, different makes and models and four-wheel drive. They were gathered at the western edge of the park and are now driving east through the park toward the coast."

"Any better description?" Douglas asked.

"Looks like two or three older Mitsubishi or Nissan-type vehicles, a large truck with a cap, an H3 that is newer than mine, and ... a Land Rover Defender. New, or almost new, and black."

Douglas said, "It sounds random enough to be deliberate. Likely someone of importance is in the Defender. Other than that, nothing out of the ordinary. If they split up, they aren't carbon copies of one another and not easy to identify."

"Right," Daniel said. He turned toward Antony. "Have them track as discreetly as they can. I'm assuming this is someone out to survey storm damage and flooding, so it wouldn't be out of the ordinary to do a couple of passes overhead. We need to know if they split up."

Antony typed a quick message, then started north. "I know a place we can pull off. They should pass us. Once I get a better description, we can back out and head to Punta Gorda."

Daniel's jaw was so tight, he thought it was going to fracture. They nestled the vehicle just out of eyeshot and padded to a rocky outcropping. It was slick and muddy, and there were any number of horrible-looking insects coming out of their hiding places. Douglas was only slightly horrified, but he rallied.

They heard the vehicles at the same time. Daniel had a no-glare covering on his high-tech phone, and as the vehicles went by, he snapped what photos he could. Douglas said it first. "There's potentially one missing. Didn't they say there were six? And I think the driver of the Defender may have been one of the guards we met in Jamaica. Arturo Rey's guard. I couldn't swear on it, but I think I recognized him. It was just so fast."

They waited, listening for a sixth vehicle. "He did say two or three for the Japanese SUVs. Maybe we aren't missing one," Airmid said.

"Antony, how well do you know this informant? I mean, he managed to get a lot of vehicle information, but he was iffy on the numbers." It hadn't struck Daniel as strange until now. He shook himself. "It doesn't matter. We need to move."

They started back toward the vehicle, Antony saying, "I'll take us back to the ruins for the second vehicle. Hang on tight because it's going to be fast and bumpy."

They loaded up, and Antony turned toward Daniel. "To answer your question, I know the man well enough. I've used him before. He's with the Belizean Defence Forces. But it is concerning that we don't have a proper count. I don't like unknown factors."

They were about three minutes into the drive back toward the ruins when Douglas looked behind him. "Goddammit! We've got company. It's a Mitsubishi Pajero. Car number six. So much for good informants."

Antony turned sharply toward the east, cursing in Spanish. Airmid said, "How the hell are we going to shake him in this muck?"

Daniel said, "Get ahead and out of sight! Do what you have to. Does your informant know how many people are with you?"

Antony shook his head. "No, but he might have been able to see two from the sky. He would have no way of knowing there were two in the back, given my black window tint."

Douglas could see where this was going. "Forget it, brother. Not happening." But Daniel wasn't listening. The vehicle had been fairly far behind them when Douglas had spotted them. Now they couldn't even see it.

Daniel said, "Faster. Like warp speed. They need time."

Airmid turned toward Douglas. "What is it? I don't understand! Someone, talk to me!"

"They know we were watching them," was all Douglas said. "Someone tipped them off."

Airmid said, "So we go to the nearest town, find the police."

Douglas said, "The man who likely tipped them off is part of the defence force, love. And with this storm, we are on our own." He looked above him. "Sky is clear of aircraft. Let's do it."

Daniel wouldn't even look at her. That's what she couldn't understand. Not until they suddenly pulled off. Daniel whipped her door open as Douglas got out on the other side. Douglas said, "Danny, you need to go. I'll stay with Antony!"

Daniel ignored him, cupping Airmid's face. "Call Morgan right away. Follow the tracker." Then he kissed her. "I love you, my Airmid." He kissed her again. "I love you both." He cupped Douglas at the nape of his neck, putting their foreheads together. "Go to the ruins. Don't forget where we put the key. Go, now."

"No!" Airmid screamed, but Douglas was pulling her into the trees, and the H3 was gone within seconds.

Douglas put a hand over her mouth without apology. "Quiet! We're no help to them if we get caught!" Douglas said against her ear. She slumped, sobbing into his palm. Then they were running.

———

They gave them a good chase. They'd almost made it out of the park, having gone away from the ruins and farther east. They caught up to them about two minutes later, and despite the ridiculous speeds, no one crashed. Even when the passenger in the Mitsubishi started shooting at them. It blasted the back windshield out first. "Dammit! Where's the fucking highway?"

Antony yelled into his phone, trying to get a message to Harry in time. The cell service was spotty at best, and Daniel held the phone for him so that he could steer with both hands. Coordinates and vehicle descriptions. That's when Daniel saw the forest open up and could see a main road about a quarter mile away. They were almost to the main road when a black Land Rover Defender pulled in front of their only way forward. Antony slammed on the breaks and went for his pistol, but the Mitsubishi crashed into the back of them.

*Fucking airbags.* That was the last thought Daniel had before he was jerked from the car at gunpoint. They were put on their knees. And suddenly, Daniel was so glad he'd called his mother. So glad he'd hired a lawyer for Airmid. Glad he'd been a good son, brother, lover, and patriot. He just wanted Airmid and Douglas safe. Whatever came next would be worth it.

They were screaming at Antony in Spanish, and one man rifle-butted him in the face. Daniel growled. "Fucking bastards." He came off his knees and started swinging, grabbing the rifle barrel of the closest man before he got a shot off. He shouldn't be taken alive anyway, and his temper was ripe. He took one knee out, bashed another in the gob, and managed to get one in a sleeper hold, choking the life out of him before he got his own blow to the head.

He picked up some of what they were saying. *Only two?* And something about Antony being an expat. Antony stiffened and Daniel looked up. Low and under his breath, Antony said, "You are familiar to the big one." That's when Daniel saw the personal bodyguard from Jamaica come forward. The one Douglas had been watching the match with during the private party. One of the men he'd fought with kicked him in the stomach, but they hadn't shot him in the head like he'd expected. God, he hoped Douglas and Airmid got the hell out of here. The man pulled his hair, taking in his face. "Blindfold them. Boss will want to question them."

———

Airmid was un-fucking-hinged. "Why would he do that? We shouldn't have split up! We have to go back!"

Douglas hissed at her. He actually hissed. "Use that fucking map or hand it over."

She wiped her face, mumbling under her breath. "The ruins should start about three hundred meters that way," she said as she pointed. Her hands were shaking so badly that she could barely read the thing.

Douglas started jogging. "We call Harry, then Morgan. Morgan will have his GPS coordinates. If they get Danny, they'll come looking for us. We have to get back to the resort and hide the 4Runner. I can pull up the coordinates on his mobile unit as well. But we need support, Airmid."

"I know. And I'm managing to reign myself in right now, but barely. He told me he loved me and then just took off! I didn't get to say it back." Her voice broke. "I didn't say it back!"

"I understand. I know you don't think I do, but I do. We've been together for almost two decades. This fucking bromance has been the most stable relationship of my entire life. Which is why the bloody-minded arsehole left me as well."

They broke through the trees, and a giant Mayan temple was towering above them. Airmid ran to the carved jaguar head that adorned one side of the temple stairway. Under the squared head, there was a small hole where the rock had fallen away. She grabbed the key fob. When Douglas gave her a look of protest, she said, "I'll drive. You make the calls and mind the map. Jesus,

Joseph, and Mary, if you don't get that look off your face, I'll beat you bloody!"

Douglas grinned and said, "I'm starting to see the appeal." And when he saw Airmid's fists grip the steering wheel, he said more softly, "We'll get them back. Or I'll die trying, love. I will not accept any other outcome." Then he started dialing as he said, "Take that access road for four miles and you'll see the first turnoff."

# 18

M organ came over the secured video call. "What the fuck do you mean they've got him?"

Douglas said, "We think the Belizean Defence Force informant was playing both sides. It's the only way they could have found us so quickly. Danny and the local operative dumped us in the bush and led them away from us. Because he's a complete asshole."

He could hear her using her other computer to send out a message. "This cannot wait until we get more of our people to you. Even if we pulled someone from another part of Central America, it could take hours we don't have. And the airlines have canceled everything because of the storm. You need to come up with some local talent. Do you understand?" Then she cursed. "I've got him! Thank God. He's still in Belize. I'm sending you the passcodes to track him on your mobile device and the coordinates for where he is right now. You don't have time to wait. If they get him over the border into Guatemala or on a ship or plane, we could lose him for good. They will torture him and dump his body."

Douglas said, "Harry is calling now. Just get me as much information as you can on that location."

Airmid answered the call from Harry. "I understand. I need manpower and weapons, goddammit."

Harry said, "This isn't the fucking army, Airmid. This is the clandestine service, and we've just had a major storm. Anyone in Mexico or the Caribbean is grounded. Honduras flights aren't up and running, and they can't carry weapons over the border through Guatemala. I can get you guns and myself, but I can't involve the embassy. We can't compromise our assets in Central America."

But all Airmid focused on was the first sentence. *This isn't the fucking army, Airmid.* She said, "Get us those weapons and meet me at the coordinates I text you. As soon as you can!"

She rang off and looked at Douglas. "The British Army has a training exercise going on as we speak. The one I told you about from the time when I was an interpreter. Douglas, Danny's cousin is a major in the British Army and he's here training. He's just outside of the Machaha Forest Reserve with a platoon of infantry troops."

Douglas shook his head. "They'll never approve it. You are talking about military action on foreign soil."

"Fuck the higher-ups, Roxburghe. This is Danny. They will kill him, and this is going to take extreme measures! Major O'Brien should have the choice at least! And I'd rather have some of my army brothers watching my ass than going in alone. And I *will* go in alone if I have to."

———

**Hawick, Scotland**

Sorcha couldn't sleep. It was the middle of the night, and something was just niggling at her. She'd taken all of her granny meds. Called Sean to check on everyone. She'd even heard from Cormac, her nephew. Apparently, Daniel had hired Cormac and Nolan to help Airmid with family court. But after having six children and extended children to mother over the years, she'd learned to trust her instincts. Something wasn't right. Like a weighted presence around her heart. She put some nature sounds on her phone. Sounds of the rainforest made her think of her time at St. Clare's. A peaceful, hidden treasure of a place with love and the presence of the Almighty. The steady sound of tapping rain and wildlife finally helped her to drift into a deep sleep.

*Sorcha was walking in the rain. The forest was dense and lush. She was surprised to come to a small clearing and see her granddaughter. "Cora, love. What are you doing here?" She was holding Finn's hand. But just as she looked away from Cora's face, something changed. Not Finn. It was Daniel. Wait, no. Her heart lurched in her chest. It was John. Young and healthy. She could feel her pulse pounding in her ears. "Am I dead, then? Did I die in my sleep?"*

*Her brother smiled at her, reaching a hand to touch her face. "It's good to see you, Sorcha. And no, you're not dead. 'Tis but a dream." Sorcha looked at her granddaughter.*

*Cora said, "It was his other da who came the first time, but ... now Uncle John is here. And I don't know why, Granny. I just know something is wrong. It's shrouded in secrets. I can't see clearly. But this place means something. There's so much rain. It's like the photos with Uncle Liam's mission, but that doesn't seem right. This is about Cousin Danny. And I think you should try to call Aidan." Cora looked at her long-dead uncle. "Is that right? She needs to call Uncle Aidan?"*

*John just nodded, his eyes never leaving his sister's face. "I think I would have loved getting older with you. And I wish I would have known him. I didn't know until I—" He looked at Cora. "Until I left and moved on. It's then that all things are revealed. I wish he knew how much I would have loved being his da. Take care of him, dear sister. Take care of my lad."*

Sorcha shot up out of bed as her phone chimed. Her face was wet, with a combination of sweat and tears dripping down. She grabbed it. "Finn! What the bloody hell is going on. Jesus, tell me that was my own nerves at work and not—"

Finn said, "Sorcha, something's not right. It was so unclear, and I got pushed out. Cora said—"

Sorcha cut Finn off. "My brother," she said, stifling a sob that boiled up in her chest. "My brother. Something is wrong." That's when she heard the wailing. It was the lassie in the nursery upstairs. Sorcha rang off and ran for the stairway.

Constance was rocking Erin, and she was inconsolable. Sorcha said, "What is it, love? What's the matter?"

"Mammy! I want Mammy and Danny! Where is Danny? He's supposed to be with Mam!" Sorcha jerked. Children could be sensitive at this age, even if they outgrew it. Pair that with her dream and what Cora and Finn had said ... Jesus wept. Where the hell was her nephew?

———

**BATSUB Headquarters, Belize**

Airmid came to the armed guard at the gate to the training headquarters. She spoke in Spanish and showed her phony passport. "Please, I am an Irish Citizen. It's an emergency. I must see Major Aidan O'Brien. My name is Tara MacMillin. He's with the Royal Irish."

The guard gave her a wary look. He left the other guard and went to the guardhouse to use the radio. It took forever, and meanwhile, they took Douglas Ruthford, a.k.a. the duke of bloody Roxburghe's fake-ass identification as well. The guard pointed at a covered structure. "Wait there. Do not return to your car unless I tell you that you can."

They were both armed to the teeth, so Airmid wasn't going to test them. She'd stand on her head if she could get Danny's cousin to come for a chat.

————

"Sir, I'm sorry to wake you, but it's important," Kearsley said as he put a hand on Aidan's shoulder.

Aidan shot out of bed, ready for a fight. Kearsley had the good sense to back up. Aidan shook himself, clearing his head. "Aye, what's goin', Lieutenant?"

"This is going to sound crazy, sir. But there's an Irish woman at the gate screaming her head off for Major O'Brien. She said ... she said she's prior army and it's about your cousin."

Aidan was running through the mud with his boots unlaced and a waterproof layer over his undershirt. He saluted the guards and then saw her. He narrowed his eyes. "This says your name is Tara?"

"Sir, can we speak in private?" Airmid asked, pleading in her eyes. "It's about Danny."

He looked at Douglas. "You look familiar. I met you—"

"Douglas Ruthford," he said lowly. "As far as anyone knows. And she means very private, Major."

————

All Airmid could think for one evil minute was that she'd love to bottle this O'Brien/Mullen DNA. Which was obviously a stress response. "My name is—"

"Airmid Roberts, six years in the British Army and the linguist for my cousin's non-profit ventures. Why the hell does your passport say Tara MacMillin, and who the fuck is Douglas Ruthford? Because last time I checked, Your Grace, you were the Duke of Roxburghe and your name is Andrew."

Douglas said, "Ruthford is my alter ego. I'm one of the Avengers. Can we dispense with the shite, Aidan?"

Aidan clenched his jaw. "Can I assume that something is amiss with Danny?" Aidan asked.

Aidan watched the woman tense and lean forward, her palms on the old conference table. "About as amiss and you can possibly get. His name, as far as everyone else in Belize knows, is John MacMillin. We are here doing counternarcotics for the British Government. I can't get into it other than to tell you that everything just went to shit. We separated in the Columbia Forest Reserve, and I think Danny and our local colleague were taken. We've been tracking activities over the Belizean border that are bringing drugs into Britain via the Netherlands. The Escobar drug cartel. And according to the GPS chip embedded in his shoe and that of our other ... friend, they were taken southwest near the Guatemalan border. We believe it is the compound of Arturo Reyes, a Belizean national married into the Escobar family. This is as bad as it could possibly have gone."

Aidan stood. "I'll get my friends from the defence force—"

Airmid grabbed his arm. "No!"

Douglas intervened. "I'm sorry, but we are almost certain the one who betrayed our whereabouts was a defence force soldier from the Belizean Army. The man was with one of the air units, and he was an asset of the colleague who was captured with

Danny. The two of them dropped us in the fucking jungle with a map and led the pursuers away. They followed the vehicle because they didn't know there were four riders instead of two. It's the only reason we got away. There is no way I can get reinforcements here from another part of Central America in time. We may already be too late. These men are stone-cold killers. They already killed two men who ended up being agents for another nation. They dumped them in the Kingston Harbor. We do not have time to wait, and we can't trust the locals. Do you understand what I am asking you?"

Aidan just nodded. He'd been here before, hadn't he? When Alanna had been taken. So, his quiet, suit-wearing cousin, Daniel, the fucking Earl of Hawick, was in the clandestine services. "I can't do this without a local. Can I just bring one soldier in here to help? They know the terrain. I'll risk everything I have to give to get my cousin back, but I can't take my lads into harm's way without some help. You are talking about armed soldiers from a foreign government raiding a private estate. They could kill us all and get away with it."

Douglas patted his pocket as his mobile went off. He answered, "Morgan, give me some good goddamn news."

He listened as Airmid tried to quell the shaking in her body. Aidan reached a hand over, cupping hers. "Be brave, soldier. Be brave a bit longer. I won't leave this country without my cousin. He's ours, but I think he's yours as well. Is he not?"

The thought terrified her. Claiming him with her words. With her heart. Only to lose him. This was no training exercise. Reyes would make sure he suffered. She couldn't bear it. But she had to. If he could sacrifice himself to get her and Douglas to safety, she could be brave. She said nothing. She just used her other hand to wipe a stray tear and said, "He's my heart. I will not abandon him. If I have to kill every drug dealer in this country, I will do it. I need weapons, a dark hat, and some camouflage paint. I'm afraid I left my ass-kicking kit in my other bag."

Douglas rang off. "Bring your man in here. And I'm going to interrogate him before I trust him with any information. Do you understand? I don't know who to trust."

Aidan said, "He has a particularly bad taste in his mouth over the Columbian cartels bringing drugs over the border into this beautiful country. He will help, and he won't bring anyone on the mission that he has questions about. His brother is here as well. I trust them with my life. I need the name of the asset you think betrayed you."

Antony hadn't told them, but maybe Harry knew. And speak of the devil. Someone pounded on the metal door. Aidan opened the door to the hut, and Harry entered without an invitation. He looked at Douglas and Airmid. "I have what you asked for. Do we have her majesty's best to aid us?"

Douglas said, "We're working on it. Morgan got leave for the soldiers to be on standby at the border of the estate. Airmid and I go in alone. And if we get murdered, this never happened. I need the name of Antony's informant. The one in the rescue helicopter. It's the only way they could have found us."

Harry hesitated. Aidan loomed over him. "I'll beat it out of you, ye wee mongrel. Fucking spooks sneaking around in the shadows. Your asset may very well have gotten my cousin tortured and fed to the pigs. Give me the fucking name." He walked over to the door, yelling for one of his men. "I need Lieutenants Ramirez and Kearsley and Lt. Colonel Mason from the dragoons—now!"

Harry, to his credit, did not shrink away from Aidan. Brave or too seasoned to let his fear show. "Well, now, you fucking Irish brute. If you'll give me a minute, I'll give it to you. We have more than one asset in the defence forces. Were any of the men training here with you in an air unit today?"

"They weren't. They were on the ground helping the villagers," Aidan said. Then they both looked up to see Ramirez walk through the door, but before he could say anything, Harry spoke.

Harry said, "Josef, it's been a week at least, I think. Have you missed your old pal?"

Ramirez froze, looking at everyone. He started spouting something off in Spanish. Airmid said quietly, "Apparently, he's another asset, and he's rightfully pissed that he just got outed." As this was happening, Lt. Kearsley and Lt. Colonel Mason came in right behind him and looked extremely confused.

Harry looked at Aidan. "Sorry. Just had to make certain it wasn't him in case I've completely lost my touch. This lad I would trust with my grandchildren's lives, but I just had to know for sure." The leak was another man whom Ramirez knew only by name. Harry filled him in briefly and he turned toward Aidan.

Ramirez said, "Your cousin? Madre Maria, protect him, amigo. This is the most terrible curse on our country, this group of men. I know the place. I can lead."

"Don't you have to get permission?" he asked.

"How do they say? It is better to ask for mercy than for permission. I don't know who we can trust outside of a select few of my men. They are all good boys, but the reach of this cartel ... they threaten the families. And after this, Harry? I am out. I'm done. I have a baby on the way. I have a wife now."

Harry said, "Understood. And after this is done, I'm going to have your comrade's nuts in a noose. Antony better make it out of this alive, or by God, I will gut Reyes myself."

Airmid turned toward Douglas. "You're quiet. What is it?"

"I'm thinking of a way past their security," Douglas said. "And it's risky."

She tilted her head, then said, "Too risky. We don't know where her loyalties lie. Actually, we do. No fucking way."

"Think about it. You never got a vibe with her? Or with Delilah? I saw Delilah nod a warning to Daniel at the table. She didn't want him to accept an escort from Reyes's men. And something is off about Rubia. She's been subtle, but she's not who she appears to be."

Airmid felt the same way. They'd all spent the day with her, and the woman had let her guard down when she wasn't under the watchful eyes of Jensen and Reyes. But they couldn't take the chance. "I don't think we should risk it. At least not until we see the security. Maybe we won't need them."

"Aye, so we get past the security, then how do we find them? That compound is big. Two stories and a subterranean level," he said.

Harry said, "They'll be below. Reyes has his own private interrogation chambers down there. Along with his guards' quarters and storage. They aren't going to be easy to get to, but I have the go-ahead to use all force necessary. The longer they have our men, the more everyone is in jeopardy of exposure. Ramirez, I think you should stay outside with the British troops. Only show your face if it's necessary. Not because I want to use you again, but because I want to protect you and your family. I'll be pulled after this. As will Antony, if he's alive. But you have to live here. In fact, I insist on it."

Ramirez shook his head. "I'm not sending my men into this and not leading. Hell no," he said as Airmid interpreted for the others.

Aidan said calmly, "You'll stay with my men. I will lead."

Douglas started to argue and Aidan rounded on him. "Do ye

think I'd stay back while my kin sits in a fucking torture dungeon? Would you stay back?" He looked at them both. "I'm goin'! It's why you came here when no one else could help. You came to me. Now let me do what I do best. I was kicking in doors through the streets of Kabul when you were having your tea parties with the queen. Mayhem is my fucking super power."

Harry actually laughed. "I think I like this Irish prick."

Lt. Col. Mason finally spoke up. "Let me see if I have this straight." After a synopsis of the current situation, and a nod from Aidan that he had everything right, he said, "By your cousin, you don't mean the Dublin garda officer. You mean the fucking Earl of Hawick?" Shit. Shit. Shit.

"That information cannot leave this room. None of the other men can know. This is officially ten steps beyond top secret," Airmid said. Before he could say her name, recognition sparking in the older dragoon's eyes, Airmid approached him and stuck out her hand. "Tara MacMillin, sir." And the look in her eyes spoke volumes. He'd already spoken Daniel's true identity. She didn't want him speaking hers. Or Douglas's. She saw right when his eyes bugged out.

Douglas said, "And I'm Tara's stepbrother. Douglas Ruthford at your service."

Mason's mouth was agape, but then he cleared his head and spoke. "I just received a secured phone call approving whatever the bloody hell you lot have cooked up in my short absence. And O'Brien, you are not cleared to—"

The look Aidan gave his superior caused the whole room to go still. Mason was not his boss, but he did outrank him. Mason said, "But if it were my cousin, I'd do the same. I'll write it up later as an unavoidable. Or not at all if I think I can pull it off."

Kearsley said, "I'm not staying back while you go in alone."

"I won't be alone, lad. I'll be with the Belizean soldiers. And I need you to be in charge of the Irish hotheads. Kenney and Cunningham are going to be a handful enough just on their own. Ramirez needs you at his six. That's an order, in case you were wondering."

————

Daniel's face felt like a piece of raw meat. They'd been at this for an eternity. First, two hours of interrogation where Reyes kept his dogs leashed and tried to use threats instead of violence. The favorite threat was all the things he was going to do to Tara, a.k.a. Airmid. Antony was next to him, and he'd fared no better. His lips were split, his left eye swollen shut. Jensen was nowhere to be found. Had he not seen the shocked look on the man's face for himself as they'd dragged him and Antony through the back entrance of the house, he'd have sworn Jensen was just as involved in all this. Apparently, Jensen was not a decision-maker. Just a very rich pawn.

The bulk of the interrogation had been about their missing friends. Other than who they were because they didn't believe for a minute that he was a non-profit CEO or that Antony was a tour guide. But they desperately wanted the whereabouts of Airmid and Douglas. He'd die before he told them. He'd been careless with his team and gotten caught. He'd trusted this poor sod next to him, a fairly new operative, to have trustworthy connections in the BDF.

He didn't regret his actions, but he regretted where he was right now. He'd likely die here. And although he hated that thought, he'd done what he needed to do when it mattered. He'd sacrificed himself to save his partners. They were more than that to him. He'd meant what he said. He loved them both. Douglas like another brother. Airmid like ... like a mate. The O'Briens waxed poetic about having one true mate. And he'd thought it was a bit much. But there was no doubt that the strong bonds between them were real. Were forever. And he knew, even though he wasn't an O'Brien, that he'd formed such a bond with Airmid. He loved her. And if he got out of this, by some miracle, he'd prove it to her. If she'd have him, that is.

Antony turned toward him. "I'm sorry, John." He wouldn't expand. They were undoubtedly on camera.

"Don't apologize. I'm here with you, Antony. You are not alone," Daniel said. He thought about his alias. Such a coincidence. If he died, would both his fathers be waiting for him? The thought seemed to soothe him.

But he couldn't die. It would kill Gregory and Elizabeth. His siblings were a good deal younger, but they were all close. He'd never had the phase some little shits went through where they were too cool to hang out with their little brother or sister. He'd beg his mother to let him carry his brother on outings. He'd been nine and his brother just one year old the first time he'd hoisted the lad up on his chest, strap him in the baby carrier, and walk around town with the little fiend. His chubby arms and legs flailing around to the rhythm of Danny's steps.

And then he'd gotten a sister. He'd helped his papa teach her to ride a pony. Helped her learn to tie her shoes. When she'd graduated from school, he'd bought her a new laptop before she went off to university to study literature and writing. They'd all gone to village schools in their youth. Douglas had attended Eton, but not them. They'd gone to the village school with the other children. He'd gone to a posh, private primary school until he'd put his foot down about things going into fifth year. He wanted to go to school with the neighboring children. It had been its own sort of education because pack laws dictated you had to prove yourself.

The earl's son got in a few clandestine fistfights, so as to thwart the schoolmaster and the parents. Once he'd proven he could take a punch and kick a little ass in return, the lads had respected him. When he went home with a black eye and hadn't talked, his father had let it go. Maybe that's when his papa had started to understand that someday, he could do this job. And just like those schoolhouse bullies, he was going to kick the guts out of Reyes and Jensen if he got the chance. And, of course, the wee bastard who had taken his fists to them both.

The main culprit was currently walking into the interrogation room behind another bloke, and Daniel cringed at what he saw. This was really going to hurt. The man said in Spanish, "Lift them up."

Daniel took the opportunity, while they untied him from the chair, to headbutt the man with the iron knuckles. The punch to the kidneys was expected, but hurt like the devil. He looked around, noticing the hose and the drain for the tenth time since they'd pulled the hoods off their heads. And the hooks above them. They taped his wrists together, as well as Antony's. Antony mumbled, "Electrocution. Fuck me, they watch too many movies."

But the reason they put this shit in movies was because it happened and it worked. By the time they were done trussing them up, Daniel's toes were touching the ground but that was it. They hooked his rope shackles to an iron loop in the floor so he couldn't kick. Then the hose started. The new man, who had dead eyes and missing teeth, asked in fairly good English, "Who do you work for? Is it a competing business or a government?"

Daniel said nothing. Giving them a witty comeback was just an excuse to hit him harder. And his head was throbbing from the stupidly timed headbutt. He couldn't avoid what was coming, so he just took a cleansing breath and met the man's eyes just as he touched him with a shit ton of electricity. Not enough to kill him.

Just enough to light him up like a Christmas tree. Pain seared through his wet skin and he growled between his clenched teeth, waiting for it to end.

A half hour later, he woke to someone slapping him in the face. Daniel swore and said, "Jensen, you piece of shit. What the fuck are you thinking getting mixed up with these people?"

The man who slapped him then punched him in the gut. He wheezed, coughing so hard he gagged. Antony writhed on his hook, hissing insults at the bastard.

Jensen said, "Enough. Leave us." The man hesitated until Jensen got up in his face. "Do we have a problem?"

The man left, closing the door. Jensen exhaled, closing his eyes. "What the fuck was I thinking? What the fuck were you thinking dragging Tara into this? Did you tell them where she was?"

"Fuck off. Don't come in here acting like you give a shit. The way you go through women? Some of them are practically slaves!" Daniel spat the words with as much venom as he could manage.

Jensen rounded on him. "I do what I have to do in order to protect mine."

Daniel sneered. "The wife who lives with her Finnish lover? Right." Daniel wanted to kill this man. He was helping bring drugs into his own country. Poisoning his country and the rest of Northwestern Europe.

"Yes, my wife. The one who lives with her lover. That's the story, and I wish it was the truth. I wish she'd left me and actually taken up with some Fin with a day job," Jensen said. "Don't assume you know anything about me, young Mr. MacMillin."

So, they had the wife. He knew something hadn't passed the sniff test with that story. "Do you really want to be responsible for kidnapping a local tour guide and a British national?" Daniel asked.

"I assure you, Mr. MacMillin, I am helpless in this situation." Jensen looked toward the camera. "It would be better if you told them what they want to know. You may not live through this, but it would make your death easier." He turned to walk away. "You shouldn't have jammed the signal in your hotel room after you'd done it on the island. Once could be explained as an outage, but when you did it again in both rooms, you drew attention to yourself. Goodbye, Mr. MacMillin."

Well, wasn't that a lesson that did him zero good now. And he'd known it was a bad idea, even though it was why they had the jammer issued to them. But he'd done it to protect Airmid's sense of safety. Not for any solid reason. He'd known it was a risk, and he'd done it anyway because loving Airmid was causing him to think with his heart and not his brain. She knew it too. Maybe that's why he felt like she kept pieces of herself from him. It was okay though. He'd told her everything he needed to tell her.

Daniel watched Jensen close the door, and he knew things were going to get fatal really fucking quickly now. And despite his love for Airmid, he knew she'd be okay. Right now, the only faces he saw were those of his sister, his brother, his mother. The loss of Daniel's papa had devastated the family. And now they'd lose him. Gregory was his heir, and he'd have to step up and take his place as earl. He'd be good at it, despite not wanting the position. And dear Elizabeth with her big imagination and sharp wit. Her fiery spirit would serve her well. He wanted to see what she'd become. And the idea that he wouldn't see it made him very sad.

He'd been so happy when he found out he was getting siblings. He'd still been young enough to curl into his mother's side and pat her tummy. To talk about what it would be like to have a real live brother. Daniel felt his eyes fill with tears. His beautiful, quiet mother. Graceful and steady. She'd loved two men in her life. And despite their differences, he knew she'd always done everything within her power to protect him. He hadn't told them he loved them enough. Not nearly enough.

The dead-eyed interrogator came in, Arturo Reyes behind him. Daniel whispered to Antony, "Be strong, saith my heart. I am a soldier. My eyes have seen worse sights than this." A quote from Homer. *Stay with me, Papa. Help me be strong until the end.*

———

It was after the third jolt of electricity that he blacked out for a time. He was suddenly somewhere else. Somewhere cool and clean, with a breeze coming off the river. He looked at the river- side and saw two men. But it wasn't possible. He approached the men who were stiff-backed, their eyes locked on each other like adversaries. His fathers. Then he saw another figure on the edge of a copse of trees. "Colin?"

———

### Doolin, Co. Clare

Finn was down with a migraine. He'd been in agony for hours. Ever since ... Brigid didn't want to think about it. Tomorrow was Colin's tenth birthday. Actually, his birthday started in two minutes. She'd had the lad at three o'clock in the morning, and it was moments away. He'd been an easy birth. And she'd felt a sort of hum through her body as he came into the world. She thought about Finn and Cora, linked in such a special way. Something niggled at her, so she poked her head into Cora's room to find her awake. Cora took her headphones off and looked at her mother. She said, "I can't sleep. How is Da?"

"The drugs knocked him out. It's a bad one. I think I may call the doctor tomorrow. This one is different." That's when it happened. The clock chimed the hour, and Cora gasped.

"Did you feel that? Did you feel that ... sort of wave go through the house? Like a pulse?" Cora's eyes were wild. "Colin!"

They both ran down the hall and Colin was on his bed, fists clenched. Eyes open and rolling toward his eyebrows. "Jesus Christ, get your da! He's seizing!"

———

**Belize**

There was no bloody way they were getting in through the front door. And the cameras around this place were everywhere. They'd have to be quick and stealthy. Jam the cameras all at once, then go in through the back where there were fewer guards.

Airmid was dressed in a pair of borrowed, black utilities, as well as a dark hat and camo paint they'd scrounged up in the barracks for her. Douglas was dressed in borrowed jungle fatigues instead of his polished, stylish clothing. She had to admit he looked hot as hell. He had murder in his eyes, and she felt the aggression rolling off him and the good major. They had to get Daniel back, and she knew there were no two men she'd rather have at her side than these two. They loved Danny as much as she did. Differently, but no less truly.

Douglas looked at his phone, and victory seemed to spark a light in his eyes. "The west entrance is a servants' entrance. It goes right to the basement. Our lovely Rubia is here."

"Be ready for an ambush," Airmid said. "We may not be able to trust her."

Harry said from behind them, "You can trust her."

They both turned around. Douglas said flatly, "And what the fuck do you know about it?"

"More than you," he said smugly. "You can trust her," he said again. "And despite what she says, try to extract her. The Belizean Government just seized the outgoing shipment in Punta Gorda. We did it. The sooner we have them all out and are cleared from the area, the better. A raid will occur within the next two hours. We have to get them out before it happens. We don't know who else we can trust."

Thank God. Airmid looked at Douglas. It was over. All they had to do was get Danny and Antony. And apparently, Rubia was coming along for the ride.

Aidan O'Brien was taking point, and he said quietly and clearly to the British troops, "You do not engage until we are off the estate, and only if you need to cover us. No one breaches the perimeter."

Kearsley said, "This could end your career, Major."

"And would you do any less for a brother?" Aidan asked.

Kearsley said, "I'd do the same. And I want to come with you. We all do."

"I have a team and so do you. Remember your responsibilities, Lieutenant. I need you right where you are." He turned toward Ramirez. "And your men are in good hands. I vow it."

Aidan said, "To the west entrance." And they all followed. Lt. Colonel Mason and a team of ten dragoons stayed to guard their retreat all the way to the vehicles. Ramirez and Kearsley would have the Royal Irish team covering the entry team from the west exit. It was game time.

He turned toward Airmid. "You are emotionally compromised. You both are," he said and looked at Douglas. "As am I. But no matter what we walk into, you keep your shit together. You can fall apart later. I'll join you. But you must keep it together until we are all out safely."

Airmid and Douglas were tight with tension. Airmid said, "I

can do this. We all three can. Together, we can get him home."
And so they went.

———

As soon as the ground team jammed the wireless security
cameras, the entry team made their move. Aidan disabled the
guard from behind with a sleeper hold as one of his team took the
other out efficiently with a blast to the skull. They dragged them
back for another man to tape and conceal. Then they were inside
the perimeter.

They passed through the wide, chain-link gate, closing it
behind them. Given the number of guards watching the exterior
of the compound, this Rubia woman had been right to choose this
entry point. Before they could even try the door, there she was.
She was a looker to be sure, and her accent was Germanic.
"Quickly, they will notice the cameras are out soon. I took care of
the security guard in the camera room, but we still have to be
quick." They actually stepped over another guard, and Aidan
wasn't sure if she'd killed him or just knocked him out. She
smirked. "Ketamine. We have about twenty minutes. There's one
at the base of the stairs, through the security door. Let me go
first."

Douglas grabbed her arm. "Who the fuck are you?"

Rubia pulled away. "Give me about ninety seconds." She
hurried down the stairs. They heard her lightly knock and say,
"Rodrigo, I snuck some sandwiches for you again." The stocky
man who opened the door didn't even look up. His eyes went from
her boobs to her empty hands, just before she struck up and broke
his nose. Aidan was behind her in a heartbeat, rifle-butting him
for good measure.

These weren't soldiers. They were hired thugs for a drug

cartel. He didn't give two shits who he had to brutalize. God help them if Daniel was dead. He watched Airmid activate a secondary jammer, in case the thick walls had shielded these interior cameras.

Rubia said, "Second door on the left. They are in there right now, interrogating him and the other boy. They will need to be carried out. I will be missed. I've done all I can. Delilah is waiting with the key."

Douglas said, "You're goin' nowhere. We have orders to extract you."

She pierced him with a glare. "I'm not leaving Delilah. She is innocent. It's my fault she's here."

Aidan said, "Then the lass comes. Now move. Tick-tock." Aidan took the lead out of the alcove, and sure enough, a tiny woman with long, black hair and multiple bruises appeared out of a doorway. Her eyes bulged at the sight of them. Aidan put a hand up. "It's okay."

Airmid spoke to her in Spanish. "We are here to help you too. Give me the key and stand back."

Delilah recoiled behind Rubia, and Airmid opened the door just enough for Aidan to kick the motherfucker open into the back of some unsuspecting piece of shit. It was mayhem then. One man pulled a gun but never had a chance to use it. Douglas had a silencer on his pistol, and the Duke of Roxburghe shot the piece of scum in the head without hesitation. The other two were on the ground with rifles pointed at their heads within seconds, the Belizean soldiers right at their backs.

Douglas said, "You horrible bastard. If you make one sound, I will rip your tongue out with those pliers."

They all took in the state of the two prisoners. They'd been severely beaten, and Danny was missing several fingernails, blood dripping from his hands. They hung from the ceiling like sides of beef, barely breathing. Two men from Aidan's team cut the ropes efficiently, while two more trussed up the other two men with duct tape.

Airmid looked at Arturo Reyes and knew it would be so easy and a gift to the world if she shot him in the back of the head right now. He narrowed his eyes on her and said, "You have no idea what you've done. I will find you, dear Tara." She kicked the piece of shit so hard, he vomited. Dirty pool, yes, but she didn't feel an ounce of regret. She went to her Daniel and held his face gently as he just kept trying to breathe. He was on his knees. "I'm here, Danny. We're going home."

Daniel croaked something unintelligible and then said, "Douglas?"

"I'm right here, brother. And a sight better off than you. Can you walk, do you think?" Douglas's tone was as gentle as he'd ever heard it. Then he saw flashes of armed military men, utterly focused and covering the backs of Airmid and Douglas.

Daniel said, "Get these fucking ropes off me, and I'll sprint out of here."

They went down the hallway in pairs. A team of eight, plus two rescued prisoners and two civilians. The guard was still knocked out, but starting to twitch. They all stepped over him.

Just as Airmid and Douglas came behind Aidan with Daniel between them, all hell broke loose. Aidan shot one guard in the shoulder as another took aim at Airmid or Danny. One or both of them. She was one-handed, helping his cousin walk. Aidan didn't think. He jumped in front of her, returning fire as the guard's rapid-speed automatic weapon hit him with high-caliber rounds to the chest and shoulder. The last thing he clearly heard was his cousin screaming over the chaos.

# 19

Daniel's head was fuzzy, but he tried to keep his weight off his partners as the estate's perimeter exploded into pandemonium. He needed a fucking weapon. He watched his cousin shoot a guard. His cousin. Where the hell had Aidan come from? Was he dreaming? No, Aidan was training in Belize. Jesus, Airmid must have gone to the army for help.

No sooner did Aidan take out the guard than another one turned his weapon toward them. Toward Airmid. *No!* Then the words came to him. *Fake left.* Daniel grabbed Airmid's shoulder and pushed left as the man readjusted his aim, then he jerked her right and curled his body around her as Douglas opened fire on the man. But not before his cousin jumped in front of them, taking the blast of the man's weapon full force. Aidan returned fire at the same time as Douglas, taking out the threat. But Daniel heard the rounds hit Aidan. He heard the impact and the breath shoot out of his cousin's lungs. "Aidan!"

He dropped to his knees, everything forgotten as Aidan gasped for breath, his eyes wide as he stared at Daniel. "Go!" he rasped. "Go, Danny. Get her and go!"

There was shooting coming from outside the gate as Douglas pulled him to his feet and then dragged him. Douglas said, "They've got him! Run, man! Or it's all for nothing." He saw Rubia running full force with Delilah under her arm, the last two out of the building.

The Belizean soldiers carried Aidan between them as troops with various uniforms lit the area up from the exterior forest surrounding the isolated compound. Some British soldiers took Aidan as the Belizean soldiers covered their retreat. Daniel could barely walk, and he noticed two of the men were carrying Antony. Arturo's men had taken a hot branding iron to the bottom of his feet, so no surprise that he couldn't walk. Thankfully, regardless of what they'd done to him, Daniel still had his shoes on his feet. That damned GPS tracker had likely saved his ass. He croaked the words, "Aidan. Where is my cousin?"

He heard one of the men yell, "We need a medic!"

Airmid was in his ear, trying to calm him. They were all loaded into two military trucks and they were off. And whatever happened after that did not involve them. It was the Belizean Government's problem. These were good people, and they didn't deserve to have their country invaded with drugs or drug workers any more than the Netherlands or the UK.

Daniel was starting to pass out, but he couldn't. Someone was crying. He focused his eyes and then saw her. "Airmid."

Airmid kissed him so gently. He was brutally beaten. The medic from the Belizean Army was treating Antony, one from the dragoons was treating Danny, and two other British Army medics were working on Aidan. *Please, God. Don't let him die.* Aidan had saved her. He and Danny. Both putting themselves in direct harm to protect her. Aidan O'Brien had a wonderful life. A sweet, intelligent wife. Three beautiful children. She watched Daniel reach for him, fighting the medics and trying to get to Aidan. Airmid said, "Move him closer! Let him talk to him. They are family."

Aidan felt someone take his hand, then he heard him. The soft burr of his lowlander cousin pleading with him. His throat was so dry. Aidan said, "Danny. I'm okay. It's okay."

Daniel whispered, "Please, Aidan. Please don't make me go home without you. Don't break our hearts." He felt his cousin hoist himself to his side, groaning with pain. Aidan looked at him. Jesus, Daniel had the Mullen eyes. He looked like Uncle John. It was like seeing a ghost.

Aidan gave him a weak grin and said, "It's okay, Danny. We'll convalesce at Mam's. Lemon cookies and good craic. It's okay. I'm not going anywhere." He was grasping for air, his words labored. But he felt where the bullets had hit his chest, luckily not penetrating, and at least one to the shoulder, which had missed his body armor. He was having trouble breathing, which he didn't understand. He was wearing his bulky vest, but he felt them gently lift it off him to get a look at his chest. He glanced at Daniel and saw his mother's face. Then nothing but the buzz of semiconsciousness.

———

## Glengormely, Northern Ireland

Alanna answered the phone after two rings. Unknown caller would normally go unanswered, but with Aidan gone, she knew an international call could come up as unknown. And something in her just felt a tug. "Hello. Yes, Lieutenant. I remember you." She watched as Davey's head turned in her direction. "Just hold on a minute, so I can get to my paperwork in my office. The kids are watching TV."

As if he knew, he just said, "I'll wait until you're alone. Thank you."

She knew he was alive. They'd never tell her something over the phone if he wasn't alive. But something was wrong. This was against protocol for a lieutenant to call her from a satellite phone. Something had to have gone to shit. She said with a smile, "Davey, watch your sister and brother for a minute. Momma has to take this call in the office."

The office was a nook in her bedroom because their house was small. She closed the door and said, "Tell me."

When he finished, she sat on her bed, shaking. Insane with the need to get there and be by his side. But it wasn't secure, and her children needed her to stay strong and stay put. It went against her very nature, but she had spoken to the colonel in Belize after Kearsley had passed off the phone. She was, under no circumstances, to come to Belize. And Daniel had been right in the thick of it. Captured and held for ransom. Beaten and tortured to gain access to his wealth. And Aidan had gone after him. They were both alive. Andrew Douglas was calling Daniel's mother.

Now, Alanna had to get her bearings and call the family. But she needed a minute. She needed to tell Davey and Isla something. She needed to do something ... anything. She should be there. She started to shake uncontrollably, going into her bathroom and turning on the shower and the faucet. She threw up, gagging and sobbing. Aidan. Her Aidan. Her mate. *You will not leave me. You will not leave me.* She sent the message across the ocean. Across the universe. And he bloody well better hear her.

She rinsed her mouth, closed the lid of the toilet, and sat. She sat and rocked and cried. Because she couldn't let the kids see her like this. She had to be strong. He was alive. The medical information was sparse, but he'd been shot. He was in surgery. But he was alive. *You will not leave me.* She repeated the words in her head, a call out to Aidan and to God and anyone else in the heavens who was listening.

Then Alanna thought of something. She wiped her face, her hands trembling as she looked at her phone. The abbey at St. Clare's Mission had finally upgraded their communications. Liam was the closest. Not close, but way closer than the rest of them. And he was a doctor. He'd want to advocate for Aidan, even if it was over the phone. She went to the app that would allow her to call him without international dialing. And thank God, he answered. Whatever time it was in Brazil, he answered.

———

Aidan was wheeled into surgery, that's all he knew. His breathing had eased a tiny bit, but his chest was on fire. They'd cut his clothes off and were prepping him. He heard machines and the voices of doctors and nurses in a language he couldn't follow. He felt like he'd run a marathon. He kept slipping in and out, and he knew he'd lost a lot of blood. As he threatened to go under again, he heard something about his BP dropping. Then everything went silent. That's when he heard her. His Alanna. With her sweet, Southern belle voice and her unrelenting strength. *You will not leave me. You will not leave me. You will not leave me.*

———

### St. Luke's Hospital, Western Belize

Daniel came awake to the sounds of a heart monitor and nurses bustling in the hall. It took him a minute to realize where he was. He was saved. He was alive.

Daniel hadn't wanted to be separated from his cousin. In fact, he'd been a proper prick about it until the nurse had threatened to give him a chemical nap. Karl Heusner Memorial in Belize City was the only trauma center in the country, so he agreed to the transfer as Aidan's next of kin. What he didn't agree to was himself being left at St. Luke's.

British Army guards were stationed at both locations, so his cousin was protected, but he needed to see him. Be with him. Daniel was being treated for his own injuries. Three missing fingernails, a few cracked ribs, a fractured wrist, two loose teeth, multiple bruises and lacerations, electrical burns to his back and chest, and so many torn muscles from hanging from the ceiling, he'd lost count. And something about bruised kidneys and them running tests on his liver and spleen. Repeated beatings and blows to the abdomen had them checking his internal organs for unseen bleeding.

Airmid and Douglas were on either side of him, stoic and tense. He finally addressed the elephant in the room. "If I hadn't done what I did, all four of us would have been taken. And they'd have used you against me. I would have talked. I would have told them anything to spare you."

Airmid's jaw was tight, and she swiped her tears away. Endless tears that he hated seeing. Douglas was the one who finally responded. "I know why you did what you did. And it freed us to go for help. I understand, Danny. It doesn't mean either of us liked it. We were afraid you were dead. So, pardon us if we need to take a minute to quell the irrational anger that we're both feeling."

Airmid stood at that, just looking out the window. More wiping those tears. Daniel wanted to hold her. But he couldn't indulge himself right now. "I need to contact Alanna."

"The army already did," Airmid said softly. "She wants you to call when you are up to it. She wanted to come, but given the circumstances, it's not safe for her right now." It had been three hours since they'd made it out of the bush and headed toward the hospital.

"What of Reyes?" Daniel asked.

Harry walked through the door at that moment, having been in Antony's room before this. "The raid happened an hour ago. Apparently, they found Reyes with his throat cut in the basement."

Douglas jerked at the words. "We did not kill him. I killed two men who were armed and fighting, that was it. Not that I didn't want to kill Reyes. Believe me, it was very tempting. We didn't kill him."

"Of course not," Harry said.

"He knows this because I killed him." Rubia entered the room, dressed in a chic, casual business suit. "It was not my imperative, but it wasn't forbidden. And after hearing him repeatedly rape Delilah through his office door, I think I'll sleep at night."

She walked to Daniel's bedside, smoothing a stray spike of hair away from his eyebrow. "I'm sorry. I didn't know you were down there for hours. Not that I could have helped, but luckily, your man Douglas reached out."

Douglas stood, his brow raised. "And I'll ask you again, Freya. Who the bloody fuck are you?"

She smirked at him. She actually smirked. Harry answered, "Agent Freya is with the German BND. She's been infiltrating this cartel for the last six months. She started with Jensen. Delilah was one of her assets."

Douglas's face grew serious. "How is she?"

Agent Freya said, "She's alive. That's all I can expect from her right now. Arturo Reyes murdered her sister after turning her into a drug mule. Six months ago, I befriended her. She was already in so deep, trying to get close to Reyes. I gave her more to work toward than revenge. And instead of getting justice, she became a permanent fixture for his nightly exploits. She refused to let me get her out. Not until we got enough to take him down. I shouldn't have listened to her."

"Is she Belizean?" he asked.

"No, she's Columbian. And she's going home to get her family. The only one left is her sister's child and a grandmother. My government will relocate them."

Delilah. Little, demure Delilah had been there, waiting with a key. Such a risk. She deserved a fresh start. Airmid said, "Thank you for getting us inside."

Freya said, "Danke schön for the ride out. I'm afraid the situation got away from me."

"What about Jensen?" Daniel finally asked.

"He's in custody. He will likely die in prison. They have his wife," she said casually. "I don't know where. Probably Columbia. It's not my problem. And Freya is my grandmother's name."

Douglas tilted his head, asking, "Are we going to be blessed with your real name?"

She smiled sweetly. "Nein." Then she went to Airmid and hugged her. "Goodbye, my dear. And rethink this life. You are too good in here." She put fingers to Airmid's heart. "Too pure for this fieldwork."

Airmid snorted. "Consider it done."

Then Agent Freya went to Douglas and pulled his neck down for a kiss. A long one considering they weren't alone. Douglas felt her slip something into his pocket, but he wasn't going to check. She said against his ear, "Goodbye, pet. I'm sorry we didn't have more time."

———

Daniel checked himself out of the hospital against medical advice within the next two hours, and Airmid was so angry, she'd actually gone silent. He said, "I need to see him."

He called his cousin's wife as soon as he took possession of his secure phone. Alanna was barely keeping it together. Daniel said, "I'm sorry, love. Christ, I am so sorry. And I can't explain everything. The most important thing I can tell you is that he's stable. The round in his shoulder went through and exited. The one to the chest never cleared his body armor, but one round entered the space closer to the armpit, between the vest panels. They were able to get it out, but his lung collapsed. He's okay. The entry wound into his lung is already starting to seal, but he has a chest tube in for now. He is strong and healthy, and he will recover."

Airmid didn't catch the entire conversation, but suddenly, Daniel shot ramrod straight, wincing in pain. "What the hell do you mean, Liam is on his way?" He let out a series of wet coughs.

Alanna said calmly, "No one is telling us everything. I know something more happened. And maybe you can't talk about it right now, but you were being treated and they wouldn't let me come. Liam is landing in Belize City in about nine hours. He took a flight out of Manaus two hours ago. I talked to one of Aidan's men. A Lieutenant Kearsley. He said there were no other injuries. What the hell happened, Danny?"

All Daniel could manage was, "He did it for me. He shielded me. This is my fault, and I'm so sorry. If I could take his place, I would. I got abducted on a jungle tour, along with my guide."

Alanna said, "I called your sister, Danny. I know you're going to be pissed about that, but you don't get a say when you are passed out with multiple injuries. I told her I didn't know what happened, but that you were injured and stable. Call home. I need to go now. I love you, Danny. We all do. This wasn't your fault. Aidan is who he is." Her voice broke. "Shielding the other guy is what Aidan does. It's why I fell in love with him. I have to go. Michael is calling me."

———

Daniel couldn't stand it anymore. He just pulled her to him in the back seat. She resisted, not wanting to hurt him. Then she finally settled, putting her face in his neck. Then they slept.

When Douglas woke them, they were at the hospital in Belize City. Daniel had a hat and sunglasses on, trying like hell to cover his battered face. The same with his partners. Douglas walked behind Harry, silent as he took in everything. They would all leave on their tourist passports, including Harry after a bit of cleanup. He'd have Antony with him. Their work here was done for good, and maybe someone else would take their place, but Britain was calling them all home before the Belizean Government detained them or caught wind of their real mission. Daniel had to get Aidan out of here as soon as he could travel. He wouldn't leave until then.

Douglas said, "I'm going to take Airmid to get something to eat and some coffee. Go, brother. See that he's well. Morgan wants everyone on a plane by tomorrow morning, but I told her you shouldn't leave."

Daniel said, "Not fucking happening." He turned toward Airmid, feeling like he could bridge the distance. He took her face in his hands. "You should get some sleep."

Airmid said, "We go together or I stay. I won't let us split up." Her jaw was tight and he understood it. She'd lost the only man she'd ever loved in a military training accident. The last two days had been a non-stop trigger, no doubt.

"Okay, just give me a bit of time with him," Daniel said. And in the morning, she was getting on that plane. He kissed her, soft and tenderly, on the forehead, and he felt her tremble. When he looked her in the eyes, she was guarded and just a little bit wrecked, and he didn't know how to fix it.

Daniel went into Aidan's room, and he was glad to see Aidan's men hadn't left him. "We sent the guard packing. It was drawing more attention than we liked," Ramirez said in stunted English. Harry agreed, and he sent Ramirez on his way.

Harry said, "You don't need the attention either. Go see that pretty wife of yours. Lay low, lad. Thank you for everything, but this is done. For now, at least."

They spoke lowly, and Daniel left them to it. He needed to see Aidan.

Aidan took a sip of his bottle of water, but he almost choked on it as he caught sight of his cousin. He'd obviously blocked out how bad Daniel had looked, but it all rushed back to him. Them lowering him to the ground, hung from the ceiling like a side of raw beef. Aidan's chest tube gave a twinge of pain as he struggled for the right amount of fatherly chastisement.

"For fuck's sake, Danny. Why are you out of the hospital?" But he couldn't maintain the indignation. His voice was raspy from being intubated. And there was also the fact that his cousin's eyes were destroyed. Not just due to bruising and swelling. He watched Danny's eyes rake over him. "I'm okay, brother," Aidan said hoarsely, even though his chest was on fire.

Daniel dumped himself into the chair next to Aidan's bed, his eyes fighting not to tear up. He put his forehead down on Aidan's good shoulder and shuddered. "Why did you do it, Aidan? Ye've got three bairns at home." And like usual, when Daniel was stressed, his Scottish heritage came through more pronouncedly.

Aidan put a hand in his cousin's hair. "Because you're my blood, mo deartháir. It's that simple. I was wearing body armor and you weren't. And there was the lass. Your woman. He could have just as easily hit her." He adjusted himself, wincing.

Daniel looked up at him, just a little bit destroyed. He cleared his throat. "She's not mine. I thought maybe there could be something, but I think I may have scared her off. She's buried one lover. I feel her pulling away." He shook himself, wincing a bit. "But that doesn't matter right now. What the hell am I going to tell Aunt Sorcha? The whole family is going to string me up all over again."

"We'll come up with something, Danny. I'm assuming no one knows why you were really here? What the three of you really are?"

Daniel said, "My mother knows. And that's only because she knew about my papa. The man who raised me. No one else knows. Not my siblings or grandparents. Just you. It has to stay that way, Aidan. I'm sorry to put that on you, but you can't even tell your wife. I'm sorry you were brought into this."

Aidan smiled a crooked smile. "Some things are just meant to happen, Danny. What the hell are the chances that I was right where I was when this happened? That we were both here in Central America? We were brought together so that we could both come home in one piece. I believe that. I should have died a few times already, but here I am. Banged up but still kicking. And your woman will come around. I saw her with you. She'd have died a thousand times over to get you out of there. Believe me, Douglas tried to get her to stay back." Daniel's chest rumbled with laughter and he actually coughed and groaned.

Daniel said, "How did that go over?"

"Your mate is fierce. It's a thing in this family," Aidan said.

Daniel's face shifted. "She's not my mate. And maybe that's better for her," he said.

Aidan said, "Go to her. Don't let her get too far into her head about this. I mean, you look like roadkill, so seduction is out. Just be with her. She'll come back to you if this is the real deal."

Daniel squeezed his arm. "I don't want to leave you."

Aidan glanced over at the recliner. "Then crank that thing back and get some sleep. I'll see if the medic can get you some over-the-counter pain meds. You are a walking injury, ye stubborn jackass."

Satisfied with that, Daniel texted Douglas.

———

Douglas gave Airmid a patient look and said, "You need to sleep. He's better off here. He checked himself out of the hospital like an idiot. Better to ride shotgun with his cousin's medical team in case he takes a turn. And O'Brien's men will watch over them both."

Airmid was too tired to argue. She just slumped in her seat in the cafeteria, staring at her untouched food. "Okay."

"You've been uncharacteristically quiet, sis," Douglas said, giving her a wink when she rolled her eyes.

"It's been a long two days. I'm processing," she said.

"Let's go, then. Call your daughter. Get some rest. It's a long flight tomorrow," he said.

She wrinkled her brow. "We can't leave Danny."

"We aren't going to leave him. You are going back as scheduled. I'm staying with him until he's well enough to fly. He's going on pure stubbornness right now, but he's going to crash. His body is going to give out, and he needs to have medical care standing by. I'd give it three days at least."

"Then I stay!" She raised her voice.

Douglas said, "You have your orders, Airmid. And you have a child. One who has never been without her mum this long. Once you get some sleep and speak with her, you will understand that I'm right. I need to concentrate on Danny right now and getting him out of here safely. I need you home, and so does Erin."

She closed her eyes. "That's not fair."

Douglas's face was almost sad. "All is fair in love and war, sister dear. Now chuck that rot in the bin and let's go."

———

Aidan woke to someone kissing his forehead. But unlike the soft lips of his mam or his beloved Alanna, the stubble was a dead giveaway. He opened his eyes to see his brother, tan and rugged, with his hair long and pulled back. "Liam," he croaked.

"Hello," Liam said, his voice trembling. He was crying.

"I'm okay, Liam. I swear it," Aidan said. He raised his bed up so he could talk to his brother better. "Did you just get here?" He was interrupted by a moan behind him. The lights were dim and Liam jumped. Startled to find someone lying down near the wall. Or lying down as much as they could in a reclining lounge chair.

"Who the—" Aidan turned the light on in his room and Liam went right to him. "Jesus Christ, is that Danny?"

"Yes," Aidan said. "He left AMA from the other hospital. He hasn't left my side."

"I don't understand any of this. How the fuck? What the fuck?" Liam was putting a hand on Daniel's forehead. Then he didn't speak as he checked his cousin. Obviously forgoing the obscenities for a more clinical assessment. "How long has he been like this? He's febrile, and there's a rattle in his breathing," Liam said.

"He wasn't this bad when he went to sleep, but it's been a few hours. They have me on pain meds and I crashed. I should have called a doctor," Aidan said.

"You've had a bit on your plate, brother. Now, call the nurse," Liam said. "With the wee button. Get someone in here. And I can get by in Portuguese, but my Spanish is kind of shite."

Aidan didn't think, he just did it. He called Airmid. She was frantic. Aidan said, "No. I just need you on speakerphone. Don't leave the hotel."

Airmid said, "I'm on my way. I don't fly out for several hours. And if I need to delay, I will."

The nurse came into the room, and Liam started trying to speak to her in Portuguese, but Airmid interrupted. "Just tell me what is going on, and I'll translate it. Tell Daniel I'm coming."

———

They'd tried to move Daniel to his own room, but he'd refused. They gave him a bed next to Aidan, as it was a double room. Due to the sensitive nature of Aidan's injuries and the lovable army goons watching him around the clock, it worked for everyone that this be the only roommate they'd agree to for the major. Aidan looked at Daniel. "You don't sound Irish, but that stubborn streak is no lie."

Airmid smirked at that, but Douglas said, "Ye've obviously not spent enough time around Scots if you need to ask where that stubborn streak came from."

Daniel was tired, but he couldn't keep the smile off his face. His two O'Brien cousins were mingling with his best friend and his ... well, he didn't know what she was. She was the love of his life. But he suspected that if he voiced that right now, like he had during that jungle chase, she'd likely run out of the room. He cleared his throat. "You've got to go back. Nolan and Cormac need you there before the court appearance. They want to fully brief you."

Airmid's eyes teared up. "I feel like I'm getting torn in two."

Daniel said, "There's no need. I'm a grown man, and I'm going to be right behind you. I'm in good hands. But who will speak for you and the child if you're not home? Erin is the first priority. I promise you, I will get on that plane as soon as they allow it." They were pumping him full of antibiotics and a fever reducer, so he was already improving. The cough was murder with the broken ribs, but he'd live.

Airmid just nodded her head. She knew he was right. She stood and so did Douglas. "It was good to meet you both," she said to Aidan and Liam. And as Douglas escorted her out, Liam whistled through his teeth.

"Ye've got it bad, brother," Liam said. Daniel just closed his eyes. Liam's chest grumbled with laughter. "Take it from someone who made a cock-up of legendary proportions when it came to their mate. It's easier to submit to your destiny."

Daniel said, "It's not that easy. Her first serious love, the father of her child, was killed in a training accident. He died and left her pregnant. And given what's happened to me, I think she's retreating. Granted, she never said she loved me. She didn't even kiss me goodbye just now." The thought gave him a pang of pain in his chest. "Even if she was starting to love me, I think I may have just sealed my fate. She has the child to worry about."

Liam said pensively, "So she's more so in the place I was in when I fell for Izzy. I buried Eve, and I thought that was it for me." Liam ran a hand over his face. "Fucking hell, that's a tough place to be. Terrifying, actually. And with a child, no less. I'm sorry, Danny. I hope she comes around."

"Should I ask her to, though? To come around?" Daniel asked absently, then shook himself. "It doesn't matter. Not now. I just need to get out of this bed and go home."

Liam narrowed his eyes on Daniel, then looked at Aidan. "Are you going to tell me what really happened? Because I'm getting the feeling this was more than a tourist abduction."

Daniel didn't bat an eye. "So, being rich and getting nabbed by a drug cartel isn't dramatic enough for you?" Aidan was stone-faced, giving away nothing.

"Oh, it is. It's just not the whole of it, I think. But I'll leave it, brother. Best get the story straight before my mother has a go at you though. She's like the fucking KGB with her interrogation tactics." And they all had to laugh because it was the truth.

# 20

## HAWICK, SCOTLAND

Cormac Carrington escorted the court-appointed social worker into the manor in Hawick, much to everyone's dismay. He whispered to Sorcha, "It's better to get a quick visit out of the way to appease the court. We have nothing to hide and everything to gain by this. The grandparents are insinuating that Ms. Roberts left her child in the wild and skipped town with a lover or some shite. I've been digging. They not only don't have a case, but they've been a bit underhanded. I can't tell, so don't ask. It's all going to come out." Cormac wouldn't tell anyone until he'd spoken with his client. Then she could share what she wanted. But his cousin Aidan had been doing some digging around, and those fools were going to have some explaining to do.

The social worker met the staff, interviewed Donna, Davis, Constance, and the housekeepers who were there for the day. She inspected the nursery, spent some time with Erin, then she was done. "I don't anticipate any issues," the woman said sweetly. "It's every child's dream, and she appears to be healthy and loved.

Her mother works. Sometimes she travels for that work, albeit rarely. She has done as well as any mother could in order to secure her safety and quality of care while she travels. Erin is a delightful, well-spoken child. You did correctly to nip the accusations in the bud and comply immediately, and my report will show all of that ... and more. I just want to go over one area of concern with regard to Erin's interview, and then we'll be done."

———

Sorcha went into the parlor to have tea with her nephew. "Cormac, thank you so much for this."

Cormac said, "Not a problem, Auntie. My father is in a trial, and it's looking like I'll have to take the lead on this. I will fight for Erin as if she were my own child. I promise."

They were interrupted by a ring of the doorbell at the front of the house, and Sorcha heard Davis say, "Madam, you know you have no need of such formality. This is your home as well. Please, it is so good to see you."

Then a female voice, English and prim, said, "Davis, my dear. After all these years, will you finally call me Molly?"

Sorcha's face went starkly white. Cormac took her hand and said, "Auntie, what is it?"

Davis had the good sense to look awkward. After all, there was nothing about this family he didn't know. "Mrs. O'Brien, please meet Daniel's mother, Lady MacPherson."

Sorcha almost pitied the woman. Almost. "Molly MacPherson. Yes, my name is Sorcha. Sorcha Mullen O'Brien."

Molly was pale, and she suspected that Davis had warned her before he brought her into the parlor. Sorcha said icily, "We were just having some tea. This is my nephew, Cormac Carrington."

Molly stepped farther into the room, head held high. "It's a pleasure." Cormac could tell something was up, but he just treated the woman with politeness. After taking another sip of his tea, he looked at Davis.

Cormac said, "Davis, I need to call the office and scan a report. Do you think Daniel would mind if I made use of his office?" And that was it. They found themselves—these two women who couldn't be more different—alone and just looking at one another.

Molly said, "Danny has spoken very highly of you. Of all of you. His grandparents and his O'Brien extended family."

Sorcha said, "I'm glad." She swallowed her resentment. She would gain nothing by lashing out at this woman. It was a long time ago, and none of it could be undone. "And he speaks highly of his family. His siblings and you. He actually speaks very highly of his papa. Daniel is the best of men. He has a good and steady heart."

Molly swallowed hard, and Sorcha was not surprised when she saw the tears mist the woman's eyes. She was close to tears herself. She raised her chin. "We cannot undue the past, Lady MacPherson. You made choices I don't agree with, but there are always extenuating circumstances when it comes to an unexpected pregnancy. If John ever talked about me, I'm sure you know I'm a midwife. I've seen a great many things in my profession. Things that perhaps will help me to muster forgiveness when the heart of a sister alone could not muster it. And you were honoring your husband's wishes. You told Daniel when you were no longer held to that promise. You raised him in a privileged, happy home. As much as I weep for our lost years with him and his lost years with my brother, I am at least grateful for that fact."

Molly Price-MacPherson looked as miserable as a woman could look. She said, "Please call me Molly." Then she said, "I think this was an inevitable meeting. And I think it would have been easier had you screamed at me. Raged and judged me. It is your willingness to set your anger aside and offer mercy that cuts me to the quick."

She took a napkin from the tea tray and blotted her face. "I did love him. I loved him with all the freeness and passionate frenzy of youth. And it may comfort you to know that I battled with my decision almost daily. Not because I didn't love my Robert. It wasn't the love between John and I, for which I mourned as much as the loss of his child. I was a thief. I knew it then and I know it now. You could not possibly hate me any more than I hate myself. But I was afraid. And I let my parents separate us. And every waking hour of every day, for nearly a month, my parents tried to get me to just terminate the pregnancy. They were breaking me, unrelenting in their verbal assaults. Then Robert came and told them all to go hang. And he took me straight to the vicar and gave me the protection of his name. His title. I didn't speak to my parents for five years. Even now, it's once a year for the children's sake. But we all did not come out of this deception unscathed."

Sorcha wiped her own eyes. "Thank God for good men. You broke my brother, Molly. And I will not absolve you of that. Perhaps John will, when it's time to see him again. But Daniel is a wonderful man, and we all love and cherish him. Hanging on to my anger is not going to do him any service, and my brother wouldn't have wanted it. We only have now. My parents are old. They have only now to love him. And we will not sully these years with old pain."

Sorcha stood and poured the tea, and Molly accepted it gratefully. Honestly, the woman looked close to a complete breakdown. Sorcha said, "Now, let us talk of Daniel. I assume you are here because of his ordeal in Belize?"

Molly nodded. "I spoke to him at the hospital. He told me about the cartel that had been kidnapping wealthy tourists for ransom. His partner is on her way back, and Douglas will remain with him." Molly was the only one who knew what Daniel really did for a living, but she stuck to the official account, knowing not to ask any questions.

"Yes, he will return, and then my Aidan, thank the Holy Mother." Sorcha crossed herself.

"Your son Aidan? And where is he?" Molly asked, and that was when Sorcha realized that this woman didn't know it all. So, she told her. Molly's hand was over her mouth, her eyes wide.

"And your boy saved my Danny?" And that's when Molly's tears transitioned into sobs.

———

Molly was staring, she knew it, but as the woman who looked just like John walked her up to the nursery, she couldn't take her eyes off the child. "She's so beautiful. Why do you think Danny went to such lengths for a colleague? I mean, to move the child here and —" Then Molly's eyes shot to Sorcha's.

Sorcha said, "I think he's in love with her. This Airmid. At least, that's what we all think. And I won't lie. Donna and I have dissected this situation like two nosey little hens. The feeling is mutual on her side of things, I believe. They're like two tea kettles, steaming up the place when they are in the same room. But the lass is wounded, terribly so, by the loss of Erin's father. And by the bloody grandparents. Apparently, they didn't like their son taking up with an Irish soldier. I mean, they are firmly middle class, and this isn't the bloody Middle Ages. But they made enough trouble that he hadn't married her before his death. She had the child alone, and then they tried to take the child."

Molly's prim demeanor was downright crumbling. She almost growled the words. "I thought things had changed, but some people just refuse to evolve. Imagine this kind of attitude still exists?" She shook her head. "Is your nephew and brother-in-law a good legal team?"

"They are," Sorcha said. "And they've had some practice, recently, with family law. We keep them busy, I'm afraid. But that's another story for another time. Right now, we have to get Daniel home. The Earl of Hawick may have some pull in the proceedings, where a prior soldier and single mother might not." And Sorcha saw the wheels turning. Yes, they were definitely turning. A nosey, interfering mother who had notions about exactly what would solve this problem.

———

**London, England**

The agency swooped Airmid up from the airport, refusing to let her go home without a full briefing. When she completed the interviews and statements to their satisfaction, Morgan rescued her and set about driving her to Hawick. She cried the whole way. Silent, but consistent. She cried for Daniel. She cried for Alanna because she must be going out of her mind. And she cried about the situation with her daughter. It all came out, and somehow Morgan had understood the way only another woman could. Sometimes your body needed the release. Grief and stress were physical as much as mental.

Morgan finally spoke. "Aidan O'Brien will be flown home in two days, along with the rest of his unit. The mission was done right. We had both governments' approval for the British forces to serve as backup. After the flooding, they were overwhelmed. And they get to claim credit for a sizable drug bust. But the British Government wants our troops out of there before anyone catches wind they were involved. We told the Belizean Government the same story. You were charity workers on a tourist passport. Daniel was kidnapped for ransom."

Airmid felt numb. "And Danny and Douglas?"

Morgan said, "They'll be home in three days, counting the travel time. They admitted Daniel while you were in the air. Apparently, he was pushing pneumonia because he's a pigheaded idiot."

Airmid closed her eyes. "I shouldn't have left."

"You didn't have a choice. This is the job. And speaking of which, I have an offer to promote you to field agent. They're looking to plant someone in—"

Airmid cut her off. "No, I want my analyst job back. No more fieldwork. I'll serve as an interpreter when you need me, but no. No way."

Morgan nodded. "Good, I'm glad. You were brilliant, truly. But this is the sort of job that will eat you alive if you don't really have the taste for it."

"And Danny and Douglas do? Have a taste for it?" Airmid asked stonily. She thought of Agent Freya. She'd actually cut Arturo's throat if her account was to be believed. Not that Airmid mourned the bastard. Especially given what he'd done to Delilah. That frail woman with haunted eyes that seemed to be playing a part at those disgusting VIP soirées.

"I think they do it out of duty, to be honest. Especially Danny. His father was MI-6. I'm sure he told you that. During the Cold War and then after. The Earl of Hawick isn't a particularly prestigious or historic house in the peerage. Roxburghe's exposure has been a lot more to manage, but they've got that certain something that seems to click with fieldwork. Douglas is brilliant and he was a very good analyst, but I think he's found his place. He'll likely leave on assignment within the next two weeks."

"I won't ask, don't worry," Airmid said. "I just want to get my daughter and go home. The hearing is Monday. The fact that I can't really tell them what I was doing overseas is the biggest stressor. I'm just hoping it doesn't come up."

Morgan said, "I know. And I don't think it'll be a problem. But if we have to pull discreet strings or call a favor in with a higher court, then we will do what we can. I just can't let you tell a roomful of people what you were doing. It likely wouldn't work in your favor, and it would expose Danny and Douglas."

Airmid said, "I know. And I appreciate it. Maybe this is all just more bluster. Tommy's parents are just troublemakers. Likely, they found us gone and started stamping their feet about it."

Morgan hoped so because that little girl belonged with her mother.

————

Airmid took the steps so fast, she was shocked she didn't trip. It was raining, and her daughter was waiting in the doorway. She scooped her up and held her. Had it really only been a week? All the air travel time, it had seemed longer. "I missed you so much, love." She couldn't quit crying.

Erin said, "It's okay, Mammy. I've been having so much fun! I missed you!" Airmid carried her to the closest chair and sat. She wiped her face and then really looked at the girl. She kissed her all over her face. She had some sort of pixie dust on her cheeks and chin. "Davis made us a secret spot in the garden. We decorated it like the fairies do and had some special magic biscuits. I want to stay and show Cora!"

Airmid smiled at the girl. "We need to go home, love. Davis is ready to take us home so we can sleep in our own beds. Wouldn't you like that?" Airmid asked.

The girl nodded. "Yes, but can we come back? Where's Mr.

Danny and Mr. Douglas? I made pictures for them. And we have to come see my pony!"

Airmid saw motion from the doorway to the parlor. It was a petite woman whom she'd seen in a photo on the second floor. Daniel's mother. The woman smiled at her. "I'm Danny's mum." *Mum? More like the Dowager Countess of Hawick. Jesus.* And Airmid had just had a maternal meltdown inside the entrance of Hawick Manor. The woman smiled at her. She looked like a countess. "I think I speak for Daniel when I say that everyone is welcome for a visit at any time. And Davis will make sure they are taking care of the ponies. I love them, too. My husband and I used to ride for hours. Even in the rain."

Airmid gave her a grateful smile. She thought about those journals Daniel had copied to his e-reader. A love story of sorts. "Thank you, Lady MacPherson."

"Davis is the only one who calls me that. I suppose it's accurate until this home is occupied by a new countess."

Davis said with a small smile, "You will still be a lady, even then. It's a title you've earned."

Molly gave him a small smile. "But please call me Molly, Airmid. I've heard a bit about you from my daughter and from Mrs. O'Brien. And it's been so nice having the sound of a child's laughter in this home again. It's always been a happy home." She stood and said, "But we won't keep you. You're exhausted. A mum knows these things. I think it'll be nice to be home around familiar things." She touched Airmid's hair and gave a gentle smile.

"And if you need assistance on Monday, the House of Hawick will be there without delay. I mean that. I know something about being bullied when you feel like you have no one. You have us, my dear. All of us." Molly turned and looked at Sorcha O'Brien, and the two women let something pass between them. A sort of peace.

Then she spun toward Morgan. "Hello again, Ms. Morgan. Please, come in and let us have a cup of tea."

———

Sorcha felt like an intruder just now, so she went upstairs to help Airmid ready the child for travel. It was minutes until the little girl was nodding off on the daybed. Airmid said, "I want to thank your family for everything. This was more like a holiday for Erin. She wasn't stressed, and I knew she was in good hands. Daniel is so fond of you all. The O'Briens and Murphys. I'm so sorry about what happened to Aidan. It was my fault. He was protecting me."

Sorcha said, "I don't know it all, love, and I suspect I never will. But Aidan would never let anything happen to Daniel, or the woman he cares for, if he was in the position to stop it. He was injured, but you could have very well been killed. It isn't your fault. Any of it." Sorcha folded a little shirt and handed it to Airmid as she talked. Her voice was tight with emotion. "That's not to say I didn't lose my bloody mind when I found out about him. I did go a bit apeshit, as my daughter-in-law would say. Aidan is my first. My sweet lad. I've come close to losing a son. My youngest, actually. They're all bloody superheroes, but they're not invincible, are they? And here I thought Daniel was safe, running a non-profit and taking care of his estate business. But trouble does have a knack for finding us."

Airmid smiled weakly. "I lost one love in my life. I don't think I'd live through it a second time. And now I have Erin."

Sorcha said, "Well, I suppose we'll have to keep Daniel at those committee meetings and checking on his tenants, and out of the bloody jungle."

Airmid said nothing. She couldn't. Daniel's aunt would likely drop into a dead faint if she knew the whole of it. Knew what her nephew was really doing in Belize. Airmid looked over at her little girl. If they stopped this now, Daniel would become a faint memory. She wouldn't have to worry about him getting killed in the Middle East or South America or somewhere in Eastern Europe. Maybe when this was all over, Airmid could find a nice, sensible man. The mere thought repulsed her. Anyone ever touching her again besides Daniel was inconceivable. The tears started again and Sorcha said nothing. She just stayed. And that was more comfort right now than anything.

————

### Newcastle-Upon-Tyne, Northern England

Davis carried their bags into the house a few at a time while Airmid took her daughter to her master bedroom and put her on the large bed. She was happy to remember she'd given the house a thorough cleaning before leaving. The sun was setting, and she wondered if Erin would just sleep through the night. She'd fallen asleep around five, and they'd left the estate in Scotland at half five. She'd been awake in the car for about a quarter hour before nodding off again. Too much excitement and all that. Airmid needed to speak to her lawyers, but first she had to sleep. She hugged Davis and found she was close to tears again. "Goodbye, Davis. Thank you for treating us like family."

Davis touched her face. "You are family, my girl. It feels like an ending, I know. But just rest. Get this custody business behind you. Everything will look brighter after that. I promise."

Airmid fell asleep next to her daughter, so happy to smell her childish scent and hear her slow, steady breathing. She fingered the blonde curls Erin had inherited from Tommy. The hair Erin's paternal grandfather had possessed in his youth. How could they do this? They'd barely been in the child's life. Something had to be driving this. And Monday, maybe she and Cormac Carrington would find out what it was.

---

Her attorney arrived early the next day, and she was surprised to see that he had an older gentleman with him. She shook both their hands. Nolan Carrington said, "The jury has five members with the flu in the trial I was working. We are in recess for a week to let it all run its course and so they don't spread it to the rest of the jurors. We're too far into the trial to just start over. But I assure you, I am healthy."

They both came in, and she was surprised when she saw a small car pull into the driveway right after them. Sorcha O'Brien came to the door. "I'll be at the local coffee shop. When the lass wakes up, call me and I'll keep her busy. Unless your mum is here?"

Airmid hugged her. "My family is flying in from Northern Ireland the night before the hearing. My parents and my brother. Just for an overnight stay, but they wanted to be here. I appreciate this. And Sorcha, you don't have to leave. Please, come in. You can just hang out on the sofa, and I'll take Nolan and Cormac into my office." It was tiny, but it would do for privacy.

Sorcha said, "I'll do that. I'm spending the night with Maeve and Nolan this evening before I fly back home, and I just thought I'd offer. I'll let you three get down to it."

---

Cormac was a handsome devil. Tall and broad with dark hair and blue eyes. After Cormac briefed Airmid on the reason for this whole mess, Airmid was stunned. He said, "They're trying to make a case for neglect and abandonment. No judge will buy either claim. You've got a career, and no one in their right mind is going to take on the feminists by saying a woman can't work and take care of a child. She's housed more than sufficiently, she has safe childcare, and when you went abroad for short periods of time, you had more than sufficient care for the child. Having your parents and brother there will show that you have a stable support system, even if they are in Ireland and the Middle East. It's good they can all be in the room. The more people who show up for you, the better it looks. Your prior childminder, your neighbors, and the social services care worker have all written statements to the judge and will all testify that Erin is in a happy, safe home and is very loved. Honestly, I don't think they'll be called to court."

Airmid rubbed her temples. "I don't understand why they are doing it."

Cormac said, "I think I may know. With the help of my cousin Aidan and one of your old commanding officers, I started looking into the survivor benefits for the children of fallen soldiers. I mean, he didn't die in combat, but he died on the job."

Airmid said, "Yes, but we weren't married. He never changed his beneficiary from his parents to me. I was pregnant, so he wouldn't have put Erin's name on anything before she was born."

"Ah, yes," Cormac said. "But they had to fill out a lot of paperwork when the benefits were being distributed. One of the questions they always ask is whether the deceased had any children."

"He didn't at the time of death because she wasn't born yet. I tried to look into it. But short of risking amniocentesis to establish paternity, I couldn't prove Erin was his."

Cormac said, "But they could have done a simple cheek swab when she was born. It was three months later. The Devons could have easily held off and received extra benefits for the child once you'd had her. Maybe they knew that, but I doubt it. They lied and said he had no children, then they never updated his veteran paperwork after Erin was born. Now that the army knows about Erin, you have sizable back pay coming to you. Not life insurance, which is what the parents received, but other things that were just for an underage child. If the Devons had custody of Erin, the British Government would be cutting the check to the Devons, not you. Which makes them the biggest rotters in the United Kingdom. My job on Monday is to show the magistrate that they deliberately lied about a child being on the way. They'll likely try to lie and say they didn't know at the time of his death."

Airmid said, "Bullshit they didn't know. Tommy told them. And I can certainly establish paternity because the court ordered a paternity test during the initial custody battle. They never gave me a dime. They told me his bastard wasn't entitled to anything. If I didn't relinquish custody and give up visitation so they could raise her, she'd be lucky if she got a birthday gift from them." Nolan hissed and Cormac's jaw was tight.

Cormac said, "I sincerely hope they make some crack like that in the judge's hearing. And if I have my way, Airmid, they are going to be paying your legal fees for this hearing and the last one. And they will not be getting the family discount."

———

They'd gone over everything until Airmid had a screaming headache. Nolan put a hand on her shoulder. "Jet lag and too much high adventure. Go spend time with your girl. I'll call you in the morning, and we'll go over some of this again. I know it's repetitive, but it's important. And what about Daniel?"

"Do we need him?" Airmid asked.

"It couldn't hurt. He's the one who acquired your full-time

childminder while you were in Scotland and abroad. And you stayed in his home during the absences the Devons are reporting. Constance will be testifying as well. They all arrive on Monday."

Airmid closed her eyes. "It's ridiculous that all these people have to stop their lives for this. Constance is job hunting," Airmid said.

"Donna, Daniel's housekeeper, has already paid her wages for next week and put her up in a local inn. And she has given her a bonus to bridge the gap between jobs. Donna and Davis will be here as well," Cormac said. "Anyone who has spent extended time with the child will be here and called to testify if I think we need them. The only people the Devons have on the witness list so far are themselves. This is not going to be a problem."

Airmid hoped so because the gloves were off. "I don't want them having visitation."

Cormac said, "They won't get visitation. You left the home so quickly, Sorcha didn't have time to talk to you about something that Erin told her. She also didn't want to spoil the reunion."

Airmid said, "Why do I have a feeling this is going to make me insane?"

Cormac said, "Well, that's why I don't want to blindside you about this particular thing in the courtroom. You need to keep your cool about it, regardless of how angry you are on the inside. Apparently, that idiot grandfather of hers gave her a cuff behind the ear for calling him Grandda. Then he told her she sounded like a papist."

Airmid shot out of her seat, screaming, "What?"

Cormac let her go. Let her vent her spleen all over the walls of her office. Then she was sobbing. Nolan put an arm around her. "There, there, lass. Get it all out. We don't want little Erin seeing you like this."

"Should we bring her in here? Should I ask her in private?" Airmid asked.

"There's no need. The social worker revealed the same thing as Sorcha. She told her the same story and said that Erin was told not to tell you. Then the social worker asked her about you. Had you ever spanked her. Had you ever pinched or hit or done any form of physical punishment. She told her no, that you made her sit in time-out sometimes, but that was it. Apparently, it only happened once with the grandfather, never with the grand-mother. It occurred while they were in the park after ice cream. I would not interrogate her about it. Once this is over, then abso-lutely open up dialogue about the incident. But for now, I am not positive there won't be another interview or some sort of deposi-tion, and we don't want the grandparents trying to say you put ideas in her head. Did Tommy Devon ever say anything about his father being abusive?"

Airmid shook her head. "No, I mean he had a strained rela-tionship with his father. He was closer to his mother. I think he said he got spanked when he was a kid, which isn't that uncom-mon. But it's certainly uncommon for a grandparent who has almost no relationship with the child to think it's okay to hit a four-year-old. I will kill that piece of shite with my bare hands!" She was spinning herself up again. Cormac didn't judge. She was entitled to her anger.

Cormac said, "When this comes up in court, you will not react. You know now, and you can curse the bastard to the fiery pits of hell after this goes our way. But you keeping your temper is going to be crucial. And my experience is that bullying assholes let their proclivity toward shows of temper come out on the stand when they are pressed. And I'm just the sort of man who likes to press."

# 21

## BELIZE CITY, BELIZE

They were going home early. The military flight was normally just for the army, but the British Government ordered the two aristocrats to hop a ride without delay. They were being driven to the airfield when Daniel said, "Stop the car!"

The driver stopped, and to Douglas's horror, Daniel started getting out of the car. "What the bloody hell are you doing?" They were passing a central market and Daniel had a mission. He limped and winced his way through the stalls, Douglas hot on his heels. "If you tell me what you are looking for, I'll help."

Daniel stopped and pointed. "That. That is what I'm looking for," he said. Douglas walked up to the booth with shelves of wood carvings. Beautiful tropical, wooden figures, mostly animals.

Douglas asked, "Which one? Who is it for?"

But Daniel just walked up and took the beautifully carved hammerhead shark and said, "Cuánto cuesta?"

The old man said, "Setenta." Seventy Belizean dollars. About thirty quid for all that work. Daniel handed him one hundred Belizean dollars and told him to keep the change. The man looked at him, then seemed to take in his injuries once more. He walked to another part of his booth, then came back with something. It was a simple, leather cord with a carved cross, made from the same ziricote wood. He slipped it around Daniel's neck, then went on to the next customer.

————

As the flight contained three army medics from the Royal Irish Regiment and the Royal Dragoons, Aidan and Daniel were monitored throughout the long flight. While the soldiers were in jump seats, the two injured men were on hospital gurneys in the cargo area, which were locked into place. The men were strapped in for the takeoff and landing.

Aidan looked at his cousin and grinned, the pain meds doing their job. "These flights usually suck. If I had known I'd get to have a lie down and auto-hydration, I'd have been shot sooner."

Daniel laughed and groaned. "Don't make me laugh."

Which, of course, got Aidan going. They took turns laughing, wincing, and groaning in a vicious cycle that neither could stop. Aidan's medic gave them both chiding looks. "Would you two please try not to blow a lung or a stitch before we land? Major, you've only had your chest tube out for thirty-six hours."

Aidan said, "Yes, Mum." Daniel had never seen Aidan so giddy. Those pain meds were doing a number on his inhibitions.

Daniel said, "If you are taking orders, I'll have what he's having."

Aidan choked on a laugh, and the medic just shook his head and looked at Douglas. "Now I see the family resemblance."

---

### Catterick Garrison, England

After landing on the RAF side of the military complex, the men were transported to the army side. They weren't going to let Aidan leave until he'd spent a night or two in the army hospital. A fact that had made him extremely testy. But Daniel had already taken care of things. Alanna was undoubtedly waiting for them at the hospital. They were loaded into ambulances, and Daniel dreaded seeing her. She'd no doubt blame him for this, despite what they'd all said. He was ready to face the jury though. He loved the O'Briens. And despite his deception that they'd never know about, he knew that they'd forgive him after a time. At least he hoped so.

Daniel was shocked as they came into the hospital to see not only Alanna, but Sorcha. And beside the two O'Brien women were his mother, Elizabeth, and Gregory. His mother's face blanched as she saw him. He knew he still looked like roadkill. Jesus, he didn't need this right now. Behind them, coming from the lav, was Morgan. Douglas was walking beside his rolling cot like a security detail. His mother, so prim and dignified, burst into complete fucking hysterics. Even his siblings were shocked at the display. "I'm okay, Mum. I promise it looks worse than it is," Daniel said.

Douglas, the rotting bastard, said, "Oh, no. It's every bit as bad as it looks. As a matter of fact, this is better than three days ago." The look he gave Douglas was murderous, but then his little sister was wiping tears, shoving Douglas aside as they were wheeled down the hallway to adjoining exam rooms. An army nurse said, "Only one family member. Sorry."

Elizabeth snapped at him, saying, "You just try to toss one of us out, soldier. I will rip your bollocks off and shove them down that hole of yours!"

Molly said, "Elizabeth!" But Daniel heard the rolling laughter go through the O'Brien crowd.

Sorcha said, "And ye best not get between a lioness and her cub. You go talk to your commanding officer and get permission because none of us are leaving."

A booming voice came from behind the entire crowd. "Sergeant, let's compromise at two at a time, rotating." They turned to see the lieutenant colonel from the dragoons' platoon coming behind them. He said, "I like my bollocks right where they are, and so do you."

———

Alanna held her husband's hand, silently weeping. He said softly, "I'm okay, love. I swear it."

She wiped her eyes and snapped at him. "I know that, Aidan." She put her face in her hands and said, "I'm sorry. I'm just feeling a lot right now." She stood because the stubborn man was now trying to get out of bed. She put a hand on his chest. "I'm okay. Don't get up, or I will have them give you a chemical nap." She smirked, wiping a tear off her chin. Aidan knew what was wrong. She'd been through this with her own father. He'd been shot in Fallujah alongside his best friend. Branna's father, Brian O'Mara, was killed and had actually died in Hans's arms. The tragedy had rocked the two families, and the emotional damage had scarred them all. He didn't ever want Davey, Isla, and Keeghan to go through what Branna had endured.

"I'm sorry I put you through this. I swore I'd be careful, and I tried. But I had to protect Danny. He was so hurt and he was unarmed and I just—"

"I understand, Aidan. You don't need to apologize. Neither does Daniel, although he has about twenty times. Everyone made it out alive. I knew what I was getting into with you. You just don't know how to sit back and do nothing. You do have an uncanny ability to get into trouble." She leaned over him, practically nose-to-nose. Her tears splashed on his face. "But you better never leave me, Aidan O'Brien. You will not leave our babies. If I have to travel to the afterlife and drag you back, I will never do without you!"

He cupped her face. "I promise, *a mhuirnín*. Forever. And"—he swallowed hard—"I heard you, Alanna. I was going in and out, and things sort of got quiet for a moment. And I heard you. And I didn't leave you. I won't leave you. Not until we are old and covered in grandchildren."

She started to cry in earnest, kissing him all over his face. Then she kissed him hard on the mouth. "Okay, then sharpen up. The two little ones are with Granny Edith, but Davey needs to see his daddy. He's not going to be okay until he sees you."

On cue, Sean O'Brien Sr. brought Davey through the curtain to see Aidan. The little boy was standing tall, chin up. But Aidan didn't need him to be tough. He just needed him to be his little boy. He opened one arm. "Come, *a stór*. Come give your da a hug. I need one of your hugs very badly just now." And Davey's chin started to wobble. He ran into Aidan's arms, and Aidan gave a grunt of pain. Two gunshot wounds and bruising from the rounds that hit his body armor. But he'd take the pain just to feel his family in his arms. Alanna smoothed a hand over Davey's cap of bright hair as he cried against Aidan's chest. They were a little worse for the wear, but their family was still whole. He looked at his father, the biggest man in the world, and Sean's eyes were teary. His da had seen a lot. And he'd stay strong for Aidan and his own young family, but he owed the big guy a hug as well.

———

Elizabeth left Daniel's bedside under protest, but he needed to see his boss. She left with their mother as Morgan came in with Douglas and shut the door. They'd moved the men to private rooms soon after they'd arrived. Daniel said, "I'm good to go home. They just need to check a few more boxes. Tell me what's going on."

Morgan said, "The Belizean Government has agreed to keep the incident out of the media. The last thing we need is photos of you and Roxburghe being linked to an international incident. The paparazzi would inadvertently end your careers if this was exposed. The Belizean Government believes you to be John MacMillin who was traveling with his wife and brother-in-law. Harry and Antony are headed home with the forensic information we need to compare the cocaine seizure in the Netherlands. For now, Arturo Reyes has been neutralized, and there have been two major seizures of Escobar drug cartel product. I think they'll be staying out of Belize, and hopefully out of the European market. I think we made a dent. We may, at the very least, get a well-earned respite."

"I should be ready to work in a week," Daniel said.

Douglas rubbed his face with both hands and said, "For God's sake, Danny. You almost died. Can't you take a bloody holiday? Stay home. Read a book and lay low. Let Donna pamper you."

Morgan nodded in agreement. She said, in her clipped, Welsh accent, "She's going to have a bloody stroke when she sees you. If she's back from Tyne and Wear in time to greet you, that is."

Daniel frowned. "What do you mean? Why would she be down there? Is Airmid okay?"

"She's got a court hearing Monday morning. There is a sizable list of witnesses. Quite a can of worms, but she has a good lawyer, thanks to you. She's sorry she couldn't be here. She just needs to get the child settled back at home and be prepped for court. The solicitors have been working with her all weekend trying to get her up to snuff."

Douglas cursed as Daniel removed his own IV. "Pull the car around, Roxburghe. I need to get home, then head down to that court hearing. Don't give me that look. I'm fine. Now get some sort of automobile or I will hire a bloody driver."

Morgan narrowed her eyes. "You are a stubborn wanker. Do you know that? You should be resting."

"I can rest when I'm dead. Let's go, Morgan. I will be there whether she wants me there or not," Daniel said. He felt responsible for her. He felt responsible for them both.

————

### Hawick, Scotland

Douglas glanced at his friend as he pulled up to the front of Hawick Manor. "I hope you prepared Donna for the sight of you."

"Davis said he warned her and my family, but you saw my mother. I'm not sure I can handle another woman crying over me. I'm knackered," Daniel said wearily. But it was too late. His brother was first, followed by Elizabeth, his mother, and the four full-time staff members. The look of horror on the faces of his mother and Elizabeth might have been funny if he hadn't felt guilty. They'd already seen him at the hospital, but getting a fresh look spun them all up again. His brother, Gregory, took his backpack and helped him out of the car. "I'm okay, brother. I can manage." And felt his own horror as he saw that his brother was close to tears. They followed him into the house, all watching him struggle with his injuries. He stood as tall and capable as he could manage. He was the head of this family, and they needed to see that he was still strong.

They sat in the informal family drawing room. The sofas were soft and a little worn. The room that didn't entertain or impress. It had books and a big tele to watch the match. A designated shelf full of his sister's published works. It was a private space. He'd allowed little Erin to play in here with Constance. Ordered a children's streaming service and had Donna stock the fridge with kid snacks. Now Erin and Airmid were gone. But his family was here, and he had never been so happy to see them.

Elizabeth broke the silence. "I don't understand, Danny. How did this happen?" And that's when Daniel made the choice. One he was authorized to make, but had always hesitated. Immediate family only.

Daniel's mother knelt in front of him, taking his hands in hers. Her face was utterly broken. She smiled sadly. "You were my first. A child of my body whom I loved more than anything or anyone. Until you two came, of course," she said to the siblings. "Because a mother's heart can be shared without it being diminished." She looked at Daniel as if she could read his mind. And maybe she could. They'd shared a body, after all. His soul had been born from her. She said, "It's your choice, my dear."

So, he nodded and she stood. She walked to the window and looked out over the gardens. Daniel glanced at his brother and sister. "Some people say their life flashes before them when they think they're going to die. And I won't lie to you. I thought I'd never come out of that underground room." Elizabeth put a hand over her mouth, but she stayed calm. "And what flashed through my mind was you. The three of you. I was sad because I wanted to see your lives in their entirety. I wanted to see you marry or conquer the world. I wanted to see your children and your grandchildren. It's so cliché, really. But that's what I thought about. You two and Mum. Because you'd already lost Papa." He took Elizabeth's hand next to him. "Being your big brother has been my greatest joy." Then he looked at his mother's profile and took a deep breath. "I've been keeping something from both of you for a long time. It started with Papa and has continued with me. But if you're going to be my heirs ... my legacy ... then you should know it all. And I trust you completely with the information I'm about to tell you."

———

Elizabeth sat between her brothers, completely stunned. Then she looked accusingly at her mother. "And you've known all of this. This whole time. Our entire bloody lives!" she said.

Molly looked at her daughter and raised her chin. "Not every agent tells their spouse. Especially thirty years ago. Your father trusted that I could handle this truth. But it was not my place to tell anyone beyond that. And before he brought your brother into service, we discussed it. If I didn't agree, he'd never have told any of you. It's how things were done back then. Especially given his position. His work was clandestine, and that kept all of us safe. He worked within the aristocracy of other nations, using his position to gain knowledge and gather assets. Your brother—" She sighed, looking at Daniel for guidance.

Daniel said, "Mine took on a bit more risk. I'm single. No wife or children. It was work I was willing to do, knowing I wouldn't be orphaning any bairns. And I love the work. I find purpose in it. I'm sorry for how you're feeling right now, but I need you to understand that most siblings never know. I could have kept you in ignorance. This is something you can never tell anyone. Not even if you marry someday. Do you understand how important that is? My life and my career depend on your silence."

Gregory nodded, quiet up until now. "I understand. And I get why Papa did what he did. You were always the most like him. Serious and with a sense of duty that would push you into service beyond the aristocracy. I wish I'd known. I have so many questions that I'll never get to ask him. But I'm proud of you both, Danny. Thank you for telling me." Gregory was always the steadiest. He didn't want to settle down with a family just now. He liked his freedom and his life. But he was like their mother in a lot of ways. Practical and clearheaded.

Elizabeth was unique. There was a fire inside her that wouldn't be quelled, and he loved that about her. Daniel squeezed her hand, and she took his other in hers. That's when she saw it. The missing fingernails that had been bandaged at the hospital but were now on full display. The tears started in earnest. "Oh, Danny. Why would you put yourself in harm's way like this? Why would Papa ask this of you?" Her tears dropped on his wrist as she kissed his hand. "I don't understand it."

"Because someone needs to do it, love. Someone has to do it, and it was my choice," Daniel said. "But I'm careful. Not careful enough in this instance, but I survived and will learn from my mistakes. And thoughts of you and Gregory and Mum? They kept me fighting."

———

Donna and Davis drove separately from Daniel. Douglas insisted on going down to Northumberland with him. "We weren't subpoenaed. Why weren't we subpoenaed?" Daniel asked.

"They weren't sure you would be released, and the attorneys thought Davis and Donna would be enough," Douglas said for the third time. "Why didn't you call and ask them? Better yet, why didn't you call Airmid just to say hello?"

"Because she's ... I don't know. Maybe I'm afraid she's giving me the push, and I want to force her to do it face-to-face? Or change her fucking mind?"

"This is why you don't dip your quill in the company ink, brother. How many times have you said the same to me?" Douglas asked.

"I was wrong. And fuck off, while you're at it," he snapped.

"You weren't wrong with a casual situation. This isn't casual though. It's worth fighting for. She's worth it. And I'm kicking myself for not getting to her first."

Daniel's look caused Douglas to smile so widely, Daniel wanted to punch him. Daniel said, "Considering you were playing the role of her brother, that would have been rather disgusting."

Douglas's mouth tipped up on one side. "True enough, old boy. Speaking of which, you drive like an old codger. Speed it up. We're going to miss the start of the show."

————

**Newcastle Family and Domestic Court**

It had taken everything in Airmid not to cling to her daughter as she relinquished care of Erin to the childcare workers in the courthouse playroom. They'd wanted the child on standby, only calling her if it was absolutely necessary. She knew this was going to go their way. It had to. But the idea that the court hearing could result in forced visitation scared her. She'd never limited their access, but they'd both had their last visit with her child. The grandmother for the way she treated Erin's mother. Because that was eventually going to morph into verbal abuse when Erin got older. Comparing her to Airmid, or simply disparaging Airmid in Erin's presence. When she could understand words like whore and papist trash. And the grandfather ... never again. He hadn't injured Erin, but he'd scared her and put harsh hands on her. He was practically a stranger. And what was next? When she got cheeky with him as she got older? When he made some sort of derogatory comment about her Irish heritage?

Airmid was seated when Tommy's parents came into the room. They both shot daggers at her, and she just looked down. She felt Cormac put a hand on her shoulder.

The judge entered the courtroom and the proceedings began. First, with the attorney who'd filed the order. The man's justification for this custody hearing was based on lies. Abandonment, unchaste behavior, and a mother who didn't make time to take care of her child, instead putting her career above Erin's welfare. They also accused her of leaving town and "hiding" their granddaughter from them.

Then Cormac Carrington stood and eloquently gave his opening statement. She could tell his father, Nolan, was proud. As Cormac laid out the timeline of events, she kept her eyes forward. Cormac said, "You'll find the court file for the first custody hearing is included."

The judge looked it over, then nodded for him to continue. "As you can see, there's no order mandating visitation to the Devons. However, Erin's mother has never kept the child from them. That will change after today, if I have anything to say about it."

Mr. Devon was on his feet in an instant. "What the hell is this?"

The judge's gavel was loud. "That's enough. You will not speak out of turn or raise your voice in my courtroom."

Cormac continued. "You'll find a restraining order in our paperwork, but we'll get to that later. For now, I would say that the list of witnesses will prove, without any doubt, that Ms. Roberts is a hardworking, attentive, loving single mother. Yes, she lost the baby's father before the child was born. She and the child were denied any veteran survivor benefits due to her unwed status and the fact that the child hadn't yet been born at the time of his death.

"But she has persevered. Her family is in Northern Ireland, and her career has brought her to England, but they are still supportive of her. Ms. Roberts ensures her daughter's safety and financial security completely on her own. I will also show the court the real motive behind the Devons pursuing custody, even though they've barely seen the girl in the four years since her birth. According to my records, they've had six visits with her in four years. No calls on her birthday. No Christmas cards. They did not attend her christening due to their prejudices against the Roman Catholic faith. They also deceived the Department of Veterans Affairs by failing to disclose that Staff Sergeant Thomas Devon had a dependent child."

Cormac looked over as the Devons' lawyer was putting a firm hand on Mr. Devon's arm and hissing at him to stay quiet. "Ms. Roberts has withstood verbal abuse, accusation, and disdain from Mr. and Mrs. Devon because she felt her deceased partner would have wanted his parents to be in the child's life. And her kindness has been repaid by the type of displays of temper that you see now." He motioned toward the pinch-faced couple whose cheeks were flushed with anger, and Airmid was suddenly so glad she wasn't on the opposing side of Cormac Carrington.

# 22

They wouldn't let Daniel and Douglas into the courtroom. Not until there was a recess. And Daniel knew he couldn't press the issue. So, they waited with one of the bailiffs until there was a break. It took two painstaking hours. In the meantime, there was a social worker who had come as well. He didn't know who had subpoenaed her—and he knew he couldn't ask—so he tried to stay calm and forget that his face looked like a prizefighter after the match was lost. No amount of ice was going to fix the bruising, but at least the swelling had gone down. Davis and Donna were sequestered in another area, as they were on the witness list. He just stared at the door, wondering what the hell was going on in that courtroom.

———

Airmid couldn't stop the tears as Tommy's parents listed all of her perceived shortcomings. And a little part of her wondered if she had missed some of these traits in Tommy. But no. He'd been a sweet man. Tough, but kind. And she wondered if the loss of him had been what gutted this couple of any warmth or compassion.

Cormac stood, ready to cross-examine Mr. Devon. Airmid had been waiting for this. And she was suddenly glad Danny wasn't here. If this came out for the first time while he was here, he'd likely go over the table and strangle the wee mongrel.

Cormac buttoned his suit coat and looked smooth doing it. He cut a dashing figure, which never hurt in any situation. Cormac said, "I'd like to bring Your Honor's attention to the results of the court-appointed social worker, as well as a statement from Sorcha O'Brien. She is a family acquaintance of Ms. Roberts who helped with childcare while Ms. Roberts was out of the country on business. Full disclosure, she is also my aunt. Both witnesses are here if there are any further questions, but we thought it was best to get the statements to you straightaway. The social worker was the one who asked Mrs. O'Brien to write the statement."

Then he turned toward Mr. Devon, who was very confused. "Mr. Devon, are you an advocate of corporal punishment?"

The man scowled and answered, "I don't know what you mean."

"Let me clarify. Do you feel that spanking, or in any way striking a child, is an appropriate form of punishment?"

Devon's face tightened. "Well, now. Sometimes. It's how I was raised. Nothing over the top, but I spanked my Tommy when he was naughty. He was a good boy most days, but he got spanked sometimes."

"I see. So, with your own child it's okay on occasion? What about someone else's child?" Cormac asked. "Let's say, a four-year-old granddaughter who barely knows you?"

"I don't know what you're referring to, but I never spanked my granddaughter. If that ... woman says I did, she's lying to try to discredit me."

Cormac said, "Let me assure you. If she'd known anything about this prior to last night, you'd have been in handcuffs, Mr. Devon. This revelation occurred while Ms. Roberts was away. The child told the social worker what happened, as well as the homeowner's aunt, who was helping care for the child. Did you, on your last visit with the girl, cuff her in the back of the head for using the term *grandda*?" Cormac said the phrase with the appropriate Irish lilt.

"I don't recall anything like that happening," Mr. Devon said, but he was starting to squirm.

"Well, then. Let me refresh your memory. Did you, after smacking a forty-pound preschooler, tell the little girl that she sounded like a bloody papist? And then did you forbid her to tell her mother you'd struck her?"

The Devons' attorney was objecting, but the judge wanted an answer. Finally, the bastard said, "It was just a bit of roughhousing. I didn't mean anything by it."

"Ah, I see. So, you feel hitting a small child in the head and screaming at her to be a good bit of fun?" Cormac asked.

"Objection, argumentative!" The other solicitor practically yelled it.

"Withdrawn," Cormac said smoothly.

The Devons' attorney was actually sweating. "Your Honor, I need a five-minute recess if you'd be so kind. I need to confer with my client," the solicitor said.

"Granted, but you must use the side chamber. Everyone else can remain seated. Five minutes and no longer. I think we all need to cool off," the judge said.

Cormac turned toward Airmid. "They are going to try to get the written testimony of Sorcha O'Brien stricken, as she was the first one the child confided in. That would leave the social worker's testimony. They will try to suppress that, but they can't. I never told the social worker about the incident until after the initial interview. So, it's not fruit of the poisonous tree. She uncovered it all on her own, bless the woman. Honestly, I don't think they'll get Sorcha's statement thrown out either, but just be prepared for them to accuse her of bias because she's related to both me and Daniel. We can always call her as a witness. This isn't a criminal trial. It's a hearing. The social worker turned in her report to the court Friday, right at close of business. She's apparently got a huge caseload, and she took her time getting the report filed."

Airmid smiled. "After their attorney would have taken his weekend off. Failing to get the report until today, I assume?"

Cormac shrugged innocently. "And it's not my fault the little fecker didn't read it before we started. It may have been buried in the middle of my file," Cormac said, "but it's nothing but the truth, so to hell with the lot of them."

A bailiff came in just as the Devons and their solicitor were entering the courtroom. The judge looked expectantly at him. "Officer Quinlan, what is it?"

The man cleared his throat. "There are two people here for the proceedings who would like to be included in the hearing, although they are not on the list."

"And who the hell would that be? Carrington, you've already called half of Scotland and Ireland for this simple hearing."

Before Cormac could answer, the bailiff did. "It is His Grace, Andrew Douglas, the Duke of Roxburghe, and Lord Daniel MacPherson, the Earl of Hawick, Your Honor." And the entire room sat motionless, their collective jaws dropped.

———

They started the testimony and cross-examination of Mrs. Devon after Cormac decimated her husband. She was the calmer head, it seemed. But it was obvious she didn't like Airmid. Cormac placed a letter in front of the woman. "Is this your handwriting, Mrs. Devon?" Mrs. Devon blushed, then nodded. "Could you read it out loud for the court?"

She looked like she was genuinely ashamed of it, which surprised Airmid. The woman cleared her throat. *"To Ms. Roberts. As you refuse to let us raise my son's daughter and insist on baptizing her in Ireland as a Catholic, we will not be attending the christening. You are a common whore who seduced my Tommy into parenthood, and you shouldn't expect a dime from this family toward the raising of his bastard. If he hadn't been distracted that day in training with the stress of the situation you put him in, he'd still be alive today."*

She folded the letter and Cormac took it. "And can you tell me, Mrs. Devon, how your son died?"

"He drowned in the river," she said as she teared up. Cormac offered her the box of tissues like a perfect gentleman. She took one, then he continued.

"Yes, according to the official report, he drowned while pinned inside an upturned vehicle. His seat belt failed to release after the rollover accident involving a military vehicle. Was he driving?"

She answered weakly, "No."

"So, this was not a case of him being distracted, was it? In fact, it was a freak accident that injured three other soldiers and killed one other soldier in the vehicle. The driver was not at fault, nor was your son. It was an equipment failure that had him pinned in and squashed under the weight of the vehicle. The other death was a man who was thrown from the back of the vehicle and sustained fatal head and spinal trauma."

"Yes, but she trapped him. She got pregnant on purpose!" She screamed and pointed at Airmid, who just flinched. Then she wiped the tears from her face. Airmid felt Daniel put a palm on her neck from behind her, and her whole body shuddered.

Cormac asked, "Did she trap him? Well then, Mrs. Devon, can you tell me what your son told you about the pregnancy? And remember, you are under oath."

She blushed. "I will not talk about my son's relations. I won't!"

"Oh, you'd call his grieving partner a whore. You'd refuse to give your blessing for him to marry the mother of his child. You'd refer to your granddaughter as a bastard. But you can't speak the simple words *'broken condom'* without playing the blushing maid?"

The judge said, "That's enough. You've made your point. Move on, Mr. Carrington."

"As you wish, Your Honor." Cormac walked to the desk where Airmid and Nolan sat. "I'd like to submit a document that has just come to me this weekend. The post was a bit delayed and I've been in Scotland." He handed one to the judge and one to the Devons' solicitor. "Madam, you'll see your signature, as well as your husband's, on this paperwork." He put it in front of Mrs. Devon. "Read line seventeen, please. Out loud."

Mrs. Devon cleared her throat nervously. *"Please list any living dependent children, stepchildren, or adopted children of the deceased service member,"* she said.

"And what did you write as an answer?" Cormac asked.

*"Not applicable.* And it wasn't. She was pregnant, and we couldn't confirm the child was Tommy's," she said defensively.

"Yes, but didn't Tommy's commanding officer come to you and plead on the surviving partner's behalf?" Cormac asked.

"Yes, but as I said, nothing I wrote on that form was incorrect," she said.

Cormac said, "Okay, we'll move on then. Did you establish paternity to your satisfaction the first time you tried to take Ms. Roberts' child from her?"

The woman lifted her chin. "We did."

"Now, Your Honor, if you will look at page forty-three of the case file, it will show you the bill passed in the Parliament providing the veterans killed in action during the recent wars in Afghanistan, Syria, Africa, and Iraq with additional benefits for surviving children. Even those who are killed during military training to prepare for these wars and military engagements, as well as disaster relief campaigns. As was the case with Staff Sergeant Thomas Devon, who was training for a deployment to the Middle East."

The woman's face blanched. Cormac asked, "Mrs. Devon, did you receive notification of this benefit?"

She squirmed. "I'm not sure. I don't remember anything like that coming."

Cormac raised his brows and asked, "Is that so? I have in the records that the document was received by your husband six months ago, as he had to sign for the delivery of the envelope. When it wasn't returned, you received another one in the early part of last month."

"Um ... yes. Now I remember. And we did return that one," she said. "I'd completely forgotten about it."

"Well, that's a coincidence. Because the back pay for this claim is substantial. It's retroactive back ten years, which means your granddaughter, and indirectly, her guardian, will be getting back pay dating back to the day the child was born. Over ten thousand pounds if my calculations are correct. And she'll receive a stipend until she turns eighteen years of age. So, is that when you decided to try to get custody again? It wasn't enough that you'd received his life insurance from the British Government. You wanted to make sure that Airmid Roberts didn't get any sort of aid from the government for Staff Sergeant Thomas Devon's surviving child?"

"That's not true! He was my son. I lost my son! She doesn't deserve anything!" She screamed the words.

The judge was smashing the gavel, threatening her with contempt. Cormac said, "I'm done, Your Honor. As a matter of fact, I find I'm speechless."

———

When Airmid took the stand, she did so with her head held high. And it was difficult. This was a sordid business. Her dirty laundry now a matter of public record. And to find out that the root of all this drama was money. It made her sick.

Cormac questioned her about her relationship with her daughter. Her extended family support system. Her friends and other people who might come into contact with Erin. Then he addressed the allegations head-on. "Did you abandon your daughter to go off with a lover?"

She stiffened, even though she'd known it was coming. "I did not, sir. I work. I am the sole provider for my household. And normally, it doesn't involve a lot of travel. At least not more than a day. This was different. I was needed as an interpreter, and it was for an overseas assignment."

"You've stated that your childminder had been getting up in years and couldn't care for the child when she was sick with a cold. The couple didn't want to be exposed to childhood illnesses. Who took care of your daughter for such an extended time?"

Airmid said, "I began by taking my daughter with me to have her close by. She needed her mother while she was ill. My employer was kind enough to pay for a nanny during my work hours in Scotland. Once Erin was comfortable and feeling better, we trusted the nanny and the household staff to care for her during two short trips to the Caribbean and Central America."

"Well, that's quite a benefit," Cormac said. "You must be very valuable." He turned toward the judge and said, "You'll see, Your Honor, that the social worker inspected the entire property and interviewed everyone who interacted with the child during the mother's absence. As did I. This was done without forewarning and while Ms. Roberts was away. I can provide the paperwork for the extensive background checks for the staff at the residence. In addition, I found them to be altogether pleasant people who doted on the child as if she were their own blood."

The judge looked over the report and asked, "Who is the owner of the residence where the child stayed?"

Cormac answered, "That is the address of Hawick Manor. The family seat for the earldom. Lord Hawick is a colleague of Ms. Roberts. He allowed the team involved in Ms. Roberts' latest work to use the manor in order to work remotely so that she could tend to the child and avoid a long commute. I have added both the Earl of Hawick and the Duke of Roxburghe to my witness list. They were detained in Central America due to his injuries, and I wasn't sure they'd be here in time for the hearing," he said before the other solicitor could object.

The judge looked at the two men, then took in Daniel's face. "I'm sure there's a compelling reason he looks like he's been beaten to within an inch of his life. This just keeps getting better. Go on, Mr. Carrington."

"Ms. Roberts, you've dealt with a lot of baseless accusations about the nature of your character over the last five years. You've been subjected to more today. All rather unkind, and you have borne them with grace and an even temper. Can you tell me how it makes you feel?"

"It makes me feel foolish," Airmid said.

"And why is that?" Cormac asked.

She took a deep breath and answered, "Erin was not planned, but I do not apologize for having brought such a beautiful child into the world. I don't regret anything about my life. I served my country. I loved Tommy Devon. After his death, I was devastated. I was pregnant and unmarried and the love of my life was gone.

"My intent had been to go to school. I'd begun my education, but then I got pregnant. I have a very good family, Your Honor. They helped while I finished university with my veterans' education benefits. I graduated with full marks in a challenging field. I did it all with a baby and no da to help raise her. I am proud of my life, and I am extremely proud of my daughter.

"My only regret is allowing those two vipers into her life. Two people who never saw her true worth. They visited her out of obligation. Once or twice a year and only for a couple of hours. A check in the box. Tommy was nothing like them. He was a good person. I know that he loved me, but not enough to stand up to them. I won't judge him for it. And I still miss him. For my sake, and for Erin's, I hold nothing but love in my heart for him. But to hear that his father laid hands on my daughter in anger makes me feel ashamed for the first time in my life. Erin is a lot like me. And a lot like Tommy, actually. She's loyal and loving. She made the decision, at four years old, to try to shield me from that man's anger," she said, pointing at Mr. Devon. "I'm so sorry for it. All I can do now is to do the same for her. I was never obligated to let them see Erin. And it was out of a misguided sense of loyalty to Tommy that I have allowed it. That is over."

———

The Devons' solicitor stood before Airmid, and she knew this was going to hurt. The portly little fucker had a gleam in his eye. "Ms. Roberts. It says here that your trips were necessary for your job. What is it that you do, exactly?"

"I'm a linguist and an interpreter. I speak several languages, but I specialize in the dialects of the Spanish language, including those—"

The solicitor cut her off rudely. "That's sufficient. And this work took you on a trip to the Netherlands, the Caribbean, and Belize?"

"It did," she said. "Is that answer short enough for you, or can I give my full answer?"

"Objection, Your Honor. Hostile witness," he said.

Cormac spoke up. "I would disagree, Your Honor. He cut her off before she could give the extent of her credentials. It's rude and unprofessional. He did ask, after all."

The judge said, "I'll have to agree. Ms. Roberts, feel free to elaborate on your field of expertise."

Daniel was so fucking proud of her, he wanted to stand up and pump his fist. Pump it right into that other attorney's cake hole. And Cormac was good. Really good.

After Airmid finished her sixty-second resume, the solicitor asked, "Do you have proof of this work overseas? Boarding passes, hotel bills, an attendance log from your meetings?"

That's when Airmid's face paled. Just a bit. The attorney misread the body language. "Isn't it true, Ms. Roberts, that your travel has been nothing more than child-free holidays with two different men? One whom you were cozy enough with that you left your daughter alone at his estate while you partied your way through three different international tourist destinations?"

Airmid didn't shout. She was so cool, it made the hair stand up on the back of Daniel's neck. "How dare you. I am a professional and an excellent mother. I served my country with honor for six years. I graduated from a good university. I take the raising of my daughter more seriously than all of those other duties. If I were a man, you would not be painting me as some promiscuous floozy. It is because I'm an unwed mother who had the audacity to succeed without a husband."

Cormac smirked and said, "Well said, Ms. Roberts. Your Honor, does the solicitor for Mr. and Mrs. Devon have any actual valid questions for my client, or is he just here to reinforce our society's mistreatment of single mothers?"

The judge said, "I believe, in between the numerous unfounded insults, he was asking for proof of her whereabouts. Do you have these things, Ms. Roberts?"

Cormac said, "We did not prepare any documents, but if you'll give me a ten-minute recess to speak with my client, I think we can arrange it for later today."

Airmid looked at Daniel and he saw the fear. Her plane tickets, other than for the Netherlands, were under the name Tara MacMillin. The hotel room was in his false name as well, and they'd been sharing a room like a married couple. The judge, thankfully, decided that they should break for lunch.

# 23

Cormac rubbed his temples. This was supposed to be an easy, clear-cut win. "What do you mean you can't tell him? You have to tell him, Airmid. You are winning. But if he thinks you are hiding something or lying, you may end up with a problem. Contempt, at the very least."

Daniel watched Airmid start to shake. Jesus. They could not reveal what they did for a living in open court. He needed Morgan here. He watched Douglas as he rang off with her. "She's on her way. If she doesn't run into traffic on the road, she'll be here in fifty-eight minutes."

"Ten minutes past the time we need her. What the bloody hell is going on here, Danny?" Cormac asked accusingly.

Daniel stopped Cormac in his tracks when he said, "She's not allowed to tell you, and neither am I."

———

Court reconvened, and Airmid was creeping up on full panic. She took the stand again, and the attorney representing her prior, almost-in-laws was a smug, little bastard. He looked as if he knew she couldn't produce the proof she needed. She said calmly, "I'm afraid I'm going to need a bit more time. We are having issues securing the requested documentation." Exactly what Cormac had told her to say.

The attorney said, "Because you were, in fact, not where you said you'd be? A bit of a tryst and some partying while a group of strangers cared for your daughter?"

"That is not true. I don't normally travel for my work, but this time, it was unavoidable. So, like a responsible adult, I did it. I will not need to travel like this again."

The judge looked at her, and Airmid knew her face was pleading. The judge asked, "How much time?"

Airmid looked at the clock, then at Douglas. He held his hand up three times. "Fifteen minutes, Your Honor," she said.

The judge said, "I'll allow it. Move on, counselor." In the meantime, they called Constance to testify. It was quick and painless. Fifteen minutes had passed when the Devons' attorney said, "In light of these additions to the witness list, I request to call Mr. MacPherson to the stand."

MacPherson stood, ready for this asshole. But Cormac couldn't resist. "Your Honor, I'd request that counsel use proper decorum. He is an Englishman last time I checked."

The attorney's ears were red. "My apologies, Lord MacPherson. I'm a bit rusty on the decorum for the antiquated peerage system."

"Objection, Your Honor. Disrespectful and argumentative," Cormac said calmly.

The judge said, "Sustained. You're on thin ice, sir."

Daniel walked to the stand, letting the bailiff swear him in.

The attorney was stopped by Cormac. "Since you've jumped ahead for no good reason, I will remind you that the Earl of Hawick is my witness. I will be the first to question him, and you can do your cross-examination in turn."

The set-down was taken silently, and the pink had spread to the top of the man's head. "Lord MacPherson, how do you know my client?"

"We met a few weeks ago. She is the Spanish linguist assigned to my work in Central America."

"And did this work also take you to the Netherlands and Jamaica?" Cormac asked.

"Yes, it did." Daniel looked up as another bailiff led Morgan into the room. Cormac's shoulders eased a bit as well.

Cormac said, "Your Honor, if I can interrupt this for now, I need an audience with you and the woman I told you about, Ms. Annabeth Morgan, in your chambers. Alone."

The judge raised his eyebrows. "It's not appropriate that you meet without the opposing counsel in the room." The asshole representing the Devons was sputtering.

Cormac's jaw tensed and he looked at Morgan. "May I approach the bench, Your Honor?"

Daniel sat quietly. Cormac approached and pinned the other attorney with a stare that caused him to plop down on his chair. Cormac whispered, "Your Honor, I promise you that this is not only appropriate, it is absolutely necessary that we speak without civilians in the room."

The judge furrowed his brows. "I don't understand. What do you mean, civilians?"

"I mean the type of people with no government security clearance. I would argue, Your Honor, that I should not even be in the room."

The judge stood, and so did everyone else. "Ms. Morgan, you

will see me in my office, along with Ms. Roberts and her attorney." He looked at the Devons. "If I think it is appropriate, I will let you in the chambers after a time. If I don't, you will be silent and submit to this court's authority. Is that clear?"

———

The judge sat, rubbing his eyes after throwing his glasses on his big desk. "I really hope you aren't yanking my chain, Carrington. I'm about at the end of my patience."

Cormac didn't pay the attitude any mind. "I assure you, Your Honor, this is very necessary. And with your permission, Ms. Roberts and Ms. Morgan have waived the necessity of me being in the room."

Morgan said, "It's not necessary for you to leave. Your Honor, this is quick and to the point. Ms. Roberts is unable to provide you with the information you seek because it is classified. Very classified. I have a letter from the Foreign Secretary, Donald Fuquay. It assures you that Ms. Roberts was indeed on Crown business during these absences. That is all I'm allowed to say, but the Foreign Secretary's extension is at the bottom if the official seal and my word are not sufficient enough."

The judge looked at the letter and read it, short and to the point. The judge set the letter on his desk, then said, "I accept this letter as evidence. The dates all line up. Now I have to go to the courtroom and explain, without explaining, why I am satisfied. And they will not be happy about it, I assure you. This part of the record, and the letter, will be sealed, per protocol. Now, do you have anything to say? Because I am slightly concerned that the Earl of Hawick was with you on this assignment, and it looks like he's been beaten half to death. When, the bloody hell, did the peerage—a duke and an earl—start sneaking about in the clan-destine service?"

"Your Honor, I am assuming that is all rhetorical. The official statement by Lord MacPherson is that he was riding a rented scooter into a village they were helping, and a truck clipped him. Hence the bruises and sling. And the limp." Morgan winced, knowing it was all a load of shite. Her good friend, the Earl of Hawick, looked like he'd been dropped off the roof of a ten-story building.

The judge sighed. "You do this job long enough, I suppose you hear it all. Okay, I will weather this storm."

Airmid spoke up then. "Your Honor, I'd like to address your concerns. You worry that I am a single-parent home and sole provider, no doubt. And I want to assure you that my normal position is in a support capacity. This was an isolated circumstance. I will not be ... accompanying His Grace or His Lordship on any more ... excursions. I will make that promise."

He looked at her and sighed. "I will not extract any such promise from you. You are entitled to make your career advances without threat of your child being taken away. Now, I would hear from your family, after the earl is done on the stand. After that, I think we can dismiss the rest of the witnesses."

Airmid smiled. "Thank you, Your Honor."

———

The attorney for Mr. and Mrs. Devon was a real dick. Full stop. "Lord MacPherson. Although your dealings overseas—"

"Objection, Your Honor. Your instructions were perfectly clear, I think," said Cormac.

The attorney smiled. "Forgive me. Let me rephrase. Is it common for you to invite your colleague for an extended stay at your manor in Hawick instead of an office or other more professional workplace? And is it common for you to hire a nanny and bring her child into the home, even though the child doesn't know you or your staff?"

Daniel put his hand up. "I'll answer it, Carrington. No bother. No, it is not. It's a first, actually. But given the circumstances, the priority was to have the child safe and near her mother. She had a cold, and Ms. Roberts' childminder cried off. I would do no less for anyone I worked with, but I think the real question should be this: Why have the child's grandparents never stepped up to help with the little girl? Knowing their granddaughter's mother was employed, never once have they offered to help her by offering childcare. They, in fact, have refused their support in any way. And I'm not talking about money. I'm talking about showing up for more than a biannual trip to the park and ice cream parlor."

"I want those comments stricken from the record. It is not what I asked." The solicitor's ears were getting red again.

The judge said, "I'm going to allow it."

"Are you involved in a sexual relationship with Ms. Roberts?" And that's when Cormac got really pissed.

"I am sorry, Your Honor. Not only is that none of anyone's business, it is a disgusting show of sexism. If she was a man, no one would be asking if she was involved. It is out of line."

The judge slammed his gavel. "I've had enough. This is not the 1950s. Women work. Single mothers work. Single mothers date. And the disgusting smearing of Ms. Roberts' character, a decorated veteran of Her Majesty's Army, stops now. This is not a criminal trial. If you don't have any appropriate questions, then let Lord MacPherson get down from the stand."

The Duke of Roxburghe actually hissed under his breath. "Brilliant."

The judge said more gently, "I want to hear from Ms. Roberts' parents. The child's other grandparents. And then I'd like to meet Erin."

———

Erin was brought in by the social worker and Sorcha O'Brien. She waved at everyone as she walked by. Then she ran to Airmid. "Mammy, I got to play with their toys. They've got a big, purple ball, and the lady let me bounce on it."

"That's so good, love," Airmid said, kissing her on the forehead. Then she turned her attention to the judge, and Erin let out a squeal.

"Danny!" She wiggled out of her mother's arms and stood before Daniel. The judge put his hand up, letting Airmid know that he wanted to see this. Erin said, "Oh, no. Danny, you're full of boo-boos!"

He smiled and rubbed a palm over her hair. "I am. I'm sorry if it scares you. I wrestled a polar bear."

Erin's brows shot up. "Ye did?" She tilted her head. "No, you're putting me on." And Daniel heard the rumble of laughter around him.

Daniel smiled. "Sorry. I am putting you on. I had an accident. It looks worse than it is. I'm okay, lass. I promise."

She turned unceremoniously and looked at the judge. "Hello, sir. Why do you get to be up so high?"

The judge said, "Excellent question. Because I'm the boss." And he winked at her. "Is there anyone else you'd like to say hello to, love? Take your time."

Erin ran to her Irish grandparents. "Granny! Grandda! I missed you. I rode a pony! And I have new friends."

She ran to her grandfather, who had tears in his eyes. "I

missed you too, love. And guess what? Your old grandda is retiring in a few weeks. I'm going to visit more."

Erin took his face in her hands. "And will you let Granny come?"

It was Douglas who cracked off a laugh, but the entire courtroom, save the three for team Devon, rumbled with laughter. Her granny said, "Do ye think I'd let him leave me behind? I'm happy to hear you've got some new friends. You'll have to tell me all about them."

The judge interrupted. "Erin, I don't know if you noticed, but your grandmother Devon and grandfather Devon are here today."

Erin looked at her granny, then at her mother. She got down from her grandda's lap, and her mother said, "Use your manners, Erin."

Erin put her chin up like a little soldier and walked to her grandparents. The parents of the father she never got to meet. "Hello, Grandmother. Hello, Grandfather."

No warmth. No fear, thankfully, but Erin barely knew them. She tolerated them, as they did her. Mr. Devon grunted a hello, giving a half smile.

Mrs. Devon opened her arms and said, "Come give your granny a hug."

And Erin said the oddest thing. "Why?"

The woman laughed nervously. "I don't know what you mean, Erin."

"I'll hug you if you want one. I like hugs. You never asked me before," she said.

She was almost five. Children knew if they were loved and wanted. The woman looked embarrassed. "It's okay, Erin. Maybe another time."

Erin's body had been rigid. Airmid saw her shoulders relax. She turned toward the judge and said, "I'm all done for now.

Danny's auntie Sorcha said she made biscuits and we'd have a tea party later."

Airmid suppressed a grin. The judge said, "I think we can let the child go back with her toys. I've seen all I need to see." And Sorcha stood, taking her hand as they met the social worker by the door to the courtroom.

———

Cormac sat at the table across from Airmid, holding her hand. "It's okay, Airmid. I know how to read the room and look past the anxiety of a client. This is going to go our way. That judge is fair, and more importantly, he doesn't like the Devons any more than we do. This is going to be okay."

Airmid exhaled, just nodding. "I don't want any visitation. I hope I made that clear."

"You did. And if it's anything else, we'll appeal it. I'll come back from Ireland if I have to, but my father is an absolute shark in the courtroom."

Airmid started at that. "Ireland?"

Cormac said, "Yes, we're expanding the practice. I took the bar in Ireland so that I could practice in both countries, just like my da. Half the family is over there. My mother is an O'Brien, as you know. So, I was ready for a change. We are looking for a lease in Dublin. I've helped my father with the family stuff, but my expertise is international law. I'm going to do some volunteer work with the Ukrainian war refugees until I get established with some more paying clients. There's a market for my skills due to some legal snags between Ireland and the UK after Brexit as well. I think it's a good move. If I can't make Dublin work, I'll branch out, but that's the goal right now. And it's where the Ukrainian families are coming into the country. Some of them unaccompanied minors whose parents stayed back to fight. I just ... I want to help while I'm arranging the rest. I'm not good with being idle. And it'll be great to be with the green side of the family for a while." Airmid laughed at that. "I mean, you've met Brigid. She's determined to rehabilitate her stuffy, uptight, half-English cousin."

Airmid smiled. Brigid was a force. So was Sorcha. And Aidan was such a man of worth. He'd saved her life. The O'Briens were as good as it got for family. She wondered, fleetingly, if she'd ever see any of them after today. She cleared a lump in her throat.

"Cormac, that is wonderful. Truly. I think Danny spent some time in the Ukraine for ... the non-profit work." She hedged. "He may be able to give you some advice."

Cormac tilted his head, reading between the lines. "Really? Now that is quite interesting. And I'll definitely talk to him about it. Thank you."

They were interrupted as the knock came on the conference door. The court clerk opened the door and said, "The judge is ready."

––––––

Airmid cried the whole way home. Full custody was retained. No visitation was mandated. The look on the Devons' faces when the judge confessed that not only was he part Irish, but he was also the son of a single mother was almost comical.

Cormac petitioned the court to have the Devons pay his fees, as this was the second time that they'd taken her to court and made her hire a lawyer. Given that they'd tried to swindle the British Government into giving them the back pay, which was owed to Airmid and Erin, the judge ordered them to pay Cormac's fees, but not the initial attorney's fees from four years ago. A good compromise.

Daniel drove her car after a stiff cup of coffee. Airmid was exhausted, both physically and mentally. She'd invited everyone to her home. Donna, Davis, Constance, and Sorcha said yes, along with Daniel and Douglas. Cormac and Nolan had to do some work at the office and didn't come. Her parents and brother were staying with her in Newcastle-Upon-Tyne, so she'd have a rather full house. Daniel didn't press her for anything. He couldn't bear to see her cry.

Airmid said, "I'm sorry. I'm not normally this much of a crier. It's just been a long, scary day. When they demanded I show travel documents—"

"I can only imagine. But you did it, Airmid. They will not come at you a third time," Daniel said.

"I can't get the look on Erin's face out of my mind," she said.

"When she saw the Devons?" he asked.

"No, Danny. When she saw your injuries," Airmid said numbly. "She saw your brutalized face. She was horrified. And even at four and a half, she knew something bad had happened to you," she said. Her voice held resignation. It broke his heart. He actually felt the crack in his chest.

"It won't always be like that. Maybe never again, Airmid," he said, pleading in his voice.

"And maybe five years down the road, someone like Reyes will dump your body in the Kingston Harbor." Daniel winced like she'd struck him. "I'm sorry, Danny, but it's the job. And she's lost a father. I've lost a partner."

"And you won't take the chance at something wonderful? You won't risk it?" he asked sadly. "Not for me?"

She said nothing. He pulled into her small driveway. Douglas pulled in behind him. "I'll just stay for a few minutes, so no one questions you. Then I'll bow out."

She choked on a sob. "Danny, you have to understand. I have a child."

Daniel just stared over the steering wheel. Then he finally said, "My father raised me with such love. I wasn't his by blood, but God, how he loved me." His voice was soft and aching. "He taught me everything I know about being a man. I was not his natural child, but he loved me unconditionally and with his whole heart. I am so very proud to be his son. And I have enough self-worth not to beg." And he got out of the car without even looking at her.

They went into the house, and he pasted a smile on his face for Erin. She ran to him and wrapped her arms around his neck, taking such care because of his bruises. It caused his heart to hurt worse than any of his other injuries.

Erin asked, "Danny, when do I get to come see you again? I miss my room and my pony." He smiled sadly. Because the memory of this child's laughter in his home was going to linger in the old, empty rooms.

Daniel said, "We'll have to see, okay? You are welcome in my home. Always. Now, I seem to remember you were in need of a very exotic-looking shark." And he pulled the shark out of his messenger bag. Erin squealed. "Look at its funny head! It's so pretty! You remembered, Danny." And she hugged him even tighter.

Airmid leaned into Douglas. "I don't remember him buying that. I'd forgotten all about it."

Douglas said, "He made the escort stop in the market square on the way to the airport. He limped through the marketplace until he found just the right one. Danny's like that. He doesn't say things he doesn't mean. He shows up. He doesn't know any other way to be."

And if that wasn't salt in the wound, Airmid didn't know what was. She looked at Daniel, kneeling down with a splinted wrist and head-to-toe injuries. He gave Erin his full attention. So, Airmid did the only thing she could do. She walked into her bathroom, turned on the faucet, and cried.

———

## Hawick, Scotland

"I'm glad to be back home, but it seems very empty just now," Daniel said.

Sorcha said, "I was thinking … instead of buying a return ticket, how about you and I take the ferry back? The weather's good. We can take it into Belfast, see your grandparents. And then I'll drive us to Doolin. Ye missed Aidan's promotion. Everyone misses you, mo chroí. You're the new hero, with all those ponies and that big nursery. Branna and Caitlyn's children are fit to be tied that they didn't get to go."

Daniel just started fumbling with the tea mugs, setting the kettle on the cooker. "I don't know. There will be a lot of questions."

"Aidan already told the family what happened. The cartel thought to hold you for ransom. And the wee bastards beat the tar out of you," she said bitterly.

Cormac was discreet enough to keep Sorcha and Airmid's parents out of the courtroom after the recess until it was time for them to testify. Sorcha was still in complete ignorance, which was better. Only Aidan knew everything, and Cormac suspected but didn't know in what capacity they worked for the British Government. Only Aidan knew the complete truth. His cousin, who had jumped into the path of a bullet even though he had three children. Daniel swallowed hard.

"Aunt Sorcha … is it possible for your heart to stop and then just start up again?" Daniel asked cautiously, like he was weighing his words.

She froze. "Um ... well, yes. I mean, not normally, but a healthy heart can sustain trauma and then correct itself. Can you tell me what happened?"

"I'm sure it was nothing. Forget I asked," Daniel said.

She put her hands on her hips, and he knew she was not going to let him back out of this. He cursed under his breath.

"That bad, eh? Well, by the looks of you, I can only imagine. Now, let's have it all. Why are you asking?"

Daniel said, "They were using electricity." He paused as her face blanched. She swallowed, then nodded, but he saw her hands start to shake until she fisted them. He continued. "After the third time, everything just ... went away. Then I was somewhere else. I was home in Hawick. And, well, I saw both of them. I saw my fathers."

Sorcha's hand went over her mouth, then she said, "I saw him in a dream. I saw John. Tell me everything."

"My papa hugged me and told me he loved me and said that he was proud. The two of them were tense. Because ... well, you know why. I mean, can you imagine?" He shook his head. "I must sound crazy, but all I can do is tell you what happened."

Sorcha remembered a time, long ago. A young medic who'd helped her during the IRA bombing campaign. A man who, it turned out, had been dead since World War II. Mick, a man with a kind face and a love so deep for his city and his family that he'd never stopped showing up when he was needed. A man who'd been killed long ago in the Belfast Blitz.

Sorcha said, "You'd be surprised, I think, to hear what I find completely believable. Go on, my dear." Her voice was thick. Her eyes were misting. Her brother. Her hero who'd saved her life as a youth. She rubbed the scar on her forearm. The blade from the

Shankill butchers. John had a hero's heart, even though he'd lived a simple life.

Daniel watched her rub the scar on her forearm. He knew who had given her that scar. And he knew who'd saved her that black day. He took her hand, squeezing it. Then he said, "I turned to John. To my ... da. He said he wished he had more time with me." His voice caught. "He said he loved me and watched over me. And then he told me it wasn't time for us all to be together. My papa nodded. A sort of peace settling between them. Robert, my father, said, 'Ye've got to go back, lad. It's not your time.'

"I woke up gasping, back in that bloody cell, feeling like I'd just resurfaced from the sea. But I think maybe I went partway to the other side. So, I was just wondering if it was a dream, or if I really saw them? If I actually died and came back? Maybe the electrocution stopped my heart, but it started back on its own or something. Or maybe I imagined the whole thing. Maybe I just wanted them there to keep me from letting go." His voice trailed off at the end, and Sorcha swallowed a sort of sob. An aching tick at the back of her throat. She crossed herself and took a breath.

Sorcha's voice was strained when she took his face in her hands and said, "You may never know whether you were just deeply unconscious or if you'd started to cross over. The important thing is that you are back. They sent you back. And yes, if you're asking, then I'll tell you. I do believe you really saw them. And I, for one, am so grateful you weren't alone"—her voice caught on a sob—"and that you weren't done with us, my sweet Danny."

Daniel was quiet for a minute, then finally said, "I think I'd like to go see everyone. I don't know that I'm particularly good company right now, but I think it's a fine idea."

Sorcha knew his heart was heavy. Mainly due to the absence of his Airmid and little Erin. She thought maybe Danny had found his mate. The woman he'd love forever. And she hoped this Airmid Roberts was smart enough to see what sort of treasure lie before her when she looked at Daniel.

She said, "Give her time, love. She's feeling a lot right now. Too much all at once. I understand her. I was young when I met my Sean. I gave him the push and went back up to the North because I had to come to it all on my own timeline. I'm stubborn, you see. Terribly so. But in that absence, I saw what life would be like without him. And I just couldn't live with the idea. I couldn't give him up. Give her time, Danny. Irish women are a handful on a good day, and you've both been through hell. If she doesn't come around, then you will survive it. And you'll find someone who can love you despite the obstacles. You'll find the person who can't give you up."

# 24

## DOOLIN, CO. CLARE, IRELAND

McDermott's was bursting with craic tonight. It was open mic night, and the locals came to sing and the tourists came to listen. Jenny O'Keefe, newly married and expecting, had the night off from Gus O'Connor's Pub and had decided to join the O'Briens for a good, old-fashioned, Doolin piss-up. She stood next to Brigid Murphy, and they were singing a comedic song about why young women shouldn't marry old men. The crowd was loving it. Cora was out tonight, a rarity. Granny Edith was in town and had agreed to watch the smaller siblings because Cora was going to make her debut at open mic night.

Daniel watched sweet Cora, such a pretty girl. Striking, really. She was turning fourteen soon, and he couldn't believe it. Her father and one of her uncles joined her on the guitar and the bodhrán. She sang an Irish tune, and Daniel's aunt whispered in his ear, "It's a war lament from the 1916 Easter Rising."

Daniel's heart was in his throat. This was a part of his history that he'd never been able to know. His mother was English, and his papa was from the lowlands of Scotland as well as having roots in England. His boyhood schools had told a different version from the side of the Crown.

All he knew was that Cora's melancholy tune was doing things to the people in this pub. Like a spell. Her sweet, youthful soprano was clear and bright. The whole crowd was on their feet. But when Daniel thought she'd step down, she looked to the side. She said, "I have a little friend who has asked to do a short song with me. Would ye mind another?" And of course, the crowd was cheering her on.

Daniel was clapping along with the crowd until he saw her. Airmid was there, off to the side of the performing area. And she had Erin in her arms. She put the child down, and Erin ran to Cora. Cora scooped her up on her hip, and the crowd was very quiet. The little girl was absolutely uncowed. *Like her mother.* Daniel looked at Airmid, and she met his eyes shyly, giving him a little wave. Then Erin spoke. "I'd like to sing a song for my friend Danny." Daniel's throat was working overtime, and Sorcha took his hand.

Airmid watched the emotion sweep over Daniel's face, and it broke her. She'd done that. She'd hurt him. She'd realized, after the dust had settled from that awful custody hearing, that she'd probably been a complete and utter fool. She'd sobbed in her pillow until her mother had come in and taken her in her arms.

Her mother realized fairly quickly that it was about more than the hearing. She knew her daughter. She'd read the two of them so easily. "Do you love him, pet? Truly? Then what the hell were ye thinking sending him on his way?" Her mother was never cruel, but she was candid. It was made so much worse over the next couple of days because Erin wouldn't quit asking if she could go see Danny. Go see Davis and Donna and her pony. It wasn't her pony. It wasn't even Danny's pony. He was boarding it for a neighbor. But Erin was nothing if not persistent.

So, Airmid finally asked her, "Erin, do you like Mr. Danny? I don't mean his ponies or his big house. Do you like Danny just for being Danny?"

Erin had answered her with a look that made her doubt her own intellect. "I love Mr. Danny. He reads to me and tells me stories from his granny. And he carries me and hugs me when I need it. And he makes me snacks. And he let me come to work with you and stay at his house when I was sick. I bet he's lonely in that big house. Can't we go see him?"

Airmid left Erin to her playing and hid in the bathroom until she stopped weeping. She was such an idiot. When she'd met him, she thought him a stuffy, arrogant aristocrat. But she'd misjudged him. He was good and kind. And he loved her. That's what he'd been trying to tell her in the car. Not just that he loved her and wanted her, but that he wanted to be a family. That he'd give to Erin what his papa had given to him. He'd be a real father to her.

And Airmid had turned her back on him. *Go big or go home* was the only way to handle this. And like a bloody coward, she'd sent her adorable four-year-old into battle to pave the way. Dirty pool, but all is fair in love and war. She watched his face take in the two girls on stage. Erin didn't know a lot of songs by heart, but Cora had probed the girl's interests and found something perfectly heartbreaking. Erin's new favorite story was the one Daniel had told her. The one his Highland grandmother had taught him.

Daniel watched Erin, very serious as she leaned into the mic. When she started to sing, he felt his chest jerk with pain. With love.

*Little Robin Redbreast sat upon a rail,*
*Niddle-noddle went his head, wiggle-waggle went his tail.*
*Little Robin Redbreast came to visit me,*
*This is what he whistled, "Thank you for the tea."*

Two more verses, and Erin and Cora did a little bow. Then

Daniel was on his feet, clapping, and Cora shushed the crowd. Erin shouted into the mic, "Mr. Danny, me and Mam love you. We want you to be in our family!"

Then he was making his way toward the little girl and Airmid. His cousin Brigid was throwing elbows and yelling, "Clear the feckin' road. Man in love on the move! Man in love on the move!"

Cora handed Erin off to Daniel's open arms. He hugged her, his face wet with tears. Then he pulled Airmid into the group hug and kissed her. "You don't fight fair, Airmid Roberts."

She laughed and said, "I love you. I'm so sorry. I was scared, and seeing you get hurt, and then the hearing happened. I am so sorry. I was a coward, but I'm not going to run away, Danny. If it's not too late, I love you. I love you!" And the pub was going absolutely apeshit because O'Briens reveled in a good love story. The women were crying, the men were catcalling, and Lord Daniel MacPherson, the Earl of Hawick, shocked the hell out of everyone by getting down on one knee.

———

Daniel woke early, despite the late night. He crept down the hallway to find Erin playing on the floor and Airmid dead to the world, starfishing in the bed. He put a finger over his lips, and Erin snuck out of the room.

When Airmid woke, she rushed to the kitchen of Sean and Sorcha O'Brien to find Daniel making Mickey Mouse-shaped pancakes on a griddle. Sorcha's parents, Michael and Edith, were smiling as they watched. Edith rose then, taking Airmid by the hand. "And you must be our Danny's love? And an Irish girl, no less. What a joy to meet you and your little girl." She hugged Airmid. "And your family is right nearby in Derry. How wonderful."

"Mam, Danny said we can go to Disney World for our honeymoon!" Erin said.

She looked at Daniel, and he was laughing. "You are shameless, girl. I said we'd talk about it. If not for the honeymoon, then just on holiday. I've never been to Disney World, so you'll have to show me the ropes."

"You have to watch aaaall the movies with me. And when we're all married, I can call you Da, right?"

Daniel froze, looking at Airmid. She had her fingers over her closed lips. He said, "Yes, sweetheart. Da or papa or daddy or father. I'll let you choose."

Erin thought about it. "What did you call your father when you were little?"

Edith's eyes were so sad, but she understood. So did Michael. Daniel hadn't even known about John. Edith gave Daniel a weak smile and a nod as she sat next to Grandda Michael. Daniel said, "Well, love, I called him Papa."

Erin said, "Then that's what I'll call you when we're all married. My da died when I was in Mammy's tummy, and I suppose I don't want to give his name away." It was like a knife in Daniel's gut. But he loved what she'd said. That she was really thinking about it. Erin was positive this was a package deal for the family and not just a marriage between two people. And in many ways, she was right.

Daniel said, "I had two fathers. Did I ever tell you that? I never knew my first father, either, and then he died. That's sad for both of us. But my second father, my papa, was such a good father. And I promise you that I'll try to be just as good."

Erin said quietly, "Danny, if I start calling you Papa before the wedding, will you get mad?"

Daniel looked at Airmid. She was crying, and he wanted to hold her. But right now, this was between him and Erin. He said,

"No, love, I won't get mad. I think that would be rather wonderful. And I'm planning on a very fast wedding before your mammy can tuck tail and run from me. We can't let her get away, can we?" This caused a rash of giggles from the little girl, and he saw Michael nudge Edith. She swatted him and told him to shush. But he saw the love between them. He wanted to grow old with Airmid. And now he had to be very careful with himself. He wanted to be here and in this family for a very long life.

He handed Airmid a plate of pancakes and winked at her. "Good morning, love. Eat up. I plan on getting you to Hawick Manor by the end of the week. And I want to stop at a jeweler in Dublin that the lads told me about."

"Why?" Airmid asked. And he wanted to laugh because he'd met a lot of British debutant types and gold-digging men who wanted to bag an heiress. He rubbed elbows with the rich and elite for his work. The women being the sort who were just used to a certain amount of luxury. "Darling, hasn't it occurred to you that I didn't have a ring in my hand when I bent to one knee? My intent is to buy you an obscenely large rock to go on your beautiful hand."

It hadn't occurred to her, which was laughable and adorable. Airmid smirked. "Aye, I turned in the borrowed set we had for work." She whispered the words, so the grandparents didn't hear. "Tara has been retired. But what makes you think we'll be going to Hawick without delay, Your Lordship? I do have a life to get back to."

He shrugged. "I've got ponies and lots of cousins. Branna is bringing her three children this weekend. You can't win, love. Don't even try." He flipped a pancake. "And I have some dust behind that one particular bookshelf in my office I need to show you. The spot is absolutely filthy." And his smile was positively devilish.

# EPILOGUE
## DOOLIN, CO. CLARE

The seizure never repeated itself. In fact, the doctors were convinced there had been no seizure activity. Finn stood over his son as he finished a letter to little Erin. The kids were all sending her short notes and some hand-drawn pictures. A congratulations, of sorts, because Daniel planned to adopt her after the wedding.

Colin looked at the letter and picture, satisfied. Then he folded it in three parts. "Da, can I have the waxy thing Mam uses for fancy notes? I think it's in her desk."

Finn found it and smiled to himself. It had been his aunt Miren's from the O'Donnell side. And the McDubh. The line from which the sight was passed down to the dark ones. He looked at Colin, seeing the mirror image of himself at ten years old. He passed the seal and wax to Colin, then went to retrieve a torch from the kitchen. When he returned, he stopped in his tracks. Colin was stark white, holding his temples. The seal was discarded on the table. "What's the matter, lad?" He knelt next to him.

"I felt a jolt. Like a pulse through my head. Then it hurt. It hurts, Da," Colin said just as Cora came skidding around the corner. She looked at Colin, then at her father.

----

**Two Months Later**

**Munich, Germany**

Andrew Douglas, the Duke of Roxburghe, looked over the crowded expanse of the Marienplatz just as the clock struck noon. The Rathaus-Glockenspiel activated, the figures moving with the chiming of midday. Every window contained a flower box that was filled to overflowing with jewel-toned flowers.

He felt her, then. Smelled expensive perfume and clean skin. "*Hallo*, Freya darling. How is the grandmother?" he asked in German. He'd met her as Rubia, knew her now as Agent Freya with the Bundesnachrichtendiens. The BND being the German equivalent of MI-6, they were officially swimming together in the community pool, so to speak. And God only knew what her real name was.

She smiled, tilting her head so that the sun shone on her golden locks. She answered in English, "Douglas, how is our friend John and his beautiful wife? Healing, I hope."

He smirked. She knew damn well they weren't really man and wife. "Engaged, actually."

She let out a low, husky giggle. "I knew it wasn't all for show. They couldn't keep their hands to themselves or their eyes off each other. Some things can't be faked. And what about you, Douglas? Do you have a little fräulein tucked away somewhere? Or perhaps a wife?"

"No, I don't. Are you offering?" Douglas asked, and she laughed.

"I'm not the marrying kind. Much too vicious," she said. But he knew better.

Douglas said lightly, "You know, I noticed you didn't have any blood on you. Not on your sleeve or hand or any across your frock. Considering you cut a man's carotid artery, you didn't get a drop on yourself." She said nothing. He continued. "Delilah did it, didn't she?"

"Did what?" she asked.

He chuffed a laugh. "I suppose you are entitled to your secrets, my dear. And she is entitled to her revenge," he said more softly.

She shook herself and asked, "So, what do you have for me?" They faced each other, leaning in close for privacy. Douglas handed her an envelope.

"You could have some questionable, new friends setting up shop in the city, I'm afraid. They came to the UK on Hungarian passports from Budapest, but they are Belarus nationals. As you know, their ruling party is in bed with the Russians, and they've been very busy. They entered on a school visa and stopped attending classes a month into the term. At the end of the term, the university started making inquiries and then alerted immigration after an unacceptably long period of time had gone by. The men must have caught wind of it because they disappeared soon after. I traced them out of Edinburgh to the Munich Airport. My trail has turned cold."

Freya asked, "Which university?"

"Edinburgh Napier University," he said with a sigh.

She wrinkled her brow. "I've never heard of this university. I'm afraid to ask ... what field of study?"

Douglas said, "Advanced cyber security and computer forensics."

Freya cursed, staring at the unopened envelope. Douglas said,

"So what do you say, Freya darling? Are you interested in some playtime?"

She tucked the envelope into her handbag. Then stood and put out her hand to shake his. "I'll be in touch." Douglas shook her hand and felt the slip of paper. *My other phone number. Give it to no one.*

# AUTHOR NOTES AND ACKNOWLEDGEMENTS

**Author Notes and Acknowledgments**

As always, I would like to first thank my family. Getting a book finished during school break and some personal challenges is always rough. They support me and understand my need to hide in my writing room. They are, as always, my rock.

I'd also like to thank my copy editor, Joyce Mochrie, and my cover designer, Christine Stevens.

Book 9 has been lingering in my mind ever since Sorcha's grown nephew came on the scene in Book 3, *Shadow Guardian*. Thank you for supporting me and allowing me to tell Daniel's story.